Publishec

An imprint of .
Saffron House, Knightoı
PL9 0JD, L

www.everybodywavesback.com

ISBN: 978 1 8384537 1 8
eBook ISBN: 978 1 8384537 0 1

This book is a work of fiction. Names, characters, businesses, organisations, places and events other than those clearly in the public domain, are either the product of the author's imagination or are used fictitiously. Any resemblance to actual persons, living or dead, events or locales is entirely coincidental.

For Lindy, who makes all this possible.

A NUMBERS GAME

A Numbers Game

RJ Dark

WAVESBACK

Contents

1

MONDAY

The week started unseasonably warm for spring and with my best friend sitting on top of me, threatening violence. From there it only went downhill. But that's what it's like when you deal with the dead; sometimes it feels like all they want is for you to join them.

Slap.

'Where's my money?'
'Jackie, I don't—'

Slap.

'Where. Is. My. Money?'
'Jackie, I can't—'

Slap.

'Your little brown friend wants his money.'

Slap

'Why do you even call yourself that, "little brown friend"?'

Slap

'To annoy lefties like you, Mal. Where's my money?'

Slap.

'You always say *you're* a lefty.'
'Don't change the subject. My money?'

Slap.

'This doesn't even hurt.'

Slap.

'That's 'cos I know you get a weird kick out of taking a beating.'

Slap.

'Jackie, will you—'

Slap.

'My money, Malachite Jones. Now. Give it me.'

So much about this situation annoyed me.

That he called himself my 'little brown friend' precisely because he knew it made me uncomfortable, even though he wasn't little, not anymore. Though he was brown, his grandparents had come from the Punjab, but the nearest Jackie had ever been to his heritage was the Jaflong Taste Indian takeaway.

That annoyed me.

The fact I had to pay him protection money, just like everyone else who ran a business in the area, even though we were supposed to be best friends because, 'I can't show favouritism, Mal, can I? People would think I was weak.'

That annoyed me.

Call Jackie Singh Khattar weak and you were liable to vanish from the face of the earth.

The fact he used my full name, Malachite, when he knew I hated it. Because what sort of person names their son Malachite when they are going to grow up on one of the roughest council estates in England?

That annoyed me. Anyone calling me Malachite annoyed me.

The fact I wouldn't be able to eat if I gave Jackie the money, and he knew that and would give it right back because 'it's about the gesture not the cash.' Well, that annoyed me almost beyond belief.

And the slapping, that was quite annoying as well.

That's the thing about friends; they know how to push your buttons. That was one of the reasons I chose not to have many. Not that I was overrun with offers, but still.

Slap.

'Alright! Fifty quid, in the top drawer.'

'Well, get it then, Mal.'

'I can't.'

'Why not?'

'Because you're sat on me.'

He stared at me. He was a weird-looking man, Jackie. He was big now, but I always saw the ghost of the kid I'd known overlaid on the man he had become. Thin, council-house thin, never-had-enough-to-eat thin, never-had-the-right-things-to-eat thin. His cheekbones were like blades, his eyes sunken and his skin, light enough he could (and did) pretend he was just a very well-tanned white boy when he wished – as long as he kept out the sun. When you saw him up close, he had wrinkles around his eyes and mouth, like laugh lines but he never laughed much. Smiled a lot, but not a big laugher, our Jackie.

He stood, pushing long, silky black hair out of his face, his arms thick with muscle after years in the army. He was wearing Fred Perry knock-offs today, in pastels; yellow trousers and a clashing pink jumper. He wasn't tall, standing five foot eight in his ugly expensive cheap clothes. He wore good shoes though; that was, he said, how you knew he had money. Good money wore good shoes, and when he said that I heard his mother's voice. Not his real mother, she died when he was two. His foster mother.

We never talked about her.

Sometimes people mistook Jackie's blasé attitude for him being a pushover. They only ever did it once though, and if they looked in his eyes first, they didn't do it at all.

I stood, chalk to Jackie's cheese. Where he was more muscular I was taller, which I liked, as it felt like a bit of an advantage. Same long black hair, but my colour came from a bottle not genetics, which he thought was funny. I didn't have the ghost of a hungry kid haunting my psyche either; I'd never wanted for anything material when I grew up. I wore black, it was an easy colour to wear and it suited my calling: vicars wore black, undertakers wore black, I wore black.

The desk in my office, the one that had Jackie's money in it, was made in 1832, the same year the second cholera epidemic struck London, and constructed from oak ship timbers, though I'd never been able to pinpoint which ship. It was heavy, dark, imposing-looking. I like old things, though I'm rarely around them. Unless you count pensioners, who are most of my clientele. I had Jackie's money in the hidden compartment in the back of the top-right drawer, always did. Sometimes I just liked to make him work for it. Payment was a foregone conclusion.

'Here.'

He took it, counted it.

'I can't believe you still count it, we've been doing this for years.'

'You're a crook, Mal. Of course I count it.'

'I am not a crook. I provide bereavement counselling.'

'Fucking crook,' he said. 'Takes one to know one. Anyway, if I take this, right' – he thumbed through the notes – old tenners, though I knew he liked twenties, or even better a fifty that he could flash about – 'can you still pay your bills?'

'Yes. I can meet my responsibilities. I just won't be able to eat.'

He slipped the money into his pocket. Smiled at me.

'You did hear me say I wouldn't be able to eat.'

He nodded.

'Well?' I held my hand out.

'You want me to give you some skin, brother?' He dropped into a cod Jamaican accent. Jackie had a remarkable talent for mimicry.

'I want to eat.'

'You can. Girl called Janine Killingham – she'll drop by later for you to con.'

'It's called a consult.' I slipped the words out between gritted teeth. Half the skill in dealing with Jackie was in not rising to the bait. 'That name sounds familiar.'

Which should have been a warning.

'Her big sister, Helen, was a model. Bit of a looker, nice tits. I 'ad her you know – or she had me, I was never sure. Night before her wedding.'

'Classy.'

'You know me, any hole in a port, innit.' Big grin, such perfect white teeth. 'Anyway, she needs help. You talk to her, help her out, and we might do alright out of it. Mates' rates too – she's from the Edge.'

'I'm trying to avoid clients from Blades Edge.'

'If you want to eat, then you'll see Janine. She'll pay you cash up front. Don't worry, you won't get stiffed.'

'I don't want to deal with the Edge.'

He stared at me. Blades Edge was the biggest council estate in the North. It sat in the shadow of a hill, half of it had been carved away in the 1960s to build the estate, creating a huge chalk cliff that loomed over the houses. That was where it got its name, from the hill, The Blade. I'd grown up on that estate, been bullied mercilessly on it, spent every day walking the sparsely grassed fields mined with dogshit or over pavements of cheap concrete that crumbled underfoot. Spent the first thirteen years of my life absolutely terrified every time I left the house.

Mostly terrified of Jackie back then. But things change; everything changes. Except Blades Edge. Or rather it does change, just not for the better.

A good half of it was derelict now. The whole place was marked for renewal by the council but that had got bogged down in legal problems with the people who had bought their houses, and there was a travellers' site that the council couldn't move. So, as ever, plans that were meant to make the place better only ended up running it further into the ground. Empty houses stood out on the streets like bad teeth in among, well, teeth that weren't too good to start off with.

A new client from Blades Edge. Should have been a warning.

I should have said no.

'Okay, I'll see her.'

'Good lad,' said Jackie, and he left, letting the door close slowly behind him. I saw a flash of red from the Ferrari he was driving this week. A second later Beryl came out of the back office. My secretary, or I called her that. She was a big woman in every way: loud, liked her food, unafraid to speak her mind.

'He took the last of your money,' she said.

'Yep.'

'And you let him?'

'Yep.'

'Ponce.'

'You mean me or him?'

'The both of you. And you better not have given him my wages.'

'I didn't.'

'Good.'

'What do you know about Janine Killingham, Beryl?'

'That model's little sister?'

'Yes.'

'That Helen Killingham has an open marriage, you know. I read it in the paper. What a slut.'

'People should do what makes them happy, Beryl.'

'You like drugs.'

'I did.'

'Try 'em again and I'll kick fuck out of you. I'm not soft-hearted like yer mate.'

'I know that, Beryl.'

'Just make sure you do bloody know.'

'I do. Now, Janine Killingham?'

'Bit of a cow, or she was.' Beryl took a cigarette from a packet in her pocket but didn't light up inside, not anymore. 'She took up with one of the Stanbecks, married him.'

'So she's not actually called Janine Killingham anymore?'

'No, Janine Stanbeck.'

I sighed. The Stanbecks ran all the crime on Blades Edge, and a lot of the surrounding areas. I decided I would kill Jackie next time I saw him.

'Married Larry Stanbeck, Mick's son,' Beryl said.

Mick Stanbeck, or Trolley Mick as most knew him, ran the Stanbecks. I decided I would kill Jackie twice when I saw him.

'He probably liked to knock her about, but that's the Stanbecks for you. Bunch of wankers think women are punch bags. Fucking Irish though, what can you expect.'

'You say the same about Muslims.'

'Aye. Arseholes.'

'Any feelings on Mormons?'

'Are they men?'

'Some of them are.

'Well, there's your problem, only reason I'm queer is men are such shits.'

'Thank you.'

She paused then. I'd like to say it was because she was aware she'd overstepped some mark with her casual racism but Beryl didn't have boundaries the way other people did. She opened her mouth and said whatever was in her mind. It made her useful to me and an absolute nightmare for anyone else.

'Why are you thanking me?' she said, 'I just called you a shit.'

'Never mind, Beryl. Janine,' I took a deep breath, 'Stanbeck?'

'I'm not sure you count as a man though,' she said to the air. I stared at her, trying to see if she was joking or not, but she was unreadable. Not a woman to play poker with.

'You were talking to me about Janine Stanbeck.'

'She one of them morons now?'

'Forget the Mormons, Beryl. Janine Stanbeck. She's coming to see me. So, who died, her mum, dad? They must be getting on now.'

'Oh no. It was her fella what died. Larry. Came off his motorbike. Died instantly, which is shit – bastard should have at least suffered a bit. Bloody Stanbecks.'

I nodded. This was exactly the reason I'd given up seeing people from the Edge. How many times can you see someone who you remember from your youth, face punched black and blue, and tell them that the man who used to beat them is on the other side; he's happy, he loves them, he always loved them and he's sorry for the things he did. Then take their money for straight-up lies without starting to feel like a fraud.

‘Word on the Edge is someone ran him off the road.’

If ever there was going to be a warning, that really should have been it.

For a psychic medium, I have always been very bad at seeing the future.

Jackie would say it was because I am a fraud.

And, of course, Jackie would be right.

My office is in a row of six lonely shops built in the 1930s on a busy main road. Half a mile one way and you’re on Blades Edge, half a mile the other and you hit Crais Curve, famous accident blackspot and the last thing about fifty per cent of the Edge’s joyriders see before the inside of an ambulance – or a hearse. We have a little lay-by that cars can park in just in front and all around us are woods. The strip of trees behind the shops is about five hundred metres deep, though it runs for miles in both directions. Behind that is a road, then a high wall and the grounds of an old country house that’s now a hotel and aggressively prosecutes trespassers. Next to my shop on the left is Mr Patel and his wife Nasreen who run an off-licence and newsagent’s. On the right is Oriental Promise, a Chinese takeaway run by Mr Wan, who speaks no English at all – unless he knows you and then he becomes fluent. After that is a big-name booky that is sucking cash out of people who can’t afford it at a rate I can only dream of.

At least I provide a service for your money.

The end shop of the row is a kebab and curry house called Spice ‘N’ Saucy that sells excellent kebabs and very bad curries and is manned by a constantly changing crew of polite and well-groomed young Asian men. They appear, work a few months, and then disappear, never to be seen again. It's also a front for a lot of class B drug dealing – 'Extra herbs on the pizza, please' – but no one seems to care.

Mr Patel used to run a shop on the Edge; it looked more like a fortress than a newsagent's but that didn't stop him getting robbed regularly. He was going to pack the business in until the offer of his premises here came up. Similar story for Mr Wan. They serve a lot of the same clientele but no one robs them because Jackie owns most of the block, bookies aside; we all pay rent and protection to him. Mine, Mr Patel's and Mr Wan's rents are far below the going rate, even if you take the protection into account. I have no idea what Spice 'N' Saucy pay but I suspect that if you dug hard enough, you'd find Jackie owns it. But I wouldn't suggest digging that hard because he would find out and then he would find you and you would have a short but unpleasant conversation about why digging into his affairs is a bad idea.

My shop is nondescript from the outside; the window is entirely closed off from the street by long red velvet curtains. Inside, it's mostly dark colours, dark-red carpet, dark desk, dark-green walls in a reproduction Victorian wallpaper that glitters in the right light, though I deliberately keep the lighting low – through faux candelabras in sconces and plenty of candles, for the mood. I did have a big chandelier, but I kept banging my head on it as the ceiling is far too low for that sort of thing.

'She'll be here soon,' said Beryl. She was standing between me and the desk, a wall of badly dressed flesh with dead eyes.

'I know.'

'Teabags.'

'What?'

'We've no teabags.'

'Go get some then?' Keeping the office stocked was meant to be Beryl's job.

'Got work to do.'

'Well, go later on then.'

'Can't work with no teabags.'

'But you just said …'

'Need some teabags.'

There wasn't really any arguing with Beryl; she was like Jackie in that way, and I wondered what god I had angered to be surrounded by such strong personalities.

'Fine, I'll go get the tea.'

'Good.' I grabbed what remained of the petty cash after paying Jackie – three pounds and fifty-eight pence – and opened the door. 'Oy.' I turned.

'What?'

'Second of June 1974,' said Beryl, as if that would mean something to me.

'Again, Beryl, what? You're going to have to give me some context'

'I saw Cat Maudy pass out front, off to Mr Patel's – she'll want you to do a trick, and that's the date of birth of her oldest son. The one that died.'

Cat Maudy was a Blades Edge legend, one of those idiosyncratic people who stuck out wherever they were but had been about for so long their strangeness was simply accepted. She must have been in her eighties, maybe older. When I was young, I heard she was a fighter pilot in the war, or maybe a spy. At least half the kids on the estate thought she was witch, so what we thought then probably shouldn't be taken as gospel. But she'd managed to raise four kids and get three of them off the Edge into good careers. And then there was one who would never leave. I'm pretty sure she could have left the estate if she wanted to, but she didn't. Instead, she stayed in her little council house, kept a beautiful garden and rescued homeless cats – high thirties at the last count. I suppose she was the stereotypical mad old cat lady in many ways, except in my mind, mad old cat ladies always smell awful. Maudy smelled of long hot summers and dry flower petals.

'Maybe I'll get the tea after Janine Stanbeck has been then.'

'Need teabags.'

Well, that was that sorted.

A good choice of slogan for Mr Patel's shop – more a small supermarket than a newsagent's – would have been 'none of the choice, double the cost', but Mr Patel had gone with the more snappy 'your local grocer.' He had the cleanest and most ordered shop I'd ever been in. Sometimes I got the feeling he was a little bit resentful of people who came in and bought things. I think he liked stacking and displaying his wares a lot more than he liked selling them. Maybe that's why everything was so expensive. When I entered, he was leaning over his counter talking to Cat

Maudy, and he almost jumped away from her when the bell rang. I don't think he liked being caught slacking.

'Mr Jones,' he said. Mr Patel had a way of enunciating every word very clearly and then raising the pitch of his voice at the end of every sentence, which turned it into a question. 'What can I help you with?'

'Just teabags, Mr Patel.' Maudy smiled at me and gave me a small wave.

'We have Tetley – they are five pounds. Or we have Mr Smart Brand's teabags, which are also very nice and just three pounds fifty.' Mr Smart Brand's teabags were anything but nice and Beryl would moan about it incessantly if I bought them, but if she wanted better teabags she should have come herself. Or maybe contributed toward the petty cash.

'Smart Brand, please.'

'They are on the top shelf – I will get my ladder.'

'Are you sure that's a good idea, Mr Patel?' said Maudy. Her voice was gentle, like a whisper, and she was wearing a thick fur coat despite the heat of the day. I hoped it wasn't made from cat. 'He hurt himself, Mr Jones.' She pointed at Mr Patel's arm, wrapped in a blue cast. 'Fell off his ladder and broke his arm. Are you sure you're all right, Mr Patel?'

'I am fine, do not fuss,' he said. He was a small but well-built man in his fifties with a thick head of greying hair, with the cast on his arm, he seemed somehow smaller. Pain can do that to you.

'I can probably reach it myself, Mr Patel.'

'It is not your shop,' he snapped. Which was true.

'Will you do a trick for me, Mr Jones?' said Maudy as Mr Patel went into the back.

'I'm a bit busy.' Sometimes I wonder why I can't just say no.

'Oh, just one trick, please.' She smiled, her face was a mass of wrinkles, but she still painted on the same make-up she must have had as a young woman, like a mask. I imagine she had been very beautiful back then; she had that air about her. I suppose that's what made her difficult to say no to.

'Okay, look into my eyes.' She did. Her green eyes were starting to cloud with cataracts. 'Now, tell me the name of your eldest boy.'

'My Peter?'

'Yes, Peter,' I said. I vaguely remembered him but he'd not gone to the school on Blades Edge, so I'd only ever seen him in passing, and then he became just a face in the paper. Articles about the accident and the scourge of drunken joyriders plaguing the estate. 'Right, I'm getting something from the spirits.'

'You are so clever,' she said. 'Have you thought of getting a cat, Mr Jones? I've got thirty-eight, but I have a black one called Magic and he'd be good for you.' I ignored her comment; Cat Maudy always wanted to give you a cat.

'I'm getting a feeling of peace, and something about him coming to you in the spring?' She continued staring intently into my eyes. 'Is it July? No, that's not spring. Definitely "J" though, so must be June?' She nodded eyes wide, a huge smile on her face. 'June the first. No, wait. Second. It's all coming through now. Nineteen seventy-four?'

Maudy clapped, like a little girl. 'Oh, Mr Jones, you are clever. You tell him I miss him so much, and I'll always love him.' She smiled up at me and I wondered if it was the memory of grief that clouded her eyes, not cataracts.

'I'll tell him, Maudy,' I said.

'Now, do another one, tell me what I am going to have for tea!'

I was about to say no to the second trick because that was considerably harder, then I noticed a little bit of paper sticking out of the pocket of her fur coat. It looked about the size and shape of the end of a receipt and, partly because I am a bit of a show-off, and partly because sometimes you have to keep practising old skills or you forget them, I decided to take a risk.

'Okay then.' I put my hands on her shoulders. 'This coat is beautiful material, Maudy.'

'Oh, it is,' she said. 'Best fake fur. It was a treat, for me. I think I deserve it.'

'I think you do too – it feels so lovely.' I ran my hand down the edge of the coat as Cat Maudy pulled up the collar against her face.

'I feel quite glamourous,' she grinned.

'You look like a movie star,' I said, and palmed the receipt from her pocket then lifted my hands in front of my face so I was looking at the receipt. I almost blurted out, 'Sardine sandwiches,' until I noticed she had bought fifty cans of sardines, so that was probably for the cats. Then the list was mostly cleaning products – also a by-product of the cats, I imagine. I started to wonder if I had made a mistake, but at the bottom of the receipt was a microwaveable lasagne for one, a ready-made salad and a surprisingly expensive bottle of champagne.

'Do you know?' she said.

'It's a bit hazy,' I said. Her face fell. 'But I'm getting, Italian, maybe?' The smile returned. 'Salad and lasagne.'

'Oh, Mr Jones!'

'Wait, wait, not finished yet. Also …'

At that moment, Mr Patel returned with my cheap teabags and slammed them on the counter. I let my hands drop to my side.

'You!' He pointed at me. 'Stop this nonsense now – I'll have no ghosts in my shop. You take your tea and get out, Mr Jones.'

'Sorry, Mr Patel,' I said, and gently pushed passed Cat Maudy to get my teabags, slipping the receipt back into her pocket as I did.

Janine Stanbeck wasn't typical of a girl in her late twenties on the Edge. She wasn't showing any flesh, for a start, and as the summer had hit a couple of weeks ago, most girls on the Edge were now walking round in what I thought looked like their underwear. Janine was covered, head to foot. She wore a light raincoat, made of blue shiny material – but it was old, threadbare, and I reckoned it wasn't hers as it was too big for her. It swamped her, making her look like a child not a grown woman. She wore trainers, old too, and jeans, not jeggings, 501s maybe or decent knock-offs, though they were worn as well, and not for fashion's sake. She was even wearing a hat; a woolly hat with a bobble on the top that was only hanging on by one bit of wool, and for some reason it got my back up. I wanted to either tear it off or to sew it on more securely. I didn't say anything, because she wasn't looking at me; she was digging in her pockets and looking anywhere but at me. When she found what she was looking for, a single well-used bank note, she held it out, still looking at the floor like I was the headmaster and she was a naughty schoolgirl.

For a minute, no one moved.

'Jackie said I should come. Said you would help.'

I took the fifty.

'I'm sorry for your loss,' I said. She looked up, the skin around her eyes jaundiced with faded bruises. If you had tried to present me with a better cliché of a women from the Edge; I don't think you could have done.

'Don't be sorry,' she said, surprisingly soft spoken. 'He was a Stanbeck – he beat me. I'm better off without him. Just find me my money.'

'Money?'

'Yeah,' she blinked, hard, and I saw nothing but scorn there. 'Jackie says you can talk to the dead – they obviously don't tell you much, do they?'

'I don't tend to do research.' This was a lie, but she had no need to know that. 'We do a consultation and see what comes through, then we go from there. There's no guarantee of—'

'All I need is for you to contact Lawrence.'

'Larry,' I said, and she flinched.

'I thought you didn't do research.'

'It just came through, together with feelings of …'

'Violence? He tended to punch people who called him Larry to his face.'

Thanks, Beryl.

'Death can change people.'

'Well, any change in Lawrence can only be for the better. Death was definitely a move in the right direction for me.'

'This isn't my usual sort of consultation.'

'Are you saying you can't help?' A sneer.

I will kill you for this, Jackie.

'Of course not. Jackie says you need the help of the spirits, and I am glad to give it.'

'Right.' She stared into my face. 'What do we do then?'

There was a level of aggression behind those words that hadn't been there when she came in. I'd taken her desire not to look at me for shyness, when the truth is I think she felt stupid. She didn't, for one second, believe I was what was written above the shop doorway: *Malachite Jones – Psychic Medium (As seen on TV)*. That didn't bother me too much, not many people did; people came to me as a last resort and I had to win them over. Janine was desperate; most people that came to me were, but mostly they were downtrodden, beaten and heavy with grief. Not her though, she might look like she was, but looks aren't everything. She needed my help, and I think she hated it.

She gave me her coat and hat. Under the coat, she wore a nondescript jumper. Under the hat, she had cut her hair short. Everything said she was a woman trying not to be seen, not to be noticed.

Cold reading, which is what I do, is an art. It's about picking up enough from someone to appear like you know everything about them when you don't. It's mostly about averages, small details and willingness for the mark to believe. The best way to get it wrong is to start off with a load of preconceptions. To cold read, you have to start cold and I'd got off on the wrong foot with Janine Stanbeck. I'd read into her what I thought a Blades Edge girl should be when she was nothing of the sort. She was hiding, that was plain. But she wasn't shy or weak or downtrodden. She was angry.

'So? What do we do?' she said.

2

HOW TO CONTACT THE DEAD

You will need:

Mood lighting
Scented Candles
Heavy fabrics (velvet is always good)
Old furniture
Crystals
Phrenology head
A soft voice
An understanding of human nature
A willingness to listen
Patience
A good researcher
An earpiece
Google

She was impatient. Not obviously so. In fact, I don't think I'd ever met anyone as contained as Janine Stanbeck, and I wondered what her home life must have been like that she had to keep so much of herself hidden. There was no overflow from her. People usually gave something away but she sat in my client's chair (Louis XV-style balloon-backed) and revealed nothing. Only stared at the desk. I waited for her to speak first.

'I thought you'd have a crystal ball.'

'That's only really for theatre. I'm not running a con.'

'I told you to get a crystal ball.' Words in my ear; Beryl, sat in the back room at her computer, listening in. She was only meant to interject with useful information, but I'd given up trying to tell her that.

'So, contact the other side or whatever and then tell me where my money is.'

'What money?'

Thanks, Beryl.

'It doesn't work like that, Janine. I can't just deliver an answer. The spirits talk in loops and riddles a lot of the time.'

She stared at me. Blue eyes, no make-up. The start of frown lines on her forehead.

'Then how does it work?'

'We need to establish contact, work up a rapport.'

'Are you trying to chat me up?'

'No.'

'You would though.'

'It sounds like you're trying to chat me up.'

'She knows you're a fraud, Mal.'

'This only works if you commit yourself to it, Janine.'

I try to use the client's name a lot, to establish a connection, but she looked at me like she was channelling every resentment she had ever felt and was passing them on to me.

'You can walk out, Janine, but you've already paid for an hour.'

She was still staring.

'So maybe give it a go?'

And more staring.

'Your husband was knocked off his bike, right? But I'm getting that it may not have been an accident.'

A small smile appeared on her face.

'If you want me to believe you can help, Malachite' – amusement in her voice at my name – 'then tell me something that isn't gossip on the estate.'

'I don't care if you believe me or not, Janine. That's not why I am doing this. Jackie told me you need help but you don't have to stay.' Calling their bluff early is always good. Because if they do walk out, you basically get an hour off.

'She did two months for selling weed when she was fifteen. Had her own little circle of dealers at her school, bloody posh one too.. Sealed records, no one knows. That should impress her.'

And that is why I pay Beryl.

'I'm wasting my time here.' She was standing, going to leave. I needed to get her attention.

'Have you ever been in prison?'

She froze. Something there on her face; not curiosity, almost anger, or maybe it was fear. People are funny about their secrets, that's why they're secret. Then she shook her head. Sat back down.

'You're fishing, saying that cos I'm from the Edge.' She picked up her bag from the floor and put it on her lap. She had the biggest handbag I had ever seen, proper shoplifters bag and it looked stuffed to the gills 'People think everyone from the Edge has been in prison, Mr Jones.'

'You weren't on the Edge then, though, were you?'

She sat a little straighter. Put her bag back on the floor. A shiver ran through her and she tapped the desk with her fingernail. It was very well manicured.

'Okay. You could have spoken to people that knew me back then.' She stared. 'But you've not had much time to do that.' She sat back and crossed her legs. Crossed her arms. 'So, I'll listen.'

'Have you brought anything belonging to the deceased, Janine?'

'Here.' She leaned over, and I heard the rustle of her massive handbag. Then she placed a black crash helmet on the desk. It had a lot of scratches down one side. 'He was wearing that when he died. He loved that stupid bike – it's even in his will that we cremate the bastard in his bloody helmet and leathers. That enough for you?'

'Well, it's a start.' I laid my hands on the crash helmet. It was icy cold. I closed my eyes for a moment.

Saw a forest full of the dead.

Every reading is a journey along an unseen path; sometimes it takes strange twists and turns. You walk, you talk, ask questions, see a sign, a broken branch that leads you in a certain direction, follow it until you find the beautiful sun-filled clearing where the client is filling out all the information for you – but thinking you have done it. It's a numbers game, really. Say enough and eventually you'll hit something. Sometimes it's easy. Especially with those who are keen to believe, who will do the work on your behalf without ever realising it.

Sometimes it's not.

Janine was the second type.

Love, career and money are the three big paths. If you wander far enough down those paths, then you will usually hit upon something that the client is looking for. Or you may not, but you might find out some interesting things on the way, branch off down those interesting paths, go the roundabout way to your destination. Sometimes I'm lucky and I hit something at the off, but I don't like trusting to luck.

It might seem like she had done me a favour by saying it was money she wanted to know about, but she hadn't. She'd closed off two paths, and there's a lot to be found just nosing around. Though she didn't look like a woman who had much time for curiosity.

'It was a lot of money,' I said.

'Of course it was a lot. Otherwise I wouldn't spend fifty quid I don't have.'

'His savings …' I said.

She rolled her eyes. Usually people are more polite, they try to hide their disbelief, but she didn't care. Not savings then.

'You've always wanted savings, right?'

She stared at me. 'Who doesn't?'

'And this money was your way out.'

She stared more.

'But you need to know where it is.' Sometimes you can feed people back things they have already told you and it impresses them because people forget what they've said surprisingly quickly.

'I told you that.' Not always though. 'I really am wasting my time here, aren't I?'

'No, but sometimes contacting the spirits is a lottery.'

Wide eyes. Shock. And there it is. The wood among the trees. The needle in the haystack. I can be gentle now because I have something. I can be calmer cos I'm not flailing about hoping for a hit.

'The spirits often drop hints, subtle hints.'

Her eyes narrowing, she picked up her bag. Reached for the crash helmet. Disappointment on her face. But's that OK; disappointment is good. Because that means, really, she wants to believe. And if she wants to, then she will.

'A lottery ticket.'

She took her hand off the crash helmet. Put her bag down. Cocked her head.

'Yes.'

From there, it's obvious.

'But you don't know where it is.' I don't let her speak, don't let her get in a cynical comment. 'Tell me the situation.'

'Can't he tell you that?'

'I get more, impressions from the spirits than actual stories. Quicker and clearer to hear it from you.'

She's wavering. Wants to believe. Wants an answer. But she can't trust. That odd look crosses her face again. She stands.

'This is lies, innit? Jackie's a grifter. You are too. It's all lies.'

'It's a slow process, Janine.' She shook her head.

'If it were real, you could tell me something really impressive, like the numbers on the ticket.'

'Zero-two …'

'Zero-two.'

'… Thirty-eight …'

'Thirty-eight.'

' … Nineteen …'

'Nineteen.

' … Six and Eleven …'

'Six and Eleven.'

Sometimes it happens like that; sometimes it feels like I'm saying the words before Beryl gives them to me, and it's easy to believe that it is more than it is. Though I don't let myself, because that's the sort of thing people who get sectioned believe, and no one wants to be sectioned.

However, that little trick is impressive enough. She's stopped in her tracks.

'That's the numbers – how did you know?'

'How do you think?'

She stared. Not as confrontational. Tapped a well-manicured nail on the desk.

'He won the Lotto,' she said. 'Eight million pounds, but he wouldn't cash the ticket. He tried to hide it from me. Said it was insurance against me "misbehaving". Bastard. We argued about it. I said he should cash the money straight away cos he might lose it. He said that would never happen. Then he died. And now it's lost.'

'And you've checked everywhere that—'

'Of course I have.' A flash of temper. 'I was sure it'd be in his lock-up – guarded that bloody place like it was full of gold – but when I got the key—'

'Got the key?'

‘Police gave it to me. From his body when they brought me his leathers and that.’ She nodded at the helmet. ‘I said I needed it to get some stuff for the kid. Anyway, the lock-up was empty.’

‘Had someone been in it?’

‘I don’t think so.’ A pause. ‘Maybe. The family are bastards.’ She leaned forward, and I saw real need in her eyes, a desperation. ‘Look, I have a kid – he’s three. You know what it’s like on the Edge. That money will get me out of there, help get him out of there. A good school, somewhere nice to live. Decent people. If you are what you say you are, and you can find the ticket, I’ll give you a percentage, Mr Jones. Just help me get the money, help me get away.’

And just like that, she had me. I wanted to help. Of course I did.

Help a young mother and her child get off the Edge? I’d have killed for that to happen to me as a kid.

How could I refuse?

3

Beryl makes tea. It's one of the things she does. I am not allowed to make tea because my tea is either too weak, or too milky, or not sweet enough, or all of the above. And anyway, I prefer coffee, which Beryl doesn't approve of.

'How did you know the numbers, Beryl?'

She paused, steaming teabag on the spoon poised above the composting pot. Beryl is very environmentally conscious.

'Last week's is claimed, week before no winners. Week before that, no winners. Week before, claimed. Week before that one winner, not claimed. Gave you them numbers.' She dropped the teabag into the composting pot. 'You bought the shit tea.'

'Well done.'

'I'm not just a pretty face.'

'Well …'

'Don't say it.'

'I wasn't going to.'

'Yes, you were. Twat.'

I was about to say it: 'You're not a pretty face at all.'

'You used to be fun, Beryl.'

'No, I didn't. Here.' She shoved a mug of tea the colour of old brick at me. 'Careful, it's hot.'

'It's tea. I know it's hot.'

'Can never be too careful with you.'

'Where's your tea?'

'I have a date. Woman called Sandra, owns a dog-walking business. Meeting her in the park. And I don't drink shit tea. You can have it, have fun.'

She left, taking the three carrier bags she always seemed to have with her but never opened or emptied, out to her car. She was right, the tea was awful.

I'm on my own a lot. I like it. I don't exactly have a lot of clients and those I do have are pretty regular, so apart from Jackie, who turns up when he feels like it, I generally know when someone is coming. Psychic medium isn't really a walk-in-off-the-street job, and I'm far enough from the Edge not to attract giggling schoolgirls who want a tarot reading.

So when my bell rang as the door opened, it was a surprise.

Two visitors; football shirts, hair shaved at the side, closely curled on top and gelled down so you can barely tell it's ginger. Sallow white skin and shaving rashes, a spattering of acne. Young, maybe not school-age young but not yet in their twenties. One's football shirt is white, the other red, but both are oversized, hanging loose on skinny lithe-limbed bodies. Thin necks with prominent Adam's apples, freckles collecting over cheeks and nose, ranging eyes. Twins, scoping out the office, checking out my things, the lights, the décor – not finding anything they like or understand.

They move like cats in new surroundings, fizzing with nervous energy.

'Where's your TV?' this was the one in white. He spoke like he wanted a bag of crisps but I wouldn't give him his pocket money.

'Yeah,' said the other. 'Where's your TV?'

'I don't have a TV.'

'Why not?'

'Because this is where I work. A TV isn't conducive to the atmosphere.'

'Conducive,' said the one in white. He mouthed the word as if tasting it.

The one in red reached into his back pocket and took out a pocket dictionary. Then he licked a finger and leafed through it. '"Adjective. Making a certain outcome possible or likely."'

The one in white nodded. 'Da says we need to better ourselves,' he said. He had cheekbones you could use to spread butter. 'But I like to watch TV when I work.'

'Can I help you boys?'

'Da wants to speak to you,' said the one in red. 'Sent us to make sure that Paki's not here.'

'He's a Sikh.'

'Fuck off.'

I knew who they were, of course – if not which of them was which. They were the Stanbeck boys. Said out loud, it always sounded kind of wholesome, though nothing could be further from the truth. They were identical twins – a fact they used to stay out of jail. No one could ever say with real certainty whether it was Kyle or Ronaldo Stanbeck they saw knifing someone or stamping on someone's head. If Ronaldo, or Kyle, was going to do something really bad, you could bet that Kyle, or Ronaldo, would be somewhere else where a lot of people would see them. They weren't clever – their dad had probably told them about that trick – but they weren't stupid either. Once they learned something worked, they didn't forget it, and that was why they were still walking about despite being a pair of violent borderline sociopaths. Everyone on the Edge called them 'The Krays', which most people thought was a smashing together of their names to liken them to the other famous gangster twins, Reggie and Ronnie. But actually it was 'cray' with a C which is short for 'crazy', among the youth and if you called them the Krays to their faces, then they would kick your head in, as more than one unfortunate had found out. Still, it had stuck in my head.

They made me nervous.

Their dad was Trolley Mick.

He made me more nervous.

I heard him coming before I saw him. Kyle, or Ronaldo, went outside and gave some signal, then the whine of an electric motor heralded Trolley Mick's arrival.

In the eighties and nineties, Trolley Mick had ruled Blades Edge; everyone had been terrified of him. When I was at school, he was the bogeyman used to ensure good behaviour: 'Trolley Mick'll come for you.' Though, if you were one of the many Stanbecks at the school, you could do whatever you wanted – unless you were in the English teacher, Miss Feeney's class, as she was having none of that. My old English teacher was the only person I ever met in my youth who wasn't frightened of the Stanbecks, and I spent many breaks hiding in her classroom because it was a safe place. Mick cracked down on his family's behaviour eventually. I think he worked out clever was more useful to him than violent, and I always wondered if Miss Feeney helped him with that realisation. Now St Jude's School – or Choppy's as we all called it on the Edge – was, if not a great school, at least not the hellhole I'd been "educated" in.

Mick was a bodybuilder back then; shell suits and mullets and arms thicker than my waist. Someone broke his legs with a baseball bat in the early nineties. Or he broke them skiing. Or he got run over. Or he was kneecapped by the Mafia. The story was always changing. But he stopped exercising, and the muscle turned to fat. He got too used to the mobility scooter he started using and never regained his old shape. Even when his legs started working, he never got off the scooter. That was the noise I heard: the mobility scooter's electric engine complaining under Mick's weight.

They didn't call him 'Trolley Mick' because of the scooter though; they'd always called him that. Started out as Off His Trolley Mick, because of his temper. I'd heard he had less of a temper now. I still had no wish to cross him.

I had no wish to meet him either, but that seemed unavoidable.

He was a grotesque, and it wasn't because of the way he looked. It was because he chose to be grotesque – or didn't care, I don't know. He rode the sort of mobility scooter you didn't see any more; bashed and rusted, blue where there still was paint. The seat, more electrical tape than vinyl, on the end of a tube of metal, handlebars the same, and it didn't look like it should support the pyramid of flesh that was

Trolley Mick. He wore green canvas trousers and a once pink shirt. Both were filthy. He'd always worn his hair long and still did, but now it was a mess of wispy, greasy grey strands smeared across the liver-spotted skin of his scalp and forehead. His face was mean, like all his features had gathered in the centre of it for fear of falling off the rolling flesh around his skull. And he stank – rumour was he just couldn't be bothered to wash, but I didn't believe that. Trolley Mick ran Blades Edge and everything on it, and no one had managed to take it off him yet. He was a man who calculated everything. He knew he was repellent; relied on it, I imagine. You saw him, you made a decision. You judged him, people wrote him off or wanted to stay away from him. He used that, his physical presence, the smell of him, to intimidate people.

He certainly intimidated me.

'That bitch has been in here,' he said.

'Sorry?'

'My daughter-in-law. Don't bother lying.' It sounded like every word was a strain, like his voice box had been burned out and the words were being forced through smoke and hurt. He took a pouch of tobacco from a pocket and started to roll a cigarette. 'You going to tell me it's no smoking in here?'

'I try not to waste my time.'

He looked up from rolling his cigarette. 'Me too.'

'He's got no TV, Da,' said Kray One.

'Says it's not con-juice-ive, Da,' said Kray Two.

'That means, "to make an outcome likely or possible", Da.'

'Well, boysm,' he said, adding an 'm' to boys, making it buzz like there was a wasp in the room 'Let's hope our visit is conducive to Mr Jones helping us, eh?'

'Yes, Da.'

'No need to talk anymore, boysm.'

'Yes, Da.'

'I know why the bitch came here, Jones. And what she's after is mine, right? One of my boys won it, so it's mine. You find it, you give it to me. Not her.'

'I can only follow the path the spirits lay out before me – I may not find anything.'

'None of your bollocks, Jones. You're a clever little shit with a way of finding things out and that's been useful to me, on occasion. But you're clean now, and good for you – I like a man that betters himself. You're up here fleecing old ladies, and that's none of my affair.' He glared at me with little piggy eyes. 'But don't interfere in my family's business, lad. Now, I'm not gonna mess about, Jones. I do not like hurting people. But sometimes, I think people feel the need to be hurt. And they choose me as the conduit of their pain.'

'Conduit,' said Kray One. And Kray Two took out their dictionary. The mobility scooter whined across the floor as Mick drove a little nearer.

'Don't hurt yourself, lad, Okay?' He reached up with a meaty hand, rolled-up cigarette smouldering between huge, nicotine-stained fingers. He gently slapped my cheek once, twice, three times. 'You do as I ask, lad. And you will, cos you are a fuck-up. Your mother was a fuck-up, a whore too stupid to charge for opening her legs, and you are too. If your brown friend hadn't dragged you out the gutter, you'd still be there now.' He smiled as he said the words, and I noticed the end of his pointed nose moved with every breath he took. 'I know fuck-ups, Jones – it only takes a little push to send you reeling back to where you came from. You find that ticket, you give it to me and we're done again. I'm not an unfair man – you'll get a finder's fee.'

'And if I don't?'

'Then I will push, Malachite Jones, and then you will fall off the edge.' The scooter whined as he reversed it. 'Boysm, you give Mr Jones here a gentle lesson – let him know we mean what we say, but no bruises, nothing broken, okay?'

'Yes, Da,' they said.

4

Steven Hitch died on the 4 May 1992. It was a bank holiday and the hottest day of the year. 'Please Don't Go' by KWS was at number one, and I was fourteen. I'd just discovered Nirvana and thought that Kurdt Cobain (sic) was the only person in the world who truly understood me.

Steve's death wasn't mysterious or violent or particularly memorable. He fell on Blades Edge Hill, hit his head, died. Most people probably don't even remember it.

He was my best friend.

Not my only friend – there were four of us. Me, Steve, Alby (short for Albert) Hersden and Sharon Shaftsbury. Though we didn't see Sharon as much, as she was just discovering she was attractive to boys and had an on-again off-again relationship with Steve that governed whether she hung out with us or not.

Me and Steve were inseparable. He shared all the sticky details of a boy's first love with his terminally uninteresting-to-girls friend. I shared all the gifts my parents showered on me. Our friendship was based around books, music and the comic *2000AD*. It never made much sense to me, our friendship; Steve was almost popular, for one of the grunge kids, and I definitely wasn't. But still, friendships are strange things.

Jackie Singh Khattar made our lives hell. He didn't have a gang or anything like that. But no one messed with him; he was wrong, everyone knew it. Bright lad, capable, and so very clearly on course to end up in prison. If he'd been white the Stanbecks would have picked him up in a flash. But he wasn't, and they didn't. A large part of my early teens was spent running or hiding from Jackie Singh Khattar's fists or his wicked tongue. There were others that made school miserable, but they weren't in Jackie's league.

Sometimes, when it's really hot, I dream of that night. Of running across Blades Edge Hill, Alby somewhere behind me, Steve behind him, Jackie behind them, chasing us. I know, in the dream, that Steve is actually dead, that he's not running. But dreams don't care about that. Steve is there, and he's trying to tell me something, but I don't know what. His face is covered in blood, his forehead dented by the rock he fell against.

I wake up, covered in sweat, feeling the same way I did when I went through withdrawal. Hot and shivery, hungry and nauseous. Sometimes I think I hear Steve's voice but I block it out, put on earphones, blast music, the radio, anything, because I don't hear voices.

I sometimes wonder who I would be if Steve had lived, who Jackie would be too, cos that night changed us both. It pushed us together, sent Jackie on a trajectory that would end in the army, doing God knows what in God knows where, and me on a course that would end in a gutter, drinking cheap cider and begging for enough spare change to buy my next hit.

Guilt is a terrible thing.

Jackie didn't want me to be an addict, and as part of not being an addict, he taught me to fight. I'm not good at it, and violence mostly scares me, but if you're not expecting it I know enough to hold my own and make enough space to run away.

That was the first thing Jackie taught me, his first rule: if you can, run away.

The reason Trolley Mick wanted his boys to check my office for Jackie is that Jackie Singh Khattar, despite his rule, has never run away from anything. If Mick started something with Jackie, then he knew it would end with someone dead because Jackie has no idea how to stay down.

It is not a part of who he is.

I, on the other hand, know exactly how and when to stay down. So when Kray One punched me in the stomach, I went down. Then when he lifted me up – my world empty of air, my stomach a black hole in my body, the pain sucking me in – and held me so his brother could have a go. I went down again. That's why, when Beryl returned, she found me lying on the floor, curled up in a ball around my aching stomach muscles.

'You drunk?' she said.

'No.' I could see her feet; she was wearing sandals and had painted her toenails an unpleasant shade of yellow.

'High?'

'No.'

'Good. You want some tea?'

'No.'

'Can't blame you. It's shit tea.'

'Yes.'

'And you should never have got involved with a Stanbeck,' she said.

'I know.'

'You better get up – Mrs Lantry is coming at four.' I sat up, had to use my hands to do it as my stomach muscles felt like old elastic bands.

'I told you to cancel that.'

'And I said if you want to cancel it, you ring her. I'm not your secretary.'

'You actually really are. That's what your contract says and everything.'

She stared at me. 'I'll make you some shit tea.'

'Don't tell Jackie about this.'

'He probably knows.' I followed Beryl into the little kitchen.

'Yeah, but if he knows I know he knows, he'll feel like he should do something.'

'No great loss if he sorts out Stanbeck and his lot.' She filled the kettle. 'Nice if they did for him too.'

I ignored that. I never quite understood why Beryl hated Jackie so much.

'How did your date go?'

'I got some action, but she was too skinny for me. I'm looking for real love.'

'Two sugars, please, Beryl.'

'One.'

The office bell rang again. And I left the little kitchen to go deal with my client.

'Mrs Lantry, I—'

It wasn't Mrs Lantry. It was two women, both in off-the-peg suits and flat shoes. One was tall, white, sharp and austere, the other small, black, round and smiling. But if she was happy that was unlikely to mean anything good for me.

'Not conning pensioners out of their savings today, Mr Jones,' she said with a grin. 'I am afraid Mrs Lantry is in the cells for shoplifting biscuits from Aldi. But she was most upset that you might think she had stood you up, so I agreed to come and tell you about it, as I was coming here anyway.'

'Why?'

The taller woman, DC Sarah Harrington, stared at me. 'To arrest you for fraud,' she said. She'd tried that before. A few times.

'Provide a service, that's all I do,' I said.

The smaller woman, DI Esther Smith, bustled over and linked her arm through mine. There was something of the mother hen to Esther, though I suspect that was a deliberate ploy to make people like and trust her.

I did not trust her. She didn't like Jackie and saw me as a way to get to him.

'Of course you do, love,' DI Smith said, and patted me on the arm. 'Of course you do. Now you, my sweet, have had an exciting day haven't you?'

'You don't have to speak to the pigs, Mal,' said Beryl from the back room. DI Smith didn't even react to her voice.

'Janine Stanbeck, Trolley Mick and his two soft lads have all been to visit you in one day,' said DI Smith. 'That's a very busy day for you, isn't it? What's happening, Malachite? Not gone back to shoplifting, have you? Supplying them with some cheap meat, are you? Or are you running your little con jobs again? Cos if you've slipped back into drugs,

I'll be very let down – we had a lot of fun when I was a constable, but let's not go through it again, right?'

'They had questions for the spirits, that's all.' I tried to get loose from her grip but she wasn't having that. 'How do you know who comes into my office?'

'I know everything that happens on the Edge.' She looked up into my face and pointed at me with an exquisitely manicured, bright-red nail.

'This isn't the Edge.'

'It's near enough.' She placed a foot on mine and leant her weight onto it.

'I think you might be police-brutalising me, DI Smith.'

'I can't see anything happening,' said DC Harrington.

DI Smith started to grind her foot a little.

'Alright,' I said and pulled my foot from under hers. 'She wanted to contact her ex. Mick wanted to know why.'

She stared at me.

'I would like to know why too, Malachite. Why don't you share your information with Aunt Esther?'

'Because we haven't got that far yet. I don't have anything to share.'

'Trolley Mick doesn't leave the Edge without a very good reason,' she said.

'I really don't know what that might be.'

'You don't know.' The register of her voice dropped with each word.

'But—'

'But, my love?' she smiled.

'Maybe I could take a guess in exchange for a look at Larry Stanbeck's autopsy report.'

She stared at me again. She wore bright-red lipstick to match her nails; some of it was smeared on one of her front teeth.

'Autopsy report?' she said. 'I can arrange that for you.'

'You can?'

'Of course I can – I'm a DI, sweet.' She grinned up into my face. 'Now, maybe in this new-found spirit of cooperation, you could share a little bit of information about your special friend, as a starter?'

'Jackie?'

'I don't think he has any other friends,' said DC Harrington.

'What could I have on Jackie?' I said. 'He is a successful local businessman, Detective Inspector.'

'My arse he is.' She leaned in close and trod on my foot again. 'He's scum, and we both know it. Though I have to admit, he's charming scum – I quite like him.' She pulled me closer to her using our linked arms, so she could speak in a whisper. 'One day, Malachite Jones, he will go down. And you know what? He will be fine in jail when he does. He's a hard one. But you will fall with him – I will make sure of it – and you are not a man cut out for jail, my love, are you? So, maybe you should think about making some more friends now, eh?'

'I don't know anything about Jackie's business.'

'Oh, come on, there must be some of your father's blood in there, right?' She touched my chest.

She was good at her job, DI Smith, and she knew she had lost me as soon as she mentioned my father, if not why. She sighed and let her arm snake out of mine, stepping away and relieving the pressure on my foot.

'I thought you were the clever one, Malachite,' she said. 'Turns out I was wrong.' She walked to the door, followed by DC Harrington, but paused in the doorway. 'Tell me, if I look in your drawers, am I going to find a load of false IDs?'

'No, DI Smith,' I said, 'and you'd need a warrant to look in my drawers.' Any trace of bonhomie fled.

'Free advice, Mal: you are not a bad man. Whatever you have got yourself into with the Stanbecks won't end well – extricate yourself from it as quickly as you can. If I end up watching some SOCO picking bits of your brain off these walls, it will ruin my day.' She pointed at me. 'You add a bit of local colour. I like it.'

5

I have never been particularly popular. It's not my thing. So, four sets of visitors in one day was a bit much. And that was why the phone on my desk was currently ringing, and I was currently ignoring it, despite occasional shouts of 'pick up the fucking phone, twat,' from Beryl in the back office.

Back office is a bit of a stretch actually. It is more a small kitchen with a desk where she keeps her computer.

But I wasn't picking up the fucking phone no matter what she said. It was keeping up a steady rhythm, ringing eighteen times before I heard the click of my old-fashioned answering machine – cassette-based that I'd picked up at a car boot sale – taking the call. Then the phone would go dead. Start to ring again.

It was on its eleventh ring when Beryl's meaty face appeared at the door.

'It's your mate.'

'Which one.'

'You only have one,' she said and slipped back into her office. I picked up the phone.

Me: Jackie, you absolute arsehole.

Jackie: What do you mean by that, Mal?'

Me: First you send Janine, who quite plainly did not want to be here. I could have done with a bit of warning about just how sceptical she was.

Jackie: Yeah. She was pretty sceptical.

Me: I know that. Then I get visited by bloody Trolley Mick and the twins.

Jackie: I've slept with one of them, you know. But I never know which one, so I can't chat up the other.

Me: I didn't know they were gay.

Jackie: Sexuality is a spectrum, Mal.

Me: Stop it! That is not the point, Jackie. After Trolley Mick came round I got a visit from Esther Smith.

Jackie: She fancies me.

Me: Jackie …

Jackie: I like police officers, they're all dirty.

Me: Jackie. That is not the—

Jackie: Still, it means Larry's money's real – that's good, innit?

Me: I'm not sure it is if Trolley Mick is involved. He wants me to find it.

Jackie: Obviously, you're good at stuff like that. A million is a physically large amount of cash, Mal, and she led me to believe it was a lot more than that. So he'd want some sort of secure lock-up – that's what you should be looking for.

Me: It's a lottery ticket.

Jackie: A what?

Me: It's not cash, Jackie. It's a lottery ticket.

Jackie: Fuck.

Me: That is pretty succinct explanation of the situation.

Jackie: How do you find a lottery ticket?

Me: I wish I knew.

Jackie: DI Smith is probably interested in Trolley Mick, not you. Or maybe me.

Me: She's definitely interested in you.

Jackie: I did say she fancies me.

Me: I didn't mean like that.

Jackie: Yeah, but she does.

Me: She wants you locked up.

Jackie: Told you, police are dirty.

Me: Jackie, what am I going to do? Trolley Mick actually thinks I can talk to the dead – he is expecting me to find this money.

Jackie: You can't give it to him. He's a bastard.

Me: I can't give it to anybody, Jackie – it's a bit of paper, I don't know where it is and there's no realistic way of me finding it.

Jackie: We'll sort something out.

A long pause.

Jackie: Did the Krays hurt you?

Me: Nothing I can't handle.

Jackie: You'd tell me if they really hurt you though?

Me: Yes.

Jackie: Good. You get some sleep or something – have a think on what we do next.

He put the phone down.

Helpful as always.

I have a client called Elsie Smallwood, and Elsie Smallwood was sure that her deceased husband, Eric – well, Eric's ghost – was stealing money from her. This upset Elsie because she and Eric had always been close, and if he wanted the money, he could just ask. Now, if I was actually dishonest, rather than someone providing an important, if admittedly slightly dishonest, service, I could have welcomed Elsie into my office, told her Eric needed the money but couldn't ask from the great beyond and Elsie would have been happy with that. Fifty quid in my pocket and a happy client who was probably going to come back to me so she could have a chat with her husband now and then.

But the whole thing felt wrong.

Elsie was sure that Eric was taking the money because there was never any sign of a break-in when the money went missing, so how else could the money be vanishing from her bedside cabinet?

How else indeed?

So, we had a puzzle, and I was determined to find out the solution.

Which that is why I spent five nights in December 2015 up a tree with a pair of binoculars watching Elsie's bungalow in the Nine Elms assisted-living park. Because, of course, Eric isn't stealing money; Eric is mouldering in a box in the churchyard. But someone was stealing money, and Elsie was eighty-two and she had paid me fifty pounds. I owed her.

It had turned out that Eric used to like a drink, and when he stayed out late, he often forgot his keys, so he hid a key under the doormat, which his neighbour and drinking partner, Clive, knew about. And Clive also knew Elsie took a lot of painkillers, so Clive liked to drop in and help himself to her savings when she was asleep and as dead to the world as her dearly departed husband.

So, I had a word with Clive, but Clive didn't really care what I thought. So, Jackie had a word with Clive, and Clive did, after a bit of persuasion, care what Jackie thought. So the next time Elsie came to see me – twenty-five pounds, because the second visit is half price – I told her how Eric was thankful for the money and had returned it to her with the key he had been using and refunded her the fifty quid of my original consultation fee as he didn't want her to be out of pocket, and she would find it all under her doormat.

I'm not a person who, presented with something unlikely, just takes the easiest option. I am quite stubborn. To the point of, maybe, not quite learning the lessons I should but I am not a quitter is the point.

Clive was not a quitter either. He died of exposure when he got stuck part way in the bathroom window of Elsie's neighbour on the other side, trying to steal from her, but that illustrates another truth of life: just cos you find a way, doesn't mean it will work.

But it doesn't mean you shouldn't try, and besides, I like puzzles. Most mysteries aren't mysteries at all, the answer is usually right in front of you.

Beryl had made me a folder on Janine Stanbeck, where she lived, her family, etc. In the file, there was a picture of her wedding from a newspaper with the word *twats* written above it – Beryl's work. Janine looked like a sad and lonely figure. There were no pictures of her husband, Larry – odd for wedding photos – but the women and men who were there all had the Stanbeck stamp on their faces. Trolley Mick was hanging round the edges of the pictures. Janine didn't look like she had anyone, and still, she stared into the cameras as though taking it on in a fight. I wondered what she had been running from at home to end up there.

I'm not sure how knowing that would help me find a lottery ticket, but there's no such thing as bad information. I stared at the picture a bit more and felt oddly melancholy. It was a while until I realised why. In my head, I've been programmed like everyone else to think of a wedding as the happiest day of someone's life, but in the picture no one was smiling. Not even Larry Stanbeck when I finally found one with him in it – he was avoiding looking at the camera the way I avoid pubs.

I didn't really like Janine Stanbeck, but if I really wanted to find this lottery ticket, then her home was where to start, and I couldn't see a way of avoiding visiting it without her being there. I liked the idea of putting it off, but I knew it would tug at the edges of my conscious until I did. So I went round to Mr Agarwal, who was the current manager of Spice 'N' Saucy and asked to borrow his car, which he was happy enough to lend me. I have a car of my own but I wasn't going to drive it into Blades Edge.

Some things are ingrained into you young, and the roads of Blades Edge are as much a part of me as the veins in my arms. It was created as a paradise, patches of green, alleyways running between the houses and fences you could talk to your neighbours over. Plenty of playgrounds with borderline lethal equipment for kids to play on, two pubs, a church, a school and a working-men's club. There were old couples on the estate who still remembered the slums that had been in the city, who remembered the sense of wonder they'd felt when they first moved to the Edge. Didn't last, of course. Cheap buildings poorly maintained, not enough investment in the space, and by the time I was growing up there, it was where the council put the problem families and then tried to forget about them.

I knew every street and back alley because, for my entire childhood, knowing where to avoid and where to hide felt like the only way to survive.

Summer had come to the Edge and the green spaces, usually tramlined with the scars of joyriding cars, were now scrubby brown spaces tramlined by the scars of joyriding cars. Rubbish collected in gutters and gangs of teenagers lounged on street corners. Younger children played in gardens around huge paddling pools and couples, old before their time, watched me drive past with suspicious eyes.

I was glad I wasn't walking.

The car broke down at the top of Hensley Lane where Janine Stanbeck lived. I rang Mr Agarwal at Spice 'N' Saucy, and he told me to leave the car where it was. He didn't seem to care that it would probably lose its wheels, but I wouldn't want to pass through the Edge just to get back a car that was ninety per cent rust if my skin was brown either. I called Jackie instead, told him where the car was and I half hoped he would come, not to pick up the car – I knew he wouldn't – but just to walk with me.

He didn't.

Jackie has a very 'what doesn't kill you makes you stronger' approach to other people's lives.

Hensley Lane was the longest street on the Edge; it curved round the outside of the entire estate with other streets branching off it. In the centre was what had been a shopping centre but had closed down and was now just a brutalist canvas for local graffiti artists, though 'artists' was a stretch. However, if you wanted to know who was a slag, then the Hensley Centre was the place to go. The road used to be a racetrack for joyriders, but traffic-calming measures had been put in that, if they hadn't stopped the races, had at least slowed the cars down. Hensley Lane also provided the only way in and out of the estate. all the other roads were blocked with concrete bollards. And, together with the hill rising behind it, they served to make the place even more like a prison. A gentle rain started to fall, but it brought no relief; the smell I associated with new rain after a warm day was absent. Somewhere a barbecue was happening and somewhere else, from the smell, I suspected someone was burning plastic. I didn't look, didn't search the skyline for a plume of black smoke – let the place do what it wants. I wanted no part of it.

I felt the van draw up, a darkening of the world as its shadow crossed me. The chug of poorly maintained diesel engine complaining as the driver geared down to slow the vehicle. I kept my hands in my jacket pockets, kept my eyes fixed on the floor. There were people here who had never left the Edge and to whom anyone who looked different or had come from outside their little world was fair game. They might shout at me, spit at me, who knows, but I knew that the best way of dealing with things like this was to ignore them.

'Mal Jones?' The voice, heavy with an Irish accent. I ignored it. 'Mal, Mal Jones, is it not?'

It didn't sound unfriendly but in my experience it was often the way things started. The people I'd known on the Edge, when I lived here in another life, were the dealers and the lifters and the small-time crooks and the drunks and the ex-cons; people whose tempers turned on a penny, who had triggers that would make no sense to most people. I once saw a man hospitalised because he'd eaten the last packet of cheese-and-onion crisps. I saw a fight start because a girl was reading a book. I hated that I had been one of them. I hated this place because I blamed it for that.

'Come on, Mal, don't be a snob, eh?'

I turned, little choice, really. If someone was really insistent, then ignoring them was as likely to end badly as engaging them.

Driving the van, an old Ford of some sort that had been hand painted a lurid purple in what looked like emulsion, was Benny Callaghan, ostensibly a scrap dealer but in reality he headed up the traveller community on the Edge and was Trolley Mick's right hand. He wasn't a physically big man, generally wore a filthy woollen beanie hat to cover up the fact he was entirely bald. His face was tan and red, weathered by sun and drink.

I knew Benny in passing, but I'd known his wife, Sheila, better. I suppose you could even say we'd been friends. She had been a barmaid at The Highlander, the biggest pub on Blades Edge before they demolished it. I'd been pretty regular there, as it was where you went if you wanted to score drugs. During the day, it was full of Blades Edge's regular drinkers, hard men and women who were smashed out of their faces by lunchtime. In the early evening, younger people went there to pick up deals from the steady stream of shoplifters and burglars coming in and out – one of them usually being me. Later, the DJ would set up and it would fill up with a mixture of the Edge's youth, eager to drink as much cider as they could, and people from outside the Edge, noticeably more affluent, dropping in to score drugs for the night's clubbing.

There were a lot of fights but it was mostly ignored by the police, until a Yardie gang tried to muscle in on Mick's territory, and there were a couple of shootings that made the papers. Then the police had to act, and The Highlander was closed down. It was derelict for a long time, slowly accruing graffiti and buddleia plants. The drug dealing still happened there, in the shadows of the mouldering building, while the council and the brewery that owned it fought over the pub's fate. While the building slowly died, so did Benny's wife, eaten away by lung cancer from the sixty cigarettes a day she put away.

They had a boy too, Callum. He'd got himself in trouble though, and his dad had seen fit to get him off the estate somehow. It must have been pretty lonely being Benny now.

'You'll be going to Janine's then?' said Benny.

'My car broke down.'

Stay non-committal.

'Odd to see you on the Edge now, Mal. You're a proper businessman now, eh? Got a shop and all.'

'Yes, Benny.'

Keep walking, keep walking.

'Only I know what you're about, Mal, the money and all.'

I stopped walking.

'Money?'

Benny brought the van to a halt, pulling on the handbrake to keep the van still on the slight incline.

'Aye, Lawrence's winnings, right? Mick told me, so don't worry yourself. I'm not like him.' He grinned.

It was true, he wasn't. I'd known Benny a long time and as long he was sober and you didn't owe him anything, he was a generally reasonable human being.

'Now listen, Mal,' Benny continued. 'I know how Mick can put people on edge, and he'll want that money, you know that. And I know you, from your wilder days, eh?' A big smile. 'We had a great time, then, didn't we?'

We really didn't. He once broke my little finger when I owed him money. Laugh a minute living on the Edge.

'We definitely had a time, Benny.'

'I just thought you should know that you can give the ticket to me, see, if you don't want to deal with Mick or the twins, and who can blame you for that, eh? But if you give it to me, I'll take it to him. I'll make sure everything is smoothed out with no trouble for anyone, eh, Mal?'

'If I find it, I'll remember that.'

He looked at me then, and it was, for a second, like all the world's sorrows rested on his face.

'Well, you do what you think is right, eh?' he said. 'It'll probably be easier for everyone if you go through me, you know what Mick's like.'

'I do.'

'Well, alright then,' he said. It took him four goes to start the van, and every time he tried it coughed out black smoke from the exhaust and he gave me an apologetic smile. Eventually, he got it going and drove off. All my life I'd been aware of Mick Stanbeck and Benny Callaghan. Best friends as kids, grew up together. Ran Mick's gang together. The thought Benny might betray his boss had never occurred to me. I mean, maybe he really did mean it, that he would act as go-between, but why would he do that? And eight million pounds – that was a lot of temptation.

Thankfully, judging the loyalty of Mick's gang members was only my problem if I could find the lottery ticket. And let's be honest, I probably wasn't going to be able to.

That was my problem.

Houses on the Edge tended to go one of two ways: they were either semi-derelict places for people with nowhere else, where you wondered how people coped, or pristine temples to the art of cleaning. I reckoned Janine Stanbeck's house would be the second; a house was a status symbol, and the Stanbecks loves their status symbols: flash cars, stone cladding, seventy five-inch TVs and booming sound systems. Jackie told me I was an idiot for acting like there was no in-between, said there were plenty of normal houses and people on the Edge, but I rarely saw them, and the fact was that the housing on the Edge was so badly built you needed money to make it liveable. The council barely kept up to them. Maybe damp had been part of the architect's design aesthetic.

Janine's house had gateposts with stone lions on top of them, which was definitely a statement. The front garden had been block paved to make room for cars, and two sat there: a four-by-four and a small convertible. It didn't look like she needed to wear hand-me-downs, so I wondered just how controlling her husband must have been that she still did; force of habit can be a powerful thing. I knocked on the door – white plastic, double glazed with an inlaid stained-glass lionesses. A burst of static made me jump.

'Who is it?' Janine's voice, distorted by the small speaker on the intercom by the door.

'It's me, Janine, Mal Jones.'

'What are you doing here?'

'Sometimes it helps to make a connection if I can look around the deceased's house. I can come back if it's inconvenient?'

Please don't make me come back.

'Give me five minutes. I was in the shower.'

'Okay.' I waited five minutes. Then five minutes more. Some very young-looking girls wandered by with babies in pushchairs. I wondered if any of them were named on the walls of the Hensley Centre. While I wondered, they called me a pervert, and one flashed her breasts at me. It wasn't unlikely that they would come back, maybe with friends who were more given over to violence, so I was pleased when Janine finally opened the door. She wore the same clothes as she had in my office, and her hair was damp from the shower.

'Come in,' she said. She didn't sound overly enthusiastic about it.

The entire floor of the house – not big, not really – had been knocked into an ultra-modern kitchen-diner-living room. It was immaculate, and the air was full of the aroma of expensive scented candles. A massive television almost obscured the front window and the long back wall was papered in dark patterned wallpaper. The other walls painted in a light blue to pick up on the wallpaper's highlights. No doubt it was very à la mode, but my interest in interior décor ended in about 1890. The kitchen was all sleek lines, gleaming white.

I hated it.

A little boy was playing on the couch, his face filthy like he'd been eating chocolate ice cream. His hair was shaved almost to the scalp.

'Hello,' I said to him. He stared at me, sizing me up, and then decided the little plastic dragons he was playing with were far more interesting.

'That's Cristophe,' she said. 'He misses his father.' At mention of his father the boy paused, then he tapped the side of his head.

'My daddy knows where it's at,' he said, then he stuck his thumb in his mouth.

'Sometimes it's like Lawrence is still here – he parrots his phrases.' She watched the boy. 'It's him you're working for, Mr Jones. It's his life you can change.'

'Did Lawrence have an office?'

'Upstairs.'

'What, exactly, did he do? Worked for his dad?'

‘Lawrence was an interior designer – he worked for Maylin and Sparrow in town.’ She glanced upstairs. ‘First door on the left,’ she said, ‘and don’t go nosying about in the other rooms.’

‘I won’t.’ I wanted to though. I hoped she’d put the TV on for Cristophe so the noise would cover me sneaking about, but she only stood there, staring at me. And the boy stared at me too, so I turned away. Before I could go up the stairs, she stopped me, calling my name.

‘Mr Jones.’

‘Yes?’

‘We take our shoes off in this house. It’s polite.’ I looked down; both of them were in bare feet.

‘I can keep my socks on though?’

She nodded.

I slipped off my boots and placed them by the door before going upstairs.

‘And if you find any notebooks, Mr Jones,’ she shouted as I went up the stairs, ‘give them to me – his work will want them back.’

Larry Stanbeck’s office wasn’t much more than a cupboard. A desk with a computer on it – with a very old-fashioned CRT monitor – and a load of paper files. I switched the computer on and perused the files while it booted up. They were sets of tax records. I presumed Janine had been through them but there was no harm in going through them again. Mostly they were dull receipts. I noticed receipts from Mr Patel’s shop coming up a lot – someone had bought cigarettes and printer paper from him. I knew Mr Patel had a Lotto machine, so I’d ask him if he knew Lawrence

Stanbeck. Going through the boxes of papers I found a notebook full of what looked like architectural drawings and notes. I balanced it precariously on top of the old-fashioned computer monitor so I wouldn't forget to give it to Janine. As I was leafing through another file, a movement caught my eye; Cristophe was standing in the doorway staring at me.

'My daddy knows where it's at,' he said again and rubbed the side of his head. 'Do you know where my daddy is?'

I span round in the chair, catching the table with the arm of it and only just catching a thick tax file as it slid off the desk.

'I … no. Sorry.'

'I love my daddy,' he said. Then I heard Janine coming up the stairs, and Cristophe turned and ran into, what I presumed was, his bedroom.

'Don't bother Mr Jones while he's working,' Janine shouted into the room.

'I want my daddy!' shouted the boy, and his voice broke into sobs. 'I want my daddy.'

She stared into the child's bedroom, shut the door and turned to me.

I felt like I was intruding in a place I should not be.

'Look what you've done.' So did Janine.

There was no coming back from upsetting a widow's child, so I changed the subject.

'I'd like to look at the computer – there might be something on there that gives me a feel for him. Do you know the password?' I said.

'Can't Lawrence tell you?'

'It doesn't …'

‘Jan1382,’ she said, with a snort. ‘My name and my birthday. I’ll shut the door.’ She tapped it closed with her foot.

I spent the entire afternoon going through Larry Stanbeck’s files and his computer, and found nothing. The only thing of interest was two regular payments to the local council. One was rent for the lock-up Janine had mentioned, but I couldn’t find any reference to the other one. It wasn’t in his accounts as a business expense – it wasn’t down as an expense at all – and I wondered if he was paying for a lock-up somewhere else.

I bobbed into the toilet and noticed that there was still three toothbrushes by the sink; little details like that bring home the fact someone is never coming home. I picked up the toothbrush in a very masculine blue and put it in the medicine cupboard, among a small pharmacy’s worth of drugs.

When I finished in the office, I made sure everything was put away neatly, then looked at the room. I couldn’t shake the feeling I’d forgotten something but couldn’t see what, so I went back downstairs.

‘Janine,’ I said, sliding my boots back on, ‘there’s a payment of thirty pounds a month to the council …’

‘Oh, I need to cancel that.’

‘What was it for?’

‘Lawrence hasn’t told you?’

‘I’m asking you.’

‘The fucking Scouts – he was saving to pay for a camping trip.’

‘Scouts?’

'He was a Scout leader. He wanted to do some good – pillar of the community and all that.'

'Oh,' I said. 'Have you still got the key to his lock-up?'

'I told you it's empty.' She glared at me.

'Physically empty, maybe. But not spiritually.'

The look she was giving me was not a friendly look. She turned and picked up an expensive-looking bag from the leather couch, rooted about in it until she found her keys and peeled one off.

'It's off the estate, on Carston's Mount, near the grammar school. Garage number five.' She gave me the key.

'If he was a Scout leader, there must be a Scout hut?'

'I never got involved in that,' she said, putting her bag back down. 'I know he wasn't allowed to leave anything there.'

'Where was it?' She shrugged. 'Well, I'd also like a picture of Lawrence, if possible, and, this is a little delicate …'

'I'm a big girl.'

'Have the police given you anything about his death? Any details, reports, anything?'

'Are you kidding? To them I'm a Stanbeck – the enemy. They can only just bring themselves not to gloat over Lawrence's death.' She walked over to a chest of drawers by the fireplace and opened a drawer. She took out a picture frame and removed the back, taking the picture from it. 'Here.'

'You don't have to give me your …'

‘I don’t really want to think about it. You should go now – I have to give Cristophe his dinner and I’m meant to keep his life as normal as possible.’ She pushed the picture at me. ‘You don’t help with normal.’

I took the picture and left.

6

It's difficult to get a taxi from Blades Edge – not many of the companies will come into the estate – but I have the number of a firm that owe Jackie a favour. Even then, I had to walk to the Hensley Centre to get picked up. While I did, I stared at the picture of Larry 'Lawrence' Stanbeck. It was much better than the wedding picture. He didn't look like a thug, didn't look at all like I expected. He was a round, comfortable and jolly-looking man. Younger than me, he would have been at St Jude's just as I was leaving, but he looked older than me in the picture because his hair was thinning. He wore a blue shirt open at the collar. The picture was posed for, with a background sheet of some sort. He had a tanned face, lines around the corner of his eyes and his smile revealed good teeth, but the smile didn't quite reach his eyes. I'd known people like that all my life; people on the edge of society, haunted people. I stared at the headshot. He didn't look like a Stanbeck, which was odd.

'Where would you hide a lottery ticket, eh?' I said. Larry didn't answer. Of course he didn't – he was dead.

I rang Beryl.

Beryl: What?

Me: Beryl, you're meant to say, "Mal Jones, Psychic Medium".

Beryl: Have you forgotten who you are?

Me: No … that … It doesn't matter.

Beryl: What do you want?

Me: Larry Stanbeck was involved in the Scouts, can you find out where his Scout hut was?

Beryl: Can't you?

Me: Research is why I have you, Beryl.

Beryl: I've got things to do.

Me: Could you do this first, please?

A long sigh, and the phone went dead just as the cab turned up. I got in and he took the quickest way out of the estate. While he drove, I gave him the address of Larry Stanbeck's lock-up, and he nodded. The suburbs of the city are full of odd, hidden little alleys and backroads and the lock-up was on one of those, at the end of a street of tall houses with pointy gables covered in fancy woodwork. I could see the grammar school where Cat Maudy's children had gone from here, more like a castle than a school. It struck me, as we turned into a weed-ridden alley between two big houses, that if you wanted to deal drugs to school kids with too much money, this would be a good place to set yourself up.

Larry Stanbeck might not look like a Stanbeck, but he was still a Stanbeck.

The taxi driver stopped at the end of the alley and I asked him how much.

'No charge, mate, on Jackie's account, innit?'

I told him to leave the meter running and wait for me. Then I strolled down the alley toward the lock-up.

There were ten garages in a little yard behind the big houses. It was exactly the sort of place that probably attracted letters of complaint to the council from the residents of the houses around it; rubbish had gathered between the concrete garages, one of which had a smashed metal door, painted blue and dotted with rust, stuck open at an angle across the doorway. I crouched down to look inside. More because I am nosy than anything else. It was empty apart from some damp-looking old bedding and a few empty bottles. Someone homeless had set up there, but it looked like they had moved on. I glanced over my shoulder and saw a stern-looking grey-haired woman watching me from the back window of the house on my right. I bet the homeless person didn't get to stay here long. I waved at the woman, and she closed the curtains. Not very friendly.

Janine Stanbeck had told me which garage was Larry's, but I had forgotten, so I had to go from garage to garage, trying the key until I found one that fitted. When I did, I turned round to find the old woman back at the window. I gave her another wave, but she didn't wave back. Really not the friendly type.

Janine had been telling the truth about the lock-up being emptied. There was no sign of life at all in the garage. A couple of shelves were on one side; there was nothing on them but dead beetles. Near the shelves was a patch of oil and a scratch on the concrete floor, which I guessed was from the kickstand for Larry's motorbike. There were plugs and lights in the garage which was odd, as most council garages didn't have electricity, and when I tried to follow the line outside, it vanished into a thicket of brambles. Past the brambles was a high fence, and beyond that was an alley with a lonely streetlight. Larry had probably hooked the electricity into that illegally. On the walls of the garage were lighter squares where it looked like there had been posters, and when I looked around the edges of the garage, I found nails from a nail gun driven into the floor, bits of material were still attached in places. It looked like there had once been a carpet in here.

'Malachite Jones, imagine finding you here.'

I turned to find DI Esther Smith leaning against the door. A golden cross sparkled against the dark skin of her chest where the top few buttons of her blouse were open. She had her arms crossed over her chest. Behind her was DC Sarah Harrington, looking as disapproving as ever.

'When we got a report of someone suspicious nosing about out here, I didn't expect it to be someone quite as suspicious as you, eh, Mal?'

'Isn't this a job for a uniform, DI Smith? Checking out suspicious-person reports from elderly ladies?'

'Mrs Jasom isn't just any elderly lady, Mal, she's head of the neighbourhood watch for this area. I'd asked her to keep an eye out for anyone tampering with Larry's lock-up.' She pushed herself off the wall of the garage. 'And here we are.'

'Yes,' I said, 'here we are.'

'And here you are, Mal. If you're running a con on the Stanbecks, you're either braver or stupider than I thought you were.'

'I'm not running a con. Janine asked for my services.'

'And you're here trying to contact the spirits on her behalf?' Gently mocking.

'Familiar spaces often contain echoes and—'

'You can save me some time by dropping the mumbo jumbo. Something is up with the Stanbecks, and Larry died because of it. I want to know what it is.'

'It was murder then?' I said.

She narrowed her eyes. 'It's a suspicious death, alright. We have questions, like why someone cleaned out this lock-up for a start.'

'You didn't then?'

'No.' She shook her head and walked in. 'This place was a home away from home originally – carpet, desks, chairs, illegal electricity supply. I wasn't happy having the Stanbecks so near a school, so I'd come and see Larry every so often. Said he just used this place for his Scouting duties. Wouldn't let me in without a warrant.'

'Imagine that, Detective Inspector, someone not trusting the police.'

She stepped closer. She was smaller than me, and rounder, but there was a fierceness to her that I utterly lacked.

'The Stanbecks are up to something,' she said.

'They're always up to something.'

'I know that, but as long as they're just dealing drugs to losers on the Edge and beating each other up about it, I don't care. If they stay on the Edge, then they're welcome to it, and Mick knows that. I've been happily ignoring the Stanbecks for most of my career. But now someone has died, Mal, so I have to pay attention.' She stared straight into my eyes. 'Something else is going on.' A gap in her sentence she hoped I would fill. 'I think you know what.'

I let the silence settle. Listened to the hiss of cars passing on the road beyond the big houses.

'If the spirits tell me anything, I will be sure to share it.'

DI Smith shook her head. Her smile dropped away. 'This is a potential crime scene, Mal, so piss off. If I see you back here, then I'll do you for obstruction of justice.'

I stood, waiting for something, but I didn't know what. After a bit, I felt a little uncomfortable. 'I better be off then,' I said, 'got a taxi waiting.'

'I sent it away.'

'Thanks.' I walked past DI Smith and up the potholed road. As I passed the last garage, she shouted after me.

'And stay away from his Scout hut too – there's nothing there!'

I had to wait fifteen minutes for another cab, and spent it watching DI Smith and DC Harrington drive past me, numerous times, to check I didn't head back to the garage.

So, I headed back to my office instead.

I might not have been able to visit the Scout hut, but if Beryl had found the address, I could look at it on internet maps and do a search for it in any recent news stories.

However, I didn't expect my office to be occupied when I got back. I generally don't expect it to be occupied at all.

Two men were waiting for me. One was small and wide – muscular wide, like someone who worked out a lot, and he stood at the back of the office. He had a head the shape of a bullet, and his hair was shaved into a silvery sheen across his scalp. When he looked at me, his eyes were such a pale blue as to seem almost blank. On his back he had a knapsack and it pulled the cheap blue suit he wore out of shape. Sat in my chair was another man; older, his suit was expensive, and he had thick dark hair, slicked back like Ray Liotta in *Goodfellas,* but where Ray's face was sharp his was soft, like he lived too well. He stood up, a big – genuine – smile on his face that revealed a golden incisor.

'Mr Jones,' he said. He had the voice and outrageous accent of a Russian bond villain. I stood where I was, unsure what to do.

'Did Beryl let you in?'

'Oh no.' He waved his hands in the air, laughing. 'We let ourselves in. But do not worry, we did not do any damage – we are very much the professionals.'

'Well …' I sat in the client's chair opposite the man. 'Thanks, I guess. Look, I've had a really busy day and—'

'I am Frank,' said the man. 'And my compatriot' – he spelled out each syllable like it was a word he had only just learned – 'is Harry. Harry, see, he is like your prince, yes?'

'He doesn't really look like P—'

'Shh!' said Frank, holding his fingers to his lips. 'Harry is very fond of your royals – it would not do to upset him.'

'Okay,' I said. 'You're Frank, and he's Harry, like the prince.'

'Exactly. Now, Mr Malachite Jones, I doubt you can tell from my speaking, but I am Russian.'

I didn't know whether he was joking or not, so didn't say anything.

'Harry is Russian also,' Frank continued, 'but he has a very strong accent and has not truly mastered your language, so I do the speaking. We like to stay incognito,' he grinned. 'You know this word?'

'Yes.'

'Good! Good! We are getting on very well.'

I looked for the right way to explain how I felt about us getting on well. I wanted to use 'uneasy' but I wasn't sure Frank would like that.

I finally opted for. 'I'm glad?'

'Yes!' he beamed. 'So am I.' He leaned across my desk, steepling his fingers. 'Now, Mr Jones, I have a problem. It is not a good problem, but it may be one you can help me with. I have a number of business interests around the city – clubs, bars, shops, etc. Many interesting things, and sometimes I come into contact with Mr Mick Stanbeck – you have heard of him, yes?' He didn't give me time to reply. 'Well, it has come to my attention that Mr Stanbeck may be about to come into a large amount of money and I am afraid that may tip the delicate balance of capitalism in this part of the world too far in his favour. Something I do not want.'

Again, searching for the right reaction. I don't think Frank wanted to hear my immediate though of, 'Oh shit.'

'Of course not,' I said.

‘So, should you come across a certain missing lottery ticket when you are speaking to the spirits, I would like you to give it to me.’

‘Won’t that tip the balance in your favour?’

‘You are a clever man, Mr Jones.’ He leaned forward, still grinning. ‘It will, yes. But that is not something I find as objectionable.’

‘The thing is …’

He held up a finger. ‘I understand, you are loyal to your clients, Mr Jones, and that is a very good trait for a man to have. But, I will let Harry explain to you why you should be helping me.’

‘I don’t think I need Harry to—’

‘Ah.’ He held a finger up again. ‘You be quiet. Just watch, please.’

Harry came forward and let his sack slip onto the desk. It landed with a thud, as though there was something very heavy in it. From the bag, he took out a ream of wrapped printer paper and opened it. Then he started laying out pristine white pieces of paper on the desk.

‘Stationery,’ I said.

‘Yes,’ whispered Frank, and it gave a sinister edge to a series of entirely unremarkable words. ‘Harry owns a number of stationers. Stationery is one of his many interests.’ He stared into my eyes. Something cold lived behind his. ‘Now, I think I told you to be quiet.’ He was no longer smiling.

Harry put out a triple layer of paper on the desk and placed the rest of the printer paper back in his knapsack. Then he took out a paper guillotine out of it. The old type. A heavy base with a long blade attached at one end that opened like one blade of a scissor. He placed the base in the centre of the white paper, the blade sticking up and turning the machine into half an arrow that pointed at Frank, who sat and watched as though Harry's actions hypnotised him.

I had a sudden and terrible need to get out.

Jackie had taught me a number of ways of hurting people, but when you are sat down and a man as big as Harry grabs your hand, there is little you can do. I'm not professionally violent in the way Jackie is, and Harry's huge paw was like a vice around my wrist.

He pulled my hand across and forced it onto the base of the paper guillotine. I tried to keep my fingers wrapped up in a fist, but he used his other hand to force mine open, like I was a child and he was an adult who had, quite frankly, had enough of my nonsense. He was firm, but not cruel. When he had my fingers splayed over the well designed for the blade to slip into, he held my hand there. Then he placed his other hand on the wooden handle of the guillotine.

'Now, Mr Jones,' said Frank. 'You know what happens if Harry pushes the blade down?'

I swallowed before I spoke. 'I lose my fingers.'

'Yes, that is exactly right.' Frank leaned forward, and this time, when he spoke, his English was perfect and unaccented. 'Harry will not push down on the handle today. But when you find the ticket, you will give it to me or I will have Harry come back and he will use his guillotine to cut off your fingers, one by one, do you understand?'

I nodded, because, at that particular moment in time, I had found I could no longer speak.

Harry stared at me impassively, and Frank smiled. Then he gently slapped my cheek.

'I think you are a good boy, I think you know what is best for you. Harry, put away your toy – let us go.'

They took the guillotine and left the paper on my desk. A stark, white reminder of their intent.

All things considered, I've had better Mondays.

7

TUESDAY

Jackie Singh Khattar first hit me when I was eight. I thought he wanted to scare me, which he succeeded in. He thought he wanted to scare me too, so he enjoyed it. I was too young, and so was he, to understand that violence was his only way of forming an emotional link with another human being.

He hit me again when I was twenty-eight, but for very different reasons.

'I'm going to hit you in the stomach,' he said.

'Please don't.'

'I'm going to hit you in the stomach, and I want you to try and stop me.'

'I don't know how.'

'I'll show you.'

And he did, and I got hit in the stomach a lot before I finally mastered the sweep of my arm that would knock away the incoming blow. Then Jackie taught me a counter that would hurt my opponent enough for me to run away. I'm not a naturally physical person, so it took me almost six months before I could do it fluidly enough to make him happy.

There was never any chance of me saying no to this – Jackie doesn't really understand the idea of no. Once he has what he thinks is a good idea in his head, then it's happening. You can not do it, but that doesn't mean he will stop trying to convince you that you should be doing it, or that he will not do whatever it is he has decided he wants to do anyway. As I didn't want to be hit in the stomach every time I saw Jackie, I had to learn to defend myself.

For similar reasons, I was staring at a paper plate of *dosa*.

'I can't eat curry for breakfast, Jackie.'

'It's not curry, it's dosa, and it's really good. It's from the sweet centre in Bradford.'

'Still spicy. Breakfast isn't spicy. I'm a Rice Krispies guy.'

'You should try it – stop being so white.'

'I'm not going to.'

'Well, I'll have to have it then.' He reached over for the paper plate containing a pancake, yoghurt, various sauces and vegetables.

'I think that's the real reason you bring it for me, isn't it? To get two helpings.'

He paused.

' … No …'

I paused.

'Take it.'

It was, of course, but he would never admit that. The thought of being greedy was anathema to him, up there with wasteful. Ideas of 'badness' drilled into him by his foster mother, of whom we did not speak. Jackie stared at me, as if searching for a lie in my face, and then slid the plate over and started shovelling food into his mouth.

'Got you another present,' he said.

'If it's another crime-family wife with a lost fortune, you can keep it.'

'Not going well?' He paused in between mouthfuls of dosa.

‘I saw more criminals yesterday, in one day, than I ever did in all the time I was doing drugs.’

‘Like you even remember,’ he said.

I didn’t give that an answer.

‘Who did you see?’ Jackie crammed more food into his mouth.

‘The Stanbecks.’

‘Twats.’

‘Benny Callaghan.’

‘He’s alright. As long as you don’t owe him. What did he want?’

‘To say I should give him the ticket, rather than give it straight to Janine or Trolley Mick.’

‘Mick’ll skin you if you do that.’ More food into his mouth.

‘And I saw DI Smith and her partner again, and two Russian men.’

‘One of them called Frank?’ He covered his mouth as he asked; he never liked to speak with his mouth full, and that he did now was a mark of how important it was for him to know. His brown eyes fixed on my face.

‘Yes.’

‘Did he hurt you?’

‘No.’

‘Did he threaten to?’

‘No more than anyone else has.’

‘Do you want me to hurt him?’

‘No.’ He stared a little longer, then shrugged and went back to eating dosa. ‘This is really good, you know.’

‘Spicy, and I don’t like raw onion for breakfast.’

'When we bring in Sharia law, you'll have to eat this for breakfast.'

'You're not even Muslim.'

'Don't you tell me what I am.' He grinned at me.

I changed the subject.

'I wonder how the Russians knew about the lottery ticket?'

Jackie started cleaning the paper plate of the last of its sauce with his finger. 'Mick's outfit leaks like a sieve – that's what happens when half your family are as thick as mince.' He licked sauce from his finger. 'Anyway, my bag under the table, present for you.' He kicked a rucksack out from under the desk with one expensive-looking shiny leather brogue then lifted it onto the desk. I expected it to thunk down on the desk – like it had a paper guillotine in it – but whatever was in there wasn't heavy. 'You look like you think it has a head in it.'

'Does it?'

'No.' Jackie looked appalled at the thought. 'You don't keep evidence like that hanging around. Did DI Smith ask about me?' He pushed over the bag.

'No,' I said, untying the toggle.

'That's cos she fancies me – doesn't want to make it too obvious. Playing coy.'

I opened the box. In it was a folder made out of blue cardboard. I took it out and opened it, surprised by what I found inside.

'Police autopsy reports?'

'Well, I knew DI Smith wouldn't give them to you cos she's playing hard to fucking get, isn't she? So I talked to a friend of a friend and sorted them out for you. You read, I'll sit and think about how good that dosa was.'

There wasn't much in the file. Larry Stanbeck had been travelling at about eighty miles an hour when he was knocked off his bike on the motorway. He never stood a chance. He'd been sideswiped, fought for control of the bike over a four-hundred-metre stretch, before he hit the central barrier, which catapulted him from the bike, and he hit a streetlight. He must have been spinning through the air as he hit it with the centre of his back. The line used in the report was 'folded him up like a piece of paper'.

'If I wasn't hungry before, I'm really not now.' I put the folder down. 'Looks like a hit-and-run.' Spatters of white marked the top of my desk. 'You've got dosa all over my desk.'

'I think you'll find I've actually added authentic Asian ambience to your desk. But read on,' said Jackie without looking up.

The next sheet was Larry Stanbeck's criminal record. A lot from when he was young – which should have been sealed but Jackie had ways and it was best not to ask – then a few collars at eighteen and nineteen for dealing marijuana; small-time stuff for a Stanbeck. Nothing after that. A little bit of background seemed to say he had cleaned up his act, gone straight. He went to sixth-form college at Choppy's and got himself a degree with the Open University. Married Janine and didn't show up on the police radar apart from in a general keep-an-eye-on-the-Stanbecks way. That didn't mean they weren't watching him closely, of course – from what DI Smith had said they definitely were – it just meant they didn't want a paper trail making a harassment case easy to prosecute.

Lastly, there were witness statements from the accident, though very little of it was actually witness statements. Mostly, it was people talking about how much they liked him; mothers of the boys in his Scout troop, parents from the nursery Cristophe went to. He didn't come across as a wife-beating criminal, but if you were any good at being a wife-beating criminal, you learned to keep it quiet. It was only at the end of the report where I found something useful. A witness had seen an older model Ford Transit, blue, she thought, coming off the next junction of the motorway at speed, and she was sure it had two fresh scratches down the side.

'When Benny Callaghan stopped to talk to me he was driving an old model Ford.'

'I think the Callaghans have a secret supply of old Ford vans.'

'The one he was driving was pretty dented.'

'They all are.'

'And it had been freshly painted. Maybe I should tell DI Smith.'

Jackie leaned forward. 'But if you do, she'll want to know how you know about the van. Then either you'll have to tell her you've got the report, which will cause problems, mate. Or you'll have to make something up, which she will see through. And then she'll want to look more closely at you.'

'I can't just look away if they were involved in murder.'

Jackie wiped yoghurt from his perfectly manicured beard with one of the wipes that came with his food.

'He was only a Stanbeck, Mal.'

'Maybe he was killed by someone who knew about the ticket? It might help us?'

He stared at me. Blinked twice. 'There is that. Shall we go see Benny Callaghan then?'

'You're coming?'

'Aye,' said Jackie, 'people can get a bit weird if you accuse them of being involved in a murder, so best I am there. I've got things to do this morning – I'll pick you up after lunch.'

Once Jackie was gone. I went into the back room where Beryl had been hiding from him. She was just leaving.

'Prick's gone then?'

'My friend.'

'He'll get you killed one day.'

'I don't need that from you as well, Beryl.'

She stared at me; she didn't like it when I answered back.

'You won't be needing me today,' she said. 'I made you shit tea.'

'What if someone rings?'

She shrugged.

'I never answer it anyway.' Then she shuffled past me with her carrier bags.

Once I was alone, I went and got the picture of Larry Stanbeck that Janine had given me, those not-quite-smiling eyes staring out at me.

'Who killed you?' I said to him, 'And why?'

He didn't answer. The dead never do – they're dead.

I took the picture round to Mr Patel at the newsagent's. I was worried he might still be cross about the trick I'd done for Cat Maudy, but he was too busy with one of his displays to be angry with me about bringing ghosts into his shop.

'Mr Jones,' he said. 'Are you familiar with square crisps? I have a number that are out of date and I am selling them at half price.'

'I'm alright for crisps, Mr Patel.' Half price in Mr Patel's shop was normal price anywhere else. 'Do you remember this guy?' I put the picture of Larry Stanbeck on the counter.

He leaned forward, wincing when the cast on his arm touched the counter.

'Ah, Larry, so sad. Sixty cigarettes – different brand each time – ten cans of Red Bull, a Lotto ticket and five scratch cards. Never had any luck with the scratch cards.'

'But won big on the Lotto.'

'Oh, you know about that?'

He glanced over at his crisps, as if worried they may escape. 'I have been told to keep it secret by the lottery people. Not that Larry will care anymore.'

'You should still keep it secret. Did he ever mention anywhere he might go to you? You know, if he needed a quiet moment?'

'No, he only ever bought his things and left.' He rubbed the cast on his arm. 'Sometimes he bought a Guardian newspaper.'

'Your arm hurting?'

‘Bloody ladders.’ His voice became quieter. ‘I was only getting down a box of pens.’

‘Dangerous job, running a shop.’

He nodded.

‘Was Larry always alone?’

‘Once he had his boy with him. A nice boy, but with sticky fingers – I had to clean the display window on my counter after they had been in. But Larry loved his child – it was a nice thing to see. Though he should have cleaned the child’s hands more.’

‘So there’s nothing you know about him?’

‘I think he was a Scout leader too – it is sad when such a man dies.’

I wandered back to my office. There were a couple of down-at-heel men smoking outside the betting shop. They stared at me suspiciously as I passed. I gave them a smile, and they avoided my eyes. They had probably been talking about me.

People often do.

Jackie rocked up at midday in a light-blue Ford Escort that was as much rust as it was car. It didn’t look like it was road legal but probably was – he was always very careful about following the small laws and avoiding anything that might get him pulled over by a traffic cop. The inside of the car smelled like someone had been soaking the seats in beer for the past four years, and the passenger seat was ninety per cent tape.

‘Is it safe to sit down, Jackie?’

‘Course it is – totally sound this baby.’

He banged the dashboard, and as he put it into gear the car let out a scream from the gearbox. Jackie liked to drive; he could be a terrifying person to drive with in one of his more expensive sports cars, but he was just as likely to drive like a pensioner, depending on what sort of mood he was in. Today was one of his over-sixty-five days. He seemed preoccupied, but I didn't fill the silence between us. It was a familiar silence, as worn and comfortable as a favourite chair. We didn't have to talk. I looked out the window at the passing world: woods, then semi-detached houses with nice gardens, then council houses with nice gardens, then council houses with less nice gardens. We skirted round the estate toward the travellers' site. Everyone called it The Scar, and the shadows of the flaking stacks of Edge Towers striped the road as we approached the turn-off.

Before we reached The Scar, Jackie parked the car at the kerb; he had to use both hands to pull on the handbrake.

'Sticks a bit,' he said, apologetically.

'Why did you even bring it?'

'Cos I've got a plan. You take this in – tell Benny you want to sell it cos you need a van.'

'You think he's going to sell me a van if he used it to murder someone?'

'No, but it might not be Benny you talk to – it might be his son, Callum.'

'He's back?'

'Yeah, but pretty recently, so he won't know the business, and he was never that sharp to begin with. Or it might be one of his employees – they might not know what it's been used for.'

'You think?'

He shrugged. 'Well, no. I suspect he's told them. Look, I just want you to keep them occupied while I sneak about. Don't buy a van by accident or cos you don't know how to say no.' He got out and slammed the door shut.

As I shuffled over to the driver's seat, he tapped on the window. I wound it down.

'What?'

'You're not to accept less than a hundred quid for this – it's got three months' MOT left.'

'Okay.'

He turned around and started to walk away. I wound up the window until it got stuck. Then I tried to release the handbrake, but Jackie had put it on so tightly I couldn't move it. A moment later there was another knock on the half-open window. Jackie was back, grinning at me.

'What?' I said.

'Do you want me to undo the handbrake?'

'No.'

'You sure?'

'Yes.'

He skipped round the car and opened the passenger side. 'You've always been very bad at asking for help,' he said, and leant over, releasing the handbrake one-handed. Then he slammed the door shut and vanished again as the car started to roll backward. The brake pedal under my foot felt spongy and barely managed to stop the car moving. I stalled twice before I got it going.

Sometimes, I wondered if the council officer responsible for naming the areas around Blades Edge had been particularly bored or impish. Though everyone called the traveller site The Scar, its proper name was Blades Carr. You could see how it got its name, but it didn't exactly make it sound like a welcoming place, and with the way the papers talked about the travellers, it wasn't somewhere people talked of fondly and there was an odd sense of distrust between its residents and the people on the Edge. No matter how bad someone's life was on the Edge, the thinking was at least you weren't 'one of them on The Scar'. This tended to make the people that lived there suspicious of anyone coming to visit – not unjustly – and it became a vicious circle of mistrust and occasional violence.

I'd known plenty of people from The Scar, and they seemed alright. If I had to come into contact with one of Mick's gang, I'd rather it was Benny – he was the least borderline sociopathic of them. Though I'd always been a bit puzzled by The Scar; it was a traveller encampment where no one travelled – which consisted of four lines of big static caravans, most of them were far grander than any houses on the estate – and it was years before I realised 'travellers' were a people, not a description of what they did.

I turned into The Scar, watched by two burly men who were cleaning a couple of very expensive-looking four-by-fours with a power washer. I gave them a cheery wave, and they turned away. At the end of The Scar were two gates: the one that led into a field where the traveller's horses lived was closed. The other was open, and that led into Benny Callaghan's scrapyard. Or we used to call it that, now the signpost read:

Callaghan Recycling Centre. But it was still a scrapyard. I let the Ford coast to stop in the middle of the Callaghan's yard and then got out. Benny Callaghan was arguing with his son, Callum. You would never tag the two men as related. Benny was thickset, small and sturdy. His son shared the same weather-beaten face – as Jackie had said he'd spent a few years working away– but he was taller than his dad and thinner; he had the posture of someone ashamed of their height.

' … and I said, Callum, I don't need a mechanic. You had a good thing on that farm, and they'll take you back. You were good with the animals, son.'

'Well, maybe I don't want to do that, Da,' said Callum, and he turned and walked away, throwing me a filthy look as he passed back toward the camp. I'd known him at school. He was in the first year when I was in the fourth. One of those kids that was always on the side, always following in the wake of a bigger kid, Stanbecks, mostly. If he'd not been Benny Callaghan's kid, they'd have used him as a punching bag, but he was, so they didn't. Instead, they made his life hell in other ways.

He was easily led. One time, he walked into the art teacher's office and took his trousers down because one of the Stanbecks had convinced him she fancied him and wanted to shag him in the cupboard. Another time I found him in a thorn bush, covered in scratches and trying to push his way right into the centre because someone had said the Stanbecks had buried a hundred pounds in the middle of it.

His dad had always been shouting at him back then. Even though I'd often take a beating from one of the kids he hung out with, and Callum was always there on the sidelines, shouting encouragement, I'd felt kind of sorry for him. In hindsight, I get the shouting his dad did now. He was Benny's only kid, while the rest of the Callaghans had big families, 'kids to spare' was the saying. But Benny only had Callum, and if ever someone was likely to get chewed up by the Stanbeck gang, it was Callum Callaghan. His father stared after him, a look I struggled to place on his features. Sadness? Anger? Regret? Maybe all of them.

'Couldn't you use another mechanic here?' I said, pointing at the shed where old cars were dismantled. Benny shrugged.

'He doesn't have the concentration for it – he's sloppy, doesn't think ahead.' He looked at the floor. 'He was good with the animals – I was proud of him for that.'

'He wants to be like his dad,' I said.

'I wish he didn't.' He looked away. 'Anyway, enough of family, Mal Jones.' And then he was all smiles; though it was false bonhomie, he was clearly rattled. I could understand that; Benny was clever enough to stay out of jail, I doubted Callum was, and it must hurt to look into your son's future and see him spending most of it behind bars. Mick Stanbeck wouldn't hesitate to use a man as easily led as Callum. 'Have you come about that thing we talked about, Mal?' said Benny.

His face fell when I shook my head. Behind him, among the forest of rusting metal and stacked cars that made up his yard, I saw a movement – Jackie.

'No, not had much luck there, Benny. I came to bring you this,' I waved at the Ford. 'It's got a couple of months' MOT left on it, but it won't make it through the next one. And I need a cheap van to move a few things. I thought you might be able to help me on both counts?'

He nodded, that strange look back on his face.

'Sure I will – it's a junker though, that car, I can't give you more than fifty for it.'

'I was looking for one-fifty.'

'You can look all you want.' Behind him Jackie slipped into the big workshop the Callaghans used for stripping down vehicles. 'Seventy-five, maybe. At the most.'

'What about part exchange against a van?'

'What type of van?'

'A Transit, maybe? Not a big one, I don't have the licence for one of those.'

'Who does,' he said. 'One-fifty against a Transit then. I've got a few around the back – come on.'

I followed him round the back of the industrial unit, built of rusting corrugated iron.

'What's in there?' I asked, even though I knew what it was.

'It's where we strip cars down – got a lot of regulations to meet now. Not as much fun as it used to be.'

He led me up to a line of vans. They all looked well kept up, had clearly recently been washed and

Benny started telling me about their various wonderful properties, not much of which I understood. The van he had been driving the day before wasn't there though.

'Which is the cheapest?' I asked.

'It's not about, cheapest. It's—'

'It is on my budget.'

He stared at me then shrugged. 'Well, in that case it's the red one – two grand.'

'That's too much. Have you taken off the money for the car?'

'Yeah, tell you what, fifteen hundred and it's yours.'

'I was looking more for something that would do one journey. What about the one you were driving yesterday? That looked like it was on its last legs.'

He narrowed his eyes. 'That's gone.'

'Was it yours?'

'No, we pick up abandoned cars for the council – it was one of those. Ditched in a farmer's field. Thought we'd have to tow it, but I managed to get it going.'

'So nothing in my price range then?'

He shook his head.

'Sorry, lad.' He shuffled nearer to me. 'Look, I don't mean to push, but any news on that other thing we talked about? Anything at all?'

'Nothing, sorry.' I put out my hand. 'Hundred quid for the car.'

'I don't think so,' he said. Then he reached into his wallet and counted seventy-five pounds off from a thick wad of notes.

I took the money and walked out. When I was out of sight of the scrapyard Callum Callaghan approached me.

'Me da was lying about that van, you know.'

'Which one?'

'The painted one he brought in yesterday. We do pick vans up for the council but not that one. We picked that one up for Mick Stanbeck.'

'Why are you telling me this?'

'Me da wants to control me, wants me to go off and spend my life covered in cow shit rather than be my own man,' he said. 'But I'll not do it. He was weird about that van though, something was off.' He stared at me. 'You were alright at school, Mal – I remember you. But it wasn't his van and we may not always get on, but I don't want my da getting in trouble for something that's not his fault, right?'

'Trouble?'

'You're not the only one asking about that van. DI Smith was asking too. I just want to make sure someone else knows if it comes to it, right? Mick Stanbeck would happily see Da in jail if it protected one of his. Da thinks it's best to be loyal, but you can't trust Trolley Mick – it's his lot first, everyone else after.' There was a sour note to his voice.

'You're not wrong there, Callum.'

'I better get back,' he said. 'Work to do.'

I walked away with plenty to think about. Further along the road, Jackie was waiting, leaning against a churchyard wall and soaking up the sun.

'How much did you get for the car?'

'Seventy-five.'

‘You owe me twenty-five quid then.’

‘Put it on my tab.’ I held out the money for him, and he waved it away. ‘He didn’t have the van out the back with the others.’

‘I know.’

‘How?’

‘It was in the workshop, mostly stripped down, but the body was there, painted with house paint like you said. Underneath that paint it was blue.’

‘Callum says they picked it up for Mick Stanbeck. If that’s the van that killed his boy, why would he protect whoever did it?’

‘Cos he’s an arsehole,’ said Jackie. ‘Now, come on – there’ll be a bus along in a minute. You’re flush, you can pay.’

8

The bus was stifling. The Edge got the worst of everything and the heating on this bus was stuck on full. Despite all the windows being open it was still like sitting in an oven. The Edge was only ten minutes by car from the city, but in its own way was cut off and we passed through long tracts of green farmland. The scent of cut grass boarded the bus with a group of pensioners who complained loudly about the heat. Jackie, for reasons known only to Jackie, decided to get off the bus in, as far as I could make out, the middle of nowhere.

'Got some business to do,' he said, standing up and ringing the bell as the pensioners sat down, grumbling, and the bus set off again.

'Here? It doesn't stop here.'

'Need to walk for a bit, clear my head. It's too hot on this bus.'

'I thought you liked the heat?'

'Don't be racist.'

'I'm not being …' but he was already gone, throwing me a grin as he vanished down the steep stairs of the bus. Then I heard him, speaking in a thick Indian accent, charming the bus driver into letting him off despite the fact there was no bus stop and they weren't really allowed to.

Once Jackie had got off, the bus continued on until it hit the suburbs, stopping and starting, never picking up enough speed to get a breeze going to blow the sweat from my skin. I sat dripping and wishing I'd worn fewer layers while the pensioners carried on complaining about the heat.

In my bag, I had Beryl's printout of all the information from the internet on Lawrence and Janine Stanbeck. There wasn't much about Lawrence, he was on the Scouts website a few times but that was it. I knew more about Janine, mostly cos her sister was almost famous. Her sister, Helen, lived in London, but her mum and dad lived just off the bus route in one of the more well-to-do suburbs of the city. You could never have too much information, and I really wanted to get off the stifling bus as quickly as possible, so I decided to go and visit them.

What harm could it do?

They lived in a house on a small 1950s estate. It was much more prestigious than living on the Edge, but because the streets had no trees, to me, it had the same sort of stark and lifeless air. The grass verges were better maintained, and there were fewer sofas rotting in gardens, but the rows of almost identical houses weren't really that different and it made getting lost in the maze of streets surprisingly easy. I had phone reception here, but no internet so couldn't connect to a maps app either. As I walked, I tied my hair back; I wanted them to talk to me, and older people generally responded well to people in positions of authority. I wasn't ever going to pass as a police officer, but I didn't intend to. People found the police intimidating and clammed up anyway. Instead, I would use my Insurance Investigator guise. It is a really good way of getting into people's houses if there's been some misfortune. It's also official enough to give me some authority, but at the same time no one is really sure what one does. There's a lot of wiggle room in 'insurance investigator'.

Eventually, I found the house. It wasn't part of the housing estate. It was one of four huge detached Victorian houses with four floors, steep slate-covered roofs and sash windows. Huge and beautifully cared-for gardens surrounded each house. Everything about it said 'money' to me. It was probably half a million pounds' worth of property. I wondered how a girl brought up somewhere like this ever ended up on the Edge. Her house on the estate was well cared for and everything, but it was definitely a step down from this.

An elderly man answered the door. He looked like he was in his eighties, stooped over. White hair and papery, liver-spotted skin. A mouth that looked like it struggled to smile. If he was Janine's father, he could only be in his sixties, and I wondered if he had some sort of disease that had prematurely aged him.

'Can I help you?' The hall he stood in had a Victorian air to it; gloomy, tiled floor, a lot of very dark brown woodwork. I liked it – not everyone's taste though.

Maybe he was the butler.

'Oh, yes, Mr Killingham, is it?'

He nodded.

Good start. 'I'm Mal Jones from Portlife Insurance, we—'

'Who is it, Arthur?' The voice that came from within the house was female and enunciated each word very clearly.

'A man from some insurance company, Alice,' he shouted back. Though 'shouted' is a bit of an exaggeration.

'Tell him we don't want any, Arthur,'

'We don't want any,' said Arthur, and he began to close the door.

'I'm not a salesman, Mr Killingham. I'm here about your late son-in-law.' I showed him my fake ID. From a room in the back, Alice appeared and strode down the hall to the door. She looked like she might have been a hippy once; her hair, though grey, was long, and she wore it tied back and partnered with large hoop earrings and a dress that was probably sold as 'ethnic'. She had the pinched face of someone who was wound tight, and from the state of the hall – show-home clean – I suspected Alice might be the reason Arthur looked so old.

'Lawrence,' she said, her voice high pitched, her eyebrows too. 'You are here about Lawrence? Is there some sort of problem with his life insurance?' And though she tried to hide both her curiosity and her delight in that by pretending to study my ID, she couldn't quite manage it.

'I'm afraid there is,' I said.

She nodded, as if that was exactly what was to be expected. 'Well, Arthur' – she reached back and twirled the grey hair of her pony tail around a ringed finger – 'get the man some tea. Bring it to the parlour. And you,' she said, meaning me. 'Please come through. Mr … Jones, was it?'

The parlour had comfortable chairs, well-padded and high enough that it was easy for older people to get up and down without too much bother. The original Victorian décor of the hall had been passed over in here for something a little more (less) pleasant; the walls were painted in muted pinks, and there was a lot of things patterned with flowers. A wooden statue of an African warrior that was almost definitely not actually from Africa stood in a corner of the room, guarding it without giving away whether he thought the décor was as ugly as I did. Arthur brought in some tea in a teapot and placed it on a small, round glass table between me and his wife. He didn't bring a cup for himself, only sat in a single seat across from us and stared at the floor.

Know your place, Arthur.

'I just have a few simple questions,' I said.

'Are there suspicions?' said Alice. 'Because it wouldn't surprise me. He was a criminal, you know.' She sat very upright, with her head tilted at an unnatural angle, like she was about to burst into song.

'I had heard rumours,' I said.

'Well, they are not rumours, Mr Jones. Most of them are criminals on the Blades Edge estate – it is not the sort of place you want to think of your daughter ending up.'

'Did you know your son-in-law well?'

'Barely at all – he wasn't welcome here, nor Janine. Not anymore.'

'She isn't?''

'No, she quite upset Arthur last time she came here.'

Arthur didn't reply, probably too upset.

'How?'

‘Oh, just by being her. She was a lovely baby, as was her sister, then they got older, and well, they became wilful girls. Do you have children, Mr Jones?’

‘I’m afraid I’ve never been lucky enough.’

‘Lucky?’ she laughed without laughing. ‘There’s nothing lucky about it.’ She leant forward, ‘Let me tell you, give them all your love, rip your heart out for them, and they just throw it in your face.’

‘How do you mean?’ I got the feeling I had hit upon Alice’s favourite topic.

‘Those girls of mine were raised right. Manners, dance classes, pretty dresses, everything a little girl could want.’ Her cut-glass accent slipped a little, something more local surfacing. ‘And all I asked was they kept their knickers on.’ She leant back, spoke more softly. ‘At least Janine kept quiet about being a slut, even if she did marry scum.’

‘Would Janine’s older sister know anything about Larry?’

‘We don’t see her. Not after the things she said in the papers. We did not bring up tarts in this house.’

‘What about your grandson, Cristophe?’

She appeared to soften a little. ‘Well, he’s one of them, isn’t he, a Stanbeck? But he has our blood too, and all I can hope is that it’s our blood that breeds true, not the Stanbecks’. If it wasn’t for the boy, I’d have cut Janine out of our will too.’ She crossed her hands in her lap, nestling in her own indignation.

‘Do you know of any specific criminal acts Lawrence Stanbeck was involved in? Unfortunately, if he was involved in any such activity at the time of his death this would, I'm afraid, invalidate his life insurance.'

Alice opened her mouth, shut it again. Tried to pretend she didn't love the idea of her daughter losing out. She licked her lips and I noticed she was wearing a very subtle lipstick. I decided I really didn't like her very much.

'Not specifically, but you mark my words, if there's something dodgy, the Stanbecks will be at the root of it.'

'This must be terrible for your daughter,' I said.

'I imagine it is,' she said. 'In fact, when you see her, could you pass on a message for me?'

'Of course.'

'Tell her "We told you so" and not to come to crying to us.'

I didn't really know how to reply to that.

'Could I see her room?' I said.

She leaned forward. 'Of course – do you think she's done something too?' It was almost as if she was willing me to say yes.

'I just like to be thorough, Mrs Killingham.'

'Arthur, take him up to Janine's room.' She turned her head away and stared at her not-African statue. 'You can search it if you want, Mr Jones. Pull it apart if you need to.'

'Yes, dear,' said Arthur, and he led me up the stairs.

At the top he unlocked a door, but before he opened it he spoke to me, very softly. 'Don't think too badly of Alice – those girls hurt her terribly.'

'What did they do?'

He smiled to himself. 'They were too like her, I think. Strong-willed. At some point in life, Alice just forgot who she was.'

He held out a lollipop to me. I stared at it. A small, sad smile crossed his face. 'It's for Cristophe, tell him Gramps says hello. Don't tell Alice about it though.'

I took the lolly from him and put it in my pocket. 'Do they ever come here?'

'Not Janine, but sometimes Larry would bring the boy round when Alice was at her book club. He's a good lad is Cristophe.'

I had a sudden spike of hope, if Larry wanted to hide something from his wife what better place than in the home she had clearly hated. I kind of wanted to give Arthur a hug.

'Do you mind if I search the room, Arthur?'

'Not as long as you put everything back – Alice gets upset when things are out of place.'

'Not a problem, Arthur. I'll be careful.'

There wasn't much in Janine's room. It still looked as it must have when she left though it was strangely spartan for a teenager. There was a bookcase full of DVDs, a small chest of drawers with an old radio on top. A single bed with a poster from the Al Pacino film *Scarface* above it. I wondered if the room was far tidier and emptier now than it had ever been when Janine lived here. It felt purged, as if only the barest bones of a personality had been left: no mess, no trinkets, no diaries (sadly) and, worst of all, no lottery ticket.

I left the Killingham house feeling deflated, not just because I'd failed to find anything, but because the house was filled with sadness, with mistakes that had somehow never been rectified and had ended up with three people – four, maybe, if you counted the sister – estranged from each other. Arthur aside there was no love in that house. I'd always imagined that other families, the ones off the Edge, had lived boisterously, in houses full of colour and noise and love. Not in old houses, cleaned within an inch of their lives, where people drank tea in disapproving silence.

It's amazing how many times the same lesson can disappoint.

I picked up the tail as soon as I left the house.

Being able to notice that he is being followed isn't the sort of skill you may expect a boy who grows up on a council estate and then pretends to be a medium to pick up, but if you spent your early life in fear of other kids then noticing when people are acting strangely or paying you unwanted attention becomes an important life skill. I've developed a kind of sixth sense for people who mean me ill.

I didn't recognise the two men following me, but I didn't need to; they were out of place here, obviously from the Edge. Dressed in sports leisurewear that needed a wash and didn't quite fit into the suburbs. They had suspicious-eyes, and slouched along in a way I am sure they thought made them look inconspicuous but only served to draw attention to them. I wandered aimlessly for a bit, turning through streets that all looked the same, bungalow after bungalow, just in case I was being paranoid, but my tail faithfully followed me. After a bit it must have occurred to them that maybe they were a little bit less inconspicuous than they had imagined and they had a quick tête-à-tête on the street. One stayed where he was, talking into his phone, or at least pretending to but it was hard to tell the difference, while the other followed me.

I wasn't sure what to do. If they intended to hurt me, then this was a bad place for it; there was nowhere quiet and there were a lot of twitching curtains in the suburbs, but at the same time it was a bad place to try to lose someone as there were no alleys or hidden places to cut through.

I rang Jackie.

Jackie: Speak.

Me: I'm being followed.

Jackie: Who by?

Me: Two blokes.

Jackie: Where are you?

Me: The suburbs. Somewhere called Alderham Crescent, at the moment, Walking up toward Alderham Avenue.

Jackie: Why are you out there? It's dead up there, unless you get the hots for grandmas.

Me: I went to see Janine Stanbeck's parents.

Jackie: Was her mum a hot grandma?

Me: Shut up, Jackie. Let's just say I can see why she ran away as a kid. The tail picked me up outside.

Jackie: So someone's watching their house?

Annoyingly, that hadn't occurred to me.

Jackie: Alright, Mal, listen. Head up toward Alderham Close. It looks like a dead end, but there's a snicket between number five and number seven – it looks like someone's gate, but it isn't. The gate is metal and painted red. Open it, follow the snicket. If they don't see you go in, they'll probably think you've gone into one of the houses, and I doubt they'll want to start knocking on doors.'

Me: And if they do see me?

Jackie: The snicket leads into a clearing. Behind a yellow-leafed bush on your right, there's a break in the fence that'll let you get into the garden of number seven. Then you can get over their back wall and you'll be on Clarence Rise. You'd never find the way through if you didn't know it was there, and as long as they're not stood behind you, they won't see you go through.'

Me: Okay, so you're not coming?

Jackie: I am, soon as I'm free.

Me: Free?

Jackie: I'm with a hot grandma, bye.

The phone went dead.

I followed Jackie's instructions and my two pursuers did a kind of amateurish leapfrogging over each other as they followed. One was always leaning against a wall and looking at his phone while the other was walking along behind me. I found Alderham Close and spotted the gate; the houses on either side of it were much older than the rest of the estate and had gardens full of mature trees. I wondered if they were the workers' cottages for whoever had owned the big houses where Janine Stanbeck's parents lived.

I turned the corner onto the close, and the second I knew my tail could no longer see me, I ran for the gate, hoping the couple of seconds where his line of sight was broken would be enough to get me through it.

It wasn't.

From behind, I heard a shout and the slap of shoes on pavement as my pursuer broke into a run. I ran down the snicket, catching myself on a bramble, swearing, and then broke into the small cleared area. It looked like it might have been an allotment once. Sure enough, there was the bush with yellow leaves, just as Jackie had said. Sometimes his local knowledge astounded me – who knew that a real commitment to dogging could be so useful. I rounded the tree and found the fence where Jackie had said there was a hole.

Newly fixed. No way through.

'Come out of there, mate.' The speaker had a thick North-East accent. I didn't really have much choice but to do what he said. I backed out of the bush, branches catching at my hair. The two men walked over. Up close, they were very different; one was tall and wiry with ears that stuck out like handles and the other was bigger, muscular once but run to fat through poor diet and, from the look of his belly, a lot of beer.

It was Jug Ears that was doing the speaking. 'We need to have a word with you about what you were doing at that house. Didn't think we'd find somewhere quiet enough round 'ere.' He grinned. 'So thanks for finding somewhere, like.'

'I was just visiting Arthur – he's a friend.'

‘Right,’ said Jug Ears. ‘A friend … Billy, grab him, like.’

Billy sauntered forward. He didn’t look particularly worried by me, why would he be? A tall, skinny guy already out of breath from a short run.

When he spoke, his accent was so thick I could barely make out the words. ‘I will hurt youse if youse don’t tell him what he wants,’ he said. Or at least I think he did.

‘Sorry,’ I said. ‘Not sure I speak that language.’

A flash of irritation in his eyes.

‘I said, I will hurt you.’ He was fighting to make each word very clear. ‘If youse don’t do, what we want.’

‘No, sorry,’ I said. ‘Not getting it.’

A flash of anger in his eyes and he reached for me with one hand. Jackie had taught me a number of things about violence. The one he said was most effective was: ‘strike first and strike hard. Do as much damage as you can and then get out of there. Most people aren’t prepared for pain, and pain is great leveller when people are bigger or more skilled than you.’

He reached out for me. I grabbed his little finger and twisted it, hard. I either broke it or dislocated it, but the effect was immediate, he screamed in pain. I didn’t stop to observe. I ran for the way out.

Jug Ears caught me.

He was much quicker than I expected. As I ran, he got near enough to kick out at me, catching me in the back of the leg. I lost my footing, had to concentrate on regaining my balance, but put too much thought into that and not enough into where I was going and ran straight into a fence. A moment later, he had his arm round my neck and was pulling me backward.

'Aww, man,' he said. 'You were just going to get a bit of a kicking, for fun like, but now you've hurt Billy, and he won't stand for that. So, you'll tell us why you were at that house, like, and we'll hurt you to make sure you're telling the truth, and I'll try and make sure Billy don't cripple you too much, man.'

Billy walked toward me, holding his mangled hand with the other. He grimaced, then straightened his finger. Shouting 'Fuck!' as he did it. I'd drastically miscalculated; he was a hard enough man to shake off pain. Which meant I'd broken Jackie's second rule of violence: 'don't miscalculate.'

'I am going to break every one of your fucking fingers, lad,' Billy said.

I had no reason to doubt him, and the thought of it made me feel like throwing up. Maybe if I vomited on him, it would scare him away. I'd heard that worked for seagulls.

'Put him down, boys.'

They turned at this new voice. Jackie stood in the entrance to the old allotment, smiling as he used a toothpick to clean his nails. He looked like he'd come straight from a rehearsal for *Saturday Night Fever*, wearing a wide-lapelled suit in deep red and a purple shirt open to his navel, exposing the smooth brown skin of his well-muscled chest. I think he'd oiled it.

'Fuck off,' said Billy. 'We've a score to settle with this bastard – don't need some Paki queer interfering.'

The smile fell from Jackie's face. He walked forward, shaking out his arms, rolling his neck.

'Why do you have to make it racist, mate? And homophobic? It could just have been a bit of a ruck, innit?' he said. With every word his accent became more Bradford Asian, the words staccato and cut short. His head moving with the rhythm of his words, eyes wide. 'Now I'm gon need hurt you, mate, right, innit?'

'Go back to fucking Islam,' said Billy.

As Jackie came within reach, Billy threw a punch. Jackie ducked and delivered two return punches to the man's kidneys that made him grunt in pain. Billy threw another punch and Jackie swayed out the way, still smiling, and then punched Billy on the nose. I heard the bone break, saw the explosion of blood. Then Jackie was in even closer, delivering one, two, three quick punches to Billy's head with a right hand thick with gold rings. And the man was down.

'You can't go back to Islam, you daft bastard,' he said, the accent gone now. 'It's a state of mind, not a place.' Billy didn't answer so Jackie turned to Jug Ears. 'I hope your theology is better than your friend's.'

Jug Ears threw me to one side and drew a knife from inside his jacket.

'I am going to cut you up, like.'

'Oh, for fuck's sake,' said Jackie, and he held his head in his hands. 'Don't draw that now.' He pointed at the knife. 'The time for drawing the knife was when I was occupied with Captain Geography here.' He pointed at Billy who was lying on the floor, groaning.

'What?' said Jug Ears. Plainly, the knife had not got the reaction he'd expected.

'If you're the type of guy that was going to use that,' said Jackie, pronouncing each word slowly and clearly as he pointed at the knife again, 'you'd have done it when it was two against one and you had the advantage. Now there's two of us and one of you so we have the advantage. For instance, my mate Mal is about to clock you from behind.'

I wasn't, of course, but Jug Ears didn't know that and turned around. As soon as he did, Jackie moved, came forward, grabbed the same arm Jug Ears was holding the knife with and twisted it behind him, making him drop the blade. Then he pushed the arm further up Jug Ears's back and used the pressure on the joint to march him forward and shove him up against the fence.

'Who sent you?' said Jackie.

'I'm not …'

'Oh, fuck this. Look, mate, I'm just going to dislocate your arm so you know I mean business then we'll talk.'

'No, wait—' The words broke off into a scream as Jackie did exactly what he said he was going to do.

'Now, who sent you, or shall I do the other one?'

'Don't fucking touch me.' He was crying, tears streaming down his face.

'Then tell me.'

'Trolley Mick sent us.' Jackie let go of him and stepped back.

'This, Mal, is a lesson in why when you want something done, you either do it yourself or you pay enough to get people who know what they are doing.' He shook his head and gently turned Jug Ears round. 'If you'd told him you were from Trolley Mick at the start' – he pointed at me, then dusted down the front of Jug Ears tracksuit – 'he'd have told you what he was doing there.'

'But …'

'No buts,' said Jackie. 'Violence is the first resort of the idiot, mate. Tell Mick that what he wants is not in that house, then go back to Geordieland. Alright?'

Jug Ears nodded.

'Come on, Mal.' Jackie walked away, and I jogged to catch up with him.

'You need to update your local knowledge. The fence had been fixed – there was no way out.'

'Yeah,' he said. 'they did it a couple of months ago.'

I grabbed his arm and pulled him to stop.

'What?'

'They fixed it a couple of months ago – Mrs Jillings at number seven is very security conscious because she smokes a lot of weed and it makes her paranoid.'

'Why did you tell me there was a way out if there wasn't?'

'Well, you wouldn't have brought them here if I'd told you there was no way out, would you?'

'Of course not.'

'Exactly,' he said, and walked off, as if it was the most logical thing in the world. I followed him back to the road.

Jackie was waiting in the driving seat of a blood-red Ferrari and I slipped into the bucket seat beside him. We were moving before I even got my seat belt on.

'Why are you dressed like that, Jackie?'

'Like what?'

'Like John Travolta.' Which he was.

'I'm not.'

'I think you are.' He really was, though the colour was different.

'You did just see me take down two armed men, right?'

'Only one was armed.'

Silence. 'You are in no position to give fashion advice, Mal.'

'Fair enough.'

More silence.

We listened to the roar of the engine as he short shifted it through streets never designed for low-slung high-performance cars.

'What happened back there doesn't make sense, Jackie.'

'That Trolley Mick doesn't trust his daughter-in-law?'

'No, that he brings in people from outside to watch her. Why not use his own people? He has enough – you can't move for Stanbecks on the Edge.'

'Thought Benny Callaghan would answer that one for you.'

'Eh?'

'Think about it, Mal. Eight million pounds.'

'He doesn't trust them?'

Jackie stared ahead and brought the Ferrari to a halt at a red light. A group of teenagers ogled the car and Jackie waved.

'But they're his family,' I said.

'One of them could be mine,' he said, staring at the kids.

'They look a bit, pale.'

'You are so racist, Mal.'

'I am not …'

'Course he doesn't trust his family. Mick's not big on trust, never has been. He can barely trust most of his family with a tenner bag of gear. Eight million pounds – that's just too much temptation.'

'But everyone's frightened of Trolley Mick.'

'He's getting old.'

'So, he's bringing people in.'

'Not good people, though,' said Jackie. 'He's always been cheap. Might change now though.'

He dropped me back at my office before driving off to do whatever Asian men dressed like John Travolta did on a Tuesday night.

9

WEDNESDAY

Jackie used to hit me in the face.

'Mal, I'm going to hit you in the face.'

'Please don't.'

'I'm going to hit you in the face, and I want you to try and stop me.'

'I don't know how.'

'I'll show you.'

And he did. At first, he threw the punches slowly. He didn't teach me to block, not yet, just taught me to dodge as the punch came in. Sway to the right or to the left. Slowly, he built up the speed of the punches and I built up a little muscle. Sometimes, he'd surprise me with a swing. At first, I got a lot of bruises, then gradually fewer and fewer. I don't remember when he started putting in the second punch. I remember my jaw aching for days though. He never taught me blocks; just said to avoid the punch.

So, I learned to avoid it. My reactions speeded up. He said that would help with the rest; I told him I didn't really want the rest, and Jackie just smiled.

Wednesday was Beryl's day off, so I had to make my own tea, which meant I had coffee which Beryl said was a ponce's drink. I spent the morning doing admin, which was also Beryl's job, but she hated admin and very rarely did it, so I put Wednesday aside to get it done. Then she couldn't hover about in the background complaining that I was 'doing her job' and 'trying to get rid of her' or feel smug that she was getting me to do work that she was paid for. I know that those two ideas seemed diametrically opposed, but Beryl is a complicated woman.

I'd had one coffee and was starting to put my expenses onto the spreadsheet when the Stanbeck twins arrived. They didn't knock, only rattled the door more and more loudly until I answered. It was like the concept of a door being locked to them just wasn't in their minds. I didn't really want to let them in after yesterday's adventures with Mick's Geordies, but the fact the Twins were, in their own way, knocking rather than just kicking the door in probably meant they weren't coming to do me harm.

Probably.

I opened the door, and they entered. They still had that wariness about them, as if they knew they weren't really welcome. I suppose they rarely were.

'Still no TV,' said Kray One.

'It's not conducive,' said Kray Two.

'Can I help you, boys?' I said. 'Or did you just come to see if I'd bought a TV?'

'Are you going to get one?' said Kray One.

'Not for the office.'

'It's not conducive,' said Kray Two. He put a lot of effort into the word 'conducive' and I think he was a little hurt that his brother wasn't complimenting him on his expanded vocabulary.

'Da sent us,' said Kray One, a little sulkily.

'To say sorry,' said Kray Two.

'Sorry?'

'For the guys,' said Kray One.

'Guys?'

'Who were gonna hurt you. Da said that wasn't their job. They've been dealt with,' said Kray Two.

'Dealt with?'

'Sent back, you know,' said Kray One. He pointed out the door. 'To wherever they came from.' He stopped and his brother filled in.

'London,' said Kray Two.

'I think,' I said, 'that they were from Newcastle.'

'Is that not London then?' said Kray One. Two pairs of pale eyes locked on to me, as if I was challenging everything they believed.

'Yeah,' I said. 'Yeah, it is London.' Some battles aren't worth fighting.

They nodded in unison.

'Da wants to know what you found at Janine's mam's,' said Kray Two.

'Nothing.'

They nodded thoughtfully again, as if they needed to chew over that revelation.

'Da wanted us to say that he won't make the same mistake twice,' said Kray One.

'What mistake?'

'Next time he'll get good people in,' said Kray Two. They looked a bit sad about that.

'Not you two.'

'Da doesn't want us to go to prison,' said Kray One.

'He loves us,' said Kray Two.

'Well,' I said, 'I better get on if I'm to find your dad's money, right? I need to get some work done.' I pointed at the back room.

'You got a TV in there?'

'Just a computer.' They looked to each other, evidently decided there was something wrong with me, and turned and left. I watched them go, then went to Mr Patel's shop and bought an overpriced and slightly stale sausage roll that I only ate half of. I put it to one side just as Beryl walked in.

'It's your day off,' I said.

She ignored me and stared at the sausage roll for a minute.

'Take it, Beryl.'

She did, then shuffled off to the back room to do whatever Beryl did back there when she wasn't helping me. I took a notepad from one of the desk drawers and started to write down what I knew. I would probably never look at my notes again, but I found it helped to get my mind in order.

I knew a lottery ticket bought by Larry Stanbeck from Mr Patel, who he called on regularly, had gone missing after Larry was killed on his bike. I knew his death wasn't an accident, but the police were keeping that quiet. I knew his wife wanted the ticket. I knew Mick Stanbeck wanted the ticket. I knew the Russians wanted the ticket. Benny Callaghan also wanted the ticket, and he didn't want his son to become a mechanic, and he had the van that had run Larry Stanbeck off the road, which he had got from Mick Stanbeck.

Killing your own son was cold, even for Trolley Mick.

Anything else?

Oh, I knew Janine Stanbeck's upbringing had probably been miserable but couldn't see how that would fit in, other than encouraging her to run off and set up with the Stanbecks in the first place. And I knew from the accounts I'd seen that Janine and her husband were skint, which was odd. I picked up the phone and rang Lucy, a friend at a credit reference agency who had access to too much information and an obsessive need to share. She checked out Larry's credit rating and made the sort of sound I usually associate with someone watching a particularly nasty fall involving bones twisting the wrong way and a lot of blood.

Me: Bad?

Lucy: Car-crash bad. Looks like he was credit-carded up to the hilt. Which is fine, if you can keep up.

Me: He didn't?

Lucy: No. I suspect he got to the point where he was juggling cards to pay off the minimum on each one, which you can do if you're organised. But not forever. Looks like his attempts collapsed about five months ago and he was midway through multiple county court judgements for debt. You didn't hear this from me though.

Me: Okay, thank you.

Lucy: We should do lunch sometime.

Me: We will.

I put the phone down, knowing full well we never would. I'd known her years ago when I was couch-surfing; she'd been escorting to fund her habit, and I was stealing what I could from chain stores because I was too wasted to run a decent con. We'd hooked up for a while when we were clean but both of us had a past we didn't want to revisit, and when I looked into her face I saw echoes of that life. I imagine it was the same for her. We had teetered on the abyss of addiction and knew how easy it was to slip back in. Going backward was never the answer; you learned that. Those people, those places, they were just weight, and the more weight you carried, the more likely it was you would overbalance and fall.

Didn't want to fall.

I shook my head, ran my hands through my hair and stared at the paper in front of me. Then felt like kicking myself and wandered back into Beryl's room. She was staring at her computer, playing spider solitaire.

'Beryl, how do I find out if Larry Stanbeck's life was insured if I don't know who the insurer was?'

'Complex. That's police or IFIG – the fraud people – stuff,' she said, and moved a virtual card across the screen without looking at me.

'Do we know anyone?'

'Leave it with me,' she said.

I returned to my desk, trying to make the words I'd written on the pad make a sort of sense, but they stubbornly refused to. I took a pair of scissors from my drawer and started cutting the sentences out so I could move them about, see if I found anything in my subconscious that my conscious mind had missed.

I didn't. I just ended up with a lot of useless bits of paper that I swept into the bin.

'He was insured.'

I turned. Beryl was standing in the doorway to the back room.

'How much for?'

She stared at me, sighed, then went back into the back room. I went back to staring at a page in my notebook that now had lots of holes in it. Five minutes later, she returned.

'A million.'

I let out a whistle.

'Who was the beneficiary?'

She sighed again, gave me a look that I could have cut my hair to the scalp with and went back into her room. She was back more quickly this time. 'Cristophe Stanbeck – goes into a trust fund with a monthly payout toward his keep. He only gets the full sum if he leaves the Edge and either goes to university and gets a degree, or works in a full-time job for longer than five years.'

I tapped my pen on the desk. 'Curiouser and curiouser.'

'I'm going out,' said Beryl, and she ambled past me with her plastic bags.

'You don't fancy sharing your source, do you, Beryl?'

She stared at me for what seemed like a long time and then turned away and headed to the door.

'No then.'

Sometimes I found myself jealous of Beryl's connections. I had no idea what she had done with her life before I met her, but I suspect it was highly illegal and specialised. There were hundreds of insurance companies that Larry Stanbeck could have been insured with and as Beryl hadn't had time to ring them all, she either struck lucky first time or had a source somewhere important. I'd tried going through the drawers in the back room to see if she kept any records of her sources; she didn't. She knew I had searched the drawers too, even though I was really careful, and she refused to speak to me for a month. Which sounds like it should be a gift but Beryl's silence is of a particularly oppressive and unpleasant kind. I never did anything like that again.

Still, at least I knew something. I didn't really like Janine Stanbeck, and the fact her husband was mired in debt made me wonder if she'd helped him on his way to get hold of his money. She plainly didn't like him much more than I liked her, but killing him without having the lottery ticket left her in a worse position; all his debts would default to her as his wife, and she didn't even have the insurance money to pay them off. If she was a murderer, she was a stupid one not to have checked out if it was worthwhile beforehand – and Janine Stanbeck didn't strike me as stupid.

But if she had knowledge of those debts, that at least showed me why she was so desperate to find that lottery ticket; she was drowning.

The debt itself made no sense though. He was a Stanbeck; he had no need to borrow money from legitimate sources because his dad always had plenty of money which was partly why the family were so loyal. Trolley Mick might be a borderline sociopath, but if you toed the line, he was a generous borderline sociopath.

If you toed the line.

But what if you didn't? He wouldn't be so generous then, would he? And you'd have trouble finding real work as a Stanbeck, unless you moved right out of the area and to a place where that name meant nothing.

Why hadn't Larry moved out of the area? He had a job, I was sure, was that why?

I went back to my un-cut up notes. Worked as an interior designer at Maylin and Sparrow in the city, a big firm and interior designer was a well-paid job. So where was all his money going? There'd been no sign of it in his accounts. Drugs? No, he was a Stanbeck; he could get all the drugs he wanted. Same for girls – or boys, if that was his thing. Mick Stanbeck had his hand in every pie and there was nothing, within reason, one of his close family couldn't get hold of.

Gambling?

I searched back through my papers and the notes I'd been keeping on my way. Nothing there, no mention of Larry Stanbeck seeming out of sorts or worried, but addicts were adept at hiding what they were doing – though that didn't mean there wouldn't be signs. Would his wife know? Probably, but she didn't like me much. Though, if this was information I could produce 'from the spirits', it might make dealing with her a bit easier. But I had to be right.

So, I'd check with his work, then I'd track down some of the parents of the boys in his Scout troop.

10

Maylin and Sparrow had offices halfway up the sort of big, glass-fronted not-quite-skyscraper-because-this-is-the-North-and-that's-a-bit-much-thank-you building that was impressive from the outside and soulless from the inside. A Victorian church was on one side and on the other was a large warehouse that used to be a brilliant music venue but was now a chain pub that sold cheap food and bad beer to career drinkers. Both the church and warehouse had been built when the city was in its woollen manufacturing heyday. Money had once streamed through here as fast as the wool filled the warehouses and mills, whose chimneys had stained the sandstone of the church and warehouse black. Underneath the sign for the chain pub, *The Millers Arms* was the washed-out sign from the original venue that no amount of sandblasting could get off. I'd spent a lot of time here when it was a venue, and in the bar when it first became a pub.

I had no wish to go in now.

I'll kick the fuck out of you if you do. Beryl's voice in the back of my mind. She really was a gift that kept on giving, and she could punch harder than Jackie when she put her mind to it.

The glass building was called The Loom; someone's idea of harking back to the city's heritage, though what weaving looms had to do with a thirty-floor glass edifice, I had no idea. It had shop fronts along the bottom, a card shop, a chain sandwich shop, a classy Indian restaurant that promised 'modern

British Indian cuisine'. I glanced at the menu: rabbit tikka masala was the speciality of the house. Very modern.

I'd have to bring Jackie here. He would hate it.

Next to the restaurant was a shop that cashed cheques and offered loans on cars.

The first ten floors of The Loom were offices. Above that were fancy apartments; the ones on the sides had balconies, but on the front, nothing had been allowed to spoil the sheer glass facade.

A year after The Loom was completed, the building developer had thrown himself out of the penthouse. I presume because his dream of people flocking to a down-at-heel Northern city hadn't come true, and the building had left him deep in debt. Now the apartments were mostly empty, and the council were engaged in a fight with the new owners to turn over the promised two floors of social housing. I didn't really understand why the owners were fighting it. Maybe they thought there were hordes of people that wanted to come and live here as soon as they made sure no one earning below a living wage was going to dirty up the building. Personally, I doubted anyone wanted to come and live here. This was the sort of city you got stuck in, not one you chose as a new home. Especially not if you could afford the prices they wanted for The Loom apartments.

You entered from the side; the lobby was painted white and rose for three storeys. The Indian restaurant was built inside a glass cube and, had it been open, I would have been able to watch the chefs and the diners, but it wasn't. The kitchen looked clean though.

The other shops clearly weren't as interesting and they had normal walls that stopped us seeing the less theatrical jobs of making sandwiches, selling cards and fleecing people in financial trouble. A long, smooth white desk ran along a central wall that had a spray of metal birds flying across it, and above them the words *The Loom* picked out in neon. It was ugly beyond belief. Behind the desk sat a security guard in a thin-looking uniform, and I wondered if he had a heater below the desk. It was warm outside but the lobby was freezing; it must be like the Arctic in winter. He stood as I approached the desk and eyed me suspiciously. I probably didn't look like I worked here. I read off the list of businesses that were on a tall plinth at the end of the desk. Maylin and Sparrow had the entire tenth floor – not a small outfit then. As I read the list, the security guard lifted a flat panel in the desk and walked out to meet me. Behind him, I saw a small fan heater.

'Can I help you, sir?' He didn't sound like he meant it when he said 'sir'.

'Yes. I'm thinking of doing some building work, and a friend of mine said I should look in on Maylin and Sparrow.'

'Do you have an appointment, sir?' he said.

'No, but I can come back if they can't fit me in. My name is Mal Jones.' He stared at me, as if he could make me go away with the power of his eyes, and when that failed, he went back to his desk and picked up the phone. He didn't do anything, only kept an eye on me. Maybe he thought I wanted to leave dirty fingerprints on the paintwork. When I still didn't leave, and he decided my bluff had been called, he made a phone call. Then he finally he told me to go up and to take the 'Yellowvater'. I wondered if that was a slip of the tongue but didn't ask. I didn't think he would welcome the invitation for conversation.

He also hadn't made a slip of the tongue.

Behind the desk, there were two lifts embedded in the white column that rose up three storeys until it hit the ceiling. One was a normal lift, and it had a sign in front of it that said *Residents only*. The other was the Yellowvater. A line of yellow was painted up the column to the ceiling directly above the lift and the words, *Take the Yellowvator to work!* were painted on the doors next to a smiley face. In case the subtle message of 'going to work should make you happy' was missed, smiley faces were also picked out all the way up the yellow column. I got in the Yellowvator and hit the button for the tenth floor. Someone had scratched, *Abandon hope all ye who enter here,* and then a smiley face next to it in the black plastic trim. I imagined there was a whole HR department working on finding this disgruntled employee.

A young woman met me at the doors to the Yellowvator; she didn't look like work filled her with joy, but she didn't look entirely worn down either. More harried and could have done without meeting me.

'I understand you are intending to do some building work, Mr Jones? We have a form for you to fill in and …'

'I'm very sorry,' I said, 'I used false pretences to get in here.' Sometimes, I find it is best to be honest rather than force her to do her job, which would probably annoy her when it turned out I had no house, never mind any building work to do on it. She became utterly still, like a woodland animal that had sensed danger. Then I saw the hint of a smile on her face and wondered just how bored she was.

'Oh really, Mr Jones?'

'Yes, I didn't think your security guard was likely to let me in if I told the truth.'

'Alans a grumpy bastard, but I would be too if I was stuck down there in the cold.' She glanced over her shoulder and whispered. 'So why are you here, Mr Jones?'

'I'm a life-insurance investigator,' I said and showed her the false ID. A shared smile, a gleam in her eye; she was interested.

'You here about Larry?'

I nodded.

'I don't know what we can tell you that we haven't told the police.'

'Sadly, the police don't give us access to their records, or I wouldn't have to bother you.'

She frowned, a thought crossing her face. 'Are you trying not to pay out?'

'No,' I said. The frown vanished. 'Strictly routine in the case of a suspicious death. Questions have to be asked, boxes ticked, that's all.'

'I know all about ticking boxes.'

'Tell me about it,' I said. We exchanged a look of frank – if false in my case – understanding. 'Did you know Mr Stanbeck, Lawrence, well?'

'Not really. I met him a few times on nights out and saw him in passing – everyone liked him. We always called him Larry. He brought his kid in a couple of times – he was nice. Quick little kid, funny. Sad he lost his father.' Her voice drifted away, then she pulled herself back to the now. 'Go to the end of the room – last bank of desk is the interiors team: Pauline, Ed, and it was Larry. They knew him best.'

'Thank you,' I said, and she walked away to get on with whatever bit of box ticking was next on her list.

Only Ed was at the interiors desk. He was a large man in his early sixties, jolly-looking with a head of thick silver hair and the brightest blue eyes I had ever seen. I introduced myself, we made small talk, and I brought the conversation round to reasons why Larry Stanbeck might have died.

'Troubled?' he said. He rubbed his face with the palm of his hand, and I heard stubble rasp against skin. 'You mean like suicide troubled?' I was about to say no, but Ed carried on. 'No, not Larry. He was happy soul, I mean he had troubles but I wouldn't say he was troubled.'

'Troubles? Like what?'

'Well, his wife mostly – she was, well, high maintenance, I suppose you would call it. He was always ready to do the overtime, if it didn't interfere with his Scouting and that, but yeah, I reckon he had to work the hours to keep her happy.'

'He said that?'

'Well, not so much, but it was the feeling I got. She came out with us once and she didn't like it – felt like she thought we were beneath her, you know?' He scratched his head. 'I'd never have put her and Larry together,' he said. 'They were a funny couple, but we can't choose those we love, right?'

'I suppose not.'

'Kid was a good 'un though,' said Ed. 'He used to bring him in when he was working late, and we'd make a bed out of our coats when the lad got tired.'

'Did he have any other hobbies, apart from the Scouts?'

'Not that I knew of. Tell the truth, he wasn't in that much, so I didn't really know him well. Worked from home a lot.'

'Any bad habits?'

'Just the wife. We went to the dogs once – he got a bit drunk and started telling us how hard it was being him, dreamed of living in the country one day. That's the only thing I can think of.'

'The dogs, did he organise that?'

Ed stared into the distance. Then nodded.

'Yeah, I think he did. The first time anyway, but he made such a hash of the orders and the numbers I took over. Then it just became a habit, go for a bet on the dogs as a company every six months – team building, they call it.'

'They do.'

Ed tapped his finger on the desk. 'Do they really think it might be suicide?'

'It's an avenue we have to investigate.'

Ed chewed on his lip.

'Why do you ask?'

'Only that, in the last few weeks, he was in work more often. Spent a lot of time in the big office too.'

'You think he was under a lot of pressure?' Ed shook his head.

'No, well, maybe,' he smiled, 'but if he was, he enjoyed it. He'd seemed happier than he had for a long time the last few times I saw him. I wondered if he was going to be promoted.'

I thanked Ed and walked away. The dogs every six months, and that was a thing that Larry started. It was slim, but if he was addicted to betting, it would have to show somewhere. And a work outing was an acceptable place to bet; the sort of thing you could get away with, were obliged to do, even. I should have asked Ed how much Larry was betting but I was being careful; you push too much and people ask questions. And he clearly doted on Larry's kid, so I doubt he'd have said anything to incriminate Larry anyway.

'Malachite Jones.'

I stopped dead at hearing my name. Stopped deader on seeing who said it.

In front of me was Frank, the Russian who had visited me in my office. The first thing I did on was look for Harry, but thankfully there was no sign of him. He must have been at his stationer's shop, fondling erasers or whatever it was stationers do. It didn't make me feel any more comfortable though.

'What do you do here, Malachite Jones?' said Frank.

'Oh, you know, just doing follow up on Larry Stanbeck.'

'Good,' he walked over and slapped me on the back, then started walking me toward the Yellowvater.

‘If I had known you wished to come here, I would have made your appointment myself.’

‘You work here?’

‘I own here, Mr Jones,’ he grinned. ‘I am Mr Sparrow.’

‘Not very Russian sounding.’

‘Oh, I find the English have problems saying my real name. So I use a pretend name for business – it is much easier.’ He leaned in close and whispered – without the accent. ‘Mention my other business interests and I will have Harry come and see you. You and he can discuss his interest in stationery, you understand?’

‘I do,’ I said. The hand on my back seemed to radiate ice through my body. ‘You never said Larry Stanbeck worked for you.’

‘My legitimate concerns are not your concerns.’

‘Did Mick Stanbeck know that his son …?’

‘As I said, Mr Jones, my legitimate concerns are not your concerns.’

‘I have questions about him.’

He stepped up to the Yellowvater with me. ‘That I cannot answer,’ he said and gently pushed me inside. ‘He was simply an employee – I had a little to do with him. Good afternoon, Mr Jones,’ he said, and as the doors began to shut, he added, ‘You will not need to come back here.’

But I knew Larry had spent a lot of time in his office recently.

I wondered what it was he was hiding.

11

Coincidences do happen. There's no denying that. But it's also foolish to overlook something that seems unlikely. I mean, how likely is it that one of Mick Stanbeck's children should end up working for a company owned by the Russian mob? It's the sort of thing that both parties would definitely be less than enthralled about.

I wondered if Larry was running some sort of long game with his father, or maybe with the Russian mob. There was no mistaking that Frank was less than pleased to find me at Larry's place of work. I couldn't see how these things tied together, or how they would help me find the missing lottery ticket, but I've found, when in this sort of position, the best thing to do is to stumble on blindly and see what happens. If nothing happens, then you're probably stumbling the wrong way, and if something does happen, then you're probably stumbling the right way. Or at least toward something. Though there's no guarantee it will be something useful.

Though I'm generally stumbling toward something a little less likely to maim me.

I passed a public telephone box, a rare thing now but there were still a few in the town centre. I dropped into the box, rang the police non-emergency number and told the lady who answered the phone that if the police were interested in the van that knocked Larry Stanbeck off his bike, they should have a look around Benny Callaghan's yard. When they started asking for details, I put the phone down and got out of the area as quickly as possible. Lunchtime was just starting, and I lost myself in among the commuters looking for a decent sandwich – harder to find than you'd think in this town.

I'd done a bit of research before I came out and it turned out one of the boys in Larry Stanbeck's Scout troop was the son of a man I knew. Well, 'knew' is a strong word; he was an outreach worker for the homeless once and we came into contact that way. I'd never liked him much – he was a bit preachy and always trying to get me into church, which isn't my thing – but if you have an existing contact, then it's easier than getting someone to trust you from a standing start. So I rang him and he agreed to meet me near the urban park in the city centre at lunchtime. His name was Will Person, which is hilariously funny when you're off your head on drugs and alcohol and still reasonably amusing when you're sober.

I think, anyway.

Will was about my age and slightly thinner and taller which took a bit of doing. He walked with a slight limp – he'd always had it – and as he waved at me from the edge of the grass, Subway sandwich in one hand, I saw he still wore Harry Potter-style round glasses. A bit closer and I saw that his short hair was greying. It had been thick and dark brown when I knew him.

'Malachite,' he said. I wondered if he knew how much it annoyed me. 'Are you well?' He offered me his hand to shake and clasped my fingers before my hand fully engaged with his, giving them a squeeze. A cheap technique that he probably thought gave the impression he had a firm handshake. Not that a firm handshake meant anything, but some people were easily pleased.

'I am, very well, William,' I said.

'Just Will.'

'Just Mal.'

He licked his lips. I'd always had the sense, back in the day, that he thought himself better than the people he was helping. He wasn't helping because it was right, he was helping them because it made him feel superior. He searched my face, looking for who I was back then and not finding him.

'Not using anymore then?' he said. Which, to be frank, was rude.

'No.' I was tempted to ask if he was still being holier-than-thou but decided to concentrate on being the better man. Now I'd seen his face, more memories of him were surfacing and I thought coming here was a mistake.

'AA, was it? You finally found your higher power?' He took a rolled-up cigarette from a pouch of tobacco and put it in his mouth.

'Could you not, please,' I said. He stared at me, and I felt a little bit of pleasure in the flash of annoyance in his eyes. But annoying him, while fun, wasn't going to help me. 'I locked myself in a cottage in a damp room and sweated it out.' Well, Jackie locked me in a damp room and forced me to sweat it out, but Will didn't need to know that.

'Oh,' he said, the rollie bobbed in his mouth, and he almost lifted his lighter to it. Remembered not to.

'You said you wanted to talk to me about something – I thought you might have needed to reach out.'

'No,' I said. 'It's about Scouts, about your son's Scout leader, Larry Stanbeck.'

'Sad what happened to him.'

'Yes.' I let a little space develop in the conversation. Watched him wanting to light his fag and not being able to because he thought it would make him look weak in front of an addict. 'Did you know him well?'

'Not really, saw him at Scouts. I helped out a bit, you know. Most of the Scout stuff happens at the church on the Edge and I'm a lay preacher there – you should come along.' He left a gap. I didn't bite. 'So I knew him from that.'

'Nothing odd? Nothing off about him?'

'Larry? No, I mean … you don't mean he was messing with the kids? Cos no one …'

'No, I don't mean that. I just mean him. How was he? What sort of things did he like?'

'He loved his bike,' he said, and took the cigarette from his mouth, looked at it, then put it back in between his lips. 'The only odd thing about him, was he was nervous.'

'Nervous?'

'Yeah, and him a Stanbeck and all. I mean, I know he didn't get on with his dad.'

'He didn't?'

'No, they fell out, about Janine, I think it was. But still, he was a Stanbeck – they're generally pretty confident, you know – even if you're not speaking to

Trolley Mick, he still looks after his own. The only person who hurts a Stanbeck is another Stanbeck.'

'He had anywhere he kept stuff, apart from the Scout hut? Somewhere the police might have missed?'

'You looking for something?'

It was too late to lie. 'Yes. Nothing much, just a family thing. It's lost and his wife asked me to find it. Sentimental value.'

'Sentimental? Janine?'

'Death changes people – you're a preacher, you should know that.'

'I suppose so,' he said and looked away. He took the cigarette from his mouth again and removed a bit of tobacco that was stuck to his lips. Then he put the cigarette back in his tobacco pouch. Out of sight, out of mind. 'If he had anything it would be at the Scout hut and the police emptied that. I know because I had the job of cleaning it up.' He didn't look at me, and I watched him as cars passed, hissing slowly along the road to the multistorey car park.

'You said he was nervous,' I said. 'Do you think he might have been hiding something?'

'Like what?'

'You know,' I said, and scratched at my arm. Then he looked at me, his eyes washed-out blue, and I knew when I looked into them that he hungered for something the way I sometimes did. I knew what I wanted; I wondered what it was for him.

A car passed.

Another.

'I never thought so,' he said. 'There were no tracks on his arms, he never turned up drunk, but there was something about him.' He stared past me. 'Like there was something in him that was empty and he couldn't fill it.' He pulled the cigarette back out of his pouch and put it in his mouth. 'When he wasn't nervous, lately, he was really up. I wondered if he was manic, to be honest. I'd spoken to the vicar about maybe giving Larry some time off from the troop.'

'I bet Larry loved that.'

'He wasn't happy, no.' He gave me a simpering smile. 'But I have a responsibility to do what is best for the kids.'

'I'm sure you do.'

An uncomfortable silence came and sat on the wall between us.

'You know, the church door is always open for you, Malachite.' I wondered if he knew that was a good way to end a conversation with me.

'You should shut it,' I said, 'or you'll let out all the heat.' I stood and walked away.

He sparked up, and I turned. 'You should quit smoking, or start vaping at least, not as bad for you. You're a father – set an example.'

I saw a flash of anger cross his face and I had to turn away to hide my grin. He'd always annoyed me and I wondered how I'd missed it before that he had been an addict too. Usually people were up front about that, especially those trying to help you out. I suppose they thought it created some sort of understanding.

I wondered where I was going and what I was doing.

Maybe I should go to church.

St Jude's, the church on the Edge that Will had been talking about shared a name with the Edge's school. It was a multi-denominational church: C of E, Catholics and a number of fringe preachers worked out of it on different days of the week. There'd been an imam for a bit, but he didn't last long: brown people were a rarity on the Edge. It was an ugly building, hexagonal, and built from concrete with a cross mounted on a short tower right in the centre of the constantly leaking roof. Inside, a corridor ran around the outside of the central space, which was impressive, and behind that were a couple of offices. It always smelled of damp and the walls were always crumbling as it had been made from cheap materials. I knew it well because my mother had been Christian, for a bit anyway.

I'm a spiritual person, Malachite.

Christianity was one among many 'paths' she had tried to walk, looking for a peace that she would never find; something to calm the shifting seas within her that coloured her moods and my childhood. I spent more time in that church than I wanted to as a moody teenager, listening to the vicar drone on, or some helper attempt an uncomfortable conversation with me about music or try to convince me to cut my hair and wear less black.

I'd hated it then, but it had also been a safe place. It was always quiet and after my friend Steve had died I'd gone there a lot, looking for answers that weren't there from a God I was reasonably sure didn't exist. I'd even had my own locker.

I stopped walking.

Turned.

Will Person was smoking his fag and walking away from me, and I ran after him. He glanced back but pretended he didn't see me coming and carried on walking. He was trying to look unhurried, as if he wasn't speeding up to get away from me. I didn't care whether he wanted to speak to me or not. I grabbed his arm.

'Will.'

'Yes, Mal?' he blew out a plume of smoke.

'Did Larry have a locker at the church? I just thought, as Scout leader, they use the church a lot, but the hut was over the other side of the estate. So it would make sense for him to keep some stuff there.'

'Maybe,' he shrugged.

'You didn't mention the lockers, Will.'

He scratched his head. 'I forgot, that's all. And I don't know if he had one.'

'Who would know?'

'The vicar.'

'I'll drop in and ask him later.'

'He's not in until this evening, and besides, the lockers have codes you put in yourself. Unless Larry wrote the code down you won't be able to get in. The church will have to get a locksmith and we don't have the money for that sort of thing.' He took a drag from his cigarette and stared at the floor.

'There's no pass key?'

'They were cheap lockers,' he said. 'We're not a rich church.'

'Okay, I'll drop in and see the vicar,' I said. 'Is it still Reverend Scanlon.'

‘No, we have a new vicar now, Canon Armitage. He’s a bit less of a pushover.’

‘I’ll drop in and see him then.’

‘Good luck,’ said Will, and he smirked at me. I hate it when people smirk.

I took the bus back to my office and got some chips from Mr Wan. When I’d eaten them, I got in my car and headed over to St Jude’s. I was wary about leaving my car on the Edge, but the church car park was about as safe is it could get, and as I only drove a Ford Ka, the effort of stealing it probably wasn’t worth the small amount of fun joyriding it might provide.

There were more cars than I expected in the church car park; it was almost full. The car park had been planted with some big tubs of flowers and it looked they had been there a while without being stolen or vandalised. Maybe miracles do happen. It was still light, but the church had four big floodlights over the door, probably there to light the car park and stop people stealing the flowers. The people coming in were carrying things, bags and boxes, and the atmosphere was a jolly one. A woman near me dropped a carrier bag and food spilled from it. Another woman stopped to help her pick it up.

I ignored the people and made my way into the church. As I passed through one of the two sets of double doors, a man stepped in front of me – big, dressed in black with a shock of white hair and a drinker’s red face. A white dog collar circled his throat. Canon Armitage, I presume.

‘If you’re here for the food bank, lad,’ he said, he had a Welsh accent as thick as cream, ‘then you’ll need to come back during the day tomorrow. We're just sorting things out tonight, but if you're starving, see Lisa.' He pointed across the doors to a small, round and poorly dressed woman who had 'do-gooder' written all over her. 'I'm sure she won't let you leave hungry, eh?'

'Do I look like I need a food bank?'

He took a step back, looked me up and down. I saw his eyes stop at my boots, which were scuffed and worn.

'A little,' he said. 'You're a bit of a scrawny one.'

'Thanks.'

'If you're not here for the food banks, are you here to join the congregation?'

I shook my head, he didn't seem concerned in the least.

'Then how can I help, young man?'

'I'm looking into the death of Larry Stanbeck, for the family.'

His face turned from one of benign peace to one of intense dislike.

'I want nothing to do with the rest of that family – they are a blight on this estate.'

'But not Larry?'

'Well, even a family of black sheep can have one white one, eh?'

'If he was.' The canon stared at me.

'I'll not have you speak ill of the dead,' he said.

'I'm just trying to find out—'

'I think you should leave' – he took a step forward so he was in my personal space – 'or I will remove you.'

Rather than cause a scene, I removed myself.

12

'So you got thrown out of a church by a vicar?' Jackie was in my clients' chair, sitting at an angle with one muscly leg over the armrest, one arm over the top of the chair as he idly tapped the wooden back, making a really irritating noise.

'I wasn't thrown out, he asked me to leave, and I did.'

'You got thrown out of a church by a vicar.'

'A canon, actually. That's more important than a vicar.'

'So you got thrown out of church by a posh vicar.'

I didn't continue to argue the point with him. There wasn't any advantage in that, really.

'It is weird though, isn't it, Jackie? Larry Stanbeck working for Russian Frank? I mean, it makes you wonder if something is going on.'

'Even Russian gangsters need interior design, Mal.'

'Do they? I thought gangster chic was just buy the most garish and expensive things you could.'

Jackie rolled his eyes. 'For their homes, yes. But it's useful to have some legit businesses if you also run illegal ones. The Russians run loads, you know, takeaways and stuff.'

'Like Spice 'N' Saucy?'

Jackie stared at me but didn't confirm or deny anything. 'Anyway, if you have a legit business, and one that provides services for a legit business, like say, a builders and architects firm, and you also own a load of takeaways, then it's a great way to launder money.

You charge the takeaways way over the odds for the services provided by the builders. They get bills but no actual money is ever exchanged, it only ever exists on the books. That way the money is brought into the system and as a bonus you end up with a load of takeaways that are pretty good-looking, as you're constantly refreshing the designs.'

Something about that was ticking in the back of my mind but I couldn't put my finger on it.

'But why let a Stanbeck get involved?'

Jackie stared at the desk.

'Maybe he was looking after family interests?'

'Eh?'

'Well, if you've got a money-laundering machine, why not hire it out to others?'

'You think the Russians were laundering money for Mick Stanbeck too?' Jackie shrugged. 'Maybe. Larry could have been there to keep an eye out, and if, as you say, he had a gambling problem?'

'You think he was skimming from his dad?'

'It's not a huge leap for someone who is desperate. Mick does not look kindly on betrayal.'

'So Mick killed him?' I tapped my pen on the desk. 'I'd believe it if Larry wasn't a Stanbeck. But Mick has different rules for family – a punishment beating, broken bones maybe. But to kill his own son?'

'Maybe he'd already had the punishment beating? Or maybe they didn't mean to kill him? Maybe they were chasing him to give him a kicking and it went wrong.'

‘Maybe,’ I said. ‘I’d still like to look at those lockers though. If the lottery ticket is in there, then I can forget all about this.’

‘Apart from who you give the ticket to.’

‘I was trying to forget about that too.’

‘Well, maybe you should think about that. We can pop over to St Jude’s – should be quiet now – and have a look.’

I looked up, Jackie was holding something in his hand: a small and shiny key.

‘You’ve got a key to St Jude’s?’ I said. He nodded. ‘Why?’

‘To get in of course, keep up.’ He stood. ‘Well, you coming?’

We drove over in an old Fiat Panda that sounded like it was in pain every time Jackie turned the steering wheel. Jackie parked it three streets from St Jude’s and passed me a black balaclava.

‘What’s this for?’

‘There are a lot of security cameras in St Jude’s. The key will stop the system calling the police, but I can’t stop them recording.’

‘How do you know this?’

‘Useful legit business, remember?’

‘You put the security system in?’

‘Not personally,’ said Jackie. He lifted his hand. ‘These hands were never meant for manual work. Now, take your hat unless you want to make DI Smith’s night.’

I took the hat.

We skirted through the streets of the Edge in the warm evening. St Jude’s was in a better area; most of the houses were owned and the gardens were neat, some even had trees which made the place feel more luxuriant. We walked hurriedly and did our best not to look suspicious, keeping relaxed and chatting as we moved.

The Edge was an odd place. There were areas near the Blade where you could walk through covered in blood holding a knife and no one would bat an eyelid; and even if they did, they definitely wouldn't call the police. Where we were, it was neighbourhood-watch central; no one is nosier than someone who thinks they're better than their neighbours. It was late enough that there were still stragglers coming back from the various pubs dotted around the edges of the estate. Some of the houses were lit up by flickering TV screens as life went on within them. We made our way up St Jude's Street, along St Jude's Avenue and up St Jude's Approach to the church.

St Jude's itself was glowing; the huge lights that illuminated the car park created a halo of light around the building, coloured lights were directed at the cross in the centre of the roof.

'Round the back,' said Jackie. He led me down a snicket that hugged the tall outer wall of St Jude's car park, running between the church and a dilapidated semi-detached that was probably not part of the neighbourhood watch. Jackie stopped at the wall between two buddleia bushes that filled the air with cloying perfume. Behind that was another scent; something foul, something rotting.

'Here,' he said. 'Give me a leg up.' I made a well with my hands and leant over. Jackie placed his shiny brogue in it, and I boosted him up so he could climb the wall and sit on top. Then he offered me a hand. 'Come on.' And pulled me up. On the other side was the explanation for the smell of rot: we were right above the church's bins.

'Delightful.'

'There are reasons no one watches some places. Stop moaning.'

We climbed down the wall, then down the bins, trying not to step in anything too squishy or get anything on our clothes. Then we were at the back of the church, in the dark and the stink.

'They call this bit God's arse,' said Jackie.

'Is there anywhere on the Edge you don't know about?'

'No,' said Jackie, and he dug into his pocket for the key as he walked toward the rear door of the church. It was a fire door, illegally locked with a chain and a padlock. 'Right, when we go through this door, I am going to run to the office and turn off the alarm. You just wait here for me to get back.' He pulled down his balaclava and stood there staring at me.

'What?'

He pointed at his balaclava.'

'Oh.' I pulled mine down over my face. Then Jackie unlocked the padlock and put it in his pocket, letting the chain hang loose.

'How do we get into Larry's locker?'

The flash of white teeth against the black of his balaclava, and Jackie twitched his shoulders, letting a crowbar slip down his sleeve and into his hand.

'All-purpose skeleton key,' he said.

‘How do we know which one is his?’ he shrugged.

‘We open them all, and that will make it look more like a normal burglary, rather than someone looking for something. You ready?’

‘Yeah.’ My heart was flittering in my chest, leaving me breathless and light-headed. I’d not done a burglary for over a decade, and never sober.

‘You don’t look ready.’

‘Just do it, Jackie.’

He grinned again. ‘I love stuff like this.’

He pushed the door open. The smell of damp hit us straight away, and then I heard the high-pitched beeping of the alarm system and Jackie was running. His feet slapping and echoing round the corridors of the church, the light from his torch vanished as he ran around the circumference of the church. I waited, counting my breaths as the alarm continued to beep.

It stopped.

Silence enclosed me and I stared into the darkness, waiting for the false dawn of Jackie’s torch as he sauntered back.

‘Come on then,’ he shouted. Then he stopped. Turned. Something about his posture was off and a thrill ran through me. He motioned me forward, and I started to walk toward him. He brought his fingers to his lips to tell me to move more quietly. I tiptoed forward.

‘Mal,’ he said, ‘I think someone else is here.’

‘What?’

‘I thought I heard someone.’ He glanced over his shoulder, and even though it was warm outside, I could see his breath in the colder air of the church.

'So we go home, right?' I said.

'Why?'

'Because someone's here.'

'So? We just sneak about more carefully than them. They obviously don't want to be found either.'

'Why do you think that?'

'Cos they didn't say anything when we came in. No "Who's there?"'

'So they might be up to no good too?'

'Probably.'

'What if we bump into them?' Jackie grinned again.

'Let's hope we don't, but I've got my all-purpose skeleton key. Come on, the lockers are this way,' he whispered, pointing in the opposite direction he had come from. We took a few steps, and he looked back over his shoulder at me. 'This place would make a brilliant set for a horror movie.'

'Thanks, Jackie,' I said.

13

We rounded the curve of the church and I saw the blocky shape of a bank of lockers in the umbra of Jackie's torch.

'Aye-aye,' said Jackie quietly as we approached. 'Seems someone was here.' He shone his torch on the lockers; they were the long type generally used in sports clubs, each tall enough to house a golf bag. All the lockers had shiny keypads on them, except the one in the middle, which swung open, squeaking on one hinge, the keypad hanging from the door. Below the locker, its contents had been strewn across the floor: a selection of muddy-looking clothes and an open sports bag. 'At least we know which one was his, right?'

'Maybe,' I said, 'but if the ticket was in there, it's gone now.'

Jackie shook his head. 'Nah, it's still here.' He gave me a grin. 'To get out, you'd have had to come past us. And I'd have seen them when I went to turn off the alarm in the caretaker's cupboard, so they're not back where we came from. That only leaves the ministry offices. Whoever did this' – he pointed at the broken locker – 'must be in there. You wait here.'

With that he was off. The door at the end of the corridor opened and shut, leaving me in darkness.

In the damp-smelling, creepy church.

Sometimes I wondered if Jackie set these things up on purpose just to test me.

A moment later, I heard a crash, then shouting, mostly Jackie's voice. Then the door opened and

Jackie emerged holding a man, also in a balaclava, by the scruff of the neck.

'Come on, matey,' he was saying as he dragged him forward, the light of his torch jerkily splashing against wall and ceiling. He stopped in front me. 'Sit down here,' he said and forced the man to his knees with a couple of well-placed kicks. In the gloom, Jackie looked at me. 'Well, do you want to be Scooby-Doo?'

'What?'

Jackie shook his head. 'Do you want to unmask the bad guy?'

'Oh, right. Yes.' I pulled off the man's balaclava only to find what I really should have expected: it was Will Person underneath.

'This is not what it looks like,' he said. Despite the chill in the building, a coating of sweat shone around his eyes where the balaclava had not soaked it up.

'I'm pretty sure it is, Will,' I said.

'You know him?' said Jackie.

'Yeah, he's a lay preacher here, used to do the drugs outreach.'

Jackie shook his head. 'You know, Will,' he said conversationally. 'Only an arsehole burgles a place of worship, and I know that doesn't look good for me and my friend here, but to burgle *your own* place of worship, that requires a very special level of arseholeness.' Something flat in Jackie's voice; something far cooler than the damp air. 'That sort of thing should be punished really, Will.'

From the look on Will's face, he heard the threat in Jackie's voice as clearly as I did; the implacability of it, the simple promise that some form of retribution was needed and that whatever the retribution was it would hurt. Will turned to me, 'Mal' he said, so much for anonymity. I knew what was going to happen next. He was going to beg, he was going to ask me to intervene, but I'd long ago learned that Jackie wouldn't be moved once he'd set himself upon a course of action. Oh, he could be whimsical, easily derailed, but if one of his lines was crossed – and I was never entirely sure where those lines were – then the consequences were generally swift and unpleasant. Will could beg me all he liked, and I could beg Jackie, but it would not change anything.

Fittingly, for a house of God, Will was saved by the intervention of the light. Before Jackie could act he was interrupted by an electrical hum, and then the flickering of old neon lights as the lights around the corridor began switching on in turn, like a bright train running toward us. When the hum had passed and we stood, blinking in the bright light, we heard footsteps. I wanted to run, but there was nowhere to run to; to get out, we would have to pass whoever was coming toward us.

'Will, did you break in to organise a party?' said Jackie. He sounded unbearably calm, but he always did when things were going wrong. It was as if he was only really himself in these moments. Calm, ready, frightening. He shook his whole body, starting at his head, rolling it around on his shoulders, flicking his hands out, kicking each foot out in turn.

'If it's the police, Jackie,' I said, 'no fighting.'

‘It won’t be the police,’ he said. I wondered how he could be so sure.

‘It might be.’

‘It won’t.’

It wasn’t.

The man that walked round, following the light, was tall, dressed in black and not looking at all happy to be here.

‘Reverend!’ said Jackie, and he pulled off his balaclava. ‘Mal, take your hat off – it’s rude to cover your face in front of a man of God.’

I did as he asked.

‘Jackie,’ said Canon Armitage. ‘You look well. Now, firstly, it is “Canon” not “Reverend”, as you well know. Secondly, may I ask what you are doing breaking into my church in the middle of the night with this gentleman’ – he pointed at me – ‘whom I met earlier when he seemed interested in getting in here himself?’

‘Purely a coincidence, Vicar,’ said Jackie. ‘This is my friend Mal Jones. We were going out when I got an alert from the alarm, and as I was with Mal anyway and we weren’t far away, we thought we would come check on the church.’

‘In balaclavas?’

‘Yes,’ said Jackie. He didn’t bother trying to explain it, he just grinned at Canon Armitage who, after a moment, shook his head and pointed at Will.

‘And why is Will on his knees?’

‘Praying,’ said Jackie.

‘Is he, indeed?’

‘God moves in mysterious ways, Canon.’

'Indeed he does, but His servant on Earth would like to know why poor Will is on his knees looking like a heathen offering a burned sacrifice.' He gave a small nod to Jackie. 'And let's have the truth, eh?'

Jackie shrugged.

'Tell him, Mal,' said Jackie. 'The truth.'

'The real truth?'

'Edit it how you wish,' said Canon Armitage. 'I know Jackie isn't always on the right side of the law.'

'Though I'm on the right side of the Lord, eh, Canon?'

'One can always hope, Jackie.' He gave him a small smile. 'Now, let your friend speak.'

I glanced at Jackie, and he gave me a nod. Will tried to smile at Jackie. Jackie raised his eyebrows at him and bared his teeth. Will stopped smiling.

'Larry Stanbeck had a lottery ticket,' I said, 'a winner, but it wasn't on him when he died. Will knew Larry through Scouts. I asked him if Larry had a locker here. He said he didn't know.'

'So you broke in to find the locker and found Will?' said Canon Armitage.

'In essence,' I said. The canon went down on his haunches so he was looking Will in the face.

'Money will not stop the fire in you burning, Will.'

'I was going to give it to the church,' he said.

'Guilt will only stoke the fire higher, Will – don't lie.' He lifted Will's head and made him look into his eyes. 'Did you find the ticket?'

Will shook his head.

'Nothing in there but dirty clothes,' he said quietly. The canon stood and turned to Jackie.

‘Right, you heard him. You can check if you want, both the locker and Will, but that sounded like a very disappointed man to me.’

Jackie nodded.

‘How did you know about the ticket, Will? I never mentioned it,’ I said.

‘I overheard him, on the phone to someone.’

‘No one likes an eavesdropper,’ said Jackie..

‘I don’t want to get Will in trouble with the police,’ the canon said, ‘and I’m sure you would rather avoid them too, so maybe we’ll just keep quiet about all this And you can be on your way?’

‘What about him?’ said Jackie, pointing at Will.

‘I’ll deal with that,’ said the Canon.

We nodded.

‘Well, on your way, boys,’ he said.

We made our way back to Jackie’s clapped out Fiat, and as I was pulling on my seat belt, he turned to me.

‘That actually went better than I expected,’ he said.

14

THURSDAY

Jackie used to try to dislocate my arm.

'I'm going to dislocate your arm,' he'd say.

'Please don't.'

'I'm going to dislocate your arm, and I want you to try and stop me.'

'I don't know how.'

'I'll show you.'

And he did. First, slowly, he went through the movements that would allow me to slip the grasp of someone trying to grab my arm and hold me. Twice we ended up in A & E, and once you've had a dislocated arm relocated a couple of times, you learn how to counter that move pretty quickly. Mostly, it's about reacting before your opponent realises you know what to do and building up the right muscle groups. But, as Jackie once showed me, if someone knows what they are doing, there's not much you can do: it's best just to go with it and not get hurt, bide your time.

My flat was above the shop and I returned home to lie on the bed with only confusion for company.

Nothing made any sense.

I had lots of bits of puzzle spinning around me, but they refused to fit together, and not one of them seemed like it would help me find the lottery ticket. For all I knew, Larry Stanbeck had it in his hand when he was hit and it had fluttered off down the motorway verge, never to be seen again. In a detective book, this would be where I would have had a contemplative whisky and I could almost feel the smoky liquid as it warmed my mouth. That led to thoughts of fragrant marijuana smoke and the way it burned the back of my throat. Those thoughts led to thoughts of other stronger drugs that took a fiercer hold and demanded you submit to them. There was a bottle of whisky downstairs, and an old syringe and an empty bottle of pills. My hand twitched.

There were no solutions for me there; only ghosts and lost days …

… weeks …

… months.

So, I tried to sleep, but sleep wasn't coming, so I tidied my flat. Sometimes Beryl came up and tidied round, but she hadn't done that for a long time, so by the time the flat – three rooms, a kitchen-sitting room, a bedroom and a bathroom that barely fit in a toilet basin and shower – was in a reasonable state, it was 3 a.m. and sleep came up and took me like a long-lost lover.

Banging woke me, and it took me a while to put together the noise I was hearing and where I was because the flat was so tidy. I thought I might be in a hospital room and experienced a moment of panic before realising I was in my own bed in my own flat. I grabbed my watch from the side of the bed – 8 a.m. Too early. It could be Beryl banging on the door, but she had a key, so she could come and go as she pleased. She could have lost it, I suppose.

No, Beryl never lost or forgot anything – which was annoying; she was like a walking encyclopaedia of every stupid thing I had ever done.

So, it wasn't Beryl.

I dragged myself over to the window; my head was throbbing, haunted by a hangover I had neither earned nor deserved. I pushed aside the blind. Below me I could see the blobby shape of Mick Stanbeck on his ragged old mobility scooter, flanked by the twins, their heads like two bright ginger moons orbiting the greasy planet of his body.

'Jones!' he shouted. 'Open up, Jones!' He looked up, some sixth sense telling him he was being watched. 'I know you're up there, come down and open up.'

Busted.

I opened the window.

'I'm coming down, Mick. Just give me ten minutes to get dressed.' That was a lie, I didn't need to get dressed as I'd fallen asleep fully clothed, but I wanted time to get my head together. Thoughts were racing through my head. What did he want at this time? An update? Maybe, but he wasn't known for being an early riser, and he hadn't looked like his usual calm self.

I hoped he wasn't angry with my lack of progress, because if he was, then I had nothing to say that was likely to make him feel any better. I smoothed my hair back. Splashed water on my face, brushed my teeth and sprayed on deodorant and stared at myself in the mirror. Too thin, haunted-looking. Nice eyes. Strong nose. Not looking too lived in despite the life I'd lived.

'You can handle Mick Stanbeck,' I said to myself and went downstairs.

Two bolts, three chains and a Yale lock. The minute the last lock was undone, one of the twins barged the door open, knocking me backward. Then the second was in through the door, ferret quick, and before I opened my mouth, he delivered a quick punch to my gut, knocking the wind from me and doubling me over. As I went over, his brother grabbed my arm and twisted it up my back, forcing me round and forward, slamming me down on my desk. I turned my head at the last minute, so he smashed my ear painfully against the wood of the desk, but I avoided a broken nose.

I couldn't help thinking Jackie would be very let down by how easily Kray One had got the drop on me.

'Mick …' I began. One of the twins' faces appeared in my vision.

'Shhh,' said Kray Two. I nodded as best I could and listened as Mick's scooter brought up its burden, whining about it all the way. The twin vanished, and Mick rolled up to my desk. He leant over, letting his weight topple the scooter forward so he was sitting with one elbow on my desk and the two side wheels off the ground. Then he brought his head down so his face was level with mine. Not only did he not wash, he didn't brush his teeth either.

'Where is he?' he hissed.

'Who?'

'Don't play games. Your friend, the Paki fucker.'

'He's a Sikh,' I wasn't even being cheeky, just words I was so used to saying.

‘I don’t fucking care,’ roared Mick and the twin holding me forced my arm further up my back. Making me scream in pain. I had a sudden flashback to the sickening sound of Jackie dislocating that Geordie’s arm.

‘If this is about those guys, Mick,’ the words came in gasps, waves of pain coming from my arm. It wasn’t dislocated, not yet, but it wasn’t in a place it should, or wanted, to be, ‘then your guys attacked me first.’

‘I don’t care about the Geordies,’ he said, his face coming nearer, foul breath wrapping itself around my head. ‘Your Paki friend can fuck Geordies dry up the arse for all I care.’ I didn’t correct him this time. ‘Just tell me where the fucker is.’

‘I don’t know.’ My arm moved another increment, ligaments and muscles screamed and I hissed. Channelling the pain out through my nose and mouth. ‘I don’t know!’ I said it again, louder, just in case they hadn’t heard. Mick’s eyes searched my face, flicking left and right, up and down. He smoothed down the greasy hair on his dappled scalp.

‘You know I love my family, right?’ I tried to nod. ‘Well, I’ve let Jackie run around doing what he wants, haven’t bothered him cos he hasn’t bothered me. But he has now, he’s gone too far.’ He took a deep breath. ‘You told him, didn’t you?’ His piggy little eyes were boring into me.

‘Told him what?’

‘About the money.’

‘He knew,’ I said, ‘he brought Janine to me.’

Mick clearly didn't know that, and he moved back a little. The smell of his breath remained.

'Well,' he said, 'maybe it just took a while for him to realise he wanted it, I don't know. But he knows the rules: you fuck with a Stanbeck, you end up in landfill. So unless you fancy a trip to the dump, I ask once more, where is he?'

'Jackie doesn't care about money.' I forced the words out. Mick moved in close again. Close enough to kiss me. I could count the open pores on his pointed nose, see the oil glistening on his skin.

'Everyone cares about money, Jones,' he said. 'It just depends on the amount. That ticket, I need it. You understand? And when Jackie stabbed Alan, he crossed a line.'

'He stabbed someone?'

That piercing gaze again.

'My nephew, not a bright boysm, see, but mine. Said a well-dressed bloke in a balaclava and with a fancy car did it. How many people like that you know on the Edge, hmm?

'When?'

'Early this morning, very early.'

'Not Jackie,' I said. 'Jackie was with me.'

'Where?'

'St Jude's.'

'Got religion, have you?' Said as a sneer.

'No, we were looking for your bloody ticket. Larry had a locker there – we had to break in. So Jackie can't have stabbed anyone, he was with me.'

Mick stared at me. Then he closed his eyes and pushed himself off my desk, righting his scooter, and I heard it complain as he reversed it away from the desk.

'Boysm,' he said, 'let him go.' The pressure released from my arm and I let out a sigh. There's nothing quite like the relief of pain stopping. I turned round, rubbing my shoulder joint, and sat on the edge of my desk. The twins stood uncomfortably close to me on either side.

'You believe me then?' I said, hoping he couldn't see I wasn't quite telling the truth.

Mick stared at me. His eyes were far too small for his face but it didn't make them any less intense. Instead, it seemed to increase their intensity, like his head was a satellite dish and the eyes were its focus, scanning you.

'You sound convincing,' he said. Then he tapped a finger on the steering stalk of the scooter and pursed his thin lips. 'But you, Malachite Jones, what about you, eh?' He coughed, and spat something out the door then turned back to me. 'You lie for a living, don't you?' He sat up straight on his scooter. 'So, best just to make sure of the truth, eh? Tell me where to find Jackie and I'll talk with him.'

Jackie would say tell him, I knew that. Jackie would say, 'Don't be a twat, Mal, I can deal with Mick Stanbeck.' And he could, I had no doubt about that. If Mick Stanbeck turned up at one of Jackie's hidey holes with his boys, intending Jackie harm, then either Jackie would walk away and Mick and the twins would never be seen again, or vice versa. There could be no in-between if you turned up intending violence against Jackie Singh Khattar. His world was simple in that way, and he had an unerring sense for when people really meant it.

'I genuinely don't know where Jackie is,' I said.

Mick nodded slowly to himself.

'I'm disappointed in you, Malachite.' He wheezed the words. 'You had me going with that church story, you really did.' He grinned, as if acknowledging a worthy opponent.

'I really don't know where he is,' I said.

'Well, let's find out. Boysm, break his fingers.'

Before I could speak the twins moved, each grabbed my wrist on their side, pinning my hand to the desk.

'Which one, Da?' they said in unison.

Mick wrinkled his nose. He leaned forward on the handlebars of his scooter.

When he spoke he sounded almost apologetic.

'I just need to know, Malachite, I'm sure you understand.' He turned his face away from me. 'He's right-handed, boysm, so?'

'We start with the left, Da,' they said in unison.

'Good boysm,' he said.

I was about to say 'no,' and indulge myself in a bit of useless begging when we were interrupted.

'Is this a private party or can anyone join in?'

I'm not usually glad to see the police, but on this occasion I made an exception. DI Esther Smith stood, round in the doorway, and behind her the ever-present dolorous shadow of DC Sarah Harrington. The twins let go of my hands and took a step away from me as their father turned around.

'DI Smith,' he said. 'I was just having a friendly chat with Mr Jones – he's an old acquaintance of mine.'

'Really?' she raised an eyebrow. Then squeezed past Mick's scooter so she could get into the shop. 'Mick, if you're looking for Mal's friend in connection with what happened to your nephew, then I can save you some time. It wasn't him.'

'You sound very sure, DI Smith,' he said. 'Does that mean you have a name for me?'

She leaned over, braving his breath without so much as a wrinkle on her forehead.

'If I had a name, I wouldn't give it to you, would I, eh?'

Mick grinned at her, it wasn't a nice grin.

'But while your boy was being stabbed, Jackie Singh Khattar was with him' – she nodded at me – 'acting very suspiciously around St Jude's – we have them on CCTV.'

'What makes you think I'm here about Jackie?' he wheezed. I noticed his wheezing became much worse when the DI was within earshot.

'Have I ever struck you as stupid, Mick?' she said.

Any semblance of a smile fell from Mick's face.

'Sadly not, Detective Inspector,' he said, and placed his hands on the handlebars of his scooter. 'Come on, boysm,' he glanced over his shoulder at the twins. 'I'm sure we'll get a chance to speak to Mr Jones another time.'

DI Smith watched as Mick left, his scooter struggling under his weight. Then she watched as the twins passed her and once DC Harrington gave her the nod from the doorway. DI Smith stepped forward.

'Where is he?' she said.

'Who?'

'Who?' she shook her head. 'Fucking hell, Malachite. Jackie, that's who. Where is he?'

'I thought you knew he didn't stab Mick's nephew.'

'That's what I told Mick so he didn't finish doing whatever he was about to do to you. But we only have witnesses for you going into St Jude's, no CCTV – that was a lie. Alan was stabbed at five this morning – there was plenty of time for your mate to do it. I can't keep that secret forever.'

'Is that a threat, DI Smith?'

She sighed. 'No, Malachite, it is just the way things are.'

'I don't know where he is.'

She stared at me, letting silence settle in the office, an uncomfortable quilt covering us all. If she hoped I'd speak because I was uncomfortable, then she was wrong. I'd been ready to have my fingers broken to protect Jackie. Social awkwardness was a breeze.

'He's going to get you killed, you know, Malachite.'

'No one calls me that.' I snapped those words out at her. Fear of the truth masquerading as annoyance.

'Jackie is a hard man, and you are not. He will take you into places you are not prepared for if you don't do something about it.' She paused, then added, 'Mal.'

I stared at her. Knew she probably spoke the truth. I'd heard the same from Beryl enough times.

‘I just need to talk to him.’

‘Jackie’s firm put in the security system in St Jude’s. Last night we went to test it – we were there all night. Canon Armitage will confirm this.’ DI Smith stared at me and I wondered if she knew I was lying.

‘Oh fuck,’ she said quietly.

‘You are desperate for him to be guilty, aren’t you?’

‘Tell him why, boss,’ said DC Harrington. ‘He likes to think he’s a good guy. So tell him why.’

DI Smith glanced over her shoulder at DC Harrington, licked her lips. Then turned back to me. ‘If it wasn’t Jackie, Mal, it was the Russians. They’ve always had some sort of agreement going with Mick, kept things sweet. But something changed recently. Relations aren’t as convivial now.’ I made a mental note to try ‘convivial’ on the twins next time they came to hurt me. ‘Now, if I can work out that the Russians are making a move on Mick Stanbeck, then he can too, cos he might stink, but he’s not stupid. And someone is going to make a move soon, a serious one, and there will be blood on the streets. It won’t all be scumbags, Mal, will it? There’ll be innocent people getting caught up in it all. So, if Jackie is involved, or if he isn’t, and you are the good guy you like to imagine you are, tell me where he is.’

She waited. And I waited. And DC Harrington waited and looked miserable about it, but that was normal for her. Truthfully, I wasn’t too happy about any of this either.

‘I genuinely, do not know where he is,’ I said.

‘Oh, come on, Mal.’

'I don't know.'

She waited a while before she answered this time.

'Very well,' she said, and took a card from her bag and held it out. 'Here's my number. You can get me at any time.'

I nodded and took the card from her, then watched her leave. When she had gone, I picked up the phone on my desk and punched in a different mobile number. Got Jackie's answering machine.

'Ring me,' I said. 'What the fuck have you got me into?'

15

I met Jackie at a little café that did a nice line in coffee and toast that was far too expensive for what you got, but Jackie liked the guy who served the coffee, so we went there a lot. I tended to sit quietly while Jackie flirted.

He put down a black coffee in front of me.

'Sugar?' he said.

'Just black, you know that.'

'You can punish yourself too much, you know,' he said.

I shrugged, picked up the coffee and burned my mouth taking a sip. I didn't let the pain show.

'It's less likely to burn you if you give it a while, or add some milk,' said Jackie. He sat and stirred two sachets of sugar into his latte with chocolate sprinkles. Usually I'd have smiled at him, but the mood between us was a little tense. Or I thought it was tense, I'm not sure Jackie was aware. Sometimes he seemed to think everything was amusing, mostly when it was going to annoy me. After explaining that the city was on the edge of a gang war, seemingly because of this lottery ticket he'd got me involved in, and that both Mick Stanbeck and DI Smith were looking for him, he'd nodded and said, 'I'd best keep away from your place for a while then.' Which was possibly the least reassuring answer he could have given me.

'I want out of this, Jackie,' I said.

'I'm not sure that's a possibility now.' He took a sip of his coffee. 'And think about Janine Stanbeck's kid. Do it for him – you might not like her, but this money could get them both off the Edge.'

'I do want to help the kid,' I said, 'but I don't want my fingers broken or cut off by Russians, or to be dead.'

'It's all bluff, Mal.' He grinned, split another packet of sugar with his thumbnail and poured it into his drink. 'They know if they hurt you, then I'd come after them.' He picked up another sachet of sugar.

'I'm not sure they're as scared of you as you think they are, Jackie.'

He put the sugar down.

'They should be,' he said, and he smiled, but it didn't quite reach his eyes.

'You didn't stab Alan Stanbeck, did you, Jackie?'

'You know the answer to that.'

'I need you to tell me, Jackie.' He stared at me and I leaned forward. 'Look, you've pulled me into something far bigger than I am, and I think I might be drowning. This is dangerous, terrifying. A murder and now an attempted murder.' Jackie just stared at me. 'Just tell me you didn't do it.'

'You know me, Mal.' He laughed, sat back. Grinned. Then he said quietly. 'I won't let anyone hurt you, Mal. You know that.'

I spun my coffee cup round on its saucer. There was a small stain on it where it hadn't been washed up properly.

'Please tell me it wasn't you, Jackie. Just say it.'

Something happened to his face, what was usually there, the mask of control, vanished. For a second, I saw the face of a boy I'd known so many years ago, terrified as the police dragged him out of school and the whisper went round he'd been arrested for murder.

Jackie stood.

'Fuck you, Malachite Jones,' he said, and walked out.

The guy serving the coffees looked kind of relieved that Jackie had left, but I felt lost. I didn't know what to do, and now I had no one to not do it with. I felt bad too, because, of course, he didn't do it. Jackie was a weapon, you aimed him, or more often he aimed himself, but he did it for a reason. He wouldn't knife some low-level thug unless they had come at him, and then he'd be proud of it. If he had a problem with Mick Stanbeck, he'd take it straight to Mick Stanbeck.

I knew all this.

Sometimes, when we're scared, we do stupid things.

I walked. When I feel like everything is too much, it is what I do. I drove back to my shop and then walked around the little row of buildings until I was in the woods at the back. They weren't big, but they were old and full of huge trees. It made you feel like you'd escaped the real world, even if you could still hear the cars on the road. It was rare to meet anyone in the wood apart from the odd dog walker, with whom I would exchange nothing but a smile or a curt hello. I felt safe here. I'd told Jackie that once. I needed solitude, and it was the nearest place to get it. My shop had been visited too many times by people who scared me in the last few days. I needed space. I liked woods too; the smell of old leaves as they dissolved into earth, the way the trees filtered the sun into a cool gloom shot through with dappled clearings where grass grew as thick and soft as moss, kept short by the deer that managed, miraculously, to live so near a city, the only proof of their existence was the odd corpse left after an unfortunate coming together of nature and motor vehicle.

I saw a deer once in these woods.

When I was at my worst, I'd often bring cheap drink and drugs here. One morning, when the mist was rising and the sun and moon still shared the sky, I'd woken to find a stag stood over me. A prince of the forest. He looked down at me and snorted, then spun around and vanished into the mist, leaving me wondering if he was a hallucination caused by withdrawal. I'd wanted to chase him, to follow him into the forest, and I was sick enough, then, to believe that if I did, I would somehow escape my life to somewhere better. But after a few steps the voices started, telling me I wasn't worth something better, and the veins in my arms started to itch, and I forgot the stag and started my long walk back toward Blades Edge to feed my habit.

I wondered if I'd see a stag today. Probably not; the wood was far busier than usual. Young mothers forcing buggies with squalling babies along root-rutted paths, joggers leaving the scent of sweat hanging in the still air as they passed. This wasn't the place I needed to be. There were too many people. I needed a quiet place away from everyone. A thin track headed off the main path and deeper into the wood. I was about to take it when I heard a voice.

'Mal Jones?'

I turned. A moment of confusion as I tried to place the face of the man I was looking at and who was looking back at me. He was wearing grey jogging pants and a grey top, his hair was slicked with sweat and his face red with effort. He ran on the spot, holding a phone in one hand, the cord of his earphones swinging as he waited for me to recognise him. But he wasn't of this place and my mind was struggling to sort him into where he fitted in my life.

'Callum Callaghan,' I said, as the memory of him arguing with his father in the scrapyard surfaced.

'You didn't recognise me?'

'No, well yes, it just took a moment, faces out of places, you know?'

He looked confused then grinned. 'You mean you didn't expect to see me here?'

'Yes, have you run all the way from the Edge?'

He shook his head, slowed his jogging on the spot and walked alongside me.

'No, I'm not that dedicated. I drove here. I'd heard it was a good place to run.'

'A good place in general,' I said, aimless, space filling words. 'I like the birdsong.'

He shrugged, pointing at the earbuds in his ears.

'Wouldn't know.' He stopped walking and did some stretches. I kept walking, hoping he would get the message and leave me to my solitude. He didn't, just jogged up behind me and then walked backward so he could see my face. 'My da says you're doing some work for him.'

'Not that I'm aware.'

'Well, for Mick then.'

'I'd better not say,' I said.

'Of course,' he grinned, 'best not to if you want to keep your knees intact, eh?' He mimed shooting me with a gun. 'Anyway, Mick's been arrested.'

'What?'

'Yeah, turns out the van we had in our shop might have been used to knock Larry Stanbeck off his bike.' He stopped stretching and caught up with me, once more walking alongside.

'His own son?'

'Proper gangster, eh?' He grinned. 'That's why I'm not at the yard – all hell's breaking loose down there while Da tries to keep everything under control. I thought it best to get away.'

'I saw you arguing with your dad about wanting to join the family firm.' He almost stumbled, his foot catching on a root in the path, and when he righted himself, he grinned foolishly at me, and I saw that gawky first-year kid I'd known at school. He'd always grinned too much.

'Da just wants everything to stay as it always has been and me out the way. Says the Edge is no place to raise a kid.'

'I suppose it isn't,' I said.

'Thought you might be interested that Mick is going down.'

'You don't sound sad about that – he's been keeping your family afloat for years.'

'Afloat, but not free,' he said. 'You always owe him, he's just like my da.' Then he nodded at me, slotted the earphones into his ears and ran on.

I wondered why Callum had come back from the farm his dad had sent him to. Maybe it was purely rebellion. It didn't sound like he liked the Stanbecks and the idea he could do any form of business around here without being mixed up with them was almost as unlikely as the idea Mick Stanbeck would go to prison because he owned the van that had killed his son. But I understood the need to be yourself. That led me to thoughts of Janine Stanbeck and her son, about to be crushed by a mountain of debt run up by her late husband, and the real difference to her life that the lottery ticket would make.

I would find it. I didn't know how, but I would. And I would find some way of getting it past Mick Stanbeck and Russian Frank that didn't involve me being permanently maimed.

There was always a way.

I should apologise to Jackie too.

I wandered back toward my shop, wondering how Russian Frank had found out about the lottery ticket. I didn't really believe that people in Mick Stanbeck's outfit had leaked the information – it was the sort of information Mick was unlikely to share. But Larry Stanbeck could have told him, or someone else in the office? I wasn't sure that made sense either. The ticket was a way out for him as much as anyone else, and he must have known who Russian Frank was, and that a man like that wasn't above taking easy money, like a lottery ticket, from someone.

But how did Mick know about it?

It was clear he didn't get on with Janine, and his son wasn't talking to him either.

Mr Patel at the shop? He had never struck me as the type to gossip; it was often difficult to get him to say more than two polite words, so that made no sense, and he hated criminals – Jackie excepted.

It felt like I'd missed something, or that something was missing. It was hard to tell which.

I unlocked the shop door to hear Beryl clattering about in the back. She brought out tea and put it in front of me.

'You're out of coffee,' she said.. Then she tapped the calendar on my desk and left. I had a client in half an hour; that I was here was more luck than planning.

I passed the half hour by watching shapes passing the window and trying to work out who they were. Some I knew. Cat Maudy in her new fur coat – I recognised her distinctive shuffle. The silhouettes of the group of lads who had taken to hanging out outside the Spice 'N' Saucy, though they would probably move on when someone came and had a quiet word with them, if they knew what was good for them anyway. Old Pete, who was a perennial fixture at the bookies. Night was falling and the shapes occasionally passing the window became starker, etched out in yellow sodium light.

My client turned up: Barry. I'd been seeing Barry for about two years, and I didn't need Beryl to help me with him. We chatted now, more than anything else; Barry was lonely and his wife, Pam, had died of cancer ten years ago. We didn't really try to speak to Pam anymore, we just tended to talk about his garden and his grandchildren and sometimes he would reminisce about his time with Pam. Today was no different. He brought a small bottle of whisky with him and knew enough not to offer me any. He poured out the liquid and swirled it round the glass, telling me about a camping trip he took with Pam to Wales where it did nothing but rain and their tent had flooded. It sounded miserable; he said it was at the time, but they laughed about it later; we laughed about it now. When his hour was up, he took out his money and I gave him half back, just like I always did. He'd never stopped offering the full amount.

When he left the shop, I started locking up, then remembered I had no coffee left, and as Mr Patel would still be open – even if I would pay double what the same coffee cost anywhere else – I would go and get some.

A siren wailed as a police car reacted to an emergency, blue light washing over me as I unlocked the door. I opened the door to find a man stood on the other side: small, a pencil-thin moustache like the bad guy out of a black-and-white film, crumbling teeth and waxy skin.

He grinned at me and when I opened my mouth to ask him how I could help, he punched me in the stomach so hard it felt like his fist came out of my back.

I doubled over and he placed a black bag over my head and through the pain and my desperate gasping for breath, I heard a car screech to a stop. Then I was pulled, stumbling across the lay-by, bundled into the back of the car and told to lie down and stay still, which I did.

Not that I had much choice.

16

Panic, first of all. Panic in the darkness, fast breaths. Suffocating. I didn't want to suffocate. The bag smelled of onions, and it conspired with the panic and ache in my stomach muscles to rob me of my breath. When I finally managed to get my breathing under control, I concentrated on taking long, slow breaths, in and out, in and out, to calm myself down.

When I stopped panicking about suffocation, I started worrying about being murdered.

People didn't kidnap you and put a bag over your head if they simply wanted a friendly chat. My hands had been bound behind my back with cable ties. It hurt. Bad men did things like this when they were serious and didn't want you knowing who they were – or getting a chance to run away. My breathing started to speed up again. I felt like a shot of whisky would somehow help me out.

Whisky doesn't help, twat. Beryl's voice, always in my head.

Breathing helps.

I concentrated on the breathing, on bringing the fear under control. My breath was loud in the hood, and the sound of my heart even louder. I started thinking of reasons to be cheerful. They hadn't put me in the boot. That was a good thing. The man who took me didn't appear to have a gun, always a plus. The car was swaying and juddering like an old boat, felt like a suburban street with speed bumps. So we weren't on a motorway and leaving the city, heading for the moors where my body would never be found. I'll take that.

With each breath my heart slowed a little.

But only a little. I listened, the hiss of my hair against the material of the bag. The stink of onions made my eyes water.

'Left here,'

'Next right.'

Accented voices. European, not sure where from. Two men. My body sliding over car seats as the vehicle turned. My head being pushed painfully against the door, tied hands stopping me bracing against anything.

What if my neck broke?

Maybe that would just save me from a lot of pain.

I didn't want to die.

The car stopped. I listened. Faint road noise, not near though – we weren't parked by the side of a road. I heard a car go past, this one sounded like it was nearer, sounded like it was behind me. I wondered if we had parked in the drive of a house, somewhere off a main road. Car doors opened and shut, but not the one I was in. Another door opened, hands grabbed my feet and before I could shout or kick out, I was pulled from the car, smashing the back of my head against the bottom of the car's door frame.

'Ow, bastards!'

'Shut up.'

A kick to the ribs that knocked all the air from me. Then I was pulled to my feet. A hand took me by the elbow, another grabbed my elbow on the other side and forced me upright, making the muscles in my diaphragm scream. Or maybe it was me.

They walked me forward.

A set of three steps that the men didn't warn me about nearly sent me sprawling onto my face, but my captors were kind enough to keep me upright, although my new-found not-very-friendly friends thought it was ever so funny. I heard them put a key in a lock; one of them swore and then the door in front of me opened and cool air flooded out. Wherever they were taking me to be murdered, clearly had air con.

'Boys, what is this?'

I knew that voice.

'I said bring him, not truss him like turkey.'

The bag was pulled off my head, and I found myself in a small office in some sort of Portakabin, nicely set out too. At the desk in front of me – a cheap IKEA thing – was Russian Frank.

'Malachite Jones!' he said, and he made it sound like we were old friends who had met unexpectedly on an all-inclusive Mediterranean holiday. He gave a nod to the man behind me who cut the cable ties around my wrists. 'I am sorry for the way you are brought here – I wanted a chat with you, me and my friend, Harry,' he added, nodding toward the huge man behind him. 'You remember Harry?'

'The stationer,' I said. I wasn't really that pleased to see Harry. Or Frank.

'You do remember Harry!' he said, with a wide grin. 'You should sit down, Malachite Jones.'

'I'd rather stand. Get my circulation going – I don't think there's any blood left in my hands.'

'I was not offering you a choice.' He pointed, unsmilingly, at the chair in front of his desk. I sat, put my hands flat on the desk. Frank grinned once more and put his feet up on the desk. Harry, looming over us on one side of the desk, turned and opened a metal filing cabinet, taking out a ream of white paper. He started putting out sheets of white paper on the desk.

A bad feeling settled in my stomach.

'I must say, Malachite Jones, I was not comfortable with you turning up at my place of work – that was not something I asked you to do. I asked you to find my lottery ticket.'

'I'm not sure it is …'

He leant forward, the smile on his face falling away, his voice lowering itself to a threatening growl. 'I am not asking you to make judgement, you know? I am not asking you to make decision. I am telling you the ticket is mine and also that you are to concentrate on finding it, not looking into Larry Stanbeck. He bought it in a shop for me, do you understand?'

I nodded.

'Good. Now, an hour ago, something very upsetting happened to me.'

Harry the stationer took out his paper guillotine and placed it on the desk, lifting up the heavy blade so it was ready to cut. The bad feeling in my stomach got markedly worse and it took all I had not to take my hands off the desk.

'Someone firebombed one of my takeaways, Malachite Jones. Now, I do not like this. And things like this very rarely happen to me, so I got to wondering who was likely to do such a thing.'

'I …'

‘Shhh,’ he said, lifting his fingers to his lips. Then he gave Harry a nod and the huge man stood to the side of the desk, looming over us.

I looked at his set-up: white paper, guillotine. This was definitely not good.

‘Most people, Malachite Jones, they know I am a very dangerous man, they wouldn’t do something like that. They are not so foolish. Then I remembered you have a friend, Jackie, yes?’

I nodded.

‘I think he is a very foolish man.’

‘Jackie did not burn down your shop,’ I said.

‘Oh? You know this? You know who did then?’

‘Well, someone stabbed one of Mick Stanbeck’s boys, there’s a train of logic there.’ Frank stared at me, raised an eyebrow.

‘I happen to know that Mick Stanbeck is currently in jail.’

‘You think that would stop him?’

Frank stared at me, then nodded and shrugged in what I took to be an affirmative manner.

‘You could be right, Malachite Jones,’ he said. ‘But Mick Stanbeck was the other reason I wished to see you.’ He leaned back in the chair. ‘See, I had another thought. You do not really know me, but you do know Mick Stanbeck.’ A smile. He picked up a pen and looked at it. ‘And it occurred to me that you may, foolishly, be more scared of Mick Stanbeck than you are of me. So, I thought, how could I kill two fowl with one rock, eh?’

‘This is going to hurt, isn’t it?’ I said.

Frank nodded.

‘Sadly, yes. Harry will cut off the little finger of your left hand. I think this will teach you to be afraid of me.’

‘I am, totally honestly, already really afraid of you.’

Frank gave me the sort of smile a kindly uncle gives you when your dad is screaming at you for something stupid you did.

‘I know that.’ He leant forward and patted my left hand with his hand. ‘I know. But we forget things so quickly, as a species, Malachite. This will leave you with a permanent reminder of who it is you should be afraid of.’

He grabbed my wrist and held it down on the desk. Harry grabbed my right hand. I bunched it into a fist. He levered out my little finger and pulled my hand toward the guillotine.

I’d always thought, in a position like this, I would scream and shout. But it all happened in silence, more like a battle of wills than a physical battle. No matter how much I stiffened my muscles and tried to become a rock, unmovable, I was outmatched by the two Russians and it only took seconds for Harry to have my finger placed over the cutting groove of the paper guillotine.

‘Please don’t do this, Frank.’

‘It will be quick,’ he said. ‘And it will also tell your friend, Jackie, if he is burning down my shops, not to. He is the sort of man who needs a real lesson, something he can touch, I think, yes?’ he put a match box lined with cotton wool on the desk.

Harry nodded. I closed my eyes and heard Frank whisper. 'Open your eyes, Malachite.'

I did. He was staring at me, eyes like chips of ice.

'Back in the old country, Malachite,' he said softly, 'my mother would take me to see a *vorozheyka*, a fortune teller. She told me I would be an important man, and she was right, you know this. But before this vorozheyka ever tried to talk to the spirits' – he grinned at me and opened a drawer in the desk, reached in – 'she would take a pin.' He held up a sewing kit in front of me and opened it, taking out a needle. 'Then, she would plunge the pin into the flesh of her arm – she said the pain helped her contact the spirits.' He smiled and looked across at Harry, my hand, and his guillotine. 'I think, cutting off a finger, that will be traumatic, unhelpful maybe. But only a little pain? This may help you, eh?'

Before I could answer in the negative, he took the needle and placed it on my wrist.

My mouth went dry.

Frank nodded at me, then he slowly pushed the needle down into my wrist between the small bones. I didn't scream. I gritted my teeth and breathed short, sharp breaths. I breathed and the needle went in further, the pain intensifying and burning through me. I turned my breathing into words.

'Bastardbastardbastardbastard.'

'Can you hear them, Malachite?' whispered Frank, something desperate there. 'Can you hear the spirits talking? Are they telling you where my lottery ticket is?' He was staring at me so intently that I was sure, at that moment, I was never going to make it out of here.

He believed. Frank, the Russian gangster, genuinely thought I could talk to dead people, and he thought pain was a gateway to the spirit world.

We were interrupted by a song. I knew that song. It was the opening bars of the song 'Going To Town' by The Afghan Whigs from the album *Black Love*.

Frank stared at me.

'What is that?' The needle stopped digging.

'My ringtone.'

'Probably best you do not answer it right now, eh? You are busy.'

I nodded, unsure what to say. The song continued playing.

'You hear anything from the spirits?'

I shook my head.

Frank let go of the needle and leaned back. He looked disappointed. 'I think,' said Frank, 'that whoever called you has ruined the mood, eh? Any spirits, they have fled?'

I nodded.

He shrugged. 'We should do your finger now then, get it over with.' He placed the sewing kit on the desk but never let go of my hand. 'We can always come back to the needles. See, this way, you get a lasting lesson in doing as I ask, and we explore the metaphysical possibilities of pain another day, eh?'

'I don't think pain helps.'

'Maybe we both learn something tonight then, Malachite Jones?' He reached out and yanked the needle from my wrist in one quick gesture. That made me scream.

Someone knocked on the door.

Frank let out a sigh and looked from me to Harry.

'I am sorry about this, Malachite,' he said. 'I had left strict instructions with Peter to guard the door and for us to be undisturbed. But Peter is not a clever man.' He raised his voice. 'What is it, Peter?' he shouted. 'We are busy in here, so this must be very important for you to bother me, yes?'

The door opened.

'I did knock, but the door was open,' said Jackie.

Frank stared at him, then blinked like a cat that had found a particularly warm place to sit.

'Where is Peter?'

'Asleep,' said Jackie.

'Where is Roman?'

'He's asleep too. You should really make sure your men are getting enough rest before you give them guard duty.'

Frank nodded.

'Why are you burning down my shops, Jackie Singh Khattar?'

'Why are you torturing my friend?'

'Because you are burning down my shops.'

'But I am not burning down your shops.'

'And why would I believe you?'

'Because if I was coming after you for something, boss,' he said, 'I'd come after you, not piss about with a few fires.'

'I doubt that,' said Frank. 'I have people like Harry here to stop anyone getting foolish ideas like "coming after me".'

'No you don't,' said Jackie, and he sauntered into the Portakabin.

'What?' Frank stood.

'I mean, no doubt you do have people to protect you, but not him.' He pointed at Harry. 'Or sleepy Peter and Roman out there. They were amateur hour. Now Harry' – he pointed at the man holding the guillotine blade poised above my little finger and took another step into the Portakabin – 'he's a frightener. You bring him in for people like Mal here. Harry's a big lad, violent no doubt, probably enjoys it from the look of him. But his suit doesn't cover that he's running to fat. I bet he's slow too.'

'Not slow,' said Harry, and he raised the blade of the guillotine a little.

I sweated a lot.

'If that blade falls and hurts Mal,' said Jackie quietly, not taking his gaze from Frank. 'I will kill you both.'

Harry's eyes widened and I think he had to physically stop himself from letting go of the blade and charging at Jackie.

'I had heard you were good,' Frank let go of my hand and stood. Then he waved at Harry. 'Let Mr Jones go for a moment,' he said. Harry let my hand go. I moved it, quickly.

'Talk is meaningless,' said Jackie. he rolled his shoulders, loosening up. 'How about I show you how good I am?' He seemed to fill with energy; it boiled off him and I found it hard to believe that Frank couldn't feel it, the danger. Maybe he did, maybe he was just used to being around violent people. Dangerous men were probably two-a-penny in Frank's world.

'Show me?' said Frank.

'Yeah,' said Jackie. He walked up to Harry, arms hanging loosely at his sides. 'Me and your big fellow. Let's go at it.'

'In here?' said Frank, a smile on his face.

'If you want,' said Jackie. 'But outside is probably fairer. A big man like Harry needs a bit of room.' He stared up at Harry and pointed at the guillotine on the desk. 'You can bring your toy, if it makes you feel better.'

Harry looked at Frank, and Frank gave him a small nod.

'There is a yard out back, with a wall around it to keep the prying eyes away from my business,' said Frank. Harry twisted a peg on the guillotine and removed the heavy blade. He held it in one hand as if it weighed no more than a kitchen knife.

'You don't have to do this, Jackie,' I said.

He turned to me, grinned. 'I know I don't have to, Mal. I want to.'

'You still don't have to.'

'Don't be daft, soft lad,' he said.

'But he's got a …'

'I know what he's got,' said Jackie. 'Now, come on, Frankie, open the back door,' he said, and smiled at me as if he wasn't about to fight for his life.

Frank stood and walked to the door. I followed, and as I passed Harry, he shifted his grip on the guillotine blade. I flinched, hating myself for it. Frank smiled at me, just so I knew he'd seen my weakness, and he led us through a little kitchen that led into a yard. It wasn't big; if three men stood with their arms stretched out, they would touch the walls on both sides. It was a lot longer than it was wide, maybe about fifteen metres, and at the end was a gate that led out into, well, wherever we were. Sodium lights threw a sickly yellow glow that leached into the yard, giving the gloom a jaundiced edge. As my eyes adjusted to the darkness, I realised that the walls were metal shipping containers. I wouldn't want to fight anyone here; my mind was already filling with images of Jackie being trapped in a corner and hacked into pieces with a guillotine blade by a psychotic stationer. Jackie came out the door behind me and put his hands on the tops of my arms, gently moving me to one side.

'Let Harry pass, Mal – he's big lad.'

'Jackie, I ...'

'It's fine, Mal,' he said.

Jackie walked down the yard until he was about halfway, then he turned, rolled his shoulders, put his hands behind his neck and stretched, bending to one side and then the other while he waited for Harry to approach.

'Are we just going to get into it,' said Jackie, 'or is someone going to say start?'

Frank came to stand by me. 'I will say start, make it more like a boxing bout, eh?' He turned to me. 'Mr Jones, are you a betting man?'

'Not really.' I don't think I could have sounded gloomier if I had tried.

'What odds?' said Jackie.

'You are the smaller man, and without a weapon,' said Frank. 'I give you ten to one.'

'Then Mal will put a tonne on me,' said Jackie.

‘Jackie, I’m skint.’ I blurted the words out before realising that saying that made it sound like I didn’t believe he could win.

Jackie grinned. ‘Stop worrying,’ he said. ‘If we’re doing this, then there’s no reason we shouldn’t make a bit of cash at the same time.’

‘Are you ready?’ said Frank. Jackie nodded and stared at Harry as he moved to stand opposite him. Harry’s hand loosened then tightened around his heavy blade. ‘Well, you may as well get to it then.’

Harry moved first. He’d been holding the guillotine blade so the sharp edge faced behind him and he twisted his wrist, bringing the blade up across his body in a move that would have cut deep into Jackie’s thigh and ended the fight right there if Jackie had not moved, but he jumped backward, like a shocked cat, the minute Frank said ‘then’. The blade whistled through thin air, its weight making Harry step forward to counter it.

‘He’s quicker than I thought, Mal,’ shouted Jackie.

Harry stepped forward and brought his blade down toward Jackie’s shoulder.

Jackie ducked beneath it, sidestepping to the left. ‘Not quick enough though, eh?’ He darted in, delivering two quick punches to Harry’s left kidney then dancing backward.

Harry didn’t seem to have felt the punches. He spread his arms out, together with the reach of the weapon he nearly filled the entire width of the yard. He walked toward Jackie, who in turn was slowly backing up.

‘Sound tactic, Harry,’ Jackie said, ‘backing me into a corner, then I’ve nowhere to go.’

Harry didn’t speak, only continued advancing on Jackie.

‘Your friend,’ said Frank, leaning over, arms folded as if we discussed a horse, ‘he talks too much.’

I shrugged. ‘He always has done.’

‘Bit boring though, Harry,’ said Jackie. ‘This slow dance.’ He darted in, Harry made a grab at him with his free hand but Jackie was already moving out of his reach, his dummy move having done its work. Harry’s hand met thin air. Jackie came forward again, at a run and bent almost double at the waist. Harry expected another attack at his kidneys and tried to cover, but Jackie ran straight past. As he did, he dug out with his elbow, landing a sharp blow to Harry’s thigh just as Harry was reacting and putting his weight on that leg to swing his blade around. The hit fouled Harry’s swing. He grunted and staggered. At the same time, Jackie came back to standing, his arms outstretched, and he jogged in a small circle around Harry until he was facing us again. ‘The master is at work,’ he shouted.

Behind him Harry turned. Lifted his heavy blade and ran forward.

‘Jackie!’

Did he grin in that moment? I was never sure. And as the blade came down, he let himself fall into a forward roll. Twisting as he fell, coming up facing Harry, whose heavy blade had buried itself in the mortar between two of the big slabs that covered the ground. The impact must have stung Harry's hand, but he didn't let go. Instead, he struggled to pull it loose.

'I planned that,' said Jackie to Harry. Then he glanced over his shoulder at us. 'Not really,' he said. 'Actually, I'm kind of bored now.' He walked up to Harry, who made a last pull at the blade, with no luck. He let go of it and came forward, hands held up like a boxer. Jackie kept his hands down, as if daring Harry to take a swing at him. Harry threw a left. Jackie swayed out the way. Harry brought his right fist round. Jackie dodged that, then he stepped inside Harry's reach and delivered a pinpoint blow to the centre of Harry's face. Harry brought both his hands up to his nose and I swear I heard Jackie say, 'Amateur,' under his breath. He moved in close, delivering punches to Harry's kidneys that were almost too quick to see. I only heard the thud of his fists against the material of Harry's suit. Harry tried to protect himself but by the time he'd moved a hand to shield his body, or throw a punch back, Jackie had moved, dancing around him, delivering punches to his back, then his side, then his ribs, always moving. It was surgical, cruel almost, the way he took the bigger man down.

'Enough,' said Frank.

Jackie punched Harry in the back of the head.

'I said enough.' Frank again. Louder.

Jackie delivered a kick to the back of Harry's leg and Harry went down on one knee.

'Enough!' Frank roared it this time.

Jackie grabbed Harry's hand, bent his arm round so it made the other man gasp in pain. Then Jackie kicked him right on the knee joint and I don't know what was louder: Harry's scream or the crack of his knee dislocating.

Then Jackie let go of Harry, who collapsed, passed out from the pain. He walked up to us. Sweat beading on his brow.

'I don't like being told what to do,' said Jackie, 'and I decide when enough is enough.' He turned away from Frank without waiting for a reply, walked up to the blade and worked it loose from the crack between the paving slabs. Then he walked over to Harry and stamped on his wrist, grinding his foot down on it. The pain brought Harry back to consciousness with a groan. 'Open your fucking hand,' said Jackie. Harry stared at him, as if he didn't understand the words. Jackie spoke again. 'Otkroi svoyu grebnuyu ruku, skazal.'

Whatever Jackie said in Russian did it. Harry closed his eyes and opened his hand. All his fight was gone. I heard him say, 'Please,' but it was so quiet as to be barely audible, and Jackie wasn't listening. He brought the blade down. Harry screamed again, rolling over, cradling one hand in the other. Left behind on the floor was his little finger.

'Now I'm done.' Jackie dropped the guillotine blade on the floor. The ring of metal on stone echoed around the little yard. 'And you owe Mal a grand,' he said to Frank.

'I won't forget this,' said Frank. No accent. No humour.

'I hope not,' said Jackie. 'That was the whole point.'

Frank stared at him. 'Well, you proved what you said, eh? Harry was not good enough.' His smile had little to no warmth. 'Next time, Jackie Singh Khattar, maybe I'll bring people who are good enough, eh?'

'If there is a next time,' said Jackie.

This time Frank's smile reached his eyes. 'Oh, Mr Singh Khattar,' he said, 'for people like us, there is always a next time, yes?' Then he went over to Harry and hauled him to his feet. 'You two should go now,' he said. 'I will take my friend Harry to the hospital.'

17

Jackie was driving my silver Ford Ka – the old type that looked like someone had forgotten about wheel arches and added them later as an afterthought. It was a car I liked – I thought they had personality – but Jackie had never been a big fan. We weren't talking; he was concentrating on driving, his hands tight on the steering wheel, so I could see the reddening and the scuff marks on his knuckles from where he'd landed punches on Harry.

'Thank you,' I said eventually.

'For what?' he said.

'For making sure I've still got all my fingers.'

He didn't reply, just drove on, the speed of the car picking up until it felt like he was pushing the little car right to the edge of what it was capable of. When he cornered, I was pushed into the seat, the tyres barely keeping hold of the greasy road surface.

'Fuck,' he said. Then he punched the steering wheel twice with the heel of his hand. 'Fuck!' he shouted it this time.

'Jackie, I—'

'No,' he said, then he shook his head. He glanced at me, the light from passing streetlights caught in his eyes, making him look devilish, tiny fires flaring in his pupils. 'I'm sorry, alright? You were right. I didn't think this would get so dangerous, but you were right. I should have told you to get out at the beginning. No. I should never have brought that woman to your door.'

'You didn't know how dangerous it was going to get.'

'I should of though, Mal.' He took in a deep breath. Let it out. 'Fucking Stanbecks.'

We drove on in silence.

'I didn't really think you stabbed Alan Stanbeck,' I said. 'I was only saying it to annoy you.'

'Worked.'

'Did you track my phone to find me?'

'Eh?'

'With the Russians. My phone rang just before you turned up, I thought …'

He shook his head, downshifted and overtook a bus; the horns of terrified motorists coming in the opposite direction squealed in panic. He swerved back onto our side of the road.

'I was sat outside your shop when they took you.'

'Keeping guard?'

'No, I was going to come in and give you a kicking. I was fucking angry.'

'I think you still are.'

'Shut up.' Overtaking an Audi which beeped, Jackie giving it the finger via the rear-view mirror. 'I saw 'em take you.' He downshifted again, and I was forced back into the Ka's seat as he accelerated around another bus. 'Listen. I have a flat in the city, maybe you should just vanish for a bit. I'll deal with any fallout.'

We drove in on silence, apart from Jackie over-revving the engine of the little car. He had at least slowed down a little now he had got his apology off his chest.

'No,' I said after a while.

'No?'

‘Something is going on, Jackie. It’s about more than lottery tickets, and if I’m not here, then Frank will go after Janine Stanbeck, won’t he?’

‘So? She’s a Stanbeck, she’ll be alright and …’ his words drifted off. ‘The kid,’ he said. Then he sighed. ‘He’d go after the kid. He’s not stupid. The kid is all the leverage he would need over her.’ He drove on, joining the main road that would take us to the shops without checking anything was coming in either direction, making me cringe. ‘She should move in with Mick, that’d keep the kid safe. Or as safe as he’s ever going to be.’ He started to accelerate again. I started to sweat. Crais Curve was on the way to the shop, the infamous accident blackspot, and Jackie seemed determined to see how fast he could take it.

‘I thought Mick was in jail?’ I braced myself against the door. ‘Maybe you should slow down.’

‘Mick’ll be out in the morning – they don’t have enough to hold him.’ The curve came up, and he threw the car around it, centrifugal force dragging me from my seat, tyres squealing, and for a moment I thought we would die and all my problems would be over. The lights around me blurred, and it was all I could do not to cry out. Then we were round, on the straight, and Jackie gave me a wild grin.

‘Did you think we wouldn’t make it?’

‘Never doubted you,’ I said.

‘Liar.’

I saw the glitter of the shop fronts further down the road and Jackie accelerated, pushing the little car until it started to shake and then breaking at the last minute, sliding to a halt on the loose gravel of the lay-by and throwing me against the seat belt. The curtains of Mr Patel's flat above his shop twitched as we got out.

Jackie leaned on the top of the Ka and the engine ticked in the warm darkness. 'Who rang you?' he asked.

I shrugged, took my phone from my pocket. My wrist ached where Frank had driven the needle in. I touched the fingerprint scanner and a text message from Beryl popped up.

butt dial

'No one,' I said. 'Wrong number.'

Jackie stared at me then laughed.

'If this was a film, Jackie, you know what would happen next?' I said.

He shrugged.

'The shop would explode.' I turned to look at the shop, holding my breath for a second before I burst out laughing. Jackie went round the back of the car, shaking his head, and took out a bag. 'What's that for?'

'Overnight bag,' he said. 'If you're not going to run, I'm not leaving you alone.'

'I'm not sharing a bed with you, Jackie.'

'You wish you were sharing a bed with this,' he said, and walked ahead of me, opening the shop with a key he always swore he didn't have. Inside, he set up a bed in the back office, which meant I wouldn't see Beryl for the duration of his stay.

'I don't know what to do, Jackie,' I said. Ghostly images overlaid my vision, bright white paper on my desk as the stationer set up his guillotine. Something caught in the back of my throat, a pain between tears and fear. Jackie sat at my desk and ran his hands along it.

'Well, we can't just sit here and wait,' he said. 'We should do something.' He tapped his hands on the desk. 'That building firm. Frank doesn't want you anywhere near it – I bet that's why he felt the need to push you away.'

'So?'

'You know what I think you should do when someone pushes.'

I nodded.

'Always push back.'

He nodded.

'I've got our gear in the Ka.'

'Our gear?'

'Breaking and entering stuff, from the church.'

'You think we should break into the building firm?'

'It's a start.'

'I'm not sure—'

'Come on.'

'Do you really need me?'

'I won't know if what I find is important. You will.' Then he stood and headed for the doors. 'Come on, Mal. Work to do.'

He didn't wait for me to agree, never did. That wasn't Jackie's way. So, I hurried after him to the Ka and we headed out into the night.

The wrong way.

'Where are we going, Jackie? The building firm is in the city – we're heading toward the Edge.'

'Always collect intel before you hit a target, Mal.'

‘Eh?’

‘We’re off to see Shaky Glen.’

‘Oh no, not Ciderman, not now. I can’t …’

‘Put your seat belt on, Mal.’

I sat back, wanting to argue but knowing it wasn’t worthwhile. Shaky Glen was one of the more famous figures on the Edge. His heyday had been in the mid-eighties; big fan of hair metal and acid. He used to be a maths teacher at the school, and when he wasn’t teaching was a regular in the metal clubs and one of the biggest dealers on the estate. Not a serious dealer, nothing hard: speed, acid and dope were Glen’s trade. And one day he went a bit too far into his stash of acid and he never really came back. Lost his job. Lost all sense of time and never managed to escape 1987. I mean, he was old now, sixties at least, but he didn’t seem to know that.

‘I’m not going into his house, Jackie.’

‘Yeah you are,’ he said, as we drew up outside Glen’s council house. It had been nice once; a teacher’s salary and his extracurricular activities had meant he could afford the best of everything. He probably owned the house, otherwise I was pretty sure the council would have moved him into one of the tower blocks in the centre of the estate – the same ones they were currently demolishing. He lived on one of the nicer bits of the Edge, among the carefully looked-after gardens, and he shared a hedge with a neighbour. His neighbour cut their side. Glen’s side looked like it had been enthusiastically backcombed, which I suppose was very on-brand for him.

Jackie got out the car and waited for me to join him. I tried sitting there and sighing as theatrically as possible to show my displeasure, but he didn't seem to care. So, I got out, and we walked toward Glen's front door.

In the garden, was a skip. There had always been a skip in Shaky Glen's front garden but no one knew what was in it cos you would have had to fight through the forest of brambles surrounding it. I only knew it was there from memories of seeing it. During the day, if you squinted, you could see hints of rusted yellow metal. At night, it looked like a mound of vegetation ready to come alive at any moment and entomb you. The only way to the door was up a single well-used path through more brambles; Jackie danced down the path to avoid getting his coat – a bizarre Adidas knock-off with *Adidot* stencilled in purple on white neoprene – snagged on any of the thorns. I wasn't as bothered and leather is harder wearing so I put my hands into my coat pockets and pushed on through, feeling the tentative pulls of the vines on my jacket as Jackie hammered on the door.

'Glen!' *Bangbangbang*. 'Glen! open up!'

There was a pause. A light went on in the front room that illuminated the filthy sheets hung up instead of curtains. It looked like they had Moomins on them.

'Glen's not here,' said a tremulous voice from behind the door. Glen's tremulous voice.

'It's Jackie, Glen,' said Jackie. 'Let us in.'

'I'm not here.'

'You are here, you are talking to me.'

A pause.

'This is someone else.'

'Glen, I will break this fucking door down if you don't open it.'

A pause. The sound of chains being taken off the door and the key scratching in a lock that needed oil. The door inched open.

'You only needed to say it was you, Jackie.'

'I did say,' he began, but Glen was already heading into his house.

'You didn't say we'd have to go in,' I hissed. 'I'll wait here.' Jackie took me by the arm and pulled me into Glen's house. The smell was like a wall.

'Fuck me, Mohammed, the Guru, Jesus and all his saints,' said Jackie. 'What is that stink?'

'I'm making dinner, Jackie,' said Glen from a side room.

'Smells like you're cooking a cat that's been dead for a month.'

'It's mince,' he said. He appeared round the door. He was a very thin man. I didn't know if he backcombed his hair now or just never washed it, but the effect was the same: a jagged thatch of brown wisps. He was wearing spandex trousers that left far too little to the imagination and a purple shirt that was open to his navel. Unlike Jackie, he didn't have the musculature to pull it off, or any musculature, in fact. He tried a hesitant smile; he had surprisingly good teeth. 'Do you want some mince?'

'I'd rather die,' said Jackie.

'It's got onions in it,' said Glen.

'I would still rather die.'

‘Okay,’ he said. The way Glen walked always reminded me of a *Thunderbirds* puppet; he kept his hands slightly out in front of him, his knees bent. The only thing that stopped the image being complete was his constant shaking. The face beneath his hair was lined, and the lines were grimy with dirt. I’d never been this close to Glen before, not sober anyway, and I wondered how I had managed to miss that what I thought was hair, was actually a cheap wig.

There wasn’t a kid on the estate that didn’t know Shaky Glen, or that hadn’t catcalled and ridiculed him as he walked about, but he seemed impervious to the ridicule, or maybe oblivious to it.

The house was cold even though it was warm outside and, despite the lights being on, it was dark too. Glen kept things. Newspapers, boxes, toys. He was also a professional lifter; he’d steal from the shops and sell it at the pubs or car-boot sales. Whatever he didn’t sell at the car-boot, joined the stockpile of rubbish in his house. It didn’t seem to bother him. He led us through into his front room. There was one chair in front of an electric fire, and by it was a small table with an ashtray and a rolling machine. Glen sat down and started trying to roll a cigarette, but the shaking of his hands meant he kept dropping the tobacco back into the little tin in his lap. He didn’t seem frustrated by it, probably just normal for him: pick up the paper. Pick up the tobacco. Grin. Drop the tobacco in the paper. Drop the tobacco from the paper into the tin. Look confused. Grin. Repeat. I wondered why he wasn’t using the rolling machine, maybe he’d forgotten he had it.

Jackie took the tin and papers from Shaky Glen and neatly rolled him a cigarette one-handed, then passed it to Glen. He had to wait a moment as Glen had made a can of cider appear from somewhere and was taking a long drink. When he finished, he balanced the can on the pile of old cigarette butts in the ashtray and took the cigarette from Jackie and lit it.

'I need some information, Glen,' said Jackie. He took another paper and some tobacco and started to roll another cigarette. Glen stared into the middle distance. 'Who stabbed Alan, Mick's lad?'

Glen turned to him. 'Were it you?'

'Would I be asking if it was me?'

'I heard it were you though.'

'It wasn't, so who else might it be?'

'Do you want to buy some sanitary towels?

'No, I want to know who stabbed Mick's boy.'

'I've got twenty boxes,' he said. 'Good ones, the ones with the song, you know, off the telly.' He didn't seem to have a TV.

'How do you shoplift twenty boxes of sanitary towels?' I said.

Glen turned to me, the thin rolled-up cigarette held between fingers stained with decades worth of nicotine. 'I wear a big coat,' he said. Something danced behind his blue eyes and I wondered if maybe he wasn't quite as far gone as he liked to pretend.

'How much are they?' said Jackie. Two cigarettes were now in the bottom of the tobacco tin and Jackie rolled a third.

'Quid a box.'

‘I’ll buy them all. Now, Mick’s lad, who did it?’ Another cigarette rolled.

‘I need the money first, Jackie.’

‘What do you need money for?’ I said, ‘You shoplift everything you need.’

‘I want to buy a ticket to see Def Leppard,’ he said.

‘Are they still going?’ said Jackie.

Glen nodded slowly. Ash fell from the fag in his hand.

‘Aye, drummer’s only got one arm, you know. You should come with me, Jackie, you’d like ‘em.’

‘Not my thing, Glen,’ he said, and rolled another cigarette.

‘Singer’s a Pakistani like you,’ said Glen.

Jackie looked at me.

I shook my head and mouthed, ‘No, he isn’t.’

Jackie mouthed back, ‘Neither am I.’

‘Mick’s lad, Glen. Stop changing the subject.’

Glen scratched at the rat’s nest of a wig on his head.

‘Mick thinks it’s the Russians, right, but they say it weren’t them. That’s why I thought it were you, like.’ He spoke slowly, as if every word required a lot of thought. ‘Some of Mick’s boys have been torching Russian takeaways – gonna be a lot more of that tonight,’ he said. He took a drag on the cigarette, but there was nothing left of it. He didn’t seem to notice.

‘Really?’ said Jackie, rolling another cigarette.

‘Oh, aye, specially cos Mick’s in jail, so he can say it weren’t him, right?’

‘Do the Russians know Mick’s torching their shops?’ said Jackie.

Glen shrugged. 'Some were here, they bought the last of me bacon, it's always a good seller, bacon.'

'When?'

'This morning. I thought it were you doing the stabbing, sorry, Jackie.'

'It's alright Glen,' he said, and he took a twenty-pound note from his coat and gave it to him along with the tobacco tin full of neatly rolled cigarettes. Glen stared at him as if he was puzzled by the money and the tin. 'Enjoy Def Leppard, Glen.'

'I will,' he said, and took another drag on the dead cigarette.

We headed out toward the city with twenty boxes of sanitary towels, and I asked Jackie what he would do with them.

'Schools, homeless shelters, they always need them.'

'Are you worried someone might hurt Glen, for telling us stuff?'

Jackie shook his head. 'You don't visit Glen if you want it kept secret, everyone knows that.' He brought the Ka to a stop at a red light. 'There are rules, Mal, you have to obey the rules.'

18

The Maylin and Sparrow building was quiet, as it should be at 2 a.m. The glass front glowed with a warm light. Behind it the desk was empty; not even a night security guard.

'How do we know that there won't be a load of Russians inside waiting for us?' I said. Jackie stared at me.

'Cos Glen told us Mick's people are going to make a run at the Russians' businesses tonight.'

'He's hardly the most reliable source.'

'If Glen knows' – Jackie turned in his seat, pushing aside boxes of sanitary towels, and finding a rucksack – 'then everyone knows.'

'How do we get in?'

'The church.'

'The church?'

'That's what I said. Come on.'

'This is the second church we've broken into in two days.'

Jackie shrugged. 'You don't believe in God.'

'Yeah but …'

'We're not breaking in, and anyway, it's been deconsecrated. Stop whining.'

I'd known this church forever. When I'd gone to the venue down the road, it had been derelict. And it was still derelict. Every so often a *for-sale* sign would go up on it, and then it would say *sold*, and then a new lock would appear on the chain that kept the doors shut and nothing would happen. Jackie had a key to the lock. Of course he did.

'You own this, Jackie?'

He shrugged. 'A friend does.'

'A friend who gives you the key?'

'A friend who owes me a favour.'

We slipped in. It smelled like an old church – old wood, some of it damp – and like Glen's house, it was much colder inside than the air was outside. Jackie flicked on a torch and cast the light about. I caught glimpses, saw a building that looked like it had remained the same ever since it had been built: lines of pews facing the front, a lectern in the shape of a large bronze eagle which stared out angrily into the disused church. To one side I saw a door; a much newer looking door than in the rest of the building. I headed towards it.

'Where you going?' said Jackie.

'I saw a door …'

'Don't worry about the door. Follow me.' He led me through the pews, past the angry eagle, then to the right. Behind a buttress was a very thin door with a very big lock. Jackie had a key for this one too, and behind the door was a steep set of stone stairs leading down into a basement that smelled strongly of disinfectant. Thick pipes ran along the floor and warmed the air. I could hear something that sounded like a boiler.

'Someone is using this place—'

Jackie's finger was on my mouth.

'I said don't worry about it – okay? Just follow me.'

We went down the corridor and into what was very obviously a boiler room; the boiler was clearly new.

Along one side were racks of electricity meters and, in a wire cage, not locked, was what looked like a cleaner's supply cupboard. On the same wall with the meters was another new door, all the stone work around it had been done recently. Recently in the life of the church anyway – maybe not in the last decade.

'Come on,' said Jackie. He walked into the supply area and pulled a set of overalls off a shelf and threw them at me, then got another pair and started putting them on over his clothes.

'What is this place?'

'Heating, meters and utilities for the building next door, cheaper for them to have this on a long-term lease and rent out their basement as more offices than to lose the space for machinery. That door' – he pointed at the new looking door – 'leads right into The Loom, and as long as we're dressed like cleaners and taking round a rubbish cart, then no one will ask questions.' He finished getting into his overalls then went over to a fuse box on the wall. He opened it and counted along the trip switches. 'Five and six and seven and eight.' He flipped them. I expected something to happen, like in a film, for all the lights to go out or for there to be a dramatic hum that slowly vanished. Nothing happened.

'Did you turn off the security system?'

He shook his head.

'And have the security firm running straight round? No, I turned off the lifts and the cameras in the shared areas. They will send someone to see to it eventually, but as long as the alarm on the doors hasn't been tripped, they won't treat it as an emergency.'

'Did you put that system in?'

He grinned at me and then went through the door, pushing the rubbish cart ahead of him, using one hand to steer it.

'So, can we just walk into Maylin and Sparrow?' I asked.

He shook his head.

'Nah, each business organises its own cleaning staff. That's why I brought this.' He tapped the rucksack on his shoulder. 'Shall we get on then?' He led me through the building. There's something mournful about an office building at night. Without the busy to and fro of people, the building dozes, and I felt unwelcome, like we were disturbing its sleep.

We had to carry our cleaning cart up the stairs as Jackie had put the Yellowvater out of action.

'Why did you switch off the lifts?'

'Gives us more time if anyone turns up.'

'My legs ache.' There were a lot of stairs. 'And my arms ache.' The cart was heavy.

'You need to get more exercise, soft lad.'

We stopped at the door of Maylin and Sparrow, and Jackie put his rucksack on the floor. He took out his all purpose skeleton key, or crowbar and then stopped on the point of breaking open the door.

'Are you still good with a lock pick?'

'Pretty good.'

'Then have a go at this.' He pointed at the door. 'Shouldn't be too hard, and it's less likely to leave signs of us having been here.'

I knelt by the door. I'd taught myself lock-picking when I was an addict, telling myself it was somehow more genteel and less harrowing for the people whose homes I burgled if I didn't smash down the doors. Lying to myself about the pain I caused.

But at least it left me with a useful skill.

The lock was a simple Yale, and as the lock gave, I stood, put my hand to the doorknob to push it open. Jackie grabbed my arm.

'What?'

He held out a balaclava and a pair of latex gloves. As I put them on he put on his own, then wiped the door handle with a cloth from his bucket and gave me a grin, white teeth against the black material, and wandered into the office. I followed.

Inside, it was simply lit, small lights in the ceiling twilit the room, and at the end of it, beyond the window, the city stretched out, veins of light, the red glow of the rear lights on cars corpuscles moving through it. Within the roads, the lights of businesses and homes, the nerves of the city, and beyond that was darkness; the city seemed to float in a lake of it – though I knew that was only the moors that edged up to the suburbs, as black as the night, cut by the odd moving light of a car, a lonely glow-worm lost in the shadow.

Jackie went forward a few steps, still pushing his rubbish cart, and then paused, held up a hand to tell me to stop and pointed upwards. A light blinked on a camera and Jackie hugged the wall, flattening his body against it and waving at me to do the same. Then he inched under the camera. Held up his hand again for me to stay where I was before he moved further into the room and down the long bank of desks, behind which was a glassed-in office, contents hidden from view by closed blinds and a blue door. Jackie stopped at the centre of the bank of desks. He leant over and dipped into the rucksack again, taking out a black box, flicking a switch and placing it as near to the centre of the desks as he could. Then he stepped back.

'Keep your hat on just in case, but we shouldn't have to worry about the cameras now.'

'Why?'

'That' – he pointed at the box – 'it's an all spectrum jammer, stops the camera signal getting to the server.'

'Have you just made that up?'

'No, I paid a lot of money to someone for it. But even if it is working, someone will notice they're not getting a signal soon. We're on the clock, Mal.'

'I'll go through Larry's desk first, you do those around him.'

'Okay.'

We did. Larry's desk was empty, totally cleaned out. We found nothing in the surrounding desks either, just diaries with appointments, dull-sounding appointments.

'I hate clear-desk policies,' said Jackie. 'Reckon you can hack the computers?'

'No, why on earth would you think I could do that?'

He shrugged. 'I might know some people, but they don't need to be here to get in.'

He looked around the office. Behind him was the only other space in Maylin and Sparrow that may hold something: the manager's office. Jackie stared at the door.

'Get your lock picks out, Mal,' he said. 'While we're here, we may as well see what Frank is up to.' He pointed at the blue door and I set to.

Inside the office was one desk – expensive, not run-of-the-mill office furniture like the rest of the place. I reckoned it was Victorian; nice workmanship, well polished. Behind it was a basket chair that had been altered so it sat on a pivot and could be reclined; modern changes to old furniture; done well, again nice workmanship.

'Stop perving over furniture and open the locks on the desk, Mal.'

I didn't deign to give that a reply and set to work on the locks on the desk drawers while Jackie fired up the computer and attached something to one of the USB sockets. In the drawers, I found nothing of any interest; a lot of cards for local sex workers in one – looked like Frank had a thing for really big girls and feet. Another drawer held cigars, one was full of pens, but that's normal; every desk has a drawer full of pens. My betting was that most of them were just on the cusp of being useless. Next drawer was general office supplies: paper, sticky tape, glue. With his bodyguard being a stationer, he probably got the lot as freebies.

One pen with every ten severed digits.

A cold shudder ran through me.

The rest of the drawers were empty.

'Anything on the computer?'

'Dunno,' said Jackie.

‘I thought you were hacking it?’ I pointed at the box.

He shook his head. ‘Nah, told you, that’s a job for better people than me, but this PC isn’t networked into the rest. No wires.’

‘Could be wireless?’

He nodded. ‘Could be. Anyway, I got the box I plugged in off my friend George, he calls it The Fuckenator.’

‘What does it do?’

‘Fuckenates things.’

‘Thanks.’ I stood, looked round the dimly lit office, nothing untoward here at all. The only other thing of interest was a plan of a house on the whiteboard. Lots of measurements and architectural shorthand, and when I stared at it I had this odd feeling that something about it was off. I just couldn’t place what.

‘Not sure whether perving over drawings of houses is better or worse than perving over furniture, Mal,’ said Jackie. ‘We should get out of here, really.’

‘There’s something wrong with that picture up there.’ I pointed at the drawing of the house.

‘It’s architecturally boring?’

‘No, more than that.’

‘‘sake, Mal – it really is time to go.’

I snapped a picture of the drawing on my phone and we left. On our way out of the building, we passed four uniformed security guards coming down the corridor. We kept our heads down as we pushed the cart past them, and they didn’t give us a second glance.

19

FRIDAY

Jackie used to trip me up.

'I'm going to trip you up.'

'Please don't.'

'I'm going to trip you up, and I want you to try and stop me.'

'I don't know how.'

'I'll show you.'

And he did. Teaching me to step over, to double step to catch my weight. But more importantly, he taught me how to fall without hurting myself. He taught me to roll, to relax my body, to aim for something soft. To take the hit on my knees or elbow or shoulders and protect my head, slamming my arms out to spread my weight. They were not fun lessons.

But I learned them.

I didn't sleep well, because Jackie snores really loudly and I don't like having people in my home. So, while Jackie – who can sleep anywhere at any time – slept the sleep of the just, I was prowling around my flat, waiting for a pair of noise-cancelling earphones to charge. Then I tried to read, but I couldn't concentrate, partly because of the buzz of Jackie's snoring and partly because of that drawing I'd seen in Frank's office. I sent the picture to my printer and printed it out as a tiny square on a large piece of paper. Then I went back to my phone and messed about with it, trying to get it to print at the right size and becoming increasingly irritated by it, and by Jackie's incessant snoring.

I gave up on the phone and emailed it to my computer, then printed it out again, this time at a decent size. I thought the noise of the printer might wake Jackie, or at least disturb him enough to stop the snoring, but if he noticed, it didn't put him off his stride or pull him from whatever dreamland he was currently occupying.

He was right about the design for the house though; it was boring – though not normal. It was taller at the front than it was at the back and was clearly special enough that Frank had felt the need to trademark it. The letters TM were liberally sprinkled over the drawing, together with a load of other initials, but I didn't know what they meant, builder stuff I imagine. It looked like the house was designed to be built on a slope. This was, as far as I could make out, a drawing of the finished article. It had all the pipework and wiring put in, bright lines of primary colour running through it. On the edges of the printout was some writing, but my printer was dodgy and it was too smudged to read. I went back to my phone and enlarged the picture, searching round the edges until I found writing.

Blades Edge Regeneration Scheme: Tranche One.

I wondered if this was how Frank laundered money. There was loads of space in a building firm to bill for services that were never made; cheaper materials bought when more expensive ones were specified. I wondered if this was the key to it. Everyone knew that the Blades Edge regeneration was bogged down in red tape. Had Frank banked on this building work coming through and was now stuck? Did he need the lottery ticket to clear his cash flow?

It made sense. A sort of sense.

'Are you still looking at that picture?'

Jackie stood in the door, a halo of sticking-up sleep-hair around his head; he wore only boxers, and his tautly muscled body was laced with the darker lines of pocks and scars from his time in the army. He pulled the tie from his long hair and let it fall loose, then smoothed it down and bundled it up with two quick movements of his hands before tying it back again.

'Jackie,' I said, 'who launders your money?'

'I' – he said grandly and with a flourish of his hand – 'am a legitimate businessman.'

'Okay, but if you weren't a legitimate businessman, who would launder your money?'

'Well, I was in the army with a guy called Pete Mac and he owns a chain of betting shops in Manchester. So if I wanted to launder money, which I don't, that would be the way to go.'

'But if you didn't know Pete Mac and wanted to keep it local? Russian Frank, right?'

'Well, I'm not sure after the last couple of days …'

'If you hadn't put three of his men in hospital and you didn't know Pete Mac and you were not a legitimate businessman, who would launder your money? Russian Frank, right?'

'Suppose so – he launders nearly everyone's money round here.'

'Even Trolley Mick's?'

'I imagine so. It's a business after all.'

I tapped my pen on the desk, wondering what was going on.

'Frank stabbing Mick's nephew. Mick burning Frank's businesses. If it's tied up in these houses and he needs it to go ahead then …' I waved the picture at Jackie and he took the picture from me, studying it.

'Nah,' he said. 'If they wanted this to go ahead that much, then Mick could just terrorise the people on the Edge who are holding on into selling up. He'd probably enjoy that.' He peered at the picture, scratching his head. 'These are going to be built on the Edge?'

'Says so.'

He nodded and handed me back the picture. 'Look at it, think about the Edge.'

I stared at the drawing, wondering what he was getting at, then it hit me.

'Blades Edge is flat – this is meant to be built on a slope.'

Jackie nodded his head.

'So this was never meant to be built.'

Jackie shook his head. 'Not on the Edge, anyway.'

'What about the other side, Blades Edge Hill – that's steep?'

Something dark crossed Jackie's face and then was gone just as quickly. He never liked talking about Blades Edge Hill.

'Green belt, innit, mate,' he said.. 'Can't be upsetting the bunnies.' He sat down in my clients' chair, still staring at the picture.

'What are we missing, Jackie?'

He shrugged. ‘I’m missing my bed, to be honest,’ he said. ‘But now I’m going to have a shower. You should too – you smell.’

‘Thanks, Jackie.’

An hour later we were both showered and in fresh clothes. Jackie had filled a carrier bag with his dirty clothes and planned to drop them off at a launderette, because he was never a man to be seen without at least two changes of, often awful, clothes on his person. I’d made us scrambled eggs, which Jackie was eating at my desk. He had soaked his in Tabasco and ate without so much as breaking a sweat. I was still staring at the picture and the more I did, the more something bothered me.

‘Jackie, when I went through Larry’s stuff at his house, there was a work notebook. I think I’d like to look at it again.’

‘Wouldn’t she have given it back to his work?’

I realised I didn’t know where the notebook was. I remembered putting it to one side to give to Janine but was sure I had never passed it to her.

‘Maybe, but I don’t think I gave it back to her.’

‘We’ll go over when I’ve finished my breakfast.’ He paused with his fork midway between plate and mouth, then lifted a finger in a way I knew meant, ‘Be quiet.’ He stood and walked over to the window, drawing back the heavy velvet curtain.

‘Aww, no,’ he said under his breath, which I knew meant it wasn’t that bad. When something really bothered him he liked to use Punjabi swearing.

‘What?’

‘Police. DI Smith and DC Horseface.’

'You should go out the back.'

He shook his head. 'I've not done anything wrong.'

'We broke into a building last night.'

'Yeah, but they won't know that was me. Wait, did you take your mask off when we were in Maylin and Sparrow?'

'No.'

'Nothing to worry about then.' There was a knock on the door. 'Just get rid of them, Mal – she's fishing and you don't have to let her in.'

'Go hide, Jackie.'

'Why?' he said, 'we haven't done anything wrong.'

'We've done two burglaries this week.'

'Just tell her to go away,' he said, and leant back in my client's chair.

I sighed and opened the door. DI Esther Smith, all four foot three of her, filled the door; her partner stood behind.

'Can I help, Detective Inspector?'

'I'd like to come in, Malachite,' she said.

'I'm a bit busy,' I said.

She tipped her head to one side and said quietly, as if speaking to someone who was a bit simple.

'I'd still like to come in.'

'I think you need a warrant to do that. As I said, I'm busy.'

'A warrant, or probable cause.' She smiled, all sunshine and daisies. 'Or to see a crime in action, or someone suspected of a crime.' She grinned at me and raised her arm. 'Hello, Jackie Singh Khattar,' she said, and gave him a little wave, bending her fingers where they met her palm like a child would do.

'Hello, DI Smith,' he said.

'I've got a warrant for your arrest, luv.' She smiled, then it fell away, and she stared at me. 'So I think I will be coming in then, eh, Mal?' And she pushed past me.

'What?' said Jackie.

'You're coming with me, Jackie,' she said. 'Frank Khlopenko had four of his kebab shops burned down last night and he says you were seen at two of them with a Molotov cocktail.'

'I do not burn down people's shops, Detective Inspector. I am a legitimate businessman.'

'Sarah, cuff this arsehole and get him in the car.' Jackie shrugged and put his hands behind his back, turning round so DC Harrington could cuff him and read him his rights. That done she turned him round and started to lead him out the office.

'You might want that bag of clothes, Officers,' he said, nodding at the carrier bag. 'It's what I was wearing last night.'

DC Harrington glanced at DI Smith who gave her a nod and she went over to grab the bag of clothes. While she did, Jackie stared at me.

'Don't do anything without me, Mal, Okay? Just stay safe.' He whispered it, but DI Smith had ears like a cat, and as soon as Harrington had taken Jackie and his clothes out of the room, she turned back to me.

'What does he not want you doing without him?'

'We're remodelling the upstairs of my shop,' I said.

‘And that’s not safe, is it?’

‘I’m not a very practical person, Detective Inspector. Jackie thinks I’m likely to brain myself with a hammer if I attempt any DIY.’

She let silence fall then stepped closer, her flowery perfume surrounding me.

‘Mal, I’ve got Jackie now. Two witnesses happy to pick him out of a line up. Got him bang to rights – he’s going down. It’ll be you next, you know.’ She reached up and touched my cheek. ‘So, have you anything you want to tell me about your friend? You should get on the right side of this now.’

‘Yes, Detective Inspector.’

‘What?’

‘It wasn’t him – he was with me last night.’

She shook her head, stared at the floor. Let out a theatrical sigh.

‘What about something true, Malachite, eh? Tell me what your friend really does.’

I nodded, took a deep breath. ‘Okay.’

She raised an eyebrow. ‘Well?’

‘He is a legitimate businessman.’

‘So many arseholes,’ she said, staring at me, ‘so little time.’ Then left.

I waited.

I paced.

I tried to sleep.

Couldn’t sleep with Jackie in jail.

I wanted a drink. How long could they keep Jackie? Twenty-four hours. Everyone knew that. Twenty-four hours and they had to charge him or release him. I needed to get out. I wanted to go to

Janine Stanbeck's, despite what Jackie said, but half eight in the morning was too early. I couldn't just sit still. I needed to do something.

Coffee.

No coffee in the cupboard. Surely it couldn't hurt to go to Mr Patel's and pay too much for coffee – it was barely twenty steps.

Go on, do it.

I did it.

No one attacked me or kidnapped me which was, so far, the best thing to happen to me in twenty-four hours. In Mr Patel's shop, Cat Maudy was there, wrapped in her fur coat, picking up her lottery ticket. Part of me felt like smashing the machine for the trouble it had caused, but Mr Patel would ban me from his shop and, despite the prices, it was near and I was lazy.

'Mr Jones,' Maudy said, and she took my hand; her fingers were brittle and cold, icy twigs wrapped in crepe paper. 'We don't usually see you in here at this time.'

'I'm not generally a morning person, Maudy.'

'Ooh, I am, Mr Jones,' she said. 'Will you do another trick for me?'

'No,' said Mr Patel. 'No ghosts in my shop!'

'Oh,' said Maudy, letting go of my hand. 'He's such a spoilsport, isn't he?' Then she headed out, stopping at the door. 'I don't think Mr Patel is a morning person either, Mr Jones. He used to call me and Mr Stanbeck his morning shift, didn't you, Mr Patel? And he was always a bit grumpy about it.' She smiled at him. Her lipstick had bled from her lips into the lines around her mouth. Her eye make-up had run as well; she wiped at her eye. 'I miss him, you know, Mr Stanbeck. He was a kind soul.' She nodded her head. 'You should let me bring you that cat round, Mr Jones, he'd help you get up in the morning,' she said. Then she left.

'Mad old bat,' said Mr Patel. 'This is not weather for a fur coat is it? She will give herself heatstroke.'

'If it makes her happy.'

'What use is being happy if you are dead, eh? She has a perfectly good old coat. And she has been buying the gold label tea!'

'Well, I'm buying own brand coffee so that should make you happy.' He stared at me.

'Own brand?' he shook his head. 'Have a bit of pride, Mr Jones.'

I didn't have much pride, so I bought my expensive cheap coffee and left.

20

Four cups of bad but very strong coffee later, it became clear I wasn't going to stay in and wait for Jackie. What I'd thought was own brand was actually a brand called Soulja Pep! that promised four times as much caffeine as normal coffee and had a picture of an angry-looking Rastafarian on the front.

I felt like ants were marching through my veins.

Nearly 10 a.m. I could go see Janine Stanbeck and see if I could find that book. Something about it was buzzing in the back of my brain. I would park right outside her house and drive straight back with the book. No way was anyone going to come and grab me in the time it took me to get to the door and back. If they tried I could run. I definitely felt like they wouldn't be able to catch me.

Not today.

Not after four cups of Soulja Pep!

I went out the back. I wore a black baseball cap I could pull down, and if I hunched my shoulders I could tell myself no one would recognise me. Maybe all the caffeine was affecting my thought processes a little. But my mind was made up. I glanced up and down outside the shops. No one there so I ran over to my Ford Ka. It took three tries to get the key in the door. I started to wonder if maybe Soulja Pep! had more than caffeine in it. I'd check when I got back.

I stalled the car twice but I wasn't going to let that stop me. On the way to Janine Stanbeck's house I stopped off at a shop to pick up chewing gum and tried to have a chat with the guy behind the counter but he wasn't interested in talking.

By the time I got to the house, the fizzing energy I'd been feeling had fled, along with the minty taste of the chewing gum. It had left behind a gnawing sense that maybe coming here had not been my best idea. Opposite Janine's house, two men were lounging against the wall.

This was almost definitely a bad idea.

I decided to throw out the Soulja Pep! when I got back home.

But the two men had already clocked me and weren't making any sort of move in my direction, so that made it likely that they worked for Mick Stanbeck, which in turn made it unlikely the Russians were going to sweep by and pick me up. I mean, Mick's men would probably stop that happening.

Hopefully.

I got out the car, crossed the road and pressed the button on the intercom. Janine opened the door.

'What do you want?' Her son was hanging back, standing in the door of the kitchen. He needed someone to wipe his nose, and I found him difficult to look at – I'm not good with bodily fluids.

'I need to look at your husband's stuff again.'

'You've looked.'

'I need to look again.'

'Are you wasted?'

'No, just too much coffee.'

'You look wasted.'

'Too much coffee and not enough sleep. Can you let me look, please? It's important.'

She rolled her eyes.

'You'll have to be quick,'

'Okay.' She moved aside and let me through.

'You should wipe your kid's nose,' I said.

She stared at me and I think she considered pushing me back out the door, but at that moment, the phone rang upstairs. She turned and went up the stairs in front of me. She was wearing a very tight skirt in a silky material, covered with flowers. I tried not to stare at her backside, which was harder than you imagine as the stairs were steep and it was right in front of my face.

She left the kid downstairs.

Maybe she did that a lot. Maybe that was how his nose stayed unwiped.

At the top of the stairs, she pointed at her husband's office room and went into her bedroom. She picked up her mobile from the bed, perfectly made, and stared at the screen, then answered it.

'Hang on, calm down,' she said and then looked up, gave me a very false smile and slammed the door shut. I tried to listen to what she was saying, but she kept her voice down. I gave up and went into the office to begin my search.

The office wasn't as I had left it. Everything was still filed away on the cheap shelves or in boxes, but I'd left it tidy. Now it looked like someone had been through it in a hurry, looking for something. The computer sat on the desk, but the keyboard was askew, as if someone had been using it. I ignored the computer; it didn't have what I was looking for. I was following a vague memory of a notebook with a picture of that house in it. Was it blue, navy blue? Or black? Was it in a drawer or in one of the box files? I couldn't remember, still wasn't sure about it or why I wanted to see it. Just a thing, tapping away at the back of my mind. I went through the box files, nothing. Then through the desk, carefully emptying out each drawer, even the one that was full of pens without tops, just in case it was somehow hiding at the bottom.

Nothing.

Had someone taken it.

Or had I imagined it?

Not in the drawers, not in the files. I sat back in the chair. There were boxes in one corner, and when I took the tops off, they were full of baby things, clothes and toys. They weren't folded carefully or sorted in any way, simply stuffed in the boxes. I picked out a pink cloth elephant.

'Mine.' I turned, the boy stood there, he still needed someone to wipe his nose. I held out the elephant, and he stepped forward and took it.

'My daddy knew the score,' he said, and tapped the side of his head.

'No doubt he did.' I fished in my pocket and found an old tissue, held it out to him. 'Wipe your nose,' I said.

He looked at me as if I was talking another language.

'My daddy knew the score,' he said again, and I realised I was either going to have to stare at the stream of mucus running down his face or clean it off myself. I didn't want to do either.

'Are you looking for your mum?'

He shrugged his shoulders and hugged the pink elephant. I had the awful feeling this was the most attention he'd had in a while. 'Come here,' I said. He stepped closer. I reached out and used the tissue to wipe his nose clean. There was no bin, so I threw it on the box. A nice reminder of his childhood for someone later on. When his nose was clean, he blinked. His eyes seemed enormous; the tears he was fighting back filling his eyes, magnifying them. Then he leaned in against me, pushing his small warm body into mine. He was all bone, and for a moment I didn't know what to do. Then I heard the noise he was making – quiet sobbing – and I remembered being small and feeling that way myself. I put my arms round him and he nestled further into me.

'You miss your dad, huh?'

I felt his head move, nodding against me.

'He asleep.' Words escaping past tears.

'Yeah, mine too.'

'Do he wake up?'

I didn't know how to answer that. I didn't understand death myself, never mind how to explain it to a kid. Fortunately, I didn't have to.

'Cristophe! Get away from him.' Janine stood in the door, mobile phone in one hand. 'Mr Jones is here to work and then go away, and we want him to go away, so don't disturb him. Go and play downstairs.'

I let go, and the boy pulled back. He gave me a look as if I'd betrayed him, then ran out the door.

Janine watched him go. 'Are you finished yet?' she said.

'Not yet.'

‘Well, be quick, and don’t mess about with my kid, alright?’

I nodded.

She stayed in the doorway looking at me, I had the distinct feeling that in another time she would have lit a cigarette and pulled hard on it. ‘You’re not going to find my money, are you?’

‘That’s why I’m here. I’m doing my best.’ She continued to stare. ‘Has someone been through this room since I was here last?’

She shook her head, and I imagined her blowing smoke into the air.

‘Finish up,’ she said, ‘I’ve got things to do.’ Then turned around and when she reached the top of the stairs, she started shouting at the boy. I wanted to find the money because I had this idea in my head of Janine using it for her and the kid to escape the Edge, but the more I saw her, the more I thought money wouldn’t help, and Cristophe was likely to end up being one of those kids who fell down the back of society. It wasn’t as much about where you were raised, sometimes, but by who. Money probably wasn’t going to help Cristophe.

Where was that book? I’d put it somewhere for Janine, because she’d asked me to give any of Larry’s work to her so she could give it back. I’d found it, but I hadn’t given it to her. I’d forgotten, because …

Because?

What had I done with it?

I had a clear image of placing it on top of the computer. Putting it aside so I would remember to give it back. I stood, moved over to the computer and closed my eyes. What had happened next?

Did something interrupt me? Yes. I remembered Janine coming in. She interrupted me. And then I banged the chair against the desk and a file fell off it.

I stared at the computer, smiled and reached down the back. The desk had a space for wires to come up through it and the notebook had slid off the top of the old-fashioned monitor and down the back, getting jammed in there. I had to stand on my tiptoes to reach over the old monitor to get it. My fingers scraped the spine. I leant in a little further, managed to grab the book and fish it out.

'Are you finished yet?' shouted Janine from downstairs. 'I really need to go out.' I opened the book, flicked through the drawings in it and found a sketch that looked like the house in Russian Frank's office. That's where I'd seen it before.

'Yeah,' I shouted back. 'I'm done.' I put the book in my inside pocket. 'I didn't find anything though,' I said as I got to the top of the stairs. Janine stood at the bottom, keys in her hand.

'What a shock,' she said, and she opened the door for me. I'm not sure it was out of politeness.

Outside, I got a surprise. Jackie was leaning against the little Ford Ka, trying and failing to do a trick with a yo-yo. He lifted his face, glared at me, and went back to playing with his yo-yo as I approached.

'I didn't think you'd be out yet.'

'Obviously, you didn't' – he tried to make the yo-yo climb back up the string and failed – 'Cos I told you to stay in.'

He stared at me.

'I couldn't. I was climbing the walls.'

He stared harder at me. Then wound up the yo-yo, put it in his pocket and walked over. Studied my face.

'Are you wasted?'

'No, I just had too much coffee.'

'You look wasted.'

'I'm not, how are you even here?'

'Good lawyer,' he said. 'No way anyone at the CPS was going to believe two known criminals over the word of a respected local businessman.' He straightened up a little. 'That's me,' he added. 'To be honest, I think DI Esther just wanted to get me alone for a bit.'

'I'm sure she did.'

'Anyway.' He took some chewing gum from his pocket and unwrapped a stick, put it in his mouth then offered the packet to me. 'You find anything?'

'I got the notebook, and someone has searched Larry's office since I was last there.' I took some gum. My hand was shaking. Thanks 'Soulja Pep!'

'But the book was still there?'

'It had fallen down the back of the computer.'

He moved in even closer to me.

'Are you absolutely sure you're not wasted?'

'Yes.' I said.

He furrowed his eyes, then let out a little 'huh' and stepped back.

'Drive us back to the office and I'll look through the book' – I tapped my chest where the book was hidden – 'see if I can work anything out.'

I'd barely opened the book as we drove before my phone rang.

Caller: Mal? Malachite Jones?

I knew the voice, but not well enough to put a name straight to it.

Caller: I need some help, Mal, and you're the only one I can think of.

Whoever was speaking sounded on the edge of hysteria.

Caller: They've taken my da.

Me: Wait, slow down, who has? And who am I talking to?

A breath. I heard the person on the other end of the phone mentally stop and gather themselves.

Caller: It's me, Callum Callaghan. From school, remember? And the yard, and then I was jogging?

Me: Yeah, course I do, Callum, sorry, bad line. Who's taken your dad? Is it the Russians?

As soon as I said that, Jackie's head turned, locking on to me.

Callum: 'Russians?'

He sounded confused.

Callum: No, it's Trolley Mick. Mick's taken him.

Me: But your dad works for Mick.

Callum: Mick thinks my da killed Larry – they're gonna kill him, Mal.

Me: You need the police, Callum.

Callum: No police.

The line was bad, and I couldn't tell if he was breaking up or the line was.

Callum: Look, Mal, I know Mick doesn't show it, but he likes you.

Me: I'm not sure he—

Callum: They'll kill him, Mal. Please. Just go, beg him for my da's life.

Me: Go where? You really need the pol—

I was nearly thrown out my seat by Jackie swerving the car over to the side of the road and slamming on the breaks. He snatched the phone from me, 'Do you know where he is?' Jackie dug open the glove compartment and about four years' worth of old sweet and crisp packets fell out. He gave me a baleful look and mouthed, 'Pen?' at me. I shrugged, and he shook his head. 'Say it again, Callum. Unit three, Richmile Estate. OK.' He turned to me. 'Mal, remember that address. How long ago?' A space and his eyes widened. 'Why did you wait that fucking long? Okay, well, I suppose Mal would be scared, so that's what normal people do. You're sure that's where they'll have him?' Jackie nodded as he listened to the reply. 'Okay. We'll go. Tell me something, Callum – your dad told us that Mick sent him to get that van, was that a lie then?' Another space. 'Alright, it's what he told you. Okay, we're going now.'

Jackie handed me back my phone, put the car in gear, checked the mirror and pulled out into traffic. He didn't look at me.

'Are we going to go help Benny Callaghan?'

'Well, we're going to find out what's happened to him,' he said. We drove on for a bit. Jackie seemed to be choosing his gears very deliberately, driving in old-lady mode, staring straight ahead as he drove.

'You're not going very fast,' I said.

He shook his head. Chewed on his gum. 'No. I'm not.' He brought the car to a stop at an amber light. He generally treated amber as a signal that meant 'speed up and you'll probably make it'.

'Not quite how I imagine a rescue mission.' He turned to me. Ran a hand through his hair then checked it in the mirror, His eyes flicked to the traffic light, seeing it was still red.

'They took him last night, Mal. I don't think arriving a couple of minutes earlier is going to make much difference to Benny.'

The light changed. Jackie put the car in gear and drove on, staring forward. He looked serious.

He looked older.

21

Calling Richmile Industrial Estate an 'industrial estate' was like calling me one of the Ghostbusters. It was four large garages; ill-kept corrugated steel over timber frames, set in the middle of a field on the moors next door to a derelict farmhouse. In the garden of the farmhouse was an overgrown tractor and two long, rusted containers – the type used on ships and trucks. The containers had once been blue, but time had left the colour as no more than a vague memory. Jackie brought the car to a stop behind the containers, so it was hidden from anyone who might be in the industrial units.

'This is going to be bad, isn't it?' I said.

Jackie's hands were locked around the steering wheel and he was pushing himself back into the car seat, staring straight ahead.

He nodded.

'Doesn't look much like an industrial estate, does it?'

'Good place to grow weed,' he said, staring at the fields and moorland where the heather had been parched brown by the sun.

'Maybe this needs the police, Jackie.'

'He called you.'

'Why me?'

'They're criminals, Mal, they don't talk to the cops. That shit runs deep.'

'What does he think I can do?'

'Talk to Mick. But it's probably too late.' I didn't say anything, and he sighed. 'No cars, no vans. Nobody here.'

'Maybe they didn't come here.'

'Maybe they've done what they need to.'

I didn't like the sound of that much.

'Maybe we should call the police then, Jackie?'

Jackie gave me a look. It was a look that said, 'We are not going to call the police.'

'Do you have a baseball bat in the boot, Mal?'

'Of course not.'

Jackie gave me another look. It was a look that said, 'You should have a baseball bat in the boot.'

'Okay, you have the kit for changing the tyre though, right?'

I shrugged. 'Never looked.'

'Fuck's sake.' He got out the car and went round the back, opened the boot and I heard him pushing things about and swearing. When he came back, he had the wrench thing for getting the nuts off the wheels in his hand. 'Come on then.'

I didn't really want to go with him, but I didn't have much choice. I had half expected Jackie to dash forward, bent over, moving from cover to cover like he was in an action movie, but he didn't. He walked straight forward, occasionally shifting his grip on the wrench and keeping his eyes locked on the doors of Unit 3. I followed.

It was incredibly quiet.

Summer quiet.

The air was still and hot, and there was no breeze. The grass around the rusting tractor was so still and so green, it was easy to imagine we were walking through a single frame in a film. Birds sang in small, high voices, chirping out tunes, while crickets rasped, and Jackie walked forward.

My phone rang.

'Shit.' I dragged it from my pocket as the first bars of the song ripped through the quiet.

Jackie shot me a dirty look.

'Sorry.'

A text from Beryl. I didn't read it, just switched my phone off.

I started to say sorry to Jackie again, but he clearly didn't want to speak to me just then, so I mouthed my apology.

He stopped in his walk toward the industrial unit, tapped his leg gently with the wrench and then strode over to the derelict farmhouse. We spent five minutes going through the dark rooms on the lower floor. They were all covered in graffiti, which I thought showed real commitment on the part of the artists – it was a long drive just to spray a penis on a wall. But apart from the spray-painted genitals and unreadable tags, there was nothing in the derelict house.

When Jackie was done with making sure no one was there, we returned to the four garages. Two of them were padlocked shut – he ignored those. The doors on the fourth one hung open, one only attached by the top hinge. Jackie had a quick look inside; I got near enough to know it smelled like a gents' toilet in a particularly rough pub and left Jackie to it. He came out grim-faced and took a couple of deep breaths of hot summer air. I couldn't shake the feeling this was something we should be doing at night.

Jackie used the wrench to hook open the door to Unit 3.

It didn't smell quite as bad as Unit 4.

But it did smell bad.

Jackie peered in. He paused, as if taking in everything around us, then pulled the door fully open. I noticed it didn't scrape along the floor. The other units had grass growing around the bottom of the door, but this one didn't. I'd not thought about it before Jackie opened the door to Unit Three. The grass there was flattened. I kept looking at the grass and thinking about that, because I didn't want to look at or think about what was inside.

'Now we call the police,' said Jackie. 'Or we do once we are well away from here.' He started to turn away. 'You can call Callum.'

Benny Callaghan was in the garage. He was sitting on a cheap chair. It was the type we used to have in school. The back, seat and front legs were made of a single curve of laminated wood. The rest was formed from a tubular metal frame. By the chair was a car battery. There was nothing else in the garage. Benny was leaning forward, only held on to the chair by the ropes that had been used to bind his hands and arms to it. His hair was soaked. His clothes were soaked. In the gloom of the garage I couldn't tell whether it was blood or water.

'Come away,' said Jackie. 'You don't need to see this.'

I nodded, barely moving my head because the scene in the garage demanded to be looked at, demanded to be witnessed and remembered. A fly buzzed. It smelled like a butcher's shop.

I had been wrong, when I said it didn't smell as bad as Unit 4. It smelled worse. Infinitely worse.

'Yeah,' I said. 'Let's go.'

Benny Callaghan took a breath. It sounded like it took everything he had to do it. Then I was moving forward, running. 'He's alive, Jackie!' and Jackie was shouting 'No!' but I didn't care. He was alive.

It was water in his hair, maybe it was sweat, maybe it was done to increase conductivity for the battery they'd used to torture him with. Nearer still, I could see there was a lot of blood too. It soaked his trousers, and he'd soiled himself, I could smell it. I didn't blame him. I think I would have done the same in his position.

And his hands, I can't even think about his hands. About what had been done to them. About how that must have felt. Must have still felt.

But Benny Callaghan was a hard man. By the time I reached him, he had managed to raise his head. His face was so bruised I couldn't see his eyes for the swellings. The teeth in his mouth had been smashed; a jagged array, like a shark, the skin of his lips stuck to them. His head lolled, then he pulled himself back up, looking in my direction.

'No,' he said. In that one word was a whole world of hurt and dread.

'It's alright, Benny. It's over. It's not them. It's me. It's Mal. Malachite Jones.'

‘Mal.’ Was it a question? Did he recognise me or was he simply lost in agony, repeating a word he recognised without understanding it.

‘Yes, it’s Mal.’ I touched his bruised face, kneeling by him, and he let his head slump against my chest. I was kneeling in his blood. I could feel it soaking through my jeans.

‘Mal,’ he said again. Did he sound relieved? It was hard to tell. He tried to say something else and though his mouth was moving, I could no longer hear him. I put my ear next to his mouth. Heard the words escaping along with his life. ‘My son. Mal. Watch out for my son.’ Then he arched his back and made a noise like nothing human. The convulsion of his muscles was so strong it knocked me to the floor, and I could do nothing but watch as the last spasms of life passed and Benny Callaghan was released from his pain.

‘What did he say?’ said Jackie. I turned to him; a dark figure, silhouetted by the bright light.

‘He wanted me to look out for his boy.’

‘Well,’ said Jackie. ‘Then that’s on you now.’

‘I didn’t …’ Jackie turned around before I could finish talking.

‘Follow me,’ he said.

I did, getting up and leaving Benny behind me. The day didn’t seem so warm or beautiful anymore. Jackie was just disappearing behind the old farmhouse when I came out, and I had to run to catch him up. When I did, he was standing by a what looked like a well, balancing a bucket on the side of it. I got to the well, and he picked up the bucket.

‘Stay there,’ he said.

'Why?'

He poured the bucket of water over my head. It was freezing. The water soaked through my clothes. Making them stick to my skin and while I was still standing there, outraged, he leant over into the well and dropped the bucket in. Quickly hauling it up and throwing another bucket of water over me.

'Why did you do that?'

He dropped the bucket back into the well and started pulling on the rope again.

'Because it's a lot easier to explain away someone wet in the passenger seat of a car than someone covered in blood.'

'You could have warned me.'

'You'd have only made a fuss.'

'No, I wouldn't.' I wrapped my hands round myself. 'I'm freezing.'

He didn't bother to answer me, mostly because he didn't need to. I would have made a fuss, and we both knew it.

Jackie walked away from me toward the tractor and started moving the grass apart with his foot. After a bit, he found what he was looking for and pulled it out of the tangle of grass that ensnared it. Then he lifted it up so I could see he held an old petrol can. He brought it over to the well and poured water from his bucket into the can, and lifted it up, studying it. I really wanted to be angry with him and to remain aloof and not talk to him, but curiosity is a powerful force.

'What are you doing?'

'Making sure it doesn't leak,' he said. Then he poured out the water, walked over to the car and went around the back. I couldn't see him, so I pretended not to be interested and took off my jacket and T-shirt. Wringing them out as best I could.

There were smears of blood on my arms. I used water from the bucket to wash them away and spread my clothes out on the grass in hope of them drying a bit. Then I sat there, ignoring Jackie as he siphoned petrol from the car tank into the can. He wasn't away for long. I heard him walking back toward the units, the sloshing of liquid in the petrol can punctuating his steps, and I hurried after him.

'What are you doing, Jackie?'

He held up the petrol can. 'Burning everything.'

'But, Benny is in there.'

'Yep.'

'The police will need to do forensics.'

'Yep,' he said, and walked into Unit 4. The sound of liquid being poured. 'And what will they find, Mal?'

I didn't go near enough to see in. I didn't want to see in.

'Evidence,' I said.

'Evidence you touched him, Mal.' He sounded a little vexed.

'I barely touched him.' The smell of petrol filled the air. Jackie was backing out of the unit, splashing fuel about.

'You don't have to touch him for long. One hair. A bit of skin. Bits of your clothes. That's all it takes. This is a murder, a torture murder. They'll throw everything they have at it.'

I suddenly felt even colder.

‘Right,’ I said. ‘Do you need some wood or anything?’

Jackie shook his head and pulled some dried grass from the ground. ‘No,’ he said. ‘Timber framed, they’ll burn well enough to hide any evidence you were here. Muddy up the knees of your trousers, Mal, there’s blood all over them.’

He lit the grass with a lighter he kept in his pocket and threw it into the garage. For a moment I thought it wouldn’t catch but I should have known better. Jackie knew all about fire. Black smoke started to seep out of the doors. When the air was starting to fill with the smell of burning meat, Jackie seemed satisfied.

‘You should get your clothes,’ he said, and started walking back toward the car.

22

Jackie Singh Khattar never talked about death. I mean, I knew, in an academic way, that he had killed people. He'd been in the army, in the SAS, or one of those other special services that you only need to refer to by its initials – though he never said which. He never talked about what he did in the army, not in any detail. Every so often, he'd say something that left me in no doubt that he'd killed, and not just at a distance with a gun, that he'd done it up close and personal.

Where it was real.

I don't know why that had made me think he'd cope easily with death, but it was clear he didn't, from the way he sat in his seat, from the way he drove, swearing under his breath at other drivers for the most minor misdemeanours. Jackie Singh Khattar was as close to being off-centre as I had ever seen him.

I didn't try to talk to him about it. If he wanted to talk, he would. He wasn't the talk-it-out type, really. He was more about putting down his personal demons with sudden and explosive violence. And at the moment, I was more about being damp and miserable, and I was never really one for violence if it could be avoided. Or even if it couldn't.

Jackie put the car radio on. News of a bomb scare in the city centre, shutting down the train station. When the newscaster started talking about Islamic extremists, Jackie turned the radio off again.

I fished the book from the inside of my jacket. It was also damp, though not as damp as I was. Water had given a wave to the edges of the pages and made the slim book feel thicker than it really was. Inside, it was full of sketches; extensions, mostly, all different types, none particularly exciting. Most of them had been crossed through, as if Larry was mentally putting each project out of his head once it was finished. They were all covered in his shorthand, initials and colours used for the various different materials within them – plumbing, electrics, insulation, whatever else builders did. There was a noticeable evolution through his notebook of the projects he was involved with; they slowly became more and more complex until I got to the final one, the house drawn in Russian Frank's office: the house he never got to finish.

I wondered if Janine knew anything about it. Then I decided she probably wouldn't tell me, as she'd specifically asked me to hand over this book if I found it. She had a funny attitude for a woman who wanted me to find a lot of money for her. Not that I could find it – I was pretty sure that lottery ticket was in the wind.

I had a sudden image of the boy, Cristophe, tapping the side of his head and saying, 'My daddy knew the score.'

I wished his dad would tell me the score.

'You should ring Callum. Tell him about his dad.'

'What?' I glanced over at Jackie. He was concentrating on the road ahead and bit the words out.

'Ring Callum, tell him about his dad. You can do it.'

'Shouldn't the police do that?'

'He rang you. You get to do the death knock.'

I didn't want to, but I knew there was no point arguing with him. My phone was in my back pocket and my trousers were tight and I was damp and had my seat belt on. It was a fight to get my phone out of my pocket. As I struggled and contorted myself, I could feel Jackie, impatient, wanting me to get the thing done, and annoyed because I wasn't already doing it.

'I can do it later if …'

'Do it now.'

'Okay.' I finally got my phone out of my pocket and stared dumbly at it. The screen was blank. Had my soaking killed it?

'You switched it off.'

'Oh yeah.' Hold down the button, wait for the screen to fire up. A cold feeling ran down my spine. 'Jackie, they'll know we are up at the units, they'll be able to track my phone.'

He let air out of his mouth. It's amazing how sometimes someone can make a thing as simple as breathing carry so much meaning. Annoyance, mostly.

'They'll need a warrant to get that information – they've no reason to suspect you would be up there.'

'Yeah, but sometimes they cheat, right?' Jackie closed his eyes and did that breathing thing again.

'Don't worry about it. I know someone. I'll sort it. Just make the call to Callum.'

'Isn't that illega—'

'I said I'll sort it.'

I didn't reply to that. He didn't want a reply. My phone booted up, and I found Callum's number, called it, got a message from Callum saying he couldn't come to the phone right now. He sounded happy. I didn't know the etiquette for this sort of situation, but leaving a message telling him his dad had been tortured to death felt like a wrong move. I asked him to call me.

'You better do it, Mal.'

'I left a message.'

'You better answer when he rings back though.'

'I'm not a monster.'

I knew this mood. Jackie was angry and looking for a target, and I was here. It wouldn't become violence, but he could wound with words as well as any weapon when he wanted. Though, thankfully, he didn't get the chance. Before he could open his mouth, the inside of the car flashed blue.

'Fuck,' he said. Which was as good as any other description. The police car behind us flashed its lights again, and I could see the officer at the wheel motioning for us to pull over. Jackie did; he was very careful about obeying the little laws. He tapped the steering the wheel while he waited for the officer to approach. I felt myself worrying. I was pretty sure he wouldn't take out his anger on a cop – as sure as I could be. That was a direct route to jail, and Jackie rarely did very stupid things.

Unless he was really angry.

And he was quite angry.

The officer, in his fifties, smart-looking with horn-rimmed glasses, tapped on the window and waited for Jackie to wind it down.

'This your car, sir?' he asked.

Jackie shook his head. Pointed at me.

'It's his.'

'And why is sir not driving?' he asked. Then he lowered his glasses and looked hard at me. 'And why is sir, damp?'

'We went for a walk,' I said. 'And we were messing about and I fell in a river. I didn't want to get the driver's seat wet, so I asked my friend to drive me back.' A shiver ran through me. I couldn't think of any reason for the police to stop us apart from what had just happened at Richmile.

'Horseplay, sir? You should be more careful,' said the officer. 'Even in hot weather, the rivers can be very cold. People drown.'

'I did notice the water was cold,' I said, but the policeman had turned his attention to Jackie.

'Are you insured to drive this vehicle, sir?' Jackie nodded. 'Can I see your driver's licence?' Jackie reached into his coat and handed it over, all without looking at the officer. The man peered at the bit of plastic, looked at Jackie. 'Your name,' he said. 'I know it. Why do I know it, sir?'

'Make a big donation to the police Christmas party, innit, mate,' he said in a Bradford Asian accent as thick as cold ghee.

'I'm sure you do, sir,' said the officer. 'One moment please – keep your hands on the steering wheel if you could, sir.' He sauntered back to his car to check Jackie's credentials.

'We're screwed, Jackie,' I said. 'They must already know about Benny Callaghan, and now they've got us.'

Jackie shook his head and his grin returned. There was nothing he liked more than a crisis.

'Nah,' he said. 'Before I left the police station, DI Esther said she were gonna make my life difficult. This is all part the game. Sit tight, Mal.' The police officer came back and gave Jackie his driving licence back.

'All seems to be in order, sir. Now, as you may be aware, there has been a suspected terrorist incident at the train station. Now, apart from your damp friend, can anyone else vouch for your whereabouts …?'

'I ain't goin' to sleep wiv 'er, mate,' said Jackie.

'What?'

'The police lady, I ain't gonna sleep wiv 'er. No chance, mate. You lot can stop me as much as you want.'

'I don't think you are going to be sleeping with the DI either, son,' he said, staring into the car. In his eyes was something dark. He didn't like Jackie, or maybe he did like DI Smith. Or maybe he was racist and didn't like either of them. He glared at me. Maybe he didn't like anyone.

When Jackie spoke again, his accent was gone. 'Officer' – he checked his badge – 'Burnham, I never mentioned a DI.'

The policeman's face went pale as he realised he'd spoken without thinking.

'But I reckon I know why someone your age is still a beat cop, eh?' Jackie continued. 'Now, you can go on pretending that you think I might be a terrorist, or maybe pretend you thought you could smell drugs, but we both know you won't find anything, and if you do it's dodgy, Officer Burnham.' He sat a bit taller in his seat. 'Badge number two-eight-nine-two, Officer

Burnham. Got that, Mal? Now, my friend is cold and uncomfortable, and I want to get him home. Can we get on our way or do you want my lawyer on the phone screaming about racial profiling? Cos I reckon, if you're still a beat copper harassing people on the say so of DI Esther Smith, you probably can't afford much in the way complaints, right?'

The officer stared into the car a moment longer. 'Maybe I'll let you get off on your business then,' he said. He glanced over at me. 'You should find yourself some better company, lad,' he turned back to Jackie. 'I look forward to meeting you again, one day, Mr Singh Khattar.' He turned around and walked back to his car.

Jackie watched him in the rear-view mirror.

'Twat,' he said, and started the car.

23

Annoying a police officer always put Jackie in a better mood. He whistled as he drove back to my flat. When we got in, I put my clothes in the wash and showered the blood, well water and quite a lot of mud off. While the hot water cascaded off me, I tried to think through everything I knew – or didn't know. A circle of information existed in my mind and around the perimeter were all these figures, criminals, police officers, wives, children, churches, Scout groups, corner shops and council houses. I could see no reason for them to be linked; in the normal world none of these things would be linked. But Larry Stanbeck hovered in the centre of the circle, a faceless figure, a misty presence that should somehow make sense of all these disparate elements.

I just didn't know how.

In fact, I didn't really know much about Larry Stanbeck at all.

Hot water flowed over my face and I realised what an idiot I had been. If this had been a normal job, if I'd simply been trying to offer Janine Stanbeck some comfort about her husband, I wouldn't have been interested in any of the peripherals. How people died was often the last thing people wanted to talk about – 'Yes, the pain is over, etc.' usually wrapped that one up. What did it matter? No, any other job, I would only have been interested in her husband. That was what mattered, but I'd been led away from him – admittedly, at some points I'd been running away from him in fear of my own safety, but I had still taken my eye off the ball. If I wanted to find the money, and really I could do with the finder's fee, then who murdered Larry Stanbeck didn't matter because it was clear that the suspects didn't have the ticket either. So, knowing who ran him off the road wouldn't help me find the ticket if Larry had hidden it.

I needed to understand Larry.

I finished my shower and dressed and found Jackie sat at my desk playing on his phone.

'Did you know your shop is full of Pokémon?'

'What do you know about Larry Stanbeck?' I sat opposite him.

He shrugged. 'Not much, never met him. He wasn't part of his dad's outfit as far as I know. Well, not the bits I come into contact with – they tend to be a bit' – he looked up from his phone and gave me a sparkling grin – 'rougher.'

'Do you even know what he looked like?'

He wrinkled his brow. 'Can't say I do. He just never crossed my path.'

'No pictures of him in his house either, people usually bring pictures of their loved ones to me. She didn't.'

'I don't think it's a big stretch to say she probably didn't love him much.'

'Yeah, but we know nothing about him, Jackie.'

'We know where he worked, we know his family, we know—'

'No, Jackie, we know about the people around him and what he did. But we don't know *him* – you didn't even know what he looked like.'

'Are you about to say he might not even be dead?' Jackie looked at me and raised an eyebrow.

'Where did that come from?'

'I just thought you were going to say he could be alive and has run off with the ticket.'

'No. We're not in an Agatha Christie book.' He nodded and went back to his phone. 'I want to go to St Jude's School and speak to Miss Feeney.'

That got his attention.

'I'm not going to Choppy's,' he said. 'I'll drop you at the bottom of the drive and wait for you, but I'm not going in.'

Choppy's was all Jackie ever called our old school. He had been expelled from the place when he was fifteen, and then he tried to burn it down. I could understand him not wanting to go in – he wouldn't get the warmest welcome.

'That's fine. Can we go now?'

'Your hair's still damp, Mal.'

'I've been damp most of the day.'

'You'll catch your death.'

We walked back to the car. It was late in the evening, but the teachers at St Jude's all stayed late. The school did a lot of outreach; late-night clubs to keep the kids off the streets while parents tried to make ends meet by working two jobs, extra tutoring for those struggling. It had been a hole when I went there but, bit by bit, it had dragged itself up and, though it would never be well funded enough to be a great school, it was doing all right.

My phone chirped as I got in next to Jackie and he started the car. I looked at it.

‘Text message from Callum Callaghan,’ I said to Jackie.

He made a sort of wordless grunt I took to mean that I should read it out.

‘Says “I know about my da. Thanks for trying.”‘ So much pain reduced to so few words. I deleted the text; I didn’t want it to be the first thing I saw when I opened my phone. The thought of Benny Callaghan, and what had been done to him, made my stomach turn.

We drove to the school in silence. Its entrance was outside the Blades Edge estate, to stop people joyriding through it, and anyone visiting in a car had to come out of the estate and drive round the busy road to get in. Jackie stopped at the bottom of the drive.

‘I’ll drop you here. How long do you think you’ll be?’ I shrugged.

‘I thought you were going to wait?’

‘No.’ He looked out of his window, away from the school. ‘I need to get the tyres off this car – we might have left prints up at Richmile. I’ll burn the old ones.’

‘Why not just burn the car?’ He looked at me like I was an idiot. ‘I mean, I’m glad you’re not going to burn my car, but you are always burning cars,’ I added.

‘Yes. But not cars I’ve been stopped by the police in or seen in by them. If we burn this after that copper stopped us, it’ll just look suspicious. I’ll put some worn tyres on it, then it won’t match anything we may have left up there, and these old Kas are common enough.’

I undid the seat belt and got out.

'Mal,' said Jackie. I leaned over to hear him. 'If I'm not here when you come out, ring the kebab shop and ask for Asif – he'll arrange a cab for you. Don't try and come home by yourself, okay'

I nodded and shut the door. He managed to make the Ford's tyres screech when he set off. I could never get it to do that.

A fence ran around the school; not high enough to stop a determined kid escaping, but tall enough to keep most of them in. The only way in was down the drive; in a car you had to stop at the barrier and one of the rent-a-cops, or 'security officers', would let you in. On foot, you had to wait at a gate while they looked at you from their little hut. I didn't mind it so much as it was a warm evening, but they still took their time before answering the intercom and grudgingly letting me in to visit Miss Feeney. Then they took their time getting me through the scanner and though I plainly didn't have a bag with me, they still asked me if I had one. I filled in the book to get my little visitor's badge.

It was quiet, and the corridors I remembered as being thronging with kids from my time here were empty. Somehow that made them feel sadder, even though when I had been here it had been a miserable experience. It wasn't the same school though; in my time, it had been falling part and now it was anything but. New parts had been built, and the old and falling-down parts had been extensively remodelled in the nineties. I'd last been in here about fifteen years ago, for reasons I'd rather not try to remember. I do remember thinking it was very shiny then, new and shiny. It wasn't so shiny now; it was starting to look more than a little frayed around the edges.

I realised I didn't know where Miss Feeney taught. I knew the classroom she'd taught me English in a long time ago, but she probably didn't have the same one now. In fact, I'm not sure that part of the school even existed any more. A cleaner was methodically making their way toward me with a mop, progressing through arcs of shining moisture. Wet the mop. Wring it out. Mop the floor. Move on and repeat. A well-practised and repetitive action that I found hypnotic. He stopped mopping and stared at me. I shook myself from my trance.

'Sorry,' I said. 'I used to come to school here. I am a bit lost. Looking for Miss Feeney, if she's still here?'

He nodded. 'Languages annex – follow the cyan,' he said, the ghost of Eastern Europe in his accent. 'Classroom twelve.'

'Thank you,' I said. And he stared at me as if he didn't know the words. I walked away in the direction he'd indicated, feeling his gaze on the back of my neck and fighting not to look back. His reference to 'following the cyan' had confused me until I looked down and saw thick colourful lines drawn on the floor. I'd noticed them when I came in, but presumed they were just a design element. Now they made more sense: they were paths for visitors to follow so they didn't get lost. The echo of my footsteps sounded impossibly loud.

I followed the cyan line and found the languages block and then followed the numbers on the rooms until I came to Miss Feeney's classroom. I knocked softly on the door.

'Come in!' There was something about her voice that made me warm inside. High, almost squeaky and with a trace of her native Liverpool. I was sure she'd been far more Liverpudlian-sounding when she taught me, but it must have faded with the years. Entering the classroom, I found her stacking chairs. Like her accent, she had faded a little; she was a tiny woman who'd been all bright clothes and black hair when she taught me, but her clothes were more subdued now and her hair, still long, was mostly grey. Her eyes were the same as I remembered though: bright blue and sparkling with mischief.

'Malachite Jones,' she said. 'Never thought to see you back here after you tried to nick that photocopier.' She smiled, letting me know she was glad to see me. 'How is your back, by the way?'

'Better, Miss Feeney,' I said. Some teachers, when you were an adult, wanted you to call them by their first names, but not Miss Feeney. She was still a teacher and I was still a pupil in both our eyes, I was pretty sure of that. 'I don't do things like that anymore.'

'Good – you were never very good at it. How's Jackie?'

'Well, Miss Feeney.'

'You should tell him to come by one day.'

'I don't think he will.'

'I know.' She lifted another chair and added it to her stack. 'So, what do you want? I doubt you'd be here if you didn't want something.'

I picked up a chair and started a stack of my own by hers. I didn't bother denying I was here for something – she never did have much time for excuses.

'I came here to ask you about Larry Stanbeck.'

'Poor Larry,' she said. 'If you're going to try and use me to fleece his wife with your nonsense, then I'm not saying a word.'

'I'm not, I promise, miss.'

She smiled. 'I've heard a lot of promises in my time, Malachite Jones.' She lifted a chair, started a new stack. 'Well, what do you want to know?'

'Anything, everything. His wife doesn't think his death was an accident. I'm looking into it.' She stopped, utterly still with a chair in her hands and stared at me. 'And he had some money, so she wants to find it.'

She nodded, then continued stacking her chairs.

'He came a few years after you left, I think. Larry was one of the ones that made Mick Stanbeck realise he was getting things wrong, had him get his brood under control.' The chair she was stacking stuck at an awkward angle and she wriggled it, filling the room with the clattering of wood on metal before it fell into place. 'He made this school, in a way.'

'What do you mean?'

'I mean Larry was clever. Very academically capable – art, music, English, history, he excelled. Mick's organisation was growing and I think Mick realised that soldiers, thugs, are ten-a-penny, he could get them from anywhere, they came to him. He could deal with them through intermediaries, withhold information, and as long as he paid them, they would do as they were told and couldn't be linked directly to him. But he could never really trust them. Then he had Larry – the boy should have gone to university really, but his dad was having none of that. Stanbecks don't get to leave the Edge. And I think he saw in Larry someone he would be able to really trust. Family, see. It matters to Mick more than he lets on.'

'But Larry wasn't involved with his dad.'

She shook her head. 'Sons and fathers, eh?' she said sadly. 'Larry was a soft boy. No one touched him, cos he was Mick Stanbeck's son, but he wasn't strong in a way his father understood. And Larry, he wanted to impress his father, but he didn't want to be like him either. I knew Mick,' she said, 'hard not to. I don't think Mick had the mental equipment to bridge the gap between him and his son, but that doesn't mean he didn't love him. And Larry loved his dad too. They'd probably have been closer if Mick had let him go to university, you know. He could have become something – historian, teacher, artist, whatever – but Mick couldn't let go. I think Mick realised in the end, but it was too late for Larry. I'd watch Mick drop him off, some mornings. They never spoke.'

'Do you have a picture of him, from back then?'

She smiled, and I swear there was the hint of a tear in her eye. 'I have pictures of you all,' she said, and headed back toward her desk. On her way, she stopped, looked at the floor and stooped to pick something up. A rolled cigarette. She sniffed it. 'Someone will be let down tonight, they dropped their joint.' She held it out. 'Do you want it?'

‘I don’t do that,’ I said, ‘not anymore.’

‘Good.’ She grinned and tucked the joint behind her ear, then she opened a big cupboard at the back of the room. It was lined with ring binders. Each had a letter of the alphabet printed on it and she picked up the one marked *S.* ‘I’ve taught a lot of Stanbecks,’ she said, and put the heavy binder down on the desk then opened it. ‘There he is, Larry – the day he qualified as an interior designer from the sixth form.’ She stared at his picture. ‘He deserved better.’

I went over and looked at the picture of Larry. He didn’t look like I expected from the few pictures I had seen; he was smaller and rounder. Soft faced and smiling.

‘He doesn’t look much like a biker,’ I said.

‘He was a Stanbeck,’ said Miss Feeney. ‘They’ve all got something wild in them.’

Her words seemed to hang in the air. It was one of those moments when someone says something so obvious and true that it feels like it lodges in the back of your mind, irritating you with the fact you had never thought of it before.

The silence was broken by a bark of static from the radio on Miss Feeney’s desk. She turned from me, picked up the radio and took a few steps away. She put one finger in her ear so she could hear what the person was saying on the other end better.

‘Yes?’ I couldn’t make out the reply, the words were lost to poor reception, and Miss Feeney had the radio pushed right against her ear to be able to hear. Her eyes flickered toward me. ‘No. He left a while back.’ More noise from the radio. ‘I presume he went out, you're the one with the CCTV system.' More noise from the radio, then the green receiving light on top went out. Miss Feeney stared at the radio. 'Jumped up little prick,' she said. 'Malachite, you had better go, Mick Stanbeck's twins just turned up looking for you.'

Something felt like it slithered down my spine.

'Okay.' I headed toward the door but Miss Feeney put her hand on my arm.

'Are you in trouble?' she asked.

'Possibly. Look, I really should go.'

She stepped toward the door and peered round the edge. 'Too late, they're on their way.'

'Did they see you?'

She shook her head. 'I've got pretty adept at hearing people walking through these corridors. You leave now you'll walk straight into them.' She glanced behind her. 'Get in the cupboard. I'll get rid of them.'

'They're dangerous.'

'I'm not scared of Mick Stanbeck's twins. Get in the cupboard.'

I got in the cupboard. I was actually quite scared of Miss Feeney, and it never really occurred to me to do anything but what she told me to. She shut the door, and I found myself entombed in the pitch black. I didn't dare move. I felt like I was in a coffin, but the feeling didn't last long. Though light could not get into the cupboard, sound could. I heard the classroom door open.

Footsteps.

Voices.

Miss Feeney: 'Hello boys, can I help you?'

A Kray: 'We're looking for Jones.'

Miss Feeney: 'I'm afraid he's gone.'

A Kray: 'Where?'

Miss Feeney: 'I don't know, boys. You seemed friendly with John on security – why don't you ask him to check the CCTV for you?'

A Kray: 'He says it doesn't work.'

Miss Feeney: 'That's government cuts for you, eh?'

A Kray: 'What?'

Miss Feeney: 'It doesn't matter. He's gone.'

A Kray: 'Was the Paki with him?'

Miss Feeney: 'We don't use that word in this school.'

A Kray: 'What do you say instead of "Paki" then?'

Miss Feeney: 'If you must refer to someone by their nationality, then "Asian gentleman" is fine.'

A Kray: 'Was the Asian gentleman with him? [No trace of sarcasm.]'

Miss Feeney: 'No, he was on his own. If you hurry down the corridor, you might even catch him.'

Silence.

The sound of my breathing.

Miss Feeney: 'I have work to do, boys, you should go now.'

A Kray: 'You're quite hot. For an old woman.'

Miss Feeney: 'You should go now.'

A Kray: 'Do you feel safe here? All alone?'

Silence.

Tension.

I wondered what I would do if they decided to hurt her. If the threat hanging in the air was carried out. Would I stay here, hiding in a cupboard?

Footsteps.

Light.

Everything swimming in brightness, eyes out of focus. Then I found myself looking at one of the twins.

'She said you'd gone,' said Kray One. Behind him, the other twin took a step closer to Miss Feeney. 'But she looked at the cupboard when she was scared.'

'You lied to us, bitch,' said Kray Two.

They reminded me of wild dogs I'd seen on a TV nature programme, stalking something weaker and excited by the weakness. Baying and yapping.

'I know your father,' said Miss Feeney.

'We're his favourites,' said Kray One. He whispered it into her face, and I could see the muscles of his neck sticking out, tight with tension. 'He gives us a lot of leeway. And he doesn't like liars. They're not conducive to business.'

'She didn't know I was in there,' I said.

Kray Two studied me.

'Then why did she look at the cupboard?'

'Maybe she thought she could hide from you in there,' I said. And Kray Two continued to study me.

'Our da doesn't like liars,' said Kray One to Miss Feeney again. Any other human would have taken a step back, but she didn't. She just glared at him.'People do like to hide though, when they think we're going to hurt them.'

‘I suppose,’ said Kray Two. He took a step back from me. ‘Why didn’t she want you in the cupboard?’

‘I wanted to look at her records – she said they were confidential.’

‘*Con-fi-den-tial,*’ said Kray One, and he reached into his back pocket for his small dictionary.

‘It means “secret”,’ said Miss Feeney.

‘We’ve got a book,’ said Kray Two.

‘She’s an English teacher – you don’t need to look in your dictionary.’

‘No, Malachite,’ said Miss Feeney, ‘you should never try to dissuade someone from reading.’

‘We’re bettering ourselves,’ said Kray One.

‘I’m glad to hear it,’ said Miss Feeney. ‘Your dad likes clever boys.’

‘Con-fi-den-tial,’ said Kray Two. ‘”Adjective. Information to be kept secret or private.”‘ He put the dictionary back. ‘You have to come with us.’ Then he glanced over my shoulder at the cupboard. ‘Is the Asian gentleman in there?’

‘No,’ I said.

He took me by the elbow and steered me toward the door, his brother followed. When we reached the door, he turned round and pointed at Miss Feeney.

‘You never saw us. You never saw him,’ said Kray One.

I had a sudden image of a ruined body strapped to a chair, but it wasn’t Benny Callaghan’s face on the body. It was mine.

24

It was dark outside. The school corridors were mostly window above hip height and, outside, the school grounds had been well landscaped. Lots of bushes and small trees grew around the playing fields and the grey squares of the playgrounds. There was a slight hill at the edge of the playground where a huge thorn bush used to grow when I came here. Jackie used to throw me in that thorn bush at least once a week and, at the time, I thought it was the most terrible, frightening, painful thing in the world. I lived in fear of the moment each week when he grabbed me and dragged me toward it.

I really hoped the Stanbeck twins weren't going to take me somewhere and torture me to death. The thought of the thorn bush seemed quite welcoming in contrast.

'Why did you come here for me?'

'You know,' said Kray One.

'I really don't.'

'Us Da wants you,' said Kray Two, as if that settled it.

We walked on through the school. All the main lighting had been turned off and only the emergency lights were on. It was pretty dismal.

'Why does Mick want me?'

The twins shrugged, in unison. Then, using that odd telepathy some twins have, both realised that I had been noticeably slowing my walk and they tightened their grips on my elbows and hurried me on.

'Da wants you,' said Kray One. 'He didn't say why. But you're coming with us, and if you try anything, then we will hurt you.'

I still tried to walk more slowly. The twins stopped walking.

'If you slow us down,' said Kray Two, 'we'll go back and hurt the teacher, you understand?'

I nodded and figured I didn't really have a choice in the matter. I let the twins lead me through the poorly lit school at their own speed. It felt like being in a horror movie. When we approached security I saw the door was open, and the office was unmanned. I remembered that Miss Feeney had referred to the security guard as a prick when it was clear he'd let the twins in. I couldn't help but agree, because there was only one way they could have known I was here and the security guard was it.

Outside, it was warm and the stars were bright; a scattering of white dots strong enough to show despite the brightness of the sodium lights that ringed the road at the bottom of the school drive. The hiss of cars passing the school was incessant, and I hoped to see Jackie waiting for me, underneath the sodium light that lit the lay-by at the bottom of the school drive, leaning against whatever he was driving now my little maroon Ka had no tyres. But the only car there was a big Range Rover with tinted windows. It must have been the twins' car because Jackie wouldn't be seen dead in one; he said they were vulgar and ugly. He preferred just straight-up vulgar.

The walk down the school drive existed in the same time zone as a dentist's waiting room when you're waiting for an unpleasant procedure – it took forever and was also over far too quickly. We were buzzed through the gate, because now the security guard was conveniently back at his desk, and we headed toward the Range Rover.

'You don't need to do this,' I said.

'Do what?' said Kray One.

And I didn't have an answer, I didn't really know how to answer. I couldn't actually bring myself to say: 'Take me somewhere private and torture me to death,' because that made it too real.

But then I didn't have to.

I heard the sound of a highly tuned engine coming round the ring road, and then something low and bright green swerved out of the speeding traffic and into the lay-by, slamming on its brakes so that it skidded to a stop just past the twins' Range Rover. Then the reverse lights glowed, and the car sped backward, stopping a hair's breadth from the front of the Range Rover before switching its engine off. A gap in the traffic gave us a moment of quiet; I could hear the engine of the sportscar ticking as it cooled. The door opened and Jackie got out.

'Nice of you to make sure Mal got down here safely,' said Jackie, walking toward us, 'but I'll make sure he gets back home.'

'No,' said Kray One. 'Da said we bring Jones to him. We got to do what Da says.'

'He's us Da,' said Kray two.

Jackie stared at him, then glanced at his brother. 'Okay,' he said. 'I'll bring him then. You drive your ugly car, I'll follow.'

'We came in a Range Rover,' said Kray Two. He sounded puzzled.

Jackie rolled his eyes.

'And Da didn't say anything about bringing you, he doesn't like …' Kray Two paused while he thought about his words. 'Da doesn't like Asian gentlemen.'

Jackie grinned.

'You really wanted to say "Paki", didn't you?'

'The teacher told us not to say that word,' said Kray One.

'Yeah,' said Kray Two, 'you should say "Asian gentleman".'

Jackie decided to ignore that.

'Are we going or not?'

Kray Two looked to Kray One and shrugged.

'Suppose so – we know where he lives though,' said Kray One, pointing at me, 'so don't run off.'

But Jackie was already walking away and the other twin shouted after him. 'We know where he lives.'

I joined Jackie in his car. It was a Lamborghini; difficult to get into, noisy, uncomfortable and overly flashy. Exactly the sort of thing he loved. He watched as the twins' Range Rover pulled ahead of us and then drew out behind it to follow. Jackie's car felt like it was angry at having to go as slow as the other cars, and he changed up and down the gears needlessly, flicking the paddles behind the steering wheel with the ends of his fingers in an annoyed fashion.

'Are we going to run, Jackie?'

He shook his head.

'Mick might kill us though.'

He shook his head again. 'He won't,' he said quietly. His eyes flashed in the darkness with reflected light from passing streetlamps.

'How do you know?'

Jackie sighed.

'He sent both twins for you. If he was planning something illegal, he'd have sent one while the other was off being seen.'

'Oh,' I said, annoyed with myself for not realising that. I knew that. I'd let fear take control of me and I had stopped thinking, and Jackie didn't approve of that sort thing, at all. 'What do you think he wants then?'

'Well we're going to find out,' said Jackie, but he didn't look at me, just kept his eyes on the road. I suspect he was thinking about Benny Callaghan, just like I had been, but for very different reasons. Jackie – adult Jackie – had a pretty definite sense of justice that he was lacking as a youth. I hoped he wasn't going to act on it when we were in the middle of Mick's territory.

In front of us, the Range Rover turned onto the estate and Jackie swore as he followed and we hit a speed bump, making us both bang our heads on the low roof.

'This is a bad car for driving round the Edge,' he said.

He was right; it wasn't a car built for potholes and speed bumps, things the roads of Blades Edge were full of, and the twins seemed to take us on a winding journey that hit every pothole and speed bump it had to offer. It wasn't a trip that put Jackie in a good mood. Eventually, they stopped outside a house on a street that was entirely lined with cars. Quite a few of them were occupied. I saw shapes in the darkness, saw the occasional glowing coal of a cigarette or joint, saw clouds of smoke being blown out of wound-down windows. The Range Rover sounded its horn and one of the twins opened the door. He leaned out and pointed at the car parked in front of them. Obligingly, it moved so Jackie could park there. We got out the car. My back ached. Security lights on the front of the nearest house came on and I saw there were men everywhere: not just in the cars: leaning on them, in the garden of Mick's house sat around a table, standing staring in a threatening fashion. Everyone smoked, and the air was summer hot. Faces were serious. It felt like being at a funeral in a foreign country.

As we walked toward Mick's house, the twins double-parked their Range Rover alongside Jackie's Lamborghini, blocking it in.

'Rude,' said Jackie.

Mick lived in a council house the same as all the others on the Edge, but he had bought the ones next door on either side and knocked it all through into a mansion. I'd never been in his house, but I'd heard talk about it, and when we entered, I found out first-hand that I hadn't been lied to. The inside of Mick's house felt like a very expensive, and tasteful, hotel; there was marble everywhere, wooden floors. Lots of antiques. I saw a couple of grandfather clocks, which I was pretty sure were Fromanteels. Clocks like that started at about a quarter of a million pounds.

Jackie always said the idea that crime doesn't pay is wrong; if you were clever about it, crime always paid. Mick Stanbeck was living proof.

'What you looking at?' said Kray One.

'The clocks.'

'They're just clocks,' said Kray Two. But they weren't. Nothing there was 'just' what it looked like. It was all exquisitely chosen: the paintings on the walls, the furniture, everything. It gave the lie to Mick's image as a smelly old invalid.

The twins led us through the hall and off to the left into a library. It was hard to imagine the scrubby, potholed streets and tatty gardens of the Edge were just outside the walls of this house. Mick Stanbeck sat in a huge, antique leather wing chair in front of a living flame fire. He had a blanket over his legs and an unlit cigar in his mouth. Opposite him was another chair. He looked up, saw Jackie and pointed at the chair in front of him.

'Better bring another, boysm,' he said. Kray One brought over another chair, and Jackie and I sat down opposite Mick. The twins shut the door; it was a thick, wooden door, dark with old varnish, Victorian from the look of it. They stood either side of the door, only looking ahead, like carved bookends.

'Malachite Jones,' said Mick. He spoke softly, gently. He looked calm, but older than I was used to. Somehow, out of his mobility scooter, he seemed more infirm. 'I asked you a simple thing. I let you know how seriously I felt about it.' He took the cigar from his mouth and looked at the wet end. 'You didn't listen, and now this situation has got a lot more complicated than it ever needed to be.' He studied the cigar a little longer before his eyes flicked up to me. He sounded tired. 'I don't like complicated – it gets in the way of my business.'

'I don't—'

Mick raised his hand to stop me talking. By my side, Jackie lounged in his chair, as if he didn't really care that he was surrounded by huge wealth and violent men. If I'd asked, he'd probably have said he was used to it.

'I am going to ask you,' said Mick slowly, not looking at Jackie at all, 'some simple questions.' He blinked and put the cigar back in the corner of his mouth. 'And you will give me simple, and direct, answers. Do you understand?' He stared at me, little eyes in a round face, wisps of greasy hair falling over his forehead. His eyebrows met in the middle and the skin beneath was red and raw-looking. Little white flecks of dry skin clinging to the hairs.

'I understand,' I said.

He nodded. Took the cigar out of his mouth.

'I don't allow smoking inside,' he said. 'It's bad for the antiques.' He put the cigar down on a small round butler's table by his chair. I was pretty sure the table was a few hundred years old and winced, because juice from where he'd chewed the end of the cigar would stain the wood. Maybe Mick thought that it only added to the patina.

'Have you found the ticket?' His eyes locked on to me.

'No.'

He continued staring at me. Leaned forward in his chair. 'Have you given the ticket, to Russian Frank?'

'I just said—'

'Yes or no answers, please.'

'No.'

'Did you give the ticket to Benny?'

I wanted to scream at him for mentioning Benny, the way Benny must have screamed when …

'No,' I said, very quietly.

'What about Janine?'

'No.'

Mick sat back in his chair and let out a long sigh. He picked up the cigar and put it back in his mouth. Then he sat there, moving the cigar about and staring at the ceiling. It was like he sank further into his chair, became smaller. I felt like I had disappeared from the room. When he spoke again, he didn't look at me.

'I want you to go to Russian Frank for me,' he said quietly. 'Tell him, if we find the ticket, we'll split it with him. He has my word on that if he gives his word to do the same. And if he agrees, everything stops.'

'What is "everything"?'

His head came slowly down so he was looking at me. 'I didn't bring you here to ask questions.'

'Why don't you go to Frank?' I said.

He opened his mouth. I thought he was going to shout, but he didn't. It seemed wrong to have raised voices in this overly warm little library. Maybe he felt the same way.

'He can't go,' said Jackie, 'cos he thinks it will make him look weak.'

'I'm letting your Paki friend in here out of courtesy, Malachite, cos I may have been a little rough with you in the past.' He motioned toward Jackie with his unlit cigar. 'But I've not given the Paki permission to speak.'

'You are sailing very close to the wind, Mick,' said Jackie. He didn't sit forward, or even move from where he lounged in the chair, utterly relaxed. He looked almost as if there were no bones in his body.

'It's my ocean – I'll sail where the fuck I like,' he said. Then he paused, glanced at his boys waiting by the door and back at Jackie, who now stared intently back at him. 'But I suppose I am trying to teach my boys how to get on the world, and it's worth them learning that a little politeness costs nothing.' He tried to smile at Jackie. 'And because I want something from your friend,' now he motioned at me with the damp cigar, 'I'll try and be a little bit polite, how's that for you? Eh?'

'Asian Gentleman,' said Kray One.

'What?' said Mick.

'It's what the teacher told us we should call Pakis,' said Kray Two.

'I'm actually A Sikh,' said Jackie.

'And what the fuck is the difference?' said Mick.

'Well,' said Jackie, and he leaned forward, putting his elbows on his knees and resting his head on his hands. 'You see, it's to do with religion, culture and the partition of India …'

'*Part-ish-on*,' said Kray One.

'Shut up!' roared Mick, 'all of you!'

The twins froze, one of them halfway through getting his dictionary out of his back pocket.

Mick took a deep breath and sat back. I discarded fanciful notions of this being a place only for quiet and Mick turned to me. 'Will you go and see Frank or not?'

'It's not really a choice, is it?' I said.

'Not really,' said Mick, 'but I am trying to be polite.'

'We'll go,' I said. He nodded. He looked miserable, and for a moment I didn't see a gangster, I saw a sad old man.

'When you see Frank,' he said quietly, 'ask him why.'

'Why what?' I said.

'He'll know,' said Mick. He turned away, as if ashamed that I'd seen a moment of weakness, and when he turned back the gangster was firmly back in place. 'You might be better going alone too – I doubt Frank wants to see your Asian-gentleman friend.'

'Frank doesn't get to choose where I go,' said Jackie.

Mick shrugged. 'As long as he gets my message' – he stared at Jackie – 'I don't really care what happens to you. You've always been trouble.' He chewed on his cigar and turned back to me, breath wheezing in and out. 'You can go now.'

We stood, and the twins opened the door for us. I went through first and Jackie followed. He paused in the doorway and turned back to Mick.

'I heard a story when I was a kid, Mick, about a nasty little fish that lived in a small pond. All the other fish were scared of it, but because he was such a little fish, he couldn't see how small his pond really was and he became convinced he was the king of the ocean.'

Everyone in the room tensed while Mick and Jackie stared at one another.

'Have you ever heard that story, Mick?' said Jackie. 'Do you know how it ends?' Before Mick could say anything Jackie carried on. 'The little fish gets into the ocean one day, and a shark eats him.'

Mick stared at Jackie, then he shook his head.

'See Mal and his Asian-gentleman friend out, lads. We're concentrating on today's business today. We'll talk about fishing with them another day, eh?'

Jackie grinned at him, and the twins escorted us out of the building and back to our car. I struggled into my seat and Jackie started the engine as the twins moved their Range Rover.

'Mick was not acting like Mick,' I said.

'I think he might have overstepped the mark, starting a war with Russian Frank,' said Jackie, and he glanced over his shoulder at the busy street, full of Mick's soldiers. 'But he looks pretty well outfitted.' He turned back to me. 'It won't save him though – I'm not Frank. And someone is going to pay for what happened to Benny. That was not right.'

'Why is he ready to deal then, if he's got an army?'

Jackie shrugged. 'He's scared.'

'But why?'

'You're the thinker, Mal.' I glanced down the street at the cars, the men. It certainly didn't seem like

Mick needed to be scared of Russian Frank, and he wasn't scared of Jackie either – he'd shown that in his house. I turned over our conversation in my head.

'Oh,' I said.

'Oh?' said Jackie.

'I don't think he needs to be scared of you, Jackie.'

Jackie's eyes widened and his head jerked back, as if shocked. 'Are you underestimating my propensity for violence and well-deserved justice, Mal?'

'No,' I said, 'not at all. I just don't think Trolley Mick killed Benny Callaghan.' Jackie turned to me. 'That's the "why", Jackie. That's what he wants me to ask Frank. Why did he kill Benny Callaghan the way he did. And that's why he's scared too, I reckon.'

'Cos if it could happen to Benny,' said Jackie, 'it could happen to him.'

We sat quietly for a few seconds.

'But Callum said Mick's men took him.' Jackie's brow furrowed in confusion. 'Callum was never the brightest lad though, was he?' I said, and Jackie gunned the car forward and onto the roads of Blades Edge. I sat back in my seat, putting one hand on the roof so I didn't bang my head when Jackie hit a pothole.

Nothing made sense anymore.

Nothing.

25

We drove into town. Jackie was very quiet.

In another man, I'd think that he was worried. That driving right into the middle of Russian Frank's territory after he'd given one of Frank's men a savage beating and cut off one of his fingers was playing on his mind, the thought of what retribution may be about to come. But that wasn't Jackie. It just wasn't the sort of thing he worried about. He had a supreme belief in his own abilities – when it came to violence, at least.

But he didn't like puzzles; he liked the world to be straightforward, and to him it generally was. Good: people Jackie agreed with. And bad: people he didn't. For a man that ran a protection racket, among other things, he had a pretty strong moral code running through him.

'I could go see Frank by myself,' I said.

Jackie shifted down a gear, overtook a cyclist, passing so near that he nearly knocked her off her bike.

'No.'

'He won't hurt me if I'm bringing a message from Mick.'

'You hope.' The engine made a noise like an angry lion.

'He won't.'

He didn't answer.

I was pretty sure I didn't sound like I believed what I was saying, but if my voice shook slightly, it was hard to tell over the rumble of the engine.

Jackie let the car come to a stop at some lights and stared ahead as cars came through the intersection. I felt like every car that passed was staring at me. They probably were, as I was sitting in a lime-green Lamborghini. If you ignored the roar of the engine, it was too quiet in the car. If the thing had been fitted with a radio, I would have turned it on, but it was far too expensive a machine to have a radio in it.

'You want to hear him answer Mick's question, don't you?'

'What?' He turned to me, a sharp, quick movement.

'When I ask why, like Mick wants me to. You want to see Frank's face, don't you?'

'What makes you think that?' He stared at me. The yellow of the sodium light played off his sharp cheekbones, and he looked like a person drawn in a comic book from a few slashes of ink.

'You do though, don't you? That was the reason you wanted me to go and see Mick too. You wanted to know if he did it.'

A car horn sounded and Jackie looked up.

'The lights have changed,' he said, and he continued to stare at me while he slipped the car into gear and pulled away slowly.

'Don't get us killed, Jackie,' I said.

He didn't reply.

Russian Frank kept court in the city's only Russian club. It was called The Russian Club. I don't know many Russians, so maybe they're not a particularly imaginative lot, or maybe it's just Russian gangsters, or maybe it's just the Russians gangsters in this particular city.

We get a lot of grey cloud and rain; it doesn't encourage flights of fancy.

Jackie parked the Lamborghini outside The Russian Club on double yellow lines. Got out, gave the finger to someone who sounded their horn at him for partially blocking the road, then shouted, 'Fuck you, arsehole!' at them for good measure. Then he wandered round to wait for me to get out. It was a really low car, and I reckon Jackie must have practised getting in and out a lot to do it as easily as he did.

I won't lie, I struggled.

The club was in an old Victorian Methodist church. It had two big doors set within an arch of stone. I remember when it was still a church, they used to be painted red, and generally covered in graffiti. You had to go up four steps to reach the doors. The doors were painted black now, and you never saw graffiti on them. Above the doors it said, *Abide by the Lord thy God.*

On either side of the door of The Russian Club stood two men. Big men dressed in black trousers and black T-shirts stretched to the point of tearing by muscles that were, more than likely, at least fifty per cent steroid.

'I'm here to see Frank,' I said.

Neither of the men on the door so much as acknowledged I existed.

'I said,' I repeated more loudly, 'I'm here to see Frank.'

I may as well have been talking to statues.

Jackie walked up to one of the men, he barely came up to the Russian's shoulder. He stood on his tiptoes so he could talk right into the man's face.

'My friend. Wants. To see. Frank,' he said loudly, like a boorish man ordering drinks from a Spanish waiter. The Russian ignored him. Jackie said it again. The bouncer ignored him again. Then Jackie said something in Russian.

'A my nei terlis drug ob druga na tanspole v kakom gay klube?'That got a reaction. A tiny movement of the man's mouth. He didn't look happy. Then he bunched his fists. His face was starting to change colour, becoming redder and redder. Whatever Jackie had said, he really didn't like it.

'Not Russian. Not get in Russian club,' said the man on the other side.

Jackie grinned and slowly lowered himself back down from his tiptoes. Then he walked over to the bouncer who had spoken while the other one got control of himself.

'That is quite a racist policy,' said Jackie.

'Not Russian,' said the bouncer.

'Is it actually because I am brown? Because my friend, Mal, is embarrassingly white,' said Jackie.

'No.' The bouncer smiled at Jackie. 'It is because you are not Russian.'

Jackie sighed.

'Look, you just tell Frank, that Mal and Jackie are here with a message from Trolley Mick,' said Jackie. He took a five-pound note from his pocket and folded it up. Then he placed it under the tight shirt sleeve of the bouncer's T-shirt. 'He'll want to see us.'

'Not Russian.'

Jackie spoke to him in Russian.

The man took the five-pound note from his shirt sleeve. I thought he was going to flick it at Jackie – as bribes went it was pretty feeble – but he put it in his back pocket instead. Then he smiled at Jackie and said, 'Not Russian.'

Jackie turned around, walked down the three steps that fronted The Russian Club. At the bottom, he turned round to face the two bouncers. He looked very small, compared to them, even though he was pretty well muscled himself.

'I put Harry in hospital.' No reaction. 'You know, the stationer? I beat him until he cried.' The bouncer on the right's head moved, coming slowly round like a stop-motion statue from an old film.

'Maybe Frank want you in the club,' he said. Then he opened one of the doors and slipped in. Jackie turned and gave me two thumbs up and a grin.

'They respect strength,' he said.

The door opened again, and the bouncer re-appeared.

'Frank see you.' He said to Jackie and then motioned toward me. 'Frank says bring him too.'

Jackie brought me.

Inside, the club was full of smoke. It was strange, I'd got so used to there being no smoking in clubs that it took me a moment to work out what the bluey-grey haze was. Incense, I thought at first, then I saw a man take a drag on a cigarette and blow smoke rings to impress the elaborately jewelled woman sat next to him. They sat at a table in a booth that curled around them, upholstered in red leather, full of people, also with fags or elaborate jewellery, often both. Next to that was another booth, then three more. The same on the other side. In the centre of the room were tables set for dinner with couples sat at them. All the booths were full and there were no spare tables.

No one in the room spoke. Not one of them.

No music played.

They watched us.

Jackie seemed oblivious to it, but I felt every eye as I hurried after him. I heard every footstep – he was wearing expensive Cuban-heeled boots, Jeffery West's, I think. I was wearing Cuban-heeled boots too, Jackie's hand-me-downs. The tap of heel on floor drew the room's gaze, heads turning to follow us until we reached the bar at the end of the room.

The bar filled most of the back wall. It was very shiny: highly polished wood, a lot of chrome, a lot of optics for spirits, and a mirror that ran the entire length of the wall behind. There was writing on the mirror but it was in the Cyrillic alphabet, so I couldn't read it. I caught sight of a man in the mirror; he looked small and scared and out of place.

I realised it was me and tried to walk a little taller.

A waiter passed with a tray of food; he didn't look at us and I couldn't smell the food for the stink of tobacco. At one side of the bar was a door and Harry, the stationer, was propped up on a stool. He was pretty bruised. One leg was in a cast as was one arm, and his hand was swollen with bandages. A crutch leaned on the wall by him.

‘Hi, Harry,’ said Jackie brightly. ‘How’s the stationery business going?’

Harry didn’t answer. He reached back with his good arm and pushed the door open and we went through. I guessed Harry had gone down a bit in the Russian gangster underworld.

Through the door, we stepped into an office, where the walls weren’t clad with dark, old wood they were covered in neatly shelved books. At a desk, similar to the one in my office, sat Frank. In the corner of the room was the man who I guessed had taken Harry’s place. He was small, and very thin, with a sharp nose, and hair that he wore long and tied into a bun on top, shaved to the skin at the sides. Young, maybe late twenties. Jackie clocked him first and as he walked in, he kept his body turned toward the man, watching him and not Frank. The man didn’t move, apart from his eyes, which followed Jackie. Jackie looked him up and down and then nodded, turned to Frank.

‘I like the new help,’ he said.

‘That is Donald,’ said Frank, ‘like the president of America. Though he is not simply help – he is more of a specialist.’

‘I thought he might be,’ said Jackie. He glanced back at Donald, and Donald opened his coat a little so Jackie could see he wore a gun underneath.

‘An SPS, nice piece. Expensive. Though, of course, I am sure Donald will be handing that in to the authorities, handguns being illegal in the UK,’ said Jackie.

‘Donald is new to this country,’ said Frank. ‘He does not speak your language, never mind knowing your laws.' Frank grinned at Jackie. 'Why don't you try and take his gun from him?'

'Not my job,' said Jackie. ' … Today,' he added.

'Try though.' Jackie shrugged and turned toward Donald.

Donald did a magic trick.

One moment he was still, studying Jackie with a detached, professional interest, and then there was a gun in his hand and it was pointed at my friend.

'Ooh, you're good,' said Jackie. He turned to me. 'He's good, Mal. I did tell Frank he needed someone good, didn't I?' He turned back to Frank. 'You know, I like a man that can take advice.'

'You are very glib for a man who might be about to be shot, eh?' said Frank.

Tension. A silence in the wood-panelled room while Jackie and Donald stared at each other.

'He's not going to shoot us though,' I said.

'Oh,' said Frank, 'Jackie, I see your pet mouse speaks. And why am I not going to shoot your friend, and then you, mouse?'

'I think Donald is the one who'd be doing any shooting,' said Jackie. Then his voice became very serious. 'Or trying to.'

Frank ignored Jackie, just stared at me, but Jackie didn't see that because he was only looking at Donald and Donald only had eyes for him.

'Well,' I said, my voice holding remarkably well considering I wasn't actually sure he wasn't going to shoot us. And I knew that Jackie might well start something because of what had been done to Benny Callaghan. 'I think, before you do anything, you probably want to know what Trolley Mick sent me to say to you.'

Frank stared at me for what felt like a very long time. Then he nodded.

'Da,' he said. 'I find that out, then maybe I shoot you?' He was a man altogether too pleased with that idea.

'No.' I shook my head.

'No?' He managed to look genuinely puzzled, even though I was starting to become sure it was all play acting.

'We drove here in a lime-green Lamborghini,' I said, 'and parked it outside your club on the double yellows. Then Jackie shouted abuse at a passing motorist. They probably reported us to the police straight away – I would. So we've been witnessed coming here, if you kill us here, now, it causes problems. And you hate problems.'

Frank steepled his hands in front of his face, nodding slowly. 'I do not like problems,' he said, 'that is true.' He then spoke very slowly, as if thinking it through. 'You do realise though,' he spoke even more slowly, 'that you are likely to end up with a parking ticket as this is a permit-controlled zone.'

'Small price, really,' said Jackie.

Frank nodded again. 'Sixty pounds,' he said, 'though if you pay it quickly, it is only thirty.' Then he said something in Russian and Donald made his gun vanish again. 'What is this message Mick Stanbeck sends me?'

'He says, if the ticket is found, he'll split it with you, fifty-fifty. But only if all the fighting stops now. No more firebombs. No more stabbings.'

Frank stared at me, I had the strangest feeling he thought I was joking. He took a deep breath, closed his eyes.

'It seems Trolley Mick has overreached himself, as you say here, eh?' He looked from me to Jackie. 'You go back, tell him eighty per cent for me, twenty per cent for him, and he can keep his little council estate.'

'He'll say no,' said Jackie.

Frank shrugged and then he leaned forward, and it was as if I had vanished from the room. All his focus went to Jackie.

'Have you ever thought, Jackie Singh Khattar, of running that little council estate yourself? You are small-time now, I know. But with my backing then …'

'Offer him sixty-forty in your favour,' I said. 'I reckon he'll go for it.'

Frank continued to ignore me, all his attention on Jackie.

'Well?' he said.

'I like being my own man.'

Frank nodded to himself. He seemed distracted, bored with us.

'Eighty-twenty,' he said. 'That is my offer.'

I stared at him, knowing Mick would never go for it. Then, I had a sudden flash, like an overlay of an older reality and something that I'd thought odd about Frank, all these trappings of the west: his name, the other names, Harry, Donald, all of it finally made sense.

‘Are you okay, Mr Jones? You look very far away?.’ he said. ‘Are you communing with the spirits?’

‘Remember when you were a kid, and you used to sit on your mother’s knee and watch American films? Remember’ – I was going to say ‘how you’ but I tripped over the words and that wasn’t what came out – ‘how she loved all the heroes? The way they chose what was best for others over what was best for themselves?’

I stopped talking and realised everyone was looking at me. Jackie, Frank, even Donald seemed slightly interested. Frank tapped his pen on the desk, nodding quietly while staring at me as if murder might be a good idea.

‘Very well,’ he said. ‘I am a fool not to listen when the spirits speak, eh? Mick gets thirty five percent, and he should be happy with that. Now, Malachite Jones, hurry and find this ticket, or you’ll have both Mick and I wanting to cut off your fingers.’ He laughed like it was the best joke ever.

It was not the best joke ever, but it was my turn to nod. I began to turn away, as if I was finished, and then hit him with the final question. Always best to catch someone off balance if you want them to betray something. Columbo taught me that.

Jackie hadn’t moved; he was watching Frank like a hawk, waiting for the moment.

‘One other thing, Frank. Mick wanted to know why,’ I said.

‘Why?’ said Frank. I could see his mind working behind his eyes.

‘Yeah, why. You know. Benny.’

Frank nodded once but kept his head down so I couldn’t see his face.

‘Benny,’ he said. ‘Benny Callaghan.’ He looked up. ‘Well, you know, lessons must be taught to some people, eh?’

I don’t know what I expected to happen. Maybe I expected Jackie to make a leap for Donald, for Frank to go for a gun under the table and for the room to erupt in gunfire.

Nothing happened.

‘Well, we better go then,’ I said, and took a breath. Frank nodded.

‘Mr Jones,’ he said, ‘tell my mother I miss her.’

‘She knows,’ I replied, because it’s always the best answer.

He nodded again and sat back in his chair, our audience definitely over.

We left, making our way back out through the smoky club where music was playing now, and past the racist bouncers into the uncomfortable but expensive, and as yet unticketed, car. Jackie put it into gear and made the wheels screech as he pulled away.

‘Bastard,’ he said. He sounded furious.

‘He didn’t do it, Jackie.’ Jackie glanced at me, chewed on the inside of his lip and looked away.

‘He said he did it.’

‘Only when I gave him Benny’s name, he put it together then. Thought he would take credit for it. It won’t harm his reputation any if people think he tortured Benny Callaghan to death. But when I asked why, I was looking into his face – he had no idea what I was talking about.'

Jackie thought about that for a bit. Then he said, 'Fuck.' It was hard to disagree.

I sent a text to Mick, telling him what deal Frank had offered, adding that he had said Benny was just business. A reply came back.

I'll deal with Frank. You find ticket.

I read it out to Jackie, and he nodded to himself.

'I'll drop you at yours,' said Jackie, his voice dull, his mind somewhere else.

'I thought you were staying?'

'You're safe now. They both want you to find the ticket, war is over, so they'll back off.'

'Until they realise I can't find it.'

'Yeah,' he said. 'That will probably annoy them. We'll deal with that when we come to it.' He was driving sedately, always a sign something was on his mind.

'What about the other player, Jackie?'

'Other?' said Jackie, though he knew exactly what I was talking about.

'If Mick or Frank didn't kill Benny. Someone else must have.'

'Yeah,' said Jackie. 'You know, the more I think about it, the less Mick and Frank make sense for it. Maybe someone in one of their organisations got big ideas, thought Benny had the money.' He shifted his grip on the steering wheel. 'A pro would never have left the body there, not alive anyway.'

'If I get kidnapped and tortured to death, is it better it's done by a professional or an enthusiastic amateur?'

'Either way, I'd avenge you.'

'That's what friends are for,' I said.

'I'd do it for anyone,' said Jackie. 'No one deserves to die like that.'

That put a dampener on the conversation, and we drove on in silence for a while. But there was something nagging at me, and I needed to ask it.

'Was Donald really good, or just a man who knew a flashy trick with a gun?'

'Donald, if I had to guess, is ex-FSB, they are the guys who took over from the KGB.'

'I knew that.'

I didn't know that.

'That gun he had, the SPS?' He glanced at me, I nodded even though it wasn't really the sort of information I retained. 'Well, that particular model of gun was only ever handed out to Vladimir Putin's bodyguards or other 'specialists' of a similar calibre. So the answer to your question, "Is Donald good?" is yes. Donald is good, probably very good.'

'Better than you?'

Jackie stared ahead. Then glanced at me, a twinkle in his eye.

'No.' I felt something in me relax. 'But,' and it tensed up again, 'I'm an all-rounder. Donald is probably a shooter, and he specialises in that. I don't get to practise as much as I'd like with a gun. So, if it was guns? Well, who knows?'

'That's comforting.'

'Well, if Donald was coming for you, it would at least be quick, there's that.'

'Thanks.'

He didn't reply, just brought the car to a stop outside my shop.

'Mal,' said Jackie as I struggled to get out.

'Yeah?'

'The film thing, with Frank, I get that. But how did you know about his mother?'

'I didn't. I just knew that the Russians are a sentimental people.'

Jackie stared at me, deep-set brown eyes beneath furrowed black eyebrows. He laughed.

'You know he's not Russian, right?'

'What?'

'Yeah, I think he's Ukrainian.' He revved the engine. 'Anyway, see you. Places to be.'

It had been a long night and I'd had no sleep. As I stumbled up to my door I heard someone inside. I glanced behind me, Jackie's car was already heading down the road and the dry heat of the night was being replaced by the dryer heat of the day.

'At least it will be quick,' I said to myself and pushed the door open.

26

SATURDAY

Jackie used to put me in a chokehold.

'I'm going to put you in a rear chokehold.'

'Please don't.'

'I'm going to put you in a rear chokehold, and I want you to try and stop me.'

'I don't know how.'

'I'll show you.'

And he did. He taught me to find purchase and push back, to try and smash my attacker into something hard to loosen their grip. Showed me how to use my height to my advantage. He told me to push my chin down as soon as I realised what was going on, to try and stop them locking their arms around my throat. He told me to go for the fingers or stamp hard on the instep of my attacker's foot; enough pain and someone will nearly always let go. Then he taught me how to throw my opponent, by ducking and pushing my hips back, which turned out to be much easier than I expected. Unless Jackie decided to make it hard, which he tended to.

We went to the hospital four times: three times because Jackie choked me into unconsciousness and once because I broke his little finger. That was also the day he said I had learned as much as I could about escaping from a chokehold.

The noise I heard was the kettle. Beryl stuck her head around the door of the back office and grunted something at me as I entered. She had a sixth sense for when Jackie wasn't here. I don't know what he had done to her, but she avoided him like the plague.

'Mrs Carling is due in at ten,' she said.

'Oh God.'

'If you've found religion she'll like that.'

Mrs Carling came once a month and paid fifty pounds to sit and share gossip with me about people I didn't know and try to get me to come to her church. The good thing was I didn't have to do much research, and I'd broached the subject a couple of times that maybe she was wasting her money, but she didn't seem to care. She wanted to come, and it was her money.

Some people come to me because they're lonely, but from the amount of gossip Mrs Carling had, I couldn't believe that was her case. She was very religious too; maybe she thought she was saving me and if it cost her fifty quid a month well, I knew people who had paid far higher prices for far worse vices.

'Is it Saturday already, Beryl?'

'Some of us don't lose track of time cos we do real work,' she said from the kitchen. 'Do you want some tea?'

'Coffee, Beryl, strong please.' I just wanted my bed, really.

'I'll make you some tea,' she said.

I went into the back and while Beryl was fussing over the kettle and got out the packet of 'Soulja Pep!'. I threw it away.

I'm going to get some proper coffee from Mr Patel,' I said.

‘Ponce,’ she said. Beryl didn’t like coffee, or people who drank coffee.

‘I need to stay awake, Beryl. Who else is due in today?’

‘No one – you’re not that popular.’

I tried to ignore Beryl, but she continued clattering about and was still clattering about when I returned with a bag of ground coffee and set my cafetiere to brewing.

‘Oh,’ she said, ‘Mrs Carling’s dog died last week. It was a cockapoo called Napoleon.’

‘Was it a nice dog?’

‘She loved it.’

‘That’s not an answer. Did it bite anyone?’

‘No one who didn’t deserve it.’ Beryl thought everyone deserved it though, so that wasn’t helpful either.

‘Was it an awful dog, Beryl?’

‘I don’t like to speak ill of the dead.’ Again, not an exact truth. ‘Mrs Carling loved it, and that’s what matters.’

‘Okay.’ I said. ‘I’m going to lie down for a bit.’

‘What about your poncy drink?’ I gave her my version of a hard stare; it had no effect. Then I poured out a cup of coffee.

‘Did you know Larry Stanbeck, Beryl?’ I can’t believe I hadn’t asked her this.

‘You already asked me that. I told you he was a shit.’

‘Yes, but you say that about all men though. Apart from me.’

‘You don’t count as a man.’

‘Thanks, Beryl.’

‘It’s alright luv.’ She slurped her tea. ‘He did stuff round the Edge, you know? Helped out. I suppose he was better than the rest of ‘em. He were still a Stanbeck though – you don’t walk away from that.’

‘I heard he fell out with his dad.’

‘True. I’d like to fall Trolley Mick off of a cliff, meself. Most people would – even his own family hate him. But he knows where all the bodies are, don’t he? Knows how everything works, who owes who, all that stuff. That family fall out as a matter of course’ – another slurp of tea – ‘but they always come back, Mal. That’s why no one ever crosses ‘em, see. Even if a Stanbeck has fallen out with everyone, they’ll go back one day and they’ll remember what you did. And Mick loves his family – I’ll say that about him – almost as much as he hates people who let him down.’

‘Thanks, Beryl, that was cheery to hear.’

The doorbell rang.

‘That’ll be Mrs Carling,’ she said. ‘You should brush your hair – you look like shit.’

Mrs Carling was more emotional than I had ever seen her be before. She clearly cared a lot more about Napoleon the cockapoo than she had ever done about Mr Carling, who I gather had been a little too quiet for Mrs Carling. I often complain about the people I see as part of my work but the truth is I like most of them, even Mrs Carling. She was in her early sixties, brassy, still dyed her hair blonde out of a bottle, liked a drink, didn’t care if suntan beds would give you cancer because she had paid for her suntan bed and she was damn well going to get her money’s worth out of it.

Skin like old leather, obviously. I'd like to add 'heart of gold' to her descriptors, but I don't think it was really true. She didn't like shirkers, or left-wingers, and I was very careful never to ask what she thought about brown people because I didn't think I'd like the answer. She wasn't an arduous fifty pounds to earn, but I wouldn't choose to go out for a drink with her.

Not that I went out for a drink with anyone now.

I'd reached the point with Mrs Carling where I could switch off. I'd been a bit worried I might get caught in the 'Do dogs go to heaven?' trap which I'd fallen foul of before with religious clients, but Mrs Carling was sure dogs did go to heaven and if the Bible said different, it was wrong, so we were fine there. Napoleon was happy. He missed her. I'd thought of saying he was with Mr Carling, but I didn't mention it. Pretty sure I'd dodged a bullet there.

Bullets made me think of Donald, and thoughts of Donald led me back to Benny Callaghan, and I didn't want to think about Benny Callaghan: *broken hands, bruised face, missing teeth*. I zoned back in to what Mrs Carling was saying.

' … and anyway, every Christmas and birthday she was sending her nephew tokens for the garden centre because she'd heard he liked that sort of thing, and he was selling them to his grandparents!' She sat back and slapped the desk. 'Can you imagine?' She clearly couldn't. 'And at only seventy-five per cent of the what they were worth! I don't know what's worse, Mr Jones, that he was selling his presents off or that his own grandparents wouldn't even give him the ticket price. And him only being fourteen too.' She stared at me, I stared back at her. What she had said about her nephew had set off a train of thought and now I needed to get her out of my office so I could see if I as right. 'Mr Jones, are you alright? You've gone pale, well, paler, love.' She cocked her head to one side. 'You know, if you ever wanted to come round and use my sunbed, you could. You could meet my vicar at the same time, Canon Armitage.'

'I know Canon Armitage,' I said, standing. 'Mrs Carling, you are a genius.' I glanced at my watch: five minutes left. 'I don't want to appear rude, but do you mind if we finish now? I know we're five minutes early, but I'll add ten minutes on to next month's session for free.'

'Well,' she said, standing. 'Usually I wouldn't, but I do like a bargain and you do look a little peaky.' She started to gather her bags from round the chair, then paused. 'I haven't upset you, have I, Mr Jones?'

'No,' I said, 'quite the opposite, in fact. I've had a problem I've been trying to solve for quite a while, and I think something you said has just let me see what was staring me in the face.'

'Well,' she said, 'I'm glad to be of service.'

'Thank you, Mrs Carling,' I grabbed her coat from the stand by the door and helped her into it.

When she was gone, I shouted into the back. 'Beryl, I'm going to ring Jackie – I think he'll be coming round.'

'I'll take the afternoon off then,' she said. Then ambled out from her little office-cum-kitchen with her collection of plastic bags. 'I still want paying though.'

I didn't answer. She didn't care.

Then I ran upstairs. I couldn't find my printouts of the picture I had taken in Russian Frank's office at Maylin and Sparrow, so I had to find the picture on my phone, send it to my computer and print it out again. Then I dug out Larry Stanbeck's notebook.

When Jackie arrived, he found me at my desk with the notebook open, printout in front of me, paper strewn everywhere and a calculator in my hand.

'What was so important?' he said. He was wearing a tweed suit.

'I worked it out.'

'Who killed Benny?'

I looked up. 'No,' I said. He seemed to shrink a little. 'But I know why the lottery ticket is so important.'

'Because they want eight million pounds,' said Jackie. 'It's not rocket science, Mal.'

'No, it's not about the money.' I stopped. Smoothed my hair back. 'Well, it is about the money, it's just not about their money.'

Now he looked interested.

'What do you mean, "not about their money"?'

I told him what Mrs Carling had said about her nephew, and he looked at me as if I was speaking another language.

'Look, this is the picture of the house on Russian Frank's wall, right?' I pointed at the printout. He nodded. 'This is the picture, the same picture, in Larry Stanbeck's notebook.' I showed him the picture in the notebook. He nodded again. 'These numbers' – I pointed at what looked like measurements in the notebook – 'are not the same as the numbers on the big drawing.'

'Well, that's a sketch, maybe it just didn't work out?'

'No, that's not it. Right, see here, it says *TM*?' Jackie nodded. 'I thought it meant "trademark". But it doesn't. I think it means "Trolley Mick". And if you follow the "TM" line, it pretty much cuts out a third of the drawing. Now, add together all the numbers of the measurements attached to initials in the book on Mick's side of the line and it comes to about the same as the length of Trolley Mick's line. Add together everything on the other side and it comes to the same length as this green line, marked *FK*. I thought that was something to do with radios at first.' Jackie was still looking at me like I was an idiot. 'TM, Trolley Mick. FK, Frank Khlopenko. Add them together, what do you get?'

'Eight thousand, so?' He looked quite puzzled. He didn't enjoy being puzzled, so I hurried on.

'If you do the same sums but using the values from the big drawing – and you can – you get six thousand four hundred.'

'I really don't know what you are getting at here, Mal.'

'And you, a respected businessman and everything.' He frowned. I got to the point. 'It's their cut, Jackie – it's twenty per cent. One drawing shows all the money invested and by whom. The other shows how much Mick and Frank have to pay back. Those thousands are standing in for millions. The difference is the cut for laundering the money for all these other people who the initials on the diagrams must stand for. They match up. Micks line is thirty five percent of eight thousand. Frank even said it, "Mick gets his thirty five percent." It's how much he invested in the scheme.' Jackie was staring, mentally totting up numbers. Then he shook his head.

'No,' he said. 'That can't work. First off, twenty per cent is not enough of a cut for money laundering.'

'It is if it's easy. Like, if someone had a lottery ticket.'

'Maybe,' said Jackie. 'But they could just give back the money. There wouldn't be any need for threatening to cut your fingers off. And more to the point, why would Larry Stanbeck share his ticket? Mick, I can see, possibly. That's family, but Russian Frank? Why only take twenty per cent of eight million when you can have it all? It doesn't make sense.'

'It can't be a coincidence, Jackie, that the amount on the first drawing scales up to eight million.' He stared at the drawing.

'But Mal, if you have eight million, why mess about with all this?' He pointed at the drawing.

'That is a good point, Jackie.' I sat back down, deflated. 'I was so sure I had it.'

He spun the drawing round so he could look at it better.

'There are a lot of coincidences in those numbers though.' He tapped the drawing ' "ESL", that could be the Eccles Silly Lads – scooter boys out of Manchester. "BPG" could be Bradford Pride Group.'

'Aren't they racists?'

'There is a racist group called that, but there's also a gay pride group with the same name. It is probably the racists though.'

'Would they deal with a Russian?'

'Well, he's Ukrainian, but I've found people get a lot less racist when money is involved, and besides, they're on Mick's side of the drawing. Nasty bastards though. I can imagine them doing Benny Callaghan – vicious, sloppy, practically their MO.' He moved his finger around the drawing. 'It could have been anyone on Mick's side of this.'

'If it was laundering.'

'If it was.' He continued to stare at the picture, and I could see him mouthing initials as he connected them to people he knew. 'We must be missing something.'

Now I felt utterly deflated. I'd been so sure when I was bundling Mrs Carling into her coat that I had solved it, and now it seemed like I hadn't really found anything but a bunch of coincidences.

'Coats,' I said.

'Sorry, Mal?'

'Coats, that's what we're missing.' Such a stupid idea in my head, and at the same time I was absolutely sure I was right. 'Come on, Jackie, we need to speak to Mr Patel.'

27

'Mal,' said Jackie, 'what have coats got to do with anything?'

I turned as we walked, so I was walking backward and looking at Jackie. He wasn't smiling, not until he saw me smiling, then he was smiling too because the grin on my face was huge enough to make my cheeks ache, and Jackie's always been easily swayed to smile.

'I was right, Jackie, I was right about the money laundering, and I can answer all your questions about why Mick and Frank are so panicked about finding that lottery ticket.'

'By going to Mr Patel's shop?'

'Yeah, but he might need a bit of persuading.'

'I can be persuasive.'

My smile slipped a little. 'Don't be too persuasive.'

'Would I?'

I didn't answer that.

The bell rang as we walked into Mr Patel's shop. He was serving a couple who looked to be stocking up on all the out-of-date crisps they could find. It was still going to be more expensive than buying them from a supermarket, but I liked that they were supporting local businesses. We waited by the door until they had left, then Jackie shut the door behind them and turned the sign to closed. After a moment's thought, he also put the latch on.

'Mr Jones,' said Mr Patel, 'and Mr Singh Khattar.' His brow furrowed in confusion, 'is it that time of the month already? It only seems like a few days since I paid my insurance.'

'It's not that time, Mr Patel,' said Jackie softly. 'Mal just wants a private word with you, that's all.'

'Then why have you shut the bloody door, man? I need to be open for customers – they rely on me.'

'We need a little bit of privacy, Raj' said Jackie.

'I do not like it when you use my first name, Mr Singh Khattar.' Mr Patel wouldn't look at him. 'It is never for anything good.' He looked smaller, shamed.

'It's nothing, Mr Patel.' I walked forward. 'just a few questions. I need you to answer them truthfully. It's alright.'

He looked from Jackie to me; he couldn't have looked more uncomfortable if he had tried.

'It's about Cat Maudy's coat.'

Mr Patel turned away, opened the locked cigarette cabinet and started tidying it up. It didn't need tidying up.

'I have told her not to wear that coat. It is far too hot. If she has collapsed from heat exhaustion, that is not my fault – I have told her many times. You know this, Mr Jones.'

'She's fine, as far as I know, Mr Patel,' I said. 'I'm interested in how she could afford a fur coat.'

He turned round. He was holding one hand in the other, kneading the fingers in the cast.

'Maybe she saved up, eh? Maybe a relative gave her some money, eh? How am I to know how she gets her money? That is not my job.'

'You do know though, don't you?' I said.

He was practically begging me with his eyes to stop.

'I do not know,' he said, and his voice was barely a whisper. Then Jackie moved. He stepped forward, grabbed Mr Patel by the front of his apron and pulled him across the desk, knocking a selection of out-of-date chocolates and snacks all over the floor.

'Tell Mal,' he hissed into Mr Patel's face, 'what he wants to know.'

Mr Patel had his eyes closed so tightly his whole face had wrinkled up. The words he spoke were so quiet I could barely hear them.

'They will hurt me again,' he said. 'And next time they will hurt my wife as well.'

Jackie's face changed then. He put Mr Patel back on his side of the counter, ever so gently lowering him. Then he brushed the front of Mr Patel's apron and straightened it up. Stepping back to make sure it looked right.

'Someone hurt you?' he said.

Mr Patel, eyes still closed, nodded, and pointed at his broken arm.

'Why didn't you tell me about this, Raj?' Jackie asked.

'I was scared.' A tear escaped from his closed eyes. Jackie stood with his mouth slightly open, as if the words would not come.

'I would have looked after you, Raj,' he said, 'and Nasreen, that's what you pay me for.'

'Youths that smash windows, Mr Singh Khattar. Foolish druggies who threaten to smash up the shop. All these things, yes, you protect me from them, and you do it very well. But this man who came' – Mr Patel's eyes opened wide as he relived something terrifying – 'he was none of those things.'

'Tell me,' said Jackie, and he gave Mr Patel a tissue. Well, he took a packet of tissues from a display on the counter. Opened them, gave one to Mr Patel then looked at the price and dug in his pocket for the two pounds marked on them, which he placed on the counter.

'I got an offer for a good deal. Off the back of lorry he said.' His words came haltingly, as if he had to work up the courage to say each sentence. 'The man turned up as I closed the shop. We went in the back to talk about the deal. When we were in the back room, he hit me. In the stomach. Then he asked me if I knew where Larry Stanbeck's ticket was. When I said no, he hit me again. And then again, and he broke my little finger with his hands. Then he seemed happy that I was not lying. He told me if I talked to anyone about Larry Stanbeck's ticket and Cat Maudy, he would come back and hurt me even more. Then he grabbed my forearm.' Mr Patel lifted the arm with the cast on it. 'He pulled me toward the door. And he smashed the door on my arm.' The last words came as a sigh. 'Hard enough to break it.'

Every muscle in Jackie Singh Khattar's body was tensed, his hands bunched into fists as Mr Patel finished his story.

'And he said, if I told anyone, he would come back and do terrible things to Nasreen.'

Jackie's eyes narrowed.

'What did he offer you a deal on?'

'Does it matter?' said Mr Patel.

'It might help me find him.'

'You do not want to find him, Mr Singh Khattar. He is a dangerous man.'

'So am I,' said Jackie.

Mr Patel stared at him. He wanted mercy. He wanted Jackie to go away, but Jackie was angry.

'No one, Raj,' Jackie said quietly, 'fucks with my people on my patch. No one. Now, what was this deal he was offering you?'

'Cut-price stationery,' whispered Mr Patel.

'Fuckers!' shouted Jackie. He almost punched the glass display case Mr Patel locked his chocolate bars behind but stopped himself. He turned to me. Walked away. Paced up and down the shop three times before coming to a stop in front of me. 'The utter fuckers, Mal. Coming here, threatening my people. Absolute bastards.' He turned back to Mr Patel. 'Right, Raj, just so you know, and can feel a bit safer, the man who hurt you was called Harry. He is a Russian gangster. I beat the living shit out of Harry a couple of days ago for threatening to hurt Mal. But if I'd known he'd done this to you.' Jackie tapped Mr Patel's arm and Mr Patel winced in pain. 'Sorry,' said Jackie, 'but if I had known what he did to you, then I would have beat the living shit back into him.'

'Please, Mr Singh Khattar.' Mr Patel stared at the floor. 'Do not tell them I have said anything.' Jackie reached across and put his hand on Mr Patel's bicep.

'Alright,' he said, 'and you don't have to pay next month's insurance, cos I didn't protect you this month.'

‘Thank you,’ said Mr Patel.

‘Now, tell Mal what he wants to know.’

Mr Singh took a deep breath, nodded. ‘I think he may know most of it,’ he said quietly. He was still struggling to speak so I let him rest for a while and told him what I thought.

‘Cat Maudy won the lottery,’ I said.

Mr Patel nodded.

‘And Larry Stanbeck bought the ticket from her?’

Mr Patel nodded again.

‘He knew she did not want all the bother of it – the begging letters, the publicity. She did not know if she had ticked the box, see, to stop all of that. Larry said he had some business friends who would buy the ticket off her. But he needed me to say he had bought the ticket, in case the lottery people checked the CCTV or something.’ He looked up. ‘I did not know, Mr Jones, that his friends were bad people or I would not have helped. Larry always seemed so nice.’

‘He’s a Stanbeck, Mr Patel,’ I said. ‘They all have something wild in them.’

‘What about Cat Maudy?’ said Jackie. ‘Is she in danger?’

Mr Patel brightened then. A little smile on his face.

‘She is cleverer than all of us, I think. When Larry bought the ticket from her. She put all her money into a Swiss bank account. Then half of it was shared among her relatives who live all over the world. The rest was shared among various cat charities. The money is gone, and Cat Maudy is old enough that she laughs in the face of death. Or that is what she told me she did when the man visited her.’

'Well,' I said, 'you get back to your shop. And thank you, Mr Patel.'

We left, and as we walked back Jackie was staring at me.

'That's why they need the ticket,' he said. 'They've already paid out the eight million.' I nodded.

'Larry must have been the go-between, for his dad and the Russians. That's what his book was – nothing to do with interior design. He was money laundering. He must have seen the lottery result announced on TV, known Cat Maudy's numbers, and got in quick to make the offer. It's practically untraceable cash. So, they go for a quick turnaround, offer a cheap rate to every criminal enterprise they know. They build up some goodwill and pull the money together quickly, cos Cat Maudy is a sly old bird, she wouldn't wait forever.'

'But they lost the ticket,' said Jackie.

'Yep, and Maudy had spent everything they gave her – they're not getting that back.' I stopped walking. 'Why didn't they hurt her, Jackie? Even if she laughed in their faces, you'd have thought they wouldn't just leave it.'

'It's unprofessional,' said Jackie. 'It sounds like Frank is the one doing the frightening.'

'He didn't really strike me as a man with an old-fashioned code of honour.'

'Of course he isn't,' said Jackie. 'He's scum. But he's clever scum. She's an old lady with nothing to lose. If he hurt her, she'd call the police. So, if he wants to get answers by hurting her, then she has to die afterwards. Murdering an old lady is going to bring even more police in, and they'll come down on it hard, and if the money is gone, it's gone. But it would come up in a police investigation when they talked to her relatives. Besides, they might need her to vouch for Larry buying the ticket, if it ever turns up.'

'And she lives on the Edge,' I said.

'Yeah. Mick's territory. Frank was probably still tiptoeing round him at that point.'

'So, Russian Frank and Trolley Mick have essentially lost eight million pounds of other people's money, other bad people's money. No wonder they want that ticket.'

'And no wonder Mick wanted to stop fighting Frank,' said Jackie. 'They're about to become the least popular criminals in Yorkshire.'

'Can't they put together enough of their own money to cover it? Mick's house was full of expensive stuff.'

Jackie shook his head. 'No, Mick's worth maybe a few million, but it's all locked up in property and investments, or hidden behind shell companies. Hard to get at quickly. Frank has maybe five or six million, but that's not really his money. He works for bigger and far more dangerous people, and if he doesn't sort this, he's likely to end up having a really unpleasant board meeting with Donald.'

'I thought Donald was his new bodyguard?' Jackie gave me a look. 'Okay. So, how does knowing what they were doing help us?'

'Not sure it does really,' he said. 'In fact, now we know that they must be really desperate for this money, it probably makes everything worse. Frank and Mick have got a lot to lose here.'

'Oh,' I said. 'Well, that's harshed my buzz.'

'Indeed,' said Jackie.

We went back to my shop. On the doormat was an envelope which I ignored as post was almost always bad. I made shit tea. Jackie opened the envelope and then busied himself with pens and pencils at my desk while I racked my brains trying to think of some way I could find the missing lottery ticket. It didn't do much good. I made us chicken sandwiches and sat at my desk.

'What you doing?' I said to Jackie.

'Making a list.'

'Oh,' I said. 'What was in the envelope?'

He passed over a bit of paper. I read it as Jackie started writing.

> *Dear Mr Jones,*
> *I have decided that you have one week to find the ticket, or I will*
> *lose faith in you and have my friend 'punch' your ticket.*
> *Yours sincerely,*
> *FK*

I read it again, just in case I had misread it and it was actually an invitation for tea. I hadn't misread it and post is always bad.

'That's not good.'

'No,' said Jackie, 'it isn't.'

'What's on your list?'

He passed it over. It was very colourful.

'I've noted down all the initials from the drawing in black. In blue, I've written my best guess at who each one is.' He tapped the paper with the back of a pen. 'The ones I have underlined in red are the ones I think are both unpleasant and amateur enough to torture Benny Callaghan to death.'

'What about the ones with red stars?'

'They're near enough for me to visit, no more than a couple of hours' drive.'

'Red and blue star?' I said.

'Near enough to visit, and probably gave their money to Trolley Mick, cos I don't reckon someone on the Russian side would have gone after Benny. It has to be someone who knows Mick's organisation.'

'Do you think they know Mick asked us for the ticket?'

Jackie shook his head. 'They don't, or they would have come after you.' Russian Frank's letter had left me feeling quite unwell, that didn't help. 'They were probably torturing Benny to try and find out where their money is, or maybe to send a message to Mick.'

'Unless Mick told them Benny was up to something and set it up,' I said. Jackie shook his head.

'Not his way, if he really thought Benny Callaghan was betraying him, he'd have dealt with Benny himself.'

'If he wasn't betraying him, why did he even want the ticket?'

Jackie shrugged.

'Oh shit,' I said.

'What?'

'I'm going to have to tell Janine Stanbeck that the money isn't hers, aren't I?' I really wasn't feeling good now.

'Good luck with that. I imagine she'll take it well.'

I was going to swear at Jackie a bit more, but Jackie stopped me speaking by holding up a hand.

I turned. Callum Callaghan was in the doorway, stooped over, hands in the pockets of his ex-army coat. I mustn't have shut the door properly when I came in and the bell hadn't gone off. Callum looked rough, as if grief was eating away it his skin.

'Callum,' I said. He looked like he hadn't slept for days. 'I'm so sorry about your dad.'

'Thanks,' he said, 'thanks for trying, you know, going up. You did go up, right?'

'Of course. I'm sorry we didn't do better. You should have called the police though.'

He nodded slowly. 'Police wouldn't have turned up in time either, too busy with that bomb scare in town.'

'How long have you been stood there, Callum?' said Jackie, his voice soft and cold.

'Just got here,' he said.

'Why would someone do that to your dad, Callum?' said Jackie.

'I guess Mick felt betrayed.' Something dark passed over Callum's face. 'I wanted to see you, Jackie, actually, I was going to ask if you could sort out…' He let the words tail off. 'I can pay you.'

'It wasn't Mick,' Jackie said. 'We wondered if you knew who else might have a grudge against your father?'

Callum shrugged, took his hands from his coat pockets and clasped his arms around himself. 'Maybe he betrayed someone else,' he said.

'Well, don't worry, Callum,' said Jackie, and he sounded as hard as I had ever heard him. 'They won't get away with, I'll see about that. And you can keep your money, this is on me.'

Callum nodded his shaggy head. 'Thanks,' he said, then again. 'Thanks.' Then he turned and walked away, his body slumped over with the weight of grief.

28

I didn't want to talk to Janine Stanbeck, but it was unavoidable. She'd paid me and, somewhere in the back of my head, I thought of that as a contract that I had an obligation to fulfil as best I could. So I set off to her house, though I didn't get far.

I was quite glad to be pulled over by DI Esther Smith. She leaned into the car and asked me to come into the station for a formal interview. Well, I was as glad as you can be when someone asks you to come into the station for a formal interview. I followed her car to the station and parked up beside her. When I got out she watched me walk toward her, probably puzzled by how pleased I seemed to be.

'Am I under arrest?'

'Should you be under arrest, Malachite?' she said. DC Harrington loomed behind her.

'Not as far as I'm aware, and I prefer "Mal".'

'I know,' she smiled and walked toward the station. 'Follow me' – she looked back over her shoulder– 'Malachite.' I followed her into the station, and she signed me in at the front desk. Introduced me as someone she 'was going to have a quick chat with' and asked which interview rooms were free. We went from there to the interview room and sat down.

'Do you want a drink?' she said. 'Coffee, tea, something cold?'

'A solicitor?'

'Do you need one?'

'I am in a police station.'

'It's just for a chat.'

‘You won’t be putting that on then?’ I pointed at the recorder on the table between us.

‘Well, I will, but that’s just to protect us both, you see?’ She grinned at me. She had the most bright and sparkly eyes of anyone I had ever seen. ‘So no one can accuse anyone of saying something they didn’t.’

‘And so you have a record of what was said.’

‘Well, that is useful too.’ She pressed record on the machine and did her little speech, giving the date and time and who was present. ‘Now, Malachite, you know Benny Callaghan, right?’

‘Yes.’ My heart sank a little.

‘Well, I’m afraid he’s dead.’

Broken fingers. Bloodied face.

‘I’d heard.’ Jackie always says, if you’re in a police interview and you did it, get a solicitor and go ‘no comment’. But if you’re in an informal interview and they’re just digging, then give short answers that are easy to keep track of and don’t offer any new information. He’s done a lot more of this than I have, so I reckon taking his advice would be a good thing. I mean, I have done quite a few police interviews, but they were mostly done in the shy haze of drug or alcohol withdrawal.

‘Bomb scares, fires, murders.’ She smiled at me and let out a little laugh. ‘It’s all go this week.’ Then she leaned forward, suddenly serious. ‘Who told you Benny was dead?’

I shrugged.

‘It must have been a shock, finding out someone you knew had died.’

‘I didn’t know him well.’

She stared at me.

'You were round Mick's house last night,' she said. 'Then you went into town to a club known to be frequented by some less-than-law-abiding Russians. What were you doing?'

'I went to give my commiserations about Benny to Mick. He asked me to drop a package off at The Russian Club, but they're not all Russian, some of them are Ukrainian.'

She raised an eyebrow. 'What was in the package?'

'I didn't ask.'

'And here's me thinking you were the curious type.'

'I'm not curious where Trolley Mick is concerned.'

She nodded and started to doodle something on the pad of paper in front of her. 'There's been some bad blood between Mick and the Russians, recently.' She stopped speaking. I almost made a joke about blood, but images of Benny's body flooded my mind and the joke died on my lips. 'Odd, that they're suddenly exchanging presents,' she said.

I shrugged.

'Odd that they both have such an interest in you as well.'

I shrugged again. I was finding shrugging very useful and had decided it was the way forward. Maybe I should tell Jackie about my new strategy.

'What were you doing up near where Benny was killed?'

'What?'

'Your car was seen up there.'

What would Jackie do? What would Jackie tell me to do? Say something plausible.

'I like to drive round the moors sometimes.'

'So you know where he was killed then?'

She never mentioned the moors. I walked right into that.

I should have shrugged, but now I needed to get myself out of this. And I realised, belatedly, that if they had me in here, and knew I had been on the moors, then they would probably bring Jackie in too. Anything I said, they would check with him.

'When I heard about Benny dying and I went to see Mick, give him my condolences. He mentioned where it happened, and I realised I'd been up there. I'd even seen the smoke from the fire.'

'But you didn't stop.'

'There wasn't any reason to.'

'Or call the fire brigade.'

'I thought someone else would already have done it.'

She nodded, then put her handbag on the table. She took out some chewing gum, put it on the table. Took out her keys. Put them on the table. Took out a tampon, put it on the table. Then she took out a rolled-up bit of paper in a plastic wallet and lay it face down on the table. Then she put everything else back in her bag and put her bag back on the floor. She turned the paper right side up in front of her and pretended to read from it. You can always tell when someone is pretending to read, they don't totally engage with the paper and get lost in the words in the same way a reader does. After a bit more pretending, she spun the bit of paper round and pushed it across the desk toward me.

I was trying to think about what incriminating bit of paper I'd had with me at Richmile Industrial Estate that I could have dropped while looking like I wasn't worried about it.

'This,' she said, leaning forward and tapping the plastic wallet. 'is a warrant.'

'I think that maybe I should talk to a solicitor if you are getting warrants.'

'Well, it won't change what's written here, Malachite' – more tapping – 'so you may as well hear me out.'

I shrugged. It was a strategy that had been working well for me until I strayed.

'This warrant allows me to access the GPS positioning data from your mobile phone. So, if you stopped at Richmile Industrial Estate, for any length of time, I will know, Malachite Jones. I' – she tapped the wallet with each word – 'Will. Know.'

I shrugged. I didn't really need to, but it felt right and it covered up the shiver that ran through me.

She leaned forward. 'You are not a killer, Mal, we both know that. But your friend is. He is bad news, we both know it. What were you doing up there?

'Am I under arrest, DI Smith?'

'Not yet,' she said, and her eyes were no longer sparkly, but intent.

'Well, I'll be going then.'

'I'll see you out.' She gave a glance to DC Harrington, who left the room. 'Just a bit of housekeeping to do first, papers and such.' She grinned and produced a form. 'This is to say we didn't coerce you into saying anything. If you could sign here' – she placed a cross on the form – 'and here' – another cross. I signed. Then she stood. 'Right then, Mal, let's get you on your way.' She smiled and led me out.

As she was leading me down the corridor DC Harrington appeared, leading Jackie up it. For all the attention he paid me, I may as well have not existed. I was never quite as poker-faced as Jackie, and I couldn't hide my surprise. Though I probably shouldn't have been surprised that they had orchestrated this. When we got to the outside door, DI Smith stopped. 'If there's anything you want to tell me, Mal,' she said, 'now is probably the time.'

I shrugged.

The visit to the police station left me unsettled, like the edges of my mind were fraying; a tiny version of DI Esther was inside, picking away at me, pulling on my strings of thought. Even though I hadn't had anything to do with Benny Callaghan's death, I had still lied to the police, and when the records from my phone came back, she would know that. And it would look bad.

Really bad.

I had a record of shoplifting and attempted burglary from a long time ago when I was a different person. The new person I was didn't want my old record updated with 'accessory to murder', which would be a real backward step for me. I was sure there were more deserving people than me for DI Esther Smith to focus on.

I even knew some of them.

Leaving the car park, I nearly backed into a police car and got shouted at by the policeman sat in it. I really didn't feel like I should be driving about; my mind wasn't on the job, but it wasn't that far from the police station to Janine Stanbeck's house on the Edge. I owed her an explanation, at least. Even if I thought she might react badly.

Halfway through my drive, my phone rang. I didn't have anything as fancy as hands-free in my little Ford, and couldn't shake the feeling that police might be following me about, so I found a place to stop before I got my phone out.

Jackie had called me. I called him back.

Jackie: What did you tell them?

Me: Nothing.

Jackie: No, I told them nothing, you definitely told them something.

Me: Only that I was on the moors.

Jackie: Mal, you never tell the police anything. How many times have I said that?

Me: They knew!

Jackie: They suspected. Now they know.

Me: Well, they'll know anyway – she's got a warrant for my phone records.

Jackie: I doubt it, but even if she has, I told you, I've sorted that.

Me: But …

Jackie: Mal, if DI Smith comes back at you, what do you say?

Me: No comment.

Jackie: Did you tell them anything else?

Me: No comment.

Jackie: Not funny. Did you?

Me: I said we took a parcel from Mick to Frank. Said we dropped in on Mick to say sorry about Benny.

Jackie: You're an idiot sometimes.

Me: Jackie, I—

But he had rung off.

The police didn't like me, Jackie was mad at me and now I was going to go and make Janine Stanbeck, who didn't like me much already, dislike me even more.

I'd always thought of myself as a people person.

Maybe I was wrong about that.

I drove to Janine Stanbeck's house, parked behind a rusty old Ford van, and rang the bell. No answer. I stood back, trying to see if there was any movement in any of the windows, because I was sure she would pretend not to be in if she wasn't in the mood, but there was no sign of anyone being home.

'She's not in, love.'

I turned. An old lady in the garden next door was doing something earthy to some roses.

'Do you know when she'll be back?'

'Dunno, love. Might be a while, considering.' She clapped her hands together to get soil off them. 'It's the kid I feel sorry for.'

'Yeah, it can't be easy losing a father.'

'And grandparents.'

'Sorry?'

She did a good job of pretending not to be elated that I clearly hadn't heard the news yet, but not good enough. 'Last night, love, police were here and everything.' She took a pair of secateurs from her apron pocket. 'Both dead from what I heard. Some sort of car accident.'

'Oh,' I said. 'Best I don't bother her then.' But it was too late. As I turned to walk away a taxi drew up and Janine Stanbeck got out, dragging her son behind her. She didn't look particularly upset, but everyone reacts differently to grief, and I knew as I got to see a lot of it.

'What do you want?' she said. She put a lot of emphasis on the word 'you' and not in a very welcoming way.

'It doesn't matter – nothing important.'

'You wouldn't be here if it was nothing. Have you found my money?'

'Well …'

She stared at me, then fished her keys out of an expensive-looking bag, made of padded golden material.

'You had better come in,' she said, 'but you can't stay long.' She walked up to the door and slid the key in. 'I've had a hard night and the boy's tired.'

'I heard what happened, I'm sorry.'

'It was my dad,' she said. She walked in and sat at the table. 'Silly old bastard.' She bit her lip. 'Do you smoke?'

'No.'

'Neither do I. I wish I did though.'

'Was it suspicious?'

'You mean like Larry?'

'Well …'

'Can't you just ask them? They're in the spirit world now, right?' She didn't let me reply. 'I know, it doesn't work like that.' She sighed. 'My dad ran a red light, and they got hit by a truck. Killed them both instantly. Put the truck driver in hospital, poor guy – he'll never be the same again, will he?'

She slumped forward a little, hands on the table in front of her. She still wore her wedding ring and was twisting it round and round on her finger.

'I suppose not.' Her son climbed onto the couch in the front room and curled up. She ignored him.

'So, bad news always comes in threes,' she sat back. 'What do you have to tell me? I'd rather get it all out of the way now.'

'The ticket Larry—'

'Lawrence,' she snapped it out.

'Lawrence had. It wasn't his.'

She sat straight. Focused herself on me.

'What?'

'It's complicated, but the money on that ticket belongs to Mick Stanbeck and a Russian mobster called Frank.'

Janine Stanbeck nodded slowly. Then she laughed.

'Bloody Lawrence, he could never get anything right.'

'I think he'd worked for Frank for a while.'

'A while?' She stood, turned and walked toward the kitchen. There was a shiny logo on the back of her jeans, designer. 'When was he doing this? He was always off, doing his bloody Scouts or his interior design for …' Her voice tailed off but she didn't look at me. 'Frank? That Frank, his boss Frank?'

'I think so. I think Lawrence was helping Mick launder money with Frank, and the ticket was part of that.'

She walked back in and sat down.

'So, he left me with nothing then? The fucking bastard. Well, I'm glad he's dead. There, I can say it now. I was glad when I heard it on the day, but I had to play the grieving widow.' She had done that very badly, but I didn't think I needed to tell her that. 'No more. He fucking lied to me. I was trying to build something and all along he was lying to me.'

'Well …'

'Fuck off, you,' she said. 'You're fired, you can stop now. And I never want to see you again. You know where the door is.'

29

SUNDAY AND EVERYTHING AFTER

The false summer heat that had stilled the air for the past week was gone. It seemed spring proper was here, and though I had no idea of how to find the lottery ticket Mick and Russian Frank were desperate for, the sound of birds singing and the scent of cut grass in the air brought a sense of promise with it that made me think that maybe, just maybe, it was possible to find it.

I had no idea how.

On my doormat the next morning was an envelope with a note from Jackie inside. At the top was the name, address and telephone number of his solicitor. The note said to memorise it and call him if the police picked me up again. Then he said he was going away for a few days and not to get into trouble. Well, it said *STAY IN!* Jackie wasn't subtle. Aftooq from Spice 'N' Saucy would be keeping an eye out, and I was to contact him if there was any trouble. Jackie's list of gangsters was missing from the desk, so I presumed he'd gone to follow up on his suspicions that someone Mick had laundered money for was responsible for the death of Benny Callaghan. I pitied them if they were; something about his death had affected Jackie. And Jackie hated anything that 'upset his poise'.

And torture, he really hated torture.

But I couldn't get my own poise back either. I kept expecting DI Esther Smith to get the results from her warrant and turn up with a pair of handcuffs. The image of her coming through my door to arrest me with a smiling DC Harrington hung over me like the sword of Damocles. On the other hand, maybe being arrested was my best option. Better than my week to find the lottery ticket running out and Frank sending Donald to visit me, anyway.

For the rest of the day, Beryl crashed around in the back room and I barely noticed her. Clients came and went and I put in minimum effort because my mind was elsewhere, but they didn't seem to notice. I jumped every time the doorbell rang, but the sword refused to fall.

I wanted, needed, something to do, to distract myself but didn't know what I could do. I had nowhere to go. I drove out to where Larry Stanbeck had died and walked along the verge of the motorway, pretending I was interested in the budding twigs and branches of the trees that lined it when really I was looking for the lost ticket.

Nothing.

So, I turned to social media.

I don't actually have a social media presence. People don't want to see photos of their conduit to the spirit world throwing up by the pool in Benidorm – it destroys the mystique. Generally, I let Beryl do social media for me, and she happily spends half her time on it, arguing with people she doesn't know about things I'm not sure either side really understands.

But, I do have some social media accounts set up under assumed names, with no content, and each one, though I never post, has, weirdly, attracted followers. Which I don't mind – it makes them look a bit more realistic. I even have one set up under the name of a guy I knew at school who moved away to America and died. I am pretty sure no one but me knows he died.

I use that one to spy on people I used to know on the Edge.

So, I did very little. I saw clients, I listened to Beryl crash about, I watched people I knew but didn't interact with on social media. I watched numerous little fights between people I didn't like and tried not to get a vicarious sort of joy from it. I saw photos of three new babies. I saw pictures of the funeral of Janine Stanbeck's parents. Not on her account, mind – she was very careful with who she let be her friends – but on Mick Stanbeck's. I don't think he even knew everyone could see them, or maybe he didn't care.

At eight o'clock that evening, I had a visitor. Beryl had gone, and I'd locked the door. I was staring at a bottle of whisky. I don't know if Beryl knew about the bottle I kept hidden in a cupboard – she probably did. She knew everything else about me.

I wasn't going to drink it. I was almost sure about that. But I was bored, and that was the worst time for me. I was bored and scared and felt like I should be doing something, but I didn't have anything to do. So, I tested myself. That was why I had the bottle. Alcohol wasn't really ever my drug of choice, but it was legal, so I could keep it on the premises and not have to worry about the police finding it if they decided to shake me down, which wasn't unlikely. I kept a syringe in the same drawer, and an empty bottle of the anti-psychotic risperidone. I often say, when I meet a new client, that it is easier to talk to the dead if you have something that belonged to them; these were the belongings of someone I liked to believe was dead.

A knock on the door shook me from my trance. For a moment, I wondered if it was the police, but it was too polite. I looked through the spyhole on the door and saw Callum Callaghan.

I unlocked the door.

'Callum?'

As I opened the door, he took a step back out of the light and into the shadows, the streetlights behind him making his face a dark hollow within his hood.

'Can we talk?' he said.

'Yes,' I said. He sounded worried. 'Come in, Callum.'

He walked in, looking around as he did, and I realised he had never been inside before, he had only ever come to the doorway of my shop. Now he was in, he looked suspicious, a bit lost. He brought his hand up and rubbed the back of his neck.

'Have you come because you want to speak to your dad?' I said.

He shook his head. 'No,' he said. 'Oh no. Da was Catholic – he wouldn't have approved of me …' He waved a hand around.

'People change when they die.'

'He wouldn't change. Ever.'

'Of course,' I said. Best not to push it.

He pulled back his hood and scratched his head. His shaggy hair was a mess. So was he, red eyed and unwashed.

'Sit down, I'll make some tea.'

‘Not something stronger?’ he said and pointed at the whisky. I shook my head and picked it up, dropping my keys on the desk.

‘Not anymore,’ I said and placed it back in the cupboard by my desk with the syringe and the empty bottle of risperidone. Stared at them for a bit before turning back to Callum. ‘Come into the back.’

His eyes wouldn’t stop moving as I made tea with cheap and awful teabags – well, cheap anywhere else, but I bought from Mr Patel.

‘We didn’t get on much. Me and Da.’

‘I remember hearing you argue.’

‘Yeah, he didn’t understand me.’

‘I think parents and their children have that argument a lot.’ He tried to smile as I led him back to the desk and sat him down but he seemed to be struggling. ‘Are you uncomfortable in here, Callum?’

‘Mam raised us Catholic,’ he said. ‘Stuff like this …’ He shrugged, sipping at his tea.

‘You must miss your dad?’

He nodded. ‘He was my da, even if he just wanted me to do what he said.’

‘You wanted to be a mechanic, right?’

He stared at me, a curious look as he tried to work out how I knew that. I don’t think he’d been aware I was listening on that day in his yard.

‘I heard you talking to your dad. In the yard.’

He smiled.

‘Yeah, he didn’t like the idea much … Did he suffer, my dad? They only told me he was dead before the fire, from trauma. Wouldn’t give me any details.’

Broken fingers.

Broken teeth.

Torn flesh.

'Your dad,' I said, but I didn't look at him. Couldn't. 'I don't think he was a man who gave in easily.'

He nodded, stood up and walked up to the Queen Anne dresser against the side wall. Ran a finger along the smooth wood before turning back.

'Do you know who did it?'

I looked up and there was something feral on his face. Something frightening, and I realised I didn't know Callum Callaghan well at all. I'd thought he would leave the vengeance to Jackie but now I wasn't so sure.

I'd not thought about how lonely he must be. Callum would have been in his mid-twenties when his mother died. That must have hit him hard.

'No,' I said. 'It must be hard for you, to lose two parents.'

Now he nodded. 'Mick and Frank are friends now, right? You helped do that?' Anger in his voice and I wondered if I had made a mistake in inviting him in.

'Why did you think it was Mick that took your dad?'

'Who else?'

'I don't think it was Mick. Or Frank.'

'Who then?' He was staring intently at me, as if searching my face for a lie.

'Jackie's out there dealing with it.'

He came back and sat down opposite me, leant forward. 'He is not the only one who can fight, you know.'

‘You were never much of a fighter, Callum,’ I said. He rubbed his mouth, took a deep breath, then nodded. ‘It’s unusual, for someone who’s part of the Stanbeck organisation to leave the Edge.’ He sat back in his seat, blinked and let out a long breath.’ Your dad sent you to work on the farm so you could escape this place, Callum. Maybe you should think about that?’

‘I was going to come back when Mam got cancer. But she said not to. Said if I did, I would never leave.’

‘She was probably right.’

‘I miss her more than my da. I was at the farm when she died. Looking after fucking cows.’ He took in a breath, pursed his lips and blinked away tears. ‘Where has Jackie gone to?’ he said.

‘Away for a couple of days.’

He nodded. ‘The police said, if it hadn’t been for the bomb scare in town, they’d have got whoever killed my da.’

I fought down a shudder; Jackie and I had so very nearly been caught.

‘Life is like that sometimes, Callum.’

‘I wish the police had got them,’ he said and stood. ‘Everything would have been simpler.’

‘It’s often the way, Callum. Life isn’t simple.’

He shrugged. ‘Thanks for seeing me.’ I walked to the door with him.

‘If I find out anything, Callum, if Jackie finds out anything, then I promise you will be the first one I share it with.’

‘You promise?’ he said. I nodded. ‘Thanks, Mal,’ he smiled. ‘It means a lot.’

I watched him walk down, past the shops and along the road. He took a phone from his pocket and made a call as he walked along, and when he was about two hundred yards away a big four-by-four came to a halt and he got in.

I wondered who it was that he'd called that had come to pick the grieving son up, but I didn't know enough about him to know his friends. We all live in our own lonely little worlds.

30

The police picked me up at 6.30 a.m. two days later.

It wasn't dramatic. Two uniformed police officers knocked on the door of the shop. They asked me to come down to the station. I made them tea that they drank in the galley kitchen while I showered and got dressed. They didn't even bother to cuff me. We passed Cat Maudy as we drove away. She waved at me, still wearing her fur coat.

Outside the station was busy – a lot of people were being brought in. Some in the casual sports leisurewear I associated with Trolley Mick's people, and some in the black suits I associated with Russian Frank's men and women. Inside the police station was even busier; there were queues at the booking-in desks. Mick and Frank's soldiers were being kept well apart. Frank's men and women sat down at one end while Mick's men were being booked in. I'd never known the station be so noisy: the rush of voices in the booking room and reception, the sound of people shouting to each other in the cells. I was taken to the front, past a queue of Mick's men who, although they didn't want to go in the cells, were still annoyed that I was jumping the queue.

'We brought Jones,' said the constable who had brought me through.

'Put in him in Interview Four with the other one,' said the desk sergeant.

'Wait,' I said, 'if I'm being arrested, you need to book me in.'

'Do you want to be arrested?' said the desk sergeant. He looked like a man who'd had a long night and was near the end of his tether.

'Not really.'

'Then go with the nice police lady.' He gave me a false smile, and I did as I was told.

Jackie was waiting for me in interview room. He was sitting in a chair, looking relaxed. There were bruises on his left cheek.

'What are you doing here?' I said.

'Waiting for my lawyer before I say anything,' he said. Then he widened his eyes at me in a kind of 'Stop talking, idiot' way.

'Okay,' I said, and sat opposite him.

It's much harder to sit silently than most people think.

'I didn't know you were …' Jackie raised a finger to his lips. I waited. 'How did you …?' I pointed at my face. Jackie raised a finger to his lips. 'I saw …' Jackie raised a finger to his lips. I decided to go for theatrical sighing rather than speaking again. Eventually, his solicitor appeared. I'd never met his solicitor before, only heard about him. He was called Imtiaz Minhas and wore suits so sharp you could cut yourself on him. He had a permanent five o'clock shadow, and when he wasn't a lawyer, he was an imam at the local mosque.

'Jackie,' he said. He put his briefcase on the table and opened it before turning to me. 'Mr Jones.' He gave me a nod. 'Jackie has asked that I represent you too. It could be said that this may be a conflict of interest. I have to make you aware of this, Mr Jones.'

‘I’m fine with it,’ I said. He smiled at me and put his hand out to shake. He wore a huge gold sovereign ring on his little finger, and his hand was very warm.

‘Good, we’ll get on then, one second.’ He walked out of the room and I heard his voice. He was a slim man, but he had the voice of someone much larger – warm and resonant. Then he came back in. ‘I’m going to go through the files out there’ – he pointed at the door – ‘which handily means no one can stand outside listening in on you. I would still suggest you try not to say anything incriminating though.’ He walked to the table and closed his briefcase, taking it outside.

‘Now you can speak,’ said Jackie.

‘You think they would listen in on us?’

‘Of course they would – that’s why they haven’t booked us in, why they put us in an interview room.’ He sat back in his chair, put his hands behind his head and grinned. ‘It’s all good though.’

‘Good? That we’ve been brought in along with every criminal in and around the Edge?’

‘Yeah,’ he nodded. ‘If they had anything, they’d have arrested us. Instead, they sat us in here and hoped we’d say something they could use. Imtiaz will have us out in no time.’

‘Why is everyone here? When did you get back? What happened to your face?’

‘One at a time, mate.’

‘Okay, what’s going on here?’

‘Whatever peace Frank and Mick had broke down last night, four firebombings and three stabbings. How did you not hear the sirens?’

‘I was asleep.’

'Well, I heard the sirens, knew they'd want to talk to me so I came here and handed myself in.' He smiled. 'No better alibi that being in a police station.'

'You've been here all night?' He shrugged.

'Slept in worse places.'

'And your face?' He grinned at me, moved so I could see his profile, all angles. 'I went looking for Benny's killer.'

'And you found him?' He shook his head.

'I found lots of likely suspects, but none that were likely enough.' He stared at the table, then lifted his head, grinning again. 'These came from the BPG in Bradford.'

'The racists? Did they beat you up for being brown?'

He made a dismissive noise, a 'pfft'. 'Nah, they were pretty polite actually, cos I have a reputation, but they had this little clubhouse, and it had a swastika on the wall.' He leaned forward. 'And a picture of Hitler too.' He shook his head. 'Not having that,' he said.

'So you fought them?'

He shook his head again. 'No, I burned their clubhouse down, then I fought them.'

'Jackie, why do you …?'

'Hitler,' he said, shaking his head. 'Anyway, what have you been up to?'

'Not much,' I said. 'I saw Callum Callaghan.'

'How is he?'

'Broken.'

Jackie nodded. 'Not a shock – I imagine he'll be worse after the inquest when he finds out what they did to his dad.'

'Right then, gents.' We both turned as Imtiaz came in. 'I think DI Smith has overreached herself a bit in having you here. This' – he waved the papers in his hand about – 'is all very vague. In fact, with Jackie being stopped so many times and brought in, but never charged, I can make a good case for harassment. I'll throw in racism too – always makes them tread more carefully.'

'So we can go?'

'Ten minutes,' he said. And he was as good as his word.

Outside we walked to the car park with Imtiaz.

'Do you know what kicked off last night's action?' said Jackie to Imtiaz.

'From what I hear, someone firebombed two of Frank's cafes. So the Russians started firebombing some of Mick's places – I think they did the fish shop on the crossroads first.'

'Terry's?' said Jackie.

'Yeah, that's it.'

'That was a good chippie,' He said.

'Anyway, then they started openly fighting in the streets. Straight-up battles around the estate. So, the police swooped in, picked everyone up before anyone got killed.' Imtiaz stopped at his car – a red BMW. 'Some of my friends are making a real killing off this, and I barely even get a chargeable hour from you.' He grinned, shook our hands then leaned in close to Jackie. 'Listen, some very dangerous people are very angry – whatever you have got yourself mixed up in, get out of it.'

'Bit late for that, mate.'

Imtiaz stared at him and sucked in air through the gaps in his perfect teeth.

'*Jackie, tuhadi apni ta nokri hegia.*'

'*Dafa ho ja, Imtiaz.*'

The lawyer laughed, and he shook his head before getting into his car and driving away.

'What was that about?'

'He was just telling me to keep my nose clean.'

Jackie led me to his car, a big Ford of some sort. As I slid in, I noticed it said *HYBRID* on the dashboard.

'Never thought to see you driving something like this.'

'I had a lot of driving to do,' he said as he started the engine, 'and I like to do my bit for the environment.'

I watched him as we drove along, waiting for him to grin or make a joke but he stared fixedly at the road ahead. After a while his frown broke and he added, 'And besides, last time I parked something decent in the police car park, the pigs keyed it.' He started to laugh. 'Jealous bastards.' As we turned onto the wooded road that led to my shop he said, 'You were right, you know.'

'Right?'

'About the money laundering. You were absolutely right. Mick's people turned up offering a great return on dirty money, but it had to be quick. So just about every decent-sized criminal group was pulling together whatever money they could to take advantage of the deal.'

'I don't understand why Mick and Frank can't just delay.'

'Because someone let it be known that the ticket is missing.'

There were clouds in my mind from tiredness and worry. I wished that they would part. There was a heaviness in my forehead, and I knew I had missed something somewhere, but could not nail it down.

'Why are they attacking each other again, Jackie?'

'What?'

'If they are both in trouble because they haven't got the money, then attacking each other makes no sense. It will only make getting the money together harder.'

'Stress,' said Jackie. 'People do stupid things when they're stressed. They lash out.'

'Stress? Seriously?'

'Being a criminal is very stressful, Mal. Mick has a heart condition.'

'Mick?'

'Yeah.'

'I didn't even know he had a heart.'

I hadn't meant that as a joke, but Jackie thought it was and he started laughing. And when he started to laugh, really laugh, it was an infectious thing, and it got to us both, so we drew up to my shop with tears of laughter streaming down our faces. We had to sit there for five minutes until we regained control. When Jackie had finally stopped giggling and I was getting out the car, he turned to me.

'We're never going to find this ticket are we, Mal? It's impossible, isn't it?'

'Pretty much,' I said, and now we weren't laughing.

'I think I'm going to have to hurt a lot of people,' said Jackie, 'to get us out of this.'

'No,' I said. 'Don't. Just wait a bit.'

'Why?'

'Because you'll end up in prison.'

'Better than you being dead – that's where this is heading, Mal. If I'm going to hit them before Donald comes after you, it needs to be quick, before they expect it.'

'Just …' I wanted to give him a reason not to, but I couldn't find one. 'Just give me a couple of days before you do anything.'

'Why?'

'Because …' I rubbed the side of my head but I couldn't rub away the clouds of tiredness. 'Because there is something, Jackie, I know there is. I just can't see it. I need a few days, that's all.'

He tapped the steering wheel of the car.

'Okay,' he said. 'But not two days. Frank will be expecting me to do something the closer we are to the deadline.' He moved his hands around the circumference of the steering wheel, bringing them apart and together again. 'I have something I need to do tomorrow, so I'll be out of town until the evening. You have until I get back, Mal. If you haven't found something that helps us out by then, well, I'll get us out of this. No matter what it takes.'

'We're in proper trouble, aren't we, Jackie?' I said.

He nodded.

‘In the local vernacular, Mal, I believe you could say that we are fucked.’

31

In one of my many short and useless sentences of community service, I met a man called Kev. Kev was small, nervous and itchy and was on the final year of a ten-year stint for armed-robbing his way across Essex. He used to say that a deadline sharpened the mind – although I don't know what sort of deadlines a man who armed-robbed his way across Essex for heroin money would have, and I didn't ask Kev because he scared the living daylights out of me.

I wasn't finding a deadline sharpening my thoughts, and I was thinking about Kev cos he was always so antsy, couldn't sit still, and that was how I felt. Maybe Kev mixed up a feeling of impending doom with a sharp mind. I'd like to ask him about it, but as soon as he got out of prison he went straight back to heroin and overdosed.

I was the only person at his funeral.

Jackie has never been to prison, as far as I was aware. He would be able to look after himself, but it would be a waste of a life. And I've never met anyone who is as full of life as Jackie Singh Khattar.

I was trying to write things down, in a notebook. Trying to get all my thoughts together in one place so I could make sense of them. Missing lottery tickets, laundered money and a murdered man. Larry's debts. His son. Books with buildings of drawings in. Benny Callaghan. Maybe if I couldn't find the ticket, I could find something else. Leverage? Motive? A smoking gun?

But I couldn't write the things down that were in my head because my hand was shaking, and the veins in my arms were burning, and my stomach was cramping with nausea. My head ached, and I felt like my temperature was soaring, then I was shivering and unable to get warm.

I'd felt this way before. Nine years ago, when Jackie dragged me out of an empty house in Bradford and locked me in a room with a bucket, ten bottles of water and a fridge full of service-station sandwiches. I'd hated him for it for the first week. Screamed abuse at him. Begged for him to let me out to get a hit, just one. The second week I changed tack. Cajoled and whined and promised I would give up the drugs. Not once, for either of those weeks, did he answer me as I raved and begged. He just came in to empty the bucket, and after the first time I tried to make a run for the door and he knocked me on my backside, I didn't try again. I'm not sure how long it was after that until the night I tried the door and found it wasn't locked. Didn't open it straight away. I took my shoes off and sneaked out, walking in that weird exaggerated way they do in cartoons when they are trying to be quiet – lifting my feet really high because I thought that might stop the floorboards creaking.

It didn't, of course.

If it had, it wouldn't have mattered.

Jackie sat in a corner of the room twinned with mine. While I was locked in the room, never getting any answer from the outside, I'd imagined he was out partying, living it up. But he wasn't. If anything, his room had less in it than mine. A sleeping bag on the floor. A camping stove. The chair he sat in, sipping tea from a metal cup.

'Can I go?' I'd asked.

He nodded, didn't say anything. Pointed at the door with the hand holding his steaming tea. I opened the door and was nearly blinded. I'd thought it was dark, that it was night. But Jackie had just covered all the windows. Outside, it was summer, the heat like a fist; kids were running up and down the road screaming and laughing. It was like a film set, hyperreal; the colours too vivid, the people too beautiful and healthy. A world I could barely remember. I took a step back.

'The physical addiction is gone now,' said Jackie softly. I turned.

'What?'

'You want to go out and score? I'm not going to stop you.' His voice was dead, and in the light streaming in from the door, he looked grey.

'Okay,' I said. Took a step forward.

'Now it's about you though, Mal. I mean, I made a decision to bring you here, rightly or wrongly. That was on me. But if you step out there and score, Mal, that's on you. You don't need it, not physically. Only up here.' He tapped the side of his head. 'So, if you go it will be on you, and I won't come for you again. You'll have made your choice.'

I remember it felt like that moment lasted for ever. The sunlight warming me. Jackie sat there, his stare boring into me with all the intensity of a bird of prey. He says that I made the decision then, that I chose to shut the door. But if he hadn't been there, sat in that corner?

I know what I would have done.

And even though he went back to the army, or whatever it was he did, for a few years afterwards, he was always there. I always knew that Jackie was sitting in the corner, sat in my corner. Now he would go to jail, for me. Cos he got us into this. But I couldn't let him go to jail, not just because I needed him there, in my corner. But because he was my friend.

Without a friend, I was lost, and I was scared of being lost, because I'd had friends before. Other friends who came when I was lost, and they weren't good for me.

So, I sat in front of my book with a pen and my hand shook and I wanted so desperately to write something down, but there just wasn't anything to write.

I woke up in a pool of my own drool. My head on the uncomfortable pillow of an empty notebook. I sat up quickly, made a comical snorting noise like someone waking up suddenly in a film. Swore. How much time had I wasted? I looked at the clock. Swore again.

I had nothing. Nothing at all.

No.

In the book I'd scrawled a word. Written it down when it was so late and I was so tired that I didn't even remember doing it. It didn't even look like my handwriting, more like Beryl's unreadable hieroglyphics.

Daddy

What did that mean? It was the sort of thing someone wrote when they wanted help, but I would never have asked my father for help. One of the few good decisions my mother ever made was to throw him out. Many of her bad ones involved letting him back in.

So why did I write 'Daddy'? I had no idea. I'd not even called him 'Daddy'. He'd always insisted on being called 'Father'. I think it made him feel like the man he never was. I couldn't ever imagine throwing myself into his arms and whispering, 'Daddy,' the way Cristophe Stanbeck did.

The way Cristophe Stanbeck did.

And just like that. Everything made sense.

The temptation was to rush out of the door and start confronting people.

I didn't.

I spent the whole day with a pen and my book, writing things down. Making connections. Checking it out and looking for weaknesses. Beryl came in at some point.

'Beryl,' I said, 'did you write this?' I pointed the scrawled *Daddy*.

'You think I come to work at night?'

'Well no … but …'

She shook her head and wandered into the back. I forgot about her almost immediately cos I was sure I was on to something now. I tried ringing Jackie, but his phone was off. It often was when he was doing 'business', but it didn't really matter. The first part of this I could do myself. I checked my watch. Five o'clock. If I went now, then I could be back by six at the latest, I reckoned. Then I could tell Jackie, present him with what I had found out. Not with what I knew. Because if I didn't go out now I wouldn't know, not really. I'd still be guessing. To know if I was right or wrong, for definite, I needed to go and see Janine Stanbeck one more time.

Even though she wouldn't want to see me.

I ran into the back, found Beryl.

'My friend Lucy at the credit agency.'

'Uh?'

'I need to know when Larry Stanbeck ran up his debts. Can you ring her?'

'Uh.'

Half an hour later, I drew up outside Janine Stanbeck's house. It wasn't the first time I'd passed her house that evening, but it was the first time I'd been brave enough to stop the car. Then I rang Jackie again, no answer. I left a message telling him to meet me back at my shop.

Then I did nothing.

Just sat in my beat-up old car and watched the house. I think part of me was hoping it would be empty, but it wasn't long before I saw movement, and then I had to decide whether I was going to go in and talk to her or go back to the office and wait for Jackie.

I knew what the sensible option was: call DI Smith, or wait for Jackie. But I had no real proof, so DI Smith wouldn't be much use. And Jackie's solution would be violent, and I wanted to avoid that, really.

So I unlocked the car door.

Crossed the street.

Knocked on Janine Stanbeck's door.
We all make mistakes.

32

She looked good when she answered the door. The bruises that had been on her face when I saw her that first time in my office had faded enough that the make-up she wore covered them completely. She was dressed in a skirt, a tight top and a small jacket. An expensive handbag on her shoulder and her short blonde hair had been styled to make it look like she hadn't bothered styling it.

'What?' she said.

'I need to talk to you.'

'I'm going out.'

If I'd just waited ten minutes, just driven once more around the block, she wouldn't have been there and things would have been so different.

'It can't wait?' I said. She tried to shut the door, and I shoved my boot into the gap, stopping her.

She stared at me. 'Well, if you're that determined, you'd better come in then.' She turned and walked into the kitchen. 'I do like a strong man.'

I followed her, she'd been cutting vegetables and had left the board, the peeler and the knives out. Something was simmering in a slow cooker.

'Where's the boy?'

'With his grandad.'

'Mick?' I couldn't keep the surprise out of my voice.

'He loves his family.'

'I thought Mick didn't like you.'

'Cristophe makes me blood, whether he likes it or not.'

I nodded and leaned against the countertop behind me. She leaned against the island opposite me, against where she'd been preparing food. 'So what do you want, Mal, it's not about the ticket, is it? Now you've decided that it isn't mine.'

'Did you kill Benny Callaghan?' I said.

She stared at me as if I'd just landed from another planet. Then her mouth creased up into a smile, genuine amusement.

'Benny? Me? No.'

She wasn't lying. But I knew that. I didn't know how Benny's death was related to all this, but I was pretty sure Janine Stanbeck didn't kill him. Worth checking though. And it put her at ease as well, for when I hit her with the next question.

'But you did kill Larry.'

The smile vanished. Only for a moment. Then it was back, but it was a mask, not real. Not like the smile when I'd asked about Benny. And her voice was missing that one hundred per cent I-can-laugh-at-you confidence.

'No,' she said. But it wasn't true. I read people. I knew.

Did I know?

'Don't lie,' I said.

Yes. I did know.

'What makes you think I killed Lawrence?' Now she wanted information, of course she did. Because up until now, she had been sure she was safe. Now she wasn't.

'Larry told me,' I said. She laughed then, a little laugh. A bit nervous, but she was a woman who believed in herself and she pushed the nerves away.

'Are you going to take that to the police, Malachite? A dead man told you? I thought the spirits didn't just speak to you? I thought it "didn't work like that"?' She rested her hands on the top of the island work surface, her arms tensing like she was going to leap off it and attack me.

'You're right, it doesn't,' I said, and the tension in her arms lessened. 'They point you in the right direction, show you things you've missed. Like your boy.'

'Cristophe?'

'Yeah. You gave me what I wanted to see in my office, another Blades Edge beaten wife dressed in awful clothes because that's all her husband would let her have.'

'He was a bastard.'

'Maybe,' I said, 'but he didn't beat you up.'

'What makes you so sure of that?'

'Because your son misses him. And he avoids you. Cristophe hugged me, you know, talked to me about his daddy. There's no way that the child of a violent father would feel that comfortable around men.' She stared at me.

'I have never hit my son.'

'What about your husband?'

She looked away.

'I thought you were so uncomfortable in my office because you didn't believe in the spirit world. But that's not true, is it? You were uncomfortable because you were worried it might be real, that Larry might tell me what happened.'

'If I believed that, why would I even come?'

'Jackie,' I said. 'Because it would look weird if he offered help and you, desperate, sad little Janine, didn't take him up on it. Because he can be really insistent if he thinks he's helping. Because I think you really do want that ticket. Just not for the reasons I thought.'

She grunted.

'And what did you think?'

'I thought you wanted it so you could run away, but it was Larry who was going to run.'

'And why would you think that?'

'Massive debts,' I said. 'He was taking cash from all his credit cards, every penny he could get his hands on. And he started doing it the day Cat Maudy won the lottery. I thought he had a gambling problem, but I forgot to check back in his records, before the lottery ticket turned up. When I did, I found he never even had a credit card before. No, he was getting ready to run.'

She stared at me.

'I think you should leave,' she said, her face hard.

'You don't want to know what else I have?'

'Nothing!' she shrieked it, and then she moved. Crossing the distance between us in a moment with the vegetable knife in her hand. She brought it up and pressed it against my throat. Her face blocked out the rest of the room. Her breath smelled of mint. 'You have nothing,' she said. 'Nothing.'

My breath came quickly, I tried to back away, to get away from the blade and the wildness in her eyes, but I couldn't go any further back and I couldn't stop myself speaking. It was like my panic was forcing the words out of me.

'Did he hit you back, is that what it was?'

She laughed, a real laugh.

'Lawrence?' she said, her voice high and mocking, 'Call me "Larry", be my friend little Lawrence, hit me? Never. I really did walk into a door.' She laughed. 'Larry always just took it. He was pathetic. I married a Stanbeck, for money and danger and excitement. I got a fucking Scout leader who was sick of crime. He was going to take my fucking boy. He wasn't even going to steal the ticket, just thought he could use it as "leverage" to get his dad to "leave us alone" and give us some cash. What world did he live in? As if Mick would ever forgive him.'

'He loved you.'

I don't think she even knew she nodded. 'Leave the Edge. Start again, he said. He had false IDs, new names for us. Wanted to bring his kid up in some shit hole, thought maybe I could get a job in call centre or something.' Her eyes came into focus and she was staring at me. The danger felt very real as her eyes scanned my face.

'If I told Mick, what you did …'

'He wouldn't believe you. Even if he did, he wouldn't care. Mick needs me, and I've got the proof. Larry's false IDs, nicely hidden away, showing his son was going to betray him. He'd have killed Larry himself if he'd known he was planning to run away with his grandson.' She stared at me, licked her lips, the pressure of the knife eased a little. 'It is not too late to save this. If you can find that ticket, I will pay you to stay quiet. My cut of the money will be pretty substantial.'

'Your cut?'

And something clicked. Larry's workmate telling me he screwed up the numbers for the office outing. Miss Feeney, reeling off the subjects he was good at and never mentioning maths. Canon Armitage telling me how badly Larry had kept the Scout troop's books.

'It was you, not him, that came up with the money laundering idea?'

Something furious appeared in her eyes. 'It was all me. I'm Mick's fucking accountant.' She laughed. 'You think you're clever and you don't know half of it! Larry couldn't count his own fingers, but Mick couldn't have some woman showing up one of his boys, could he? And believe me, you'd have beaten Larry up if you had to brief him on the figures so he could get them past Russian Frank once a week. He had to make those bloody stupid diagrams to remember any of it. He just wanted to play with the kid, never gave a thought to how he would provide for me further down the line.' She stared at me. I said nothing. Then she leaned in close so she could whisper in my ear. 'If I cut you, here and now,' she said, 'Mick would clear it all up. You'd just vanish, Malachite Jones. No one would ever know.'

'The police …'

'You. Have. Nothing,' she said. She pushed the knife against my neck. I felt the cold pain of the blade opening my skin. 'And will the police really care if another small-time scam artist vanishes from the streets?'

'Jackie knows I'm here,' I said, lifting my head as if it could get me further away from her knife. 'He's expecting me at the office at six. He'll come looking.'

'That fucking Paki.' She hissed each word. My answer came automatically.

'He's a Sikh.'

'Shut the fuck up.' She screamed it into my face.

I did. Then I was staring into her eyes as she decided what she was going to do. And even though I thought I was good at reading people, I had no idea. But I suppose that shouldn't really have surprised me, because I'd had no idea all along.

She let the knife drop. Took a step back. Smiled.

'You have nothing,' she said. 'Nothing at all. Now fuck off, I'm going for a drink with some friends.'

I did as she said.

33

I drove back, annoyed with myself. What had I expected to happen? Had I seriously thought I could confront Janine Stanbeck and she would, would what? Hand herself in to the police in tears because she'd been caught out?

Of course not.

I hadn't quite expected what I had found, and it had thrown me, so I took the long way round on my way back to the shop, only to find my usual parking place filled by a rusty, old green Ford van. Which irritated me. I parked as closely as I could to its back bumper to make getting out of the space difficult for the driver, which was petty, but that was the way I was feeling.

Nothing I had done had brought me any nearer to finding the lottery ticket.

I locked the car and wandered over to the shop. The door was open, which was a relief. I needed to talk to Jackie. Maybe he would see a way of using what I had found out to stop Frank sending Donald to murder us; or a way to stop both of us ending up in prison because Jackie had killed Donald to stop him murdering us.

'Jackie?' I had to squint. He'd not put the lights on, but I could just make out his figure at my desk. Sat in my chair, which I knew he did to infuriate me.

'No,' said a voice, and I stumbled, trying to stop myself mid-step. No?

'Jackie?' I said again, though it was stupid thing to say, because it wasn't Jackie.

‘Sit down, Mal.’

I did, sliding into the client’s chair, more confused than anything because Callum Callaghan was sitting in my seat.

‘Callum,’ I said, ‘how did you get in?’

‘With a key.’

‘I didn’t give you a key.’

‘No, I stole it last time I was here. You left them on the desk.’

‘I wondered where they had gone,’ I said. ‘Why would you need my keys, Callum?’

‘To get in, of course.’

‘Why would you need to get in?’

I was being very slow.

‘You’re the detective, Mal.’

‘I’m not a detective.’

‘Well, you seem to have been acting like one.’

My mind wasn’t working.

‘But I’d always let you in, Callum. You know that.’

He let out a laugh. ‘Yeah, you really would. You’re such an idiot, how did you figure any of it out?’

‘Any of what?’

So very, very slow.

Callum flicked on the desk lamp. On my desk was the bottle of whisky I kept hidden away, next to that was the syringe kept in the same cupboard and the empty pill bottle. He picked up the pill bottle.

‘Ris-pe-ri-done.’ He sounded out every syllable. ‘I had to google these. Everyone always said you were a nutter, a clever nutter. But still a nutter. I didn't think they meant it properly.'

'Callum …'

'You really think we can risk you telling Mick about what happened to Larry?'

Oh.

What a fool I had been.

'You work for Janine,' I said.

'Not for!' he shouted, and he slammed the pill bottle down on the table. 'Not for,' he said again, more quietly. 'With. I work with her. We work together.' He sat back. 'You're not even meant to be here. You were meant to go down for what happened to my dad.'

Ice in my stomach.

Benny Callaghan's voice.

Look out for my son.

Not a request. A warning.

'You killed him? You tortured your own father to death?'

'He deserved it,' said Callum. No doubt there. No emotion. 'He hated that I wanted to come and work with him. Wanted me to go to some stupid farming college.' A crack in his voice. 'He made out like I wasn't good enough to work with him. Like I was too stupid.' His eyes met mine, and I saw the anger flare. 'He let my fucking mum die!' Then his voice became quiet again. 'But he was scared at the end.'

'Scared?'

'He knew I had more backbone than him. He was always, "Don't do that, Callum, don't do this, Callum." Cos he was scared of being a real gangster.'

'And you killed him for that?'

He looked confused. 'No, I killed him because he was going to betray me.' He stood and raised his voice. 'His own fucking son!' He was going to tell Mick about me and Janine! Tell Mick we were going to run away once we got the money.'

'That was why he wanted the ticket,' I said. 'To stop you and Janine getting it.'

Callum sat back down and leaned toward me, something desperate on his face.

'I had to know if he had it, you see? That's why I had to hurt him. Do you understand?'

'Yes,' I said. I didn't. But I don't think Callum wanted to hear that.

'But now we have the money from her parents' estate, see?' He smiled. 'We can get away. She'll be the brains. I'll be her muscle. We don't even need the ticket.'

Another piece, clicked into place.

'That's what you meant, isn't it, when you said "mechanic"? Not for cars, you meant a hitman, a killer.'

He nodded. 'Talking of which,' he said quietly, 'I have a gift for you. I think you'll like it.' He dug in his pocket, took out a spoon and a small clingfilm pellet full of a brown substance that made me swallow and want to reach out, to hold it, touch it, own it. Heroin. He put the spoon and drugs down and pushed them forward with the syringe.

'I don't do that anymore.'

'You could do though, one last time.'

'I don't want to.' I did. In the dim light of the Anglepoise, I only had eyes for the pellet of drugs. I wasn't kidding myself; I knew what he intended. What he was offering me wasn't a gateway into addiction, it was a way to end my life.

'You saw what I did to my da.' *Broken hands.* 'You saw.' *Broken teeth.* 'He always said I'd never be anything, wasn't strong, wasn't clever. He said Mick's gang ate up people like me. He wanted me to work on that fucking farm, with fucking cows. Knee-deep in shit cos that's what he thought I was.'

'He was proud of you for it.' I said. 'For getting out.'

'No!' shouted Callum, and he stood, leaning over the desk. In his right hand was a gun. He pushed it against my forehead. 'You shut up! Fucking shut up!'

Now I couldn't look at anything but the gun. My mouth went dry. The gun filled my world. I didn't know its make. That was my first thought, because you never know how you'll react to a gun until you see one. It was something dark and ugly and blocky. Jackie would know what it was, know its name, know how many bullets were in it, know its effective range. He would be able to reel all those things off.

I didn't need to know those things because I knew something more important. It was more than a gun. It was Callum Callaghan's self-worth.

'I am giving you an opportunity to go easily, Mal,' he said. 'Cos I like you, Mal.' He was looking straight at me. 'I didn't like my da, but I didn't enjoy what I did to him.' Was there something there, some note of desperation? 'Janine said I had to make sure he didn't know where the ticket was, cos he was close to Larry.'

'Did Janine give you the gun?' I sounded far calmer than I felt.

He nodded. 'She loves me. It was a gift.'

I looked at Callum, sad, downtrodden Callum. And I knew, for sure, he was as much a tool as the gun he held in his hand. It didn't make me feel any safer.

'If you kill me, Callum, you'll never get the ticket.' How much did he know?

'We don't need the ticket,' he said and pushed the gun harder against my forehead, forcing my head back. 'Why aren't you listening?' His voice full of frustration. 'Her parents are dead – she'll get all the money they had, and the house. We can run away with that.'

'Did you do that too, Callum, her parents?'

A little smile on his face. The pressure of the gun on my forehead lessened a little.

'You learn a lot on a farm, Mal.' He took a step back, dropping the gun to his side. 'It's heavy,' he said, lifting it again to show me. 'I loosened the break cables a bit on her dad's car. He shrugged, 'Little hole in this, little hole in that. Suddenly a car is out of control.'

'And she knows you did it?'

'She asked me to do it.'

Of course she did.

'She's using you, Callum.'

'She loves me.' He seemed so very sure.

'She has no intention of running away, Callum. She's Mick's numbers girl. All the stuff that everyone thought Larry did for Mick, that was her. She's not going to run away – she has a place in Mick's organisation.'

He stared at me, shook his head. 'That is not true,' he said.

'It is. She told me.'

'No!' A sudden flash of temper and he raised the gun, pointed it at me again. I turned my head away. 'If it's true, Mal, why has she got me keeping that gang war going then, eh? Making Mick weak, eh? Why would she even do that, eh, clever lad?'

I didn't know. Not straight away. Callum was right – it made no sense. Why put the machine that provided for her in jeopardy? But, like drops of water falling from a tap to form a pool, it started to come together. Larry, Mick's son, gone. Benny, Mick's right hand, gone. The organisation crippled and in desperate need of money.

'Oh Callum,' I said. 'I am so sorry.'

'Sorry?'

'You're a dead man.'

'Don't you fucking threaten me,' he said. 'I've got a gun.'

'I'm not threatening you.'

'And don't think I'm frightened of your Paki friend – I have plans for him.' The gun in his hand was wavering.

'I'm not talking about Jackie.'

'What then?' He looked so confused.

'Janine's used you to clear a path, make Mick weak so he needs cash. She's going to use her money to buy in, make herself Mick's new second in command. She'll probably take over at some point.

How long do you think you'll last, knowing the things you know? Because me and you, in this room, we're the only people that know the truth. That she had Mick's son killed. And she is careful, and she is clever.'

He stared at me over the barrel of the gun, and I thought he saw it. Thought he saw the truth, and that the only way this could ever end for him was in an unmarked grave somewhere on the moors.

The gun started to come down.

Then he shook his head.

The gun came back up, pointed at my forehead, his hand no longer shaking.

'She said you were full of weasel words, said you'd come up with something to try and save yourself. Well, I'm not stupid, Mal. You can't fool me.' He lowered the gun and tapped the syringe with the barrel. 'I'm going to give you one more chance. Okay? You can go easy' – he pushed the syringe forward with the gun barrel – 'or you can go hard' – he pointed the gun at me. 'Your choice.'

I waited a moment, hoping Jackie would come running through the door to save me.

He didn't.

I felt terribly cold. Knowing you are about to die is not a pleasant sensation. But the heroin, I knew that would warm me up. I would slip away in a warm infinity and I wouldn't care about Callum Callaghan or Janine Stanbeck or Cristophe or Trolley Mick or Russian Frank.

'What'll it be then, Mal?'

'Easy,' I said. Defeated.

Callum nodded, lowering the gun.

'I knew you'd go for that,' he said. 'Da always said, "Once a junkie, always a junkie."'

I stared at him, wondering if he realised he had quoted his father, but he seemed completely unaware.

'Do it then,' he said.

I remembered Jackie, sat in the corner of an empty room.

It's your choice.

I heard the voice of Callum's dad.

He never thinks ahead.

Time. I needed time. Jackie might turn up.

Something might turn up.

'I can't just do it, Callum.'

'Why?'

'It's the last time I'll ever get to do this.' I picked up the syringe and stood up. Took my coat off and hung it on the back of the chair. 'It has to be right, Callum. There are rituals I need to do, stuff to make it right.'

'You mean, like witchcraft,' he said. He was very calm now, sure of himself, conversational even. In his mind, he'd won.

'No, just things I need to do to make it right.'

He scratched his head with the gun barrel, ruffling up his thatch of brown hair.

'Like the whisky,' I said. 'It's there cos before I fix my shot, I need a drink.'

'Well,' he said, 'bottle's right in front of you.'

'No, not swigging it out a bottle. I need it from a glass, a tumbler. Lead crystal is the best …'

'Well, get one then.'

‘I haven’t got any. But there’s a mug in the bottom drawer of the desk.’ He stared at me, then reached down. I heard the drawer open, and he took out the mug – white with a black pair of antlers on it. He pushed it across the desk with his gun.

‘There you go.’

‘Thanks. I’m going to have plenty,’ I said, and I filled the mug two thirds of the way up. ‘Now I need a candle.’

‘A candle?’

‘Yeah, I like the light. And I need it to melt the heroin on the spoon with. There’s one on the desk, by you. Just light it – matches are in the top drawer.’ He stared at me. ‘Please, Callum. A shot of whisky, candlelight.’ Callum had gone back to staring at me. ‘Come on, mate. This is the last thing I’ll ever do.’ He shrugged and lit the candle. ‘Could you hold the candle, Callum? I’ll need you to pass it to me in a bit, so I can heat the spoon. Make my fix.’

He nodded and picked up the candle, holding it in front of his chest.

‘This is very good whisky,’ I stared into the mug. ‘High alcohol content.’ I lifted the mug up. ‘Cheers, Callum,’ I said.

‘Cheers’ he said.

He looked a little puzzled.

‘Your dad once said something to me, Callum.’

‘What?’

‘He said you never think ahead,’ I grinned, ‘and he was right.’

I threw the whisky in Callum’s face. The liquid hit him. The candle ignited it, coating him in flaming alcohol. He screamed, dropped the gun and started batting at himself. I threw the syringe in the corner of the room and ran.

First, I ran to my car. But someone had parked right up against the back of it and because I'd parked so near the van it was blocked in. I swore, kicked the car behind mine and headed down the road as fast as I could. I heard the door open behind me.

'Bastard!' shouted Callum, and he must have been shooting at me. It didn't sound like gunshots in a film. It was quieter than I expected. Quieter than balloons popping. Then it felt like someone punched me in the arm and I was swung around, fighting to keep my balance as I ran around the edge of the kebab shop. I thought of running in, but it was Monday and all the lights were out.

I headed for the woods. Running for the trees, not thinking about the growing ache in my arm or the pain in my lungs from running. Hearing Callum behind me but not near enough to catch me. Then I was among the trees, in the gloom. I headed in as far in as I could. Careening off the path. Crashing through waist-high bracken, hiding behind a tree. Willing my breathing to slow.

Phone.

I needed my phone. Got it. Dial. Answer it, Jackie. Answer it.

Jackie: Speak.

Me: Jackie I need you here.'

Words coming out in a rush.

Jackie: Chill out, I'm about five minutes away.

Me: Callum Callaghan did it.
Jackie: What?
Me: He killed Benny, and he's got a gun and I'm hiding in the woods behind the shop.
Jackie: Fuck! What type of gun?
Me: A black one.
Jackie: Listen to me. Turn up your phone and chuck it as far away as you can. Then hide. And Mal …
Me: What?
Jackie: Don't die.

He rang off. I stared at the phone, wondering what he was planning.

'Mal! Come out, Mal! This can still go easy, Mal!'

I dialled the volume up to full and threw the phone as far as I could from me, peered around the edge of the tree. I could see Callum; he was silhouetted at the treeline, and it looked like he was reloading his weapon. I got down low. The bracken was coming up thick. I had to force my way through sharp stalks, and I couldn't put any weight on my left arm. Blood running down my arm from my bicep. I was shot. He shot me. It hurt. I didn't want to die. I crawled on. Found another tree. Sat with my back against it.

I was shot.

Callum was loud coming through the wood. From where I sat, I could see the road on the other side of the wood as he strode through the bracken, gun in one hand.

'Come out, Mal. There's not much wood to hide in.' He was right. 'I'll find you eventually.' Also right. 'I'll make it fucking hurt! It can still be quick.' I peered round the tree, through a screen of gently shivering bracken. No sign of him to my left. I leaned around to the right. No sign of—

'I see you!'

Fuck.

He'd got in front of me somehow. Illuminated by a shaft of light breaking through the trees. Looking straight at me. Pointing the gun at me. I rolled as he fired. Bullets sent splinters flying from the tree and I pushed forward, first on all fours, then up. Zigging and zagging, keeping low until I hit a gulley that ran across the strip of woodland. Turned right. Trying to keep my feet out of the small stream so I didn't make too much noise. Back up into the bracken on the same side I had gone in. I heard Callum land in the stream with a splash.

'Mal?'

Don't answer.

'Come out, Mal.'

He took a step. Couldn't tell the direction. Toward or away?

'Come on, Mal. Still a chance for it to be quick.'

Two more steps. Coming toward me. Definitely. The bracken here was low.

If I moved, he would see me.

'Ma-aaal.'

If I didn't move, he would see me.

'I'm coming for you, Mal.'

So near. Sounded like he was by my feet.

'I'm going to kneecap you first, Mal.' The splash of feet in the stream. 'Then shoot out your elbows.'

Another splash of movement. 'This is your last chance, Mal.'

I nearly stood up.

Despite what Jackie thought, I didn't enjoy pain. Not even slightly. I could weather it if I had to, for a beating. But the thought of Callum Callaghan standing over me, calmly putting bullets into my joints and the ensuing agony was more than I could take.

If it had to happen. I wanted it to be quick.

I took a deep breath.

Heard a sound. An alien sound. Something not at home in this wood.

The sound of The Afghan Whigs. Tinny riffs echoing through the wood from the rubbish speaker on my mobile phone. I heard Callum laugh.

'You dumb fucker, you left your phone on.' Footsteps, splashing down the stream. Then I heard him running through the woods away from me, leaping over waist-high bracken shouting, 'You dumb fucker! You dumb fucker!'

A body landed beside me and I nearly had a heart attack.

'What a dumb fucker,' said Jackie. He grinned at me. 'You look pale, Mal – well paler.'

'I'm shot, in the arm.'

He put his hand on my forehead. 'Do you feel nauseous?'

'No.'

'Then you'll be alright.'

'What do we do, Jackie?'

'Do?' He looked surprised. 'We run.'

'Run?'

'He's got a gun, Mal.'

'I thought you'd do your action-man thing.'

'A gun is a great leveller, Mal. So, right now, we're going to run like fuck. Get ready.' He rolled onto his front and lifted his head. 'Still looking for you over there. Daft bastard. Right, let's go. Back toward the shop.'

Jackie grabbed my good arm and pulled me up, forcing me to run through the bracken, pushing me on. I heard Callum shout something but couldn't make it out for the sound of the snapping twigs against my clothes. Then we broke out of the wood, into the light. A hyperreal world full of colour and life and beauty. I heard four or five pops as Callum fired at us. Jackie let out a small cough, stumbled, but didn't stop running. Parked in front of the shop was his lime-green Lamborghini.

'Get in.' He had one hand on his chest.

'Jackie …'

'I said get in,' he shouted. I slid into the Lamborghini and Jackie revved the engine. Looking in the rear-view mirror until he saw Callum run from the wood. Then he hit the accelerator, sending us fishtailing out of the lay-by. He didn't speed though. I turned. Saw Callum climb into the van that I had blocked in. A moment later it came to life in a cloud of thick black diesel smoke and he rammed it back into my Ford Ka to get out.

'He'll catch us, Jackie.'

'I want him to.'

'What?'

He coughed again.

'How bad are you hurt, Jackie?'

'I'm alright, just tell me what's going on.'

'Janine Stanbeck – she was the money woman, for Mick. Larry was a front to save face with the Russians. She killed her husband. Had Callum kill Benny. Kept the war going to make Mick weak. Killed her parents for the inheritance.'

'Fucking cold,' he said.

'Yes.'

'Why do all this?'

He was gritting his teeth between words, as if to stop himself shivering. I could see his jaw muscles standing out.

'Larry was going to run off with the kid. She is going to buy in to Mick's organisation, become his second, take over in the end, I imagine. Callum won't make it out alive.'

'You're right about that,' he said. 'He definitely killed his own dad?'

I nodded. Glanced back. The van was catching up with us. Callum's hand came out the open window and fired off a shot. The van swerved from side to side.

'Definitely,' I said.

'Right,' said Jackie, and the Lamborghini leapt forward. Up ahead was Crais Curve and Jackie was accelerating toward it, but he wasn't really pushing the supercar. The van on the other hand was doing all it could to keep up. We hit the bend, G-forces pushed me back into my seat and I felt the grip of the bucket seat holding me in place. I moved my head. Looking through the slit that was the sportscar's rear window, I saw Callum taking the bend in the van. Too fast. Far too fast.

'You dumb fucker,' whispered Jackie.

What happened was inevitable. The van couldn't hold the road. It slipped sideways. Callum tried to correct. Couldn't. The van hit the barrier, bounced off it. Then, in a scream of rending metal, it spun around, hitting the barrier again and throwing off bits of metal as it disintegrated. Eventually, coming to stop, a smoking heap in the middle of the road. Jackie slammed on the breaks, skidded the car round in a tight circle and drove back, stopping fifty or so metres from the van. He got out. It took him a couple of seconds to straighten up. There was blood high on the back of his jacket. I got out and followed him.

I could hear Callum Callaghan shouting for help from the wrecked van. The closer I got to the van, the more I could smell petrol. That didn't make sense – it was a diesel.

'What's that smell, Jackie?'

'Petrol,' he said. Coughed. 'Probably from Molotov cocktails, or whatever he's been using to burn places down with.' Jackie was forcing himself on now, limping, his dark skin looking grey. He took a lighter from his pocket.

'What are you going to do, Jackie?'

'You go back to the car, Mal,' he said.

'But Jackie …'

'Go back to the car.' His voice. I knew that tone. No arguing with it. I turned back. Heard his voice again, low. Too low for me to make out the words. I heard Callum begging. Then I heard the ignition. The sound of flames and I heard Callum screaming. I turned. Jackie was backing away from the broken van with the lighter in his hand. He watched the burning vehicle for a moment, then turned back to me, forced a smile onto his face and tottered forward. He was only a few feet from me.

'He might have hurt me more than I said.' He coughed, blood stained his beard. 'You might want to call an ambulance now.'

'Jackie …'

'Tell Frank …' He was struggling with his words. 'Tell him … Callum had the ticket. That it burned. We did our best.' He smiled. 'That should get you off the hook.'

He fell forward. I caught him. His weight dragged me to the ground.

I pulled him over. His eyes were closed, and, despite the heat of the burning vehicle and the night, he felt cold.

So very cold.

Epilogue

I'd always hated funerals. I hated this one more than most.

The bullet hit Jackie high in the back. It passed straight through his lung, nicked an artery and cracked a rib on its way out. If we'd gone straight to hospital, he'd have been alright, apparently.

But we didn't.

So, Jackie was placed in an induced coma due to blood loss. He was in intensive care for two weeks, and it was touch and go for most of it. I visited him every day, didn't really have anyone else to talk to.

'What you looking so morose about, Mal? I'm the one in a wheelchair.'

He'd got out of hospital two days before. I'm not sure how being shot in the lung meant you had to be pushed about in a wheelchair, but I wasn't going to argue with Jackie about that, not yet. I hadn't wanted to come to Larry Stanbeck's funeral, but Jackie said I had to; and when I said no, he said in that case I could pay Imtiaz Minhas's fees for keeping me out of jail. Imtiaz Minhas was one of the best lawyers in the North, and so, also one of the most expensive.

So we went to Larry Stanbeck's funeral.

Though, actually, by the time we got there, I'd changed my mind about attending. There are some things that hide in plain sight; you see them, but you don't notice them. They walk straight by you, and admittedly, a lot had walked straight by me. But there was one last thing, one thing that I thought I had realised, and I was sure no one else had.

I wanted to find out if I was right about it.

So, even though I knew this funeral would be full of people I'd rather not see, I was still here. I mean, I was safe, no one was going to break my fingers or murder me. The story had been agreed: Callum Callaghan had gone rogue, killed Larry, killed Janine's parents, killed his father and then tried to kill me and Jackie for getting too close. The ticket had burned up with him. I shook hands with Janine as we went into the funeral home, and she leaned in close so she could whisper into my ear.

'Stay quiet, stay safe,' she said and then took a step back. 'Thank you for coming, Malachite,' she added. She looked every inch the grieving wife, albeit one very expensively dressed. Mick didn't say anything, he just sat on his dilapidated mobility scooter and stared at Jackie. Maybe he was jealous of his shiny new wheelchair.

Of course, Russian Frank wasn't there. But I'd known he wouldn't be. I'd been visited by Donald and a Russian man called Dino. They came to tell me that I didn't have to worry about Frank anymore. Dino was taking over because Frank had gone back to Russia, where he'd been involved in an unfortunate accident that involved shooting himself five times in the head. I didn't get the feeling Dino was a subtle man, but he had Donald with him, so he probably didn't need to be.

We were among the first people into the funeral home. It was likely to be standing room only because Mick had let it be known he wanted his son to have a good send off. It would take a while for everyone to get here, but that suited me.

'You're sure they'll let us in?' I whispered to Jackie.

'Yeah, Matt's a big petrol head. Honestly, you would not believe the engines in some of his hearses. I've promised him a go in a Ferrari if he lets us in the back.'

One of the funeral home's ushers wandered over.

'Mr Jones, Mr Singh Khattar?' We nodded, but we didn't need to; he knew who we were. 'If you could follow me.'

He led us out of a side door of the chapel and down a corridor into a very clinical room that held one coffin. Matt Warrell, who owned the funeral home, was a big, effusive and funny man who could turn on the funeral-director seriousness at the drop of body. He had lifted up one of the half lids on the coffin and propped it open. Now he stood in front of the body with Larry's crash helmet in his hands, as if unsure what to do with it.

'Jackie,' he said, 'we'll be taking him through in a minute, to get set up behind the curtain, so you don't have long.' He glanced at me. 'You're not going to do anything that'll get me killed, are you? I mean, like draw on his face or anything? This is an open-coffin funeral, you know.'

'We're not,' I said.

'Okay' He nodded. There was silence for a minute and then Jackie spoke.

'But we do need a moment alone, to pay our respects, to Larry.'

Matt looked from Jackie to me and back to Jackie, who twitched his head toward the door. 'Oh, right,' he said and started toward the door.

'I'll take that,' I said, pointing at the crash helmet.

'Oh, right.' He passed it to me. 'They wanted him to go into the fire in his bike leathers,' he said. 'I've never burned a crash helmet before,' he looked a bit worried about it, then he left.

'So,' said Jackie, 'what's your big revelation then?'

I lifted the crash helmet and stared into the darkened visor.

'Sometimes the dead really do talk to us,' I said. A look of concern ghosted across Jackie's face. 'You never met Larry Stanbeck's kid, did you?' I added and turned the helmet so it was on its top and I was looking down into the padded interior.

'No, but he's going to grow up so screwed with her for a mother. Not much we can do about that though.'

'We should try and keep an eye out for him,' I said, slowly turning the helmet, studying it. 'He's really going to miss his dad. He kept telling me, "My daddy knows where it's at," then tapping the side of his head.' I found what I was looking for: a place where the stitching had come undone and been restitched. I took a penknife from my back pocket and opened the blade with my teeth, then slipped the tip of the knife into the stitching, opening the padding up. Inside was a slip of paper. I showed it to Jackie and tapped the side of my head. 'My daddy knows where it's at.'

He let out a long, low whistle.

'That what I think it is?'

'Yeah,' I said.

'That's a lot of money, Mal.'

'Yeah,' I said, and I pulled the lottery ticket from its hiding place in the padding of the helmet.

'We probably earned that,' said Jackie.

'Probably,' I said.

'It's your choice though,' said Jackie. I stared at the ticket and thought about it, thought about all the blood spilled for this bit of paper.

Broken hands. Broken teeth. Bloodied face.

I crossed to the coffin and looked down at Larry Stanbeck. He looked peaceful, laying there in his biker leathers. I unzipped one of the pockets on his leather jacket and slid the lottery ticket into it. Then zipped it back up.

'I think you were probably alright, you know, for a Stanbeck,' I said to Larry's corpse. Then put the crash helmet on his chest and left him, pushing Jackie's wheelchair back into the chapel. It was full now. Lots of unfriendly eyes watched us as I pushed Jackie to the back of the chapel so we could endure the service.

Later, as Janine Stanbeck stood, stoically watching Larry Stanbeck's coffin move into the flames, she put a supportive hand on Mick Stanbeck's shoulder. Jackie looked up at me.

'There was an article in the paper this morning,' he whispered, 'about how expensive funerals are getting.'

We got thrown out of the funeral home for giggling.

The canon said it was unseemly.

Hard not to agree.

END

Acknowledgements

I depend on and must thank many people for helping bring Jackie and Mal to the public. Some indirectly: my mum and dad for instilling a love of words in me. And some more directly: my wife for supporting me in this, my agent Ed Wilson at Johnson & Alcock for his belief in this book, and my editor at Wavesback, Nick, for loving it as much as I do. Also, Alex Khlopenko of Three Crows Magazine and Dr Sam Hirst for helping me out with Russian*. Stewart Hotston who put some 'Asian eyes' on the book and Fiona, Richard and Matt who, as always, provided excellent sounding boards during the writing.

It's a funny thing, being a writer and having people live in your head, and of all the characters who have taken up residence in my mind, Jackie and Mal have lived there the longest. Probably longer than a decade. I've always loved the 'mismatched buddies' thing that American crime writers do – Robert B. Parker's Spenser and Hawk and Robert Crais' Elvis Cole and Joe Pike being the two who I have dragged around with me – and I've always had this dream of doing a British version. Jackie and Mal have their genesis in that wish, and in a desire to write about the place I live in and the place I grew up in and the place I love most in the world: the north of England and its people.

But I could never get it right. Mal was always set and has never changed much, but Jackie never quite made sense until I stumbled across this version. Earlier versions were much harder, and the whimsy was missing, and I think it's that which makes the friendship seem real, possible. This Jackie is a mixture of people I know and people I've worked with in the past, and with Jackie in place, the book was a breeze to write (also helped by realising I'd been trying to write the wrong book for the pair and starting something completely new.)

I like Jackie and Mal, and they occupy a strange place as their Yorkshire is not actually Yorkshire; Blades Edge estate doesn't actually exist. And even if it did, it wouldn't be half as bad as Mal makes it sound because he is a person trapped in the past. He sees Blades Edge through that past and it's that blindness to change that leads him to get everything so disastrously wrong. But it turns out all right in the end.

I think what I like most about Jackie and Mal is they are people struggling to do the right thing. They may do foolish or downright stupid things, but it's from a place of wanting to do the right thing, and I think that's an important quality. One I try to live by, while staying well away from psychotic gangsters and anyone who may want to kill me.

I really hope you've enjoyed spending time with Jackie and Mal as much as I've enjoyed writing about them, and I hope you'll join me for the next book when they come back and blunder into danger once again.

*The two things Jackie says in Russian are: 'I said open your fucking hand' (P158) and 'Didn't we rub each other up on the dance floor in some gay club.' (P231)

About the Author

RJ Dark spent his youth as an underground musician and occasional club promoter. He then moved on to stints as an advertising copywriter, trainer, playwright, music reviewer, amateur historian, TV cameraman, anarchist, contrarian, engineer and fraud investigator.

After a long battle with chronic illness, RJ finally settled on a career in writing. He lives in a crumbling ancient mansion somewhere in Yorkshire and is surrounded by books, music, animals and his family.

www.rjbarker.com

@dedbutdrmng

Printed in Great Britain
by Amazon

14934190R00221